YOUR POWER OVER ME

YOUR POWER OVER ME

MISSY HEART

WARM PUBLISHING

WARM PUBLISHING
El Paso, Texas
www.warmpublishing.com

Original title: *Dark domination*
published by Edisource
Paris, France

Interior design by Warm Publishing
Cover design by Angela Haddon
Art by Scarlett Lovell
Translated from French by Iris Clark

ISBN: 978-1-958447-01-7

!ABB5

Trigger Warning

WARNING: Although Your Power Over Me is a romance please note that there are several themes within this book that may trigger those who have experienced similar trauma. If you are easily triggered by dark content like violence, sexual assault, drug, grief, and other proceed with caution and at your own discretion.

Author's Note

To align the events taking place there, the city of Kiruna in Sweden has been modified.

Prologue

I have always admired the Northern Lights, considering this natural spectacle as unique and extraordinary. It's the sky's expression. Every night, the Earth communicates to us through these dances how beautiful, unique, and precious it is. And despite this beauty, I can't help but feel sadness at the thought that this will be the last time, the last image I'll see before I die. And that my world will never again be made of these pretty colors, as I sink deeper into the darkness of these icy waters.

1

Lovisa

Water. A beneficent element that brings life. Without it, nothing would exist. It can also be a source of much misery when the oceans rage to destroy everything in their path.

For my part, I see it as a painful element that serves as punishment.

Lying in my filled bathtub, I watch the drops fall from the faucet with extreme slowness.

The calm before the storm. This phrase has never seemed more true to me than at this moment.

My cell phone rings, breaking the religious calm of the bathroom. Using a towel placed near my head, I dry my hand and pick up my phone placed on the wicker cabinet behind me.

Unknown number.

Who could it be?

"Hello?"

"Miss Granberg? Mr. Linderoth, I'm the lawyer for the Ekman family."

Ekman.

A shiver electrifies my entire body at the mention of that name. long time since I heard it. My heart tightens, painful emotions try to resurface. *No, no.*

How did he get my number?

"What can I do for you?"

Movement in the room catches my attention, it's my boyfriend, his curiosity must have pushed him to come. He questions me with his eyes. In response, I just shrug.

"I have bad news."

Oh, no... what's happening? Did he... Did he...

"Your father has unfortunately passed away."

I sit up abruptly, the water around me ripples and almost overflows from the tub.

Hendrik is dead?

How? Why? I never thought I would receive such a phone call. Hendrik the immortal, as we used to call him when we were teenagers. This day has come.

How... How is he feeling?

"Are you still here?"

"I... Yes, I'm sorry."

"The funeral will be this Friday."

Already?

"I don't think—"

"Your presence would be appreciated. Right after the ceremony, your father's will—"

"Stepfather."

"Sorry?"

"He's my stepfather, I mean, he was."

It's necessary for me to clarify this, I refuse to let anyone thinks we were related by blood.

A moment of silence creates a slight discomfort between us. Mr. Linderoth hastens to continue, "It's essential for you to be there for the reading of the will."

Hendrik left me something? He never did anything good for me. This man ruined my life.

"All right, I'll be there," I resign myself.

"I'll see you on Friday. The funeral service will start at one in the afternoon. My condolences, Miss Granberg."

"Thank you."

What else to say in such circumstances? I never knew and yet I experienced the deaths of my parents.

"Who was it?" my boyfriend Rikard asks.

"The Ekman family lawyer, Hendrik is dead."

He falls silent, compassion is not part of his personality. Once, this trait attracted me; he didn't treat me like a fragile thing, but now this cold side makes me sick.

Rikard sits on the edge of the bathtub and runs his fingers through the water.

"Damn, it's freezing. Why do you do this?"

The cold water punishes me for being so stupid, so weak.

I look away at my screen, where there's a picture of the two of us; we look so in love I could almost believe it.

"Are you going?"

"I have no choice and then—"

"And then what?" he asks abruptly.

"I'm in the will."

He leers at my body lasciviously, I feel too vulnerable right now to feel flattered.

"Will he be there?"

"Who?"

His stern demeanor sends shivers down my spine. Playing dumb would only irritate him.

"It's his father's funeral, so yes, he'll be there."

"Then, I'm coming," he declares, getting up.

"Rikard…"

"I'm coming. And I'm taking this from you."

Rikard grabs my phone and slips it into the pocket of his jeans.

Damn jealousy.

"My parents are waiting for us, don't linger," he says.

He glances at my face, making me blush with shame.

As he exits, I refrain from showing him my middle finger. He deserves much more than that.

With my body trembling and chilled, I finally step out of the bathtub. I wrap myself in a towel, previously placed on the wall heater. Its gentle warmth hugs my body delightfully, replacing the warm arms my boyfriend should have given me.

As I make my way to the sink, above which sits an oval mirror, no surprise registers on my face. The top of my right cheekbone is a slightly swollen and pink from the blow it received.

He couldn't control himself.

Usually, he always careful not to leave any visible marks.

You have such a beautiful face, it would be a shame to damage it.

Yet, that's what he did. I hate him when he's like this.

A good layer of makeup and any traces of his *love* will disappear.

"Lovisa!"

"I'm coming, just a minute!"

At this moment, my appearance and my living condition alongside Rikard matter little to me.

Soon things will change. Soon I will see *him* again.

At the prospect of being in his presence again, after all this time, my heart clenches. The wound closed for nine long years will soon reopen.

2

Lovisa, 13 years old

She's selfish and only thinks about herself. I hate her and I'll hate her new boyfriend too. I know she's forgotten about Dad, but I haven't. He's still in my heart and I don't want to replace him. She's taking me away from everything I love and know. I won't see my friends again. She says in return, I'll gain a brother, but I don't want to see or get to know him, he's older than me and I'm sure he'll boss me around. Mom doesn't understand that I want to stay in Gothenburg and continue studying with Jan Sörvik, Sweden's most talented violinist! She doesn't think about my ambitions as a musician.

I hate my life!

***

Packing a suitcase is very simple and yet, I've had to start over a dozen times. What to bring for a funeral? And then? It's very cold in Kiruna, much colder than in Stockholm. It's one of the coldest cities in Sweden. Fortunately, that bastard Hendrik didn't die at the beginning of winter; temperatures can drop to minus twenty. In early March, the weather is very cold, but bearable; nonetheless, warm clothing is a must.

All week, I've been thinking about today. I tremble at the thought of returning to the places of my adolescence. Those three years spent there were the most memorial, the most painful, but also the most wonderful.

Rikard took care of the plane tickets as well as the rental of a private car. Kiruna airport offers this service, but the cars aren't sophisticated enough for my boyfriend. Since birth, he's been driven in the most beautiful cars that exist. His parents run several luxury car dealerships.

The flight lasts four hours. While Rikard dozes off beside me, his head resting on the window, I connect to the plane's WiFi via my laptop. Nowadays, everyone is on the internet, it's easy to look someone up. I'm on Instagram myself, where I post videos of me playing the violin, whether on stage with other musicians or in quieter places like a forest, by the river, a lake, and even on the beach. I also post pictures of my meals, my travels, of just me. My favorites are the ones where I pose in the snow, because my long red hair contrasts with the white of winter. I pose a lot with Rikard. He's taller than me, his hair is dark brown and cut short. He likes me to regularly post pictures of us together to show that I belong to him. We give the impression we have a perfect life.

It's just a facade.

The other side of the story is quite different, and it's probably the same for many people. Is it the same for *him*? I often find myself spying on his photos. A part of me has never been able to forget him. Yet, there was a time when I would have given anything not never see him again.

✳✳✳

All along the way to Iron House, I can't help but dwell on what I know about him. According to social media, he loves playing airsoft in the wilderness, going to nightclubs, running, and hanging out with his friends, especially Gunkil and Fredrik, his best friends. We went to the same high school.

"Are you sure this is the right address?" Rikard asks.

"Absolutely, it's a very isolated area."

Rikard sighs again, the car ride is taking too long for his liking. He absolutely doesn't want to damage the rental car, and driving surrounded by trees doesn't reassure him.

With sweaty hands and feeling sick. I feel very small as long-repressed memories resurface.

The gates of the Ekman estate loom over us like sharp claws about to snatch our lives. Their sight has always frightened me, especially at night.

Our car stops in front. The designs on the gate depict a forest with thin, leafless trees and fierce wolves at their feet. Above is the name of the property, *Iron House*. The gate end in spikes so sharp that I wouldn't risk putting my finger over them. On each side, a wall about 6 feet high runs along the vast property. There is no houses for miles around. To my right, a man with an old burn covering the entire right side of his neck comes out from a small house no bigger than a shed.

Rikard lowers his window.

"We're here for the funeral."

The man leans in to look inside the vehicle. When our eyes meet, his face softens.

"Hello, Lovisa. I'm happy to see you again. Despite the circumstances."

"Hello, Oscar," I squeak, uncomfortable having to talk to him in front of Rikard.

"You can come in."

He steps away and signals to his colleague inside the guardhouse. The gates open automatically, letting us come in.

"Did you screw him?" Rikard asks.

His question surprises me, yet coming from him, it shouldn't.

"Are you serious? He's twice my age!"

"That didn't stop your mom with Hendrik. Like mother, like daughter."

His attack breaks my heart. How dare he smear my mother's name? His cruelty knows no bounds. My lips tremble under the harsh words that I'd like to throw at him. Nothing comes out, as always.

Rikard looks at me sternly. "Got something to say?"

You're just a bastard. I hate you!

"No, nothing."

A ball of anger clogs my throat and makes it hard to breathe properly. My confused thoughts seethe with rage. In these moments, I'm capable of imagine the worst things to do to him without ever acting on them. I often feel guilty afterwards, and then only ice-cold baths can calm me down. And…

… I feel like I'm getting closer to him.

We drive half a mile, crossing the snowy forest of the estate before arriving at a huge brown brick mansion. A little further on our right, a dozen parked cars indicate where to park. Rikard slots in between a black Volvo and a red Volkswagen.

My boyfriend helps me to get out of the car, my heels not ensuring a steady walk. For the occasion, I'm dressed in a black dress that reach just above the knee; the sleeves extend to my elbows. With the biting cold, my outfit is enhanced with thick dark ties and a suede coat with a fur collar. Rikard slips a possessive arm around my hips. A whistle escapes his lips as he admires the size of the house.

"You didn't tell me your family was rich. He could've have given you more."

"Hendrik only gave me what I needed to live, not a penny more."

"I hope he left you something. So I didn't come for nothing," Rikard says.

Money plays a big role in his life. He's been in it since he was born. At the beginning of our relationship, he financed absolutely everything. We might think that my bank account is full, thanks to all the concerts the orchestra performs, but Rikard makes sure I spend every last penny. Sometimes I feel like he does it to keep me with him.

And it works.

I love him, but I can't stand being by his side anymore.

The funeral service takes place inside the mansion. The burial happens in the Ekman family mausoleum, about hundred feet away. We climb the stairs to the porch. From there, an employee opens the door for us, I don't know who she is. She's dressed in a black pantsuit with a white shirt. On her blazer, her first name *Crystal* is written on a badge.

"Rikard Rapace and Lovisa Granberg," my boyfriend introduces us.

Crystal checks her list and ticks our names with a beautiful brown pen with a gold edge.

"Please, come in."

We don't hesitate to enter the impressively hall. I immediately notice the familiar smell of burnt wood and sage. The latter is placed in the ashes to spread its good smell. In nine years, the decoration hasn't changed. A feeling of finally coming home wash over me.

The entrance is modest, just like I remember. A huge canvas adorns the wall to my right, a mix of blue, gray, and black paint. This painting has always made me think of a forest shrouded in mist; a sense of calm would wash over me every time I looked at it. It's still the case today.

"May I take your coat?" Crystal offers.

"Thank you," I accept, taking off my jacket.

The warmth from the fireplace is enough to heat the living room where all the guests are gathered. A large buffet sits in front of the bay window overlooking the front of the house. As Rikard and I enter the room, several eyes turn in our direction before the guest return to their conversations.

"We won't stay long," Rikard murmurs in my ear.

I nod as quickly scan the crowd around us. Damn it! *Where is he?*

"I'm going to get myself a drink. Want something?" Rikard asks me.

"No, thank you," I decline. "I'm going to offer my condolences."

I make my way into the living room, weaving through the guests. The brown leather sofas are still arranged around the fireplace with a coffee table in the center. Portraits of Hendrik and his ancestors proudly adorn the walls around us. A true tribute to the Ekman family. There's almost no trace of my passage visible; I appear in only one photo. It's on a small table against the wall, below a shelf containing encyclopedias on the history of the Nordic countries. In the frame, my mother, Hendrik, him, and I pose solemnly. Our parents on a beautiful leather couch, while he and I are behind them. My mother and I share this flamboyant red hair, while the two men beside to us have a brown lock with golden highlights. We all look so distant and serious that it's hard to believe we're a family.

"Lovisa?"

That voice.

I turn sharply, smiling brightly, and welcome the old lady who rushes into my arms.

"Alfrida!"

Our burst of joy seems out of place in such circumstances, but I've held this woman in my heart for years. Despite the distance, we've never lost touch. Every month, I write her a letter; she's my confidante, a surrogate mother.

"I was hoping to see you, sweetie."

Alfrida is the housekeeper of Iron House. She makes delicious meals and ensures that the house is always spotless even when the staff comes to clean and take care of the maintenance. At sixty-five, this woman has been working here for decades.

"You've grown so much," says Alfrida, looking me up and down.

"I couldn't stay the little girl you once knew forever."

"For me, you'll always be that thirteen-year-old girl."

She generously kisses my cheeks before hugging me again into her warm and comforting arms. Alfrida is a slightly smaller than me, and I'm not very tall, five feet four at most. Heels give me a boost of just four inches.

"I missed you," I confide, brushing my hand over her cheek as thin as paper.

She's aged; her face is more wrinkled than before, and her brown hair has more gray strand. Only her green gaze has kept this mischievous sparkles from before.

"It's heartbreaking to see each other in this condition."

Her words are only a form of politeness, because she hates Hendrik as much as I do. Alfrida only stayed for *him*. I look over her shoulder, she easily guesses my intentions.

"He's standing near to the casket," she says.

I thank her and make my way, feeling anxious. I pass through two large glass doors framed in black-stained wood and find myself in the library transformed into a funeral room. The armchairs are replaced by a few high tables decorated with white floral arrangements. To my left, the wall bookcase is still there, filled with books older than tie itself. Most of them probably have never been read.

Unpleasant tingling crawl up my neck.

He's looking at me.

Even after nine years, he still has the same effect on me. One day, during a violin solo on stage while we were performing in Stockholm, I felt the same shivers that only his eyes provoke in me. I could have sworn he was in the audience that day.

Apprehensively, I turn and look up at him. His cold blue gaze pierces through me, making me feel entirely exposed. The gazes directed at us only worsen the situation.

He's even more handsome and imposing than in his photos. Having him in front of me changes the image I had of him. More handsome and… terrifying? A new shiver runs through me as I approach him. His cold and distant expression is unfamiliar to me. He hasn't looked at me like this in a very long time.

I stop less than a foot away from him. His body tenses at this proximity, his square jaw clenches.

This is what you've been waiting for all these years.

I gather my courage, tilt my chin slightly to face him.

"Hello… Niklas."

3

Lovisa, 13 years old

Niklas is horrible! He was rude to my mother and didn't even speak to me. Yet we're both in the same boat. The welcome was cold and distant. I was so uncomfortable walking into that huge house that all I wanted was to be shown to my room so I could lock myself in there forever. This palace gives me the creeps; it's like nobody lives here. Everything is impeccable, and there's no sign that a family reside here. Who are these people? I fully intend to talk to Mom about moving back home. Maybe she'll let me go back to Gothenburg to live with one of my friends.

* * *

His response is slow in coming, and I almost feel like he'll insult me by ignoring me, but finally he decides to speak.

"Lovisa."

His tone astonishes me. I didn't imagine our reunion would be so cold. Maybe he's like this with everyone. After all, we're at his father's funeral. He must be suffering from his death. I myself was devastated by my mother's the death.

Don't let it shake you.

"I... 'm sorry for your loss…"

Hesitant, I over the last inches that separate us, I kiss his bearded cheeks. This tingling sensation is unfamiliar to me. When I knew him, there was no hair on his face. Nevertheless, I can still feel the softness of his skin. My lips linger longer than necessary on his cheeks. I soak in his musky scent, which makes my heart race. Niklas has become a man. A *true* Viking.

A painful memory resurfaces at the sight of the scar that marks his right temple. Suffering seems to permeate the entire house. Hendrik's death is proof of that.

"I understand the pain you're going through."

His gives a smile that doesn't reach his eyes and lock his gaze with mine.

"What do you know of pain, huh?"

More than you think…

"My mother, I— you know."

I don't like the discomfort between us. But can I blame him? I left him with a horrible letter, and we're meeting again for his father's funeral. His grudge is strong, I've always known that. But toward me? I bite my lip.

"I'll stay until tomorrow, we could talk?"

I owe him the truth.

"Yeah, for the inheritance, that's all you're interested in," he spits out.

"It… it's not just about that. Niklas, I—"

"There you are."

Rikard places himself at my side and puts an arm on my slender waist. Niklas and Rikard size each other up. They're both the same height, but Niklas is the stronger one. Their difference in style is striking. Rikard is clean-shaven, dressed in a fine black suit. He exudes sophisticated beauty; he's a man of the aristocracy. My stepbrother, on the other hand, sport golden-brown hair tied up in a bun, and he wears a well-groomed beard, a few inches long, giving him a Viking-like appearance. A sensual, even wild, beauty emanates from him. His new look doesn't leave me indifferent.

A surge of testosterone radiates from them and makes my hair stand on end.

"My condolences," Rikard offers, extending his hand.

If Nik's eyes could kill, my boyfriend would be dead instantly. Seeming to restrain himself, the last descendant of the Ekman family finally takes his hand. I don't know how much force they exert, but the knuckles of their fingers turn white, each trying to gain the upper hand.

Men, I sigh inwardly.

Finally, Niklas breaks this exchange with a small, wicked grin on his lips.

"So, he's the one taking care of you?"

"I'm her boyfriend," Rikard clarifies, grunting.

"Does that change anything?"

Niklas lifts his head and stares at a point above me. Without announcing it, he walks around us and joins a couple in their fifties, shaking their hands generously.

"What a son of a bitch," Rikard snaps.

"Rick!"

"What?" he growls. "Have you seen how he spoke to me?"

"He's grieving, he might not know what he's saying."

At least, I hope so.

Niklas can be rude when he's not well. I forgave him every time because I knew who he was deep down.

I approach, hesitant, toward the open casket. Hendrik lies solemnly in a black suit. Seeing him makes my stomach churn. I've never been comfortable with the concept of death. Seeing him laid down gives me cold chills. I've wished many times for him to die, and now that it's happened, I feel guilty for having had such thought.

Twelve years ago

This room, far too big for me, has a neutral decoration, begging to be personalized. The king size bed is huge, I can't help but sit on it to appreciate the plushness. A large bay window brings natural light to the room.

It must be nice to wake up here every morning.

"Don't get too comfortable. You'll be out of here soon enough."

On the threshold, my new stepbrother size me up with a stern expression. If I wasn't thrilled to be here, it's even worse for him. From the moment we arrived, he's been austere toward us.

"Your mother and you are just temporary, like all the others."

His attitude doesn't affect me; I'm in the same mindset. I remain seated as he approaches my luggage; he grabs my case containing my violin.

"Be careful, don't break it."

"All pretty things break someday."

Is he only talking about the violin? He eventually puts it down. His icy blue eyes lock at me. He's trying to be intimidating, but all I see is beauty. They stand out against his dark hair and fair complexion.

"Were there been many?"

"What are you talking about?"

"Women, before my mother."

A wicked grin stretches his lips.

"Quite a few, indeed. All money- grabbing. Your mother will be the same. If I were you, I wouldn't unpack my suitcase."

With these sharp words, he leaves my room.

Who does he think he is? I'll make him swallow that arrogant expression. I won't let him crush me.

****

Rikard rages while drinking his drink in his corner. The insult was intended for me, my boyfriend took it personally. His egocentricity will always amaze me. He would have wanted to leave, but the reading of the will is my excuse to stay. And there's no way he's leaving me alone.

It's been an hour since we've been at the funeral, and I've been able to see familiar faces. Like classmates, especially those who were part of our group with Niklas. I was surprised to see Lucia; I thought she would have left Kiruna, but she preferred to stay here to work as a veterinarian. As for Gunkil and Fredrik, Nik's two best friends, they barely spoke to me.

"I need to go to the bathroom," I say to Rikard after a while.

"Fine, I'll go get another drink."

Four drinks. When he drinks too much, he's even more unbearable than usual. I can't stop him, but I can distance myself a bit. Besides, the gloomy atmosphere is getting to me, I need some fresh air. I leave the library and find myself in front of a wide staircase made of black wood. The railing, made of the same material, worn by the years, is still pretty. My fingers brush against the carved flower reliefs as I climb to the second floor. The house has two floors and an attic converted into a bachelor apartment for Niklas.

This room...

I shiver as memories long repressed come back to mind. *No, I* refuse to think about it. I shake my head and head straight for my old room.

Opening the door, I expected to find a layer of dust several inches thick, but nothing. Everything is clean. This place reminds feels like a mausoleum, nothing has changed. The atmosphere is filled with memories assaulting me. Sitting on my bed is a plush red fox. It seems so small to me. I run my finger over its fur, smiling. My hasty departure didn't allow me to take it.

"Hello, my old friend."

"He missed you."

I jump, spinning around. Niklas is watching me with a smirk on his lips. I blush, clutching my stuffed animal.

"What are you doing here?" I ask, looking at him.

"I followed you. Snooping around?"

"It's my room, I have the right. And I'm not snooping around."

He chuckles and walks into the room, looking around. He has grown a lot since our teenage years; the room seems too small for him now. His sudden mood change unsettles me.

"You left, it's not your room anymore. Nor your stuff. Everything belongs to me now."

Niklas snatches the stuffed animal from me and examines it. This fox had been a gift from him to me.

"Give it back to me."

"Why?" he asks. "By leaving it here, you lost the right to take it back."

What a kid! Some things never change.

He hands me the plush back. As I take it, he grabs my wrist and pulls me toward him. His unexpected move takes my breath away.

"What are you doing?"

He remains silent, wrapping his muscular arms around my waist. His dominant stance makes me feel small and fragile. His icy gaze scrutinizes me carefully, seeming to imprint my image. Initially on guard, I eventually relax. In turn, I observe him. The expression on his face has hardened over the years. A small white scar runs horizontally across his left cheek. It's not a recent injury. What happened?

Niklas slips his hand into my bun and releases my hair. His gaze darkens as he grabs it.

"Nick..."

"You abandoned me," he hisses.

His grip tightens, causing me to grimace.

"It's not what you think. I'll explain."

"It's too late for explanations."

He forces me to step back, exerting more pressure on my hair. My body collides with the wall next to the large bay window. My heart is beats fast and too loud. My cheeks flush as his touch allows me to feel each of his muscles, particularly his member pressed against my thigh.

What is he trying to do? I dare not look him in the eyes; his dark aura makes me uneasy. Trapped against him, I can't escape. This feeling of being ensnared suffocates me and reminds me of many unpleasant situations I've experienced with Rikard.

Rikard!

He must not see us. The situation could mislead him, and provoking him in his drunken state is not part of my plans.

"Stop… Back off."

A new laugh escapes from his throat. A joyless, mocking laugh. I shiver and try to push him away.

"What's wrong? Are you afraid that your little lapdog will catch us?"

Yes!

What I've learned from living with Niklas is that the more he's hurt, the crueler he becomes.

"Please."

"Yes, beg me."

Niklas leans his face into my hair, inhaling it. This simple gesture makes my heart race and increases my anxiety. I've dreamed of this moment, but it was before I met Rikard, and he slowly destroyed me. Conflicting emotions rage within me, preventing me from thinking clearly.

With trembling lips, I finally dare to raise my head to look him in the eyes. I don't know what he reads on my face, but he backs away. All wickedness leaves his features.

"You should go."

"The will—"

He cuts me off.

"I'm not in the mood. I'll ask for the reading be postponed until Monday."

"Oh, I… Okay. We've booked a hotel room. I guess we can stay two more days."

"Which hotel?"

"The Royal Ruby Hotel."

His thick eyebrows furrow before he leaves me alone in my room. I exhale deeply, leaning forward.

Shit!

Why does he have this hold on me? After all this time, it hasn't evaporated. I don't know what to think about what just happened. Does he hate me? His abrupt action toward me proves it. He hasn't always been kind to me, but not like this. Will he let me explain the real reasons for my departure? Things are going to be more complicated than I thought.

I need to go back downstairs before Rikard start asking questions. I leave the fox on the bed and gently close the door.

My boyfriend is in the living room, near the buffet. Engaged in conversation with a young woman, he only notices my presence when I stand beside him. My gaze falls on the blonde who is keeping him company.

"Jonna?" I exclaim, surprised.

"Lovisa!"

Jonna throws herself into my arms, laughing. I hadn't seen her for a long time.

"I didn't expect to see you here," I admit, smiling.

"I'm here to support Niklas, poor thing. He has no one left now."

He has me.

"You're right, he's lucky to have you."

"It's true," Jonna chuckles, nudging me with her shoulder. "I suggested to your boyfriend that we go for a drink to catch up on old times."

How did they start talking? Among all the guests, they had to meet.

"I want to hear all about Lovisa when she was fifteen," says Rikard, pulling me close to him.

In my memories, Jonna never held back. Is she still the same? I don't want her to give away information that would give Rikard a reason to blame me.

"If you both want, we can leave now?" she suggests.

"I wouldn't say no, this place is boring," Rikard agrees.

"I'll let Niklas know we're leaving," she says.

Seeing her again is unexpected. We were best friends back then. My sudden departure could have made her resentful, like Niklas, but it is quite the opposite. What a relief!

"You let your hair down," Rikard observes, running his hand through it.

"Oh, I… um, yes, the bun was too tight, I has a headache."

"You look pretty like this," he tells me, kissing me eagerly.

He reeks of whisky. I place my hands on his chest to gently push him away.

"Do you want me to drive?"

"Why?"

"I think you've had too much to drink."

He smiles and places a kiss on my lips while grabbing my butt with one hand.

"I've got this under control. And even drunk, I drive better than you. Come on, let's go."

4

Niklas, 15 years old

He assigned her my mother's studio to make it her bedroom. How dare he? It was the last place where I felt her presence, and now there's nothing left. My father threw everything away without even asking for my opinion. It's like she's dead, and this feeling of complete abandonment messes me up even more. I want to destroy everything, especially that stupid violin Lovisa seems to care so much. Her mother will never replace mine, and Lovisa will not take my place. I will never consider her my sister, no matter what my father wishes. I will destroy them.

***

Locked in the bathroom of my room, I splash my face with water repeatedly.

Damn it.

Hands presses against the sink, I examine what my reflection sends back to me. Features strained with fatigue, I try to see what could have scared Lovisa so much. Nothing. I can't find the explanation, but I scared her. Good. That's all she deserves after what she did to me. I wish I never had seen her again. Yet, a part of me i   o throw her on my bed and fuck her wildly.

Fucking Lovisa.

She makes me feel things I swore I'd never feel again. It doesn't change anything, he'll leave soon. When she cashes in her inheritance, I won't see her anymore. I just have to hold on a few days; then she'll go back to her life, and I'll go back to mine.

Someone knocks on my door of my room. I straighten and leave the bathroom. Oscar, my father's right-hand man, and now mine, steps aside as I pass.

"Are you okay, sir?"

"I'm fine," I reply curtly, unimpressed by his age, which is twice mine. "What's up?"

"She's leaving, I thought you'd like to know."

He knows. He knows the effect she has on me; he always has. Oscar has been working for my family since I was born, that's twenty-seven years ago. He's a man I would trust with my life without hesitation.

I quickly descend to the entrance hall and see Lovisa and that jerk leaving. Seeing his hands on her ignites a surge of rage within me.

"Royal Ruby Hotel, tell Goran to cancel their reservation. Let no hotel open its doors to them."

"Right away, Sir."

I acted impulsively. As usual. What possessed me to do that? Hell, this won't help my situation.

Oscar disappears, and Jonna replaces him immediately, wrapping her arm around arm, ready to leave, with her coat on her back and her bag in her hand.

"I'm going to have a drink with Lovisa and her boyfriend. I can come by after, when everything's over, if you want?"

When I look at Jonna, I think of those overly sweet treats that make your mouth water before becoming bland and being spat out. A fleeting taste.

"Why not. I'll send you a message."

Her face lights up, she kisses me before rushing outside. With Rikard having already started the car, he drives off after Jonna when she climbs into her own vehicle.

Shitty day. I can't wait for it to be over.

Back at my father' side, I look at his face. The work was well done; the funeral home made him look younger. Probably a request from him. He doesn't look like he's sleeping, as I've often heard said. No, my father is dead. He's cold and looks like a wax statue.

I've had enough.

I step out to smoke a mint cigarette. Clad in a simple black sweater and pants of the same color, I feel the cold seep into my bones. The smoke dissipates into the air. Everything is calm, the forest of the estate is peaceful, undisturbed by what's happening inside the house. The chatter of the guests doesn't pass through the doors; the glass is so thick that a scream would turn into a whisper. I know what I'm talking about; for a long time, my childhood screams were muffled within these walls. It's over now; I won't scream anymore.

Fourteen years ago

"Take a drag, hold the puff for a second, then exhale at ease," explains Gunkil, holding a lit cigarette.

My best friend shows me how to do it. When he exhales the smoke, a smell of mint reaches me. He stole them from his mother, who swears by them.

"How is it?"

"Here, try it."

I take the cigarette between my index finger and thumb and pull a little too hard. I start coughing under the laughter of my friend.

"Don't laugh!"

He hits me on the back. I push him away and try again. It goes down better. I soak up the nicotine wrapped in mint. I close my eyes. Without asking for permission, I finish it while making sure to exhale the smoke outside. Sitting on the windowsill, feet dangling in the void, we are enveloped by the coolness of the night, like an icy coat. We are in the attic. My hideout, as my friends call it. We spend a lot of time in front of the TV playing video games or playing foosball. The mini-fridge is always raided. Lucky for us, Alfrida remembers to check what's missing and to restock. The house wouldn't run properly without her.

"That sucks, Gun, these are women's cigarettes!"

"Don't complain, it's all I could find. Why don't we raid in your dad's stash?"

"He smokes cigars. They stink, unlike these."

I crush the cigarette butt in a small ashtray between us and look at my best friend.

"And besides, he'd beat me up. He cares more about those shitty cigars than me."

"What a bastard," declares Gunkil, lighting another cigarette.

I have many friends, but he's the only one who truly knows what my father is like. Sometimes, it's just us against the world.

"I hope you're not talking about me," interrupts Hendrik.

I turn around sharply, eyes widening. Immediately, my heart beats faster, and a sheen of sweat forms on my back.

Shit.

"Father! What are you doing here?"

I leave the windowsill without waiting for a response.

"I smelled the low-quality cigarettes," my father asserts disdainfully.

Gunkil's laughter behind me elicit a grimace. Since we were kids, he's always been the boldest of us. Standing up to my father should be my job, but every time, I chicken out. My friend stands next to me, looking at my father defiantly.

"It's not crap." says my friend.

"At thirteen, what do you know about the quality of an object?"

"I know a lot more than you think."

My father approaches us. His smile doesn't bode well.

"I'd love to chat with you, but it's getting late. My driver will take you home."

"My bike is downstairs—"

"He'll put it in the trunk. Have a good evening."

His tone is final. Gunkil looks at me, I signal him to leave.

Now We're alone. My father then heads to the window, where Gunkil's pack of cigarettes is resting on the sill. He takes it and passes one of the white sticks under his nose.

"You smoke now?"

"We just wanted to try. All the kids our age are doing it."

Hendrik lights one up, to my surprise.

"Since you want to follow the crowd, go ahead and smoke."

"What?"

"Smoke this cigarette."

He forces me to take it with just a stern look. He despises weakness. If I refuse, he will make me pay for it. So, reluctantly, I take long drags to finish it as quickly as possible. I struggle to hold back a cough.

"Good boy."

"I'm going to bed," I say, crushing the cigarette butt.

I immediately walk around him and tense my shoulders when he calls out to me.

"One moment."

Hendrik lights up another cigarette.

"You're not done."

"Dad..."

"Don't use that girly tone with me. You're going to smoke it all even if you end up puking."

***

Back then, my father wanted to teach me a lesson.

After this, either you won't smoke anymore, or you'll finally start smoking quality stuff.

He was wrong. I love these fucking menthol cigarettes. Even after what he put me through and the suffering endured that day, they're ingrained in me.

"Sir, we're taking the body to the family vault," says Oscar behind me.

"All right, let's bury that bastard once and for all."

5

Lovisa, 13 years old

Dad, why did you abandon us? Couldn't you fight harder against the illness? For mom, for me? I feel like I'm alone in the world, my friends are far away, mom doesn't pay attention to me anymore, and my stupid stepbrother hates me. In my new school, everyone avoids me, I know Nik ordered it, he has a lot of influence. Dad, please come back or take me with you.

***

The city of Kiruna boasts no fewer thirty thousand inhabitants. In the past, this area was industrialized. Its resident making a living from mining. The Ekman family gradually bought out the company forty years ago. Following this, the city modernized. Malls popped up, luxurious hotels were built, and that's how they had Iron House build, one of the biggest houses I've ever seen. Its architecture is modern, avant garde. It's doesn't resemble any Swedish house, and it been for several decades now.

Jonna guided us to a coffee place where we sat on the terrace. A fire nearby warmed it up. We have a view on huge snowy mountains. Tall and majestic, they make me feel small and insignificant. Nature dominates us with its beauty. Upon closer observation, we can see all its potential, its danger, but also its brightness.

"Lovisa? Are you with us?" my friend says, snapping her fingers under my eyes.

"Sorry, I was lost in thought. What were you saying?"

"I was telling Rikard about the time I stole my brother's motor scooter. We drove all around the city before being arrested by the police."

This anecdote makes me smile. It's one of the craziest things I've ever done with Jo.

"I thought you were going to pee your pant that day when your dad showed up," I add, thinking back to her defeated expression.

I haven't always been the wise young woman that I'm today. There was a time when I had a lot of fun. I often miss those days; adult life isn't what I expected it would be.

"If we'd been with the gang, the cops would never have messed with us," Jonna says, taking a sip of her coffee.

Seeing the state of my boyfriend, I was relieved when she suggested this strong drink. As for me, I took a simple herbal tea.

"The gang?" Rikard, sitting next to me, asks.

"Yeah. Lovisa, me, Gunkil, Fredrik, Lucia, Sven and Niklas. Britt was also here, but she didn't stay with us for long."

"Wow, that's a quite group. I would have liked to be part of it," Rikard remarks.

I didn't know Rikard as a teenager, but if he was anything like he is now, I wouldn't have wanted him with us.

"You're hot, no doubt we would have had you join us," Jo says.

That superficial side has been present in her since I've known her. Jonna is a stunning woman; her long blonde, almost white, hair gives her an angelic air. Her almond-shaped hazel eyes sparkle with mischief and passion that I've never possessed. She was always the one who to find the best ways to have fun. My friend is a little taller than me, and her curves have always made me envious. Even back then, she had a body that made boys turn their heads.

"Lovisa must have looked adorable in her uniform."

Rikard slips a kiss under my ear, sending shivers down my spine. I blush and lean into him as he wraps his arm around me.

We were in a private high school. The uniform consisted of a skirt with a blue blazer, a tie of the same color, and a white shirt.

"I looked ridiculous."

"You're kidding! Guys couldn't stop staring at her! With that fiery hair, she couldn't go unnoticed."

She's exaggerating, she was the star. No one could near me; I was Niklas' stepsister. Even in the beginning, when he hated me, he had forbidden all the boys from approaching me.

"Did she have a boyfriend?" Rikard suddenly asks.

Not that question.

I feel the discomfort creeping in as my blood runs cold. Jonna doesn't know him; she can't know that this kind of information will piss off my boyfriend.

"Just one," Jonna begins. "Everyone wanted him, and he chose her."

"Who's that?" Rikard asks.

"Do we have to dwell on the past? That's old story," I say, feeling uneasy.

I give my friend a stern look to signal that shouldn't continue. I don't want to argue with him. She seems to understand the message because she changes the subject and talks about her family. Her parents have several restaurants in Sweden, including one in Kiruna. Her mother, a former Michelin-starred chef, hung up her apron to run the business with her husband, and now only cooks for her two children.

"Is Erik still into photography?"

"Oh, yes," Jonna sighs. "He thinks he's the photographer of the year since a gallery offered to exhibit his shots. You should see him strutting, it's enough to make you puke."

Sibling conflicts have always been part of their relationship. They bicker constantly, and yet, they stick together. I've always wanted to have a sister or a brother. I never saw Niklas as such; we have always been different. What happened between us is proof of that.

Rikard tightens his embrace around me, pulling me away from the memory of the handsome Viking.

"And you, Jonna, what do you do?" he asks.

I recognize the tone of his voice: indifferent. He doesn't care about her answer. So why?

"I'm in charge of mum's restaurant in Kiruna," she replies.

"You never left?" I intervene. "You talked about moving to Australia; I remember it was your dream at the time."

"Yes, well… Some things kept me here and I could never bring myself to leave."

"Someone, you mean?" retorts Rikard.

He can be very insightful about others, but when it comes to me, he's often wrong. His jealousy and love for me blinds him. He imagines a lot of things about me.

"Maybe. Your boyfriend is curious!" Jonna remarks, laughing.

I just smile and place my hand on his. He quickly squeezes it, a little too hard, but I don't object.

"Lovisa, on the other hand, plays music. It doesn't pay much, so luckily I'm here."

Bastard.

Why does he take such pleasure in putting me down? I'm his girlfriend; he should support me!

"Oh! That's right, you played the violin. I loved listening to you. Where do you perform? I could come by sometimes."

"Pretty much everywhere. I'm taking a break here, but I'll keep you posted."

Music keeps me alive. When I play, I feel free and so happy that my heart swells with joy. I don't know what would happen if I were deprived of it. It's also a way to stay connected with my mother. She sacrificed everything for me.

"The trip has been long; we should head to our hotel," Rikard suddenly says.

"Already? Well, Lovisa, we'll see each other before you leave, right?"

"Yes, can you give me your phone number?"

"I don't know it, but can you give me yours," Jonna suggests, handing me her phone.

I do it and kiss her cheeks before leaving. My friend always manages to lift others' spirits. Talking with her made me smile, and I feel somewhat lighter.

Once in the car, I fasten my seatbelt and look at Rikard.

"That was nice, wasn't it?"

Before I can react, his fist shoots out and lands a violent blow to my stomach. I bend in two, gasping for breath. The instant pain shakes my body and threatens to make me vomit.

"Why?" I cry out, on the verge of tears.

"You dare to ask me?"

"Yes! Tell me what I did!"

I don't deserve this!

Tears blur my vision and eventually stream down, smudging my makeup under my eyes. The stabbing pain wracks my body and seems relentless.

"I can't stand knowing that you've been with other guys before me."

"But that was before! I'm with you now! With you!"

"Exactly," he growls, forcefully pulling my chin up.

He presses his forehead against mine and stares into my eyes. His breath, loaded with alcohol and coffee, forces its way into my nostrils. Rikard prevent me from turning my head by sliding his fingers into my hair, gripping it tightly.

"You belong to me, if another man dares to touch you or even look at you, you'll pay for it."

I really don't deserve this!

His threat isn't just talk. He would be able of breaking me to prevent anyone from showing interested in me.

"Do you understand me?"

Why does he have to ruin everything every time? We were having a good time, and it flies away. He destroys everything beautiful in my life. The only thing he hasn't been able to take away from me so far is my music.

"Lovisa."

This can't go on. I've been living in fear of upsetting him for too long. This miserable existence can't continue. Maybe one day his blows will be more violent, and I won't get up again? Swallowing hard, I put on a determined expression and stare ahead when he releases me.

"Yes, I understand."

As Rikard starts the car, I take out a tissue and silently wipe my face. As always, I erase the traces of his love only to put on a fake smile in front of the others. *Smile, Lovisa, smile.* Hopefully, soon I won't have to do it anymore.

***

"What do you mean, canceled?" Rikard explodes at the receptionist of the Royal Rubis Hotel.

With my suitcase in hand, all I want is to sleep for few hours. This day is ending badly.

"We're fully booked. Your booking was an error."

"This hotel is ridiculous. Get the manager!"

"He's not available right now. We're sorry for this inconvenience," the receptionist says calmly. "I'll call nearby hotels to see if they can accommodate you."

"Right! It's the least you can do," my boyfriend grumbles as he walks away.

Just what we needed. Patience isn't Rikard strong suit; he's used to being served right on time. I'm the opposite. I've learned to take whatever comes my way, and disappointment constantly looms over me. I wasn't expecting anything. If I had, I would have exploded on the guy standing beside me a long time ago. I would have left at the first blow, at the first argument, at the first jealous rage. But I stayed. Why? I still ask myself the question.

"This kind of thing would never have happened back home."

"Everyone makes mistakes."

I try to calm him down by taking his hand. His skin is thin and soft. He has the hands of a man of letters, not of a laborer. He never had to work hard to get where he is. I almost feel ashamed of my musician's hands, with fingertips that have become hard and often injured.

"Calm down, it's ok, they'll find a solution."

"They better, or their reputation will take a hit."

Don't act like an asshole.

Rikard has been unpleasant in other hotels and restaurants before. He has influence because of his family. He's a listened-to man. Unfortunately. No one sees what he truly is. He always displays an impeccable image of himself, and it's often me, when we're alone, who bears the brunt of his wrath. I dared to speak up once to his mother. She glared at me and sided with her son, scolding me, saying I was lucky that a man like him was interested in me given my social status. Since then, I've never mentioned the hell I live through every day. What's the point when people bury their heads in the sand?

We wait about ten minutes before the receptionist returns to us. His dismay expression doesn't announce anything good. His confidence from earlier has completely vanished. I feel sorry for the poor guy; he doesn't know Rikard's temper when he's drunk.

"I'm sorry. All the hotels are full."

"Ad so? What do we do now?" Rikard snaps.

Manners are gone; he reveals his true face.

"I'm truly sorry," the dark-haired man repeats.

Rikard explodes. He insults the receptionist. Drunk, my boyfriend is out of control. I prefer to distance myself by taking my suitcase. Outside, the temperature is gradually dropping; I don't want to linger here, but if I leave without him, he'll make me pay for it.

To waste no time, I ask the valet to bring back our rental vehicle. When I can lighten Rikard's mood, so he doesn't take it out on me, I don't hesitate.

If all the hotels are full, where will we sleep? I don't know where Jonna lives, and I have no way to contact her. What do we do?

No. No, I can't.

And yet… Do we have other choices? When Rikard returns, his face is red with anger, and the veins in his neck stand out. I wouldn't want to be in the poor man's shoes who bore the brunt of his fury.

"What a bunch of incompetents! They can't do anything for us!"

To emphasize his words, he throws his suitcase against mine. Both crash to the ground. The handsome gentleman disappears to make room for the man behind the scenes. His good looks once fooled me.

"Every problem has a solution," I say.

"And what do you suggest, huh?"

I'm used to his disdainful tone, but every time it's like he's pushing a needle into my heart. It shouldn't be like this between us.

"We can stay at Iron House. My room is still there."

"What, with Niklas?"

"No, not with him. It's also my home."

Well, sort of, because I'm not a true Ekman. I'm just a young dog that Hendrik agreed to keep after my mother's death.

Please don't let his jealousy interfere, I pray with all my might. I bite my lip and add, "There're motels too, I saw one on the highway about an hour from here."

He hates motels, they're not good enough for him. He seems to weigh the pros and cons. I see his shoulders relax despite his closed-off expression.

"Fine. It's better than those crappy motels."

We've been together for four years, I know how to talk to him. Sometimes it doesn't work, but then there are those blessed days, like tonight, when my words still reach him.

"Let's no delay, it's cold."

Just like your heart.

The valet parks in front of us and quickly puts our suitcases in the trunk. Without a thank you, we leave the place with tires screeching, making me grimace.

On the way, I keep silent, trying to make myself as small as possible. Staring into the landscape, I let my mind wander to arrive faster at Niklas'. What will he say when he sees us arrive? We didn't attend his father's burial. Will he hold it against us? What happened in the bedroom makes me believe that he hates me. He's bitter about what happened nine years ago.

He can't just leave us at the door.

A small voice deep inside me laughs at my naivety and urges me to remember an old memory.

Twelve years ago

I knock on the glass door to the garden with all my strength. My palms, red and painful, are frozen in the cold.

"Let me in!" I shout for the hundredth time.

Niklas and I are alone in the house. He's inside, warm, while I've been freezing outside for about twenty minutes.

I hate him!

It's been two months since my mother and I moved in with him and his father. Our relationship keeps getting worse. It's a perpetual fight. Tireless, Niklas always finds a new way to make my life worse. The first week, he focused on denying my existence, which suited me fine. But then, seeing that it didn't affect me, he started playing dirty: releasing his snake into my room, hiding my schoolbooks, wetting my bed or even eating everything I like at the table to leave me with unappetizing dishes. Today, his new idea is to throw my violin in the snow. He has no sense of money.

While I rushed to pick up my instrument and check that it was okay, Niklas took the opportunity to lock all the doors. I'm stuck outside with no one to help me. Hendrik went to town with my mother. He wanted to show off his new young and pretty conquest to his old friends with undoubtedly ugly wives. As for Alfrida, the housekeeper, she's at the checkpoint at the entrance to the estate, bringing a basket of supplies to the bodyguards.

"You'll pay for this!" I shout again.

Niklas taunts me from behind the door. Sipping a hot drink, he takes wicked pleasure in seeing me freezing. He's doing everything to make us leave, by targeting me. Hasn't he realized that it's not up to me? I begged my mother on my knees to leave this awful place, but she doesn't listen to me. She only cares about Hendrik, who showers her with gifts and compliments. He spoils her so much that she turns a blind eye to his illegal activities. Worse, she takes advantage of them.

"What are you going to do?" Niklas taunts with a smirk.

"I... I don't know yet, but I'll figure it out, and you'll regret it!"

Exhausted, I stop banging on the window. It's so thick that I'll never be able to break it. Besides, Niklas has to raise his voice to talk to me.

I'm going to lose my fingers, and that be the end of my dream of having a career in music. Wearing a thin emerald green sweater and close-fitting black nylon pants, I shiver. I made the mistake of going out barefoot, thinking it would be a quick round trip. But I didn't think about Niklas' trickery. I sway from one foot to the other on the doormat, trying to wake up my numb toes.

"You're in no position to threaten me."

"Shut up and open up!"

I'm about to cry. All I want is to go back inside and lock myself in my room to let my grief out. What have I done to deserve this? I suffer as much as he does from this cohabitation; we should support each other instead of waging war. Every retaliation from me feeds his unhealthy pleasure in tormenting me. I've tried ignoring his existence, but he always manages to knock me off my feet.

I breathe in and out, weary. Shoulders hunched, I force myself to calm down and look at him. My bottom lip trembles with anger and sadness. Whatever I say, he does as he pleases. Whatever I do, it encourages him to continue. I decide to stop this fight, for now. I don't have the strength to carry on; all my extremities are tingling and numb.

I spend long minutes staring at him. Niklas study me, analyzing my behavior, I can tell from his curious expression. Is he wondering what he should do? Should he let me in? Should he leave me there until Alfrida comes back, or our parents? Finally, he sets down his cup and unlocks the door. I sigh with relief and pick up my violin, leaning against the doorframe. I almost push Niklas aside as I walk in. Immediately, the heat attacks me and bites my skin. A sensation of unpleasant tingling runs through my body.

Before leaving the kitchen, I turn to my stepbrother. We size each other up for a moment. I don't know why he finally opened the door, but I'm glad he did. Without further ado, I flee to my room, where my thick blanket awaits.

✳✳✳

When Rikard parks in front of the house, there are only two cars left. Everybody is gone.

"Don't let him think he's doing us a favor by accepting us here. He'll be paid for every day we stay."

What could I reply? I'm too exhausted to argue with him. Either way, he'll do as he pleases.

Suitcases in hand, we climb the few steps, and the light on the porch flicks on. Niklas is already behind the door, which he opens. Before he hides his emotions, I see a feigned, forced surprise pass over his face, and for a brief moment, I glimpse relief.

At his feet, a big black and white Bernese Mountain dog, with a brown spot around his mouth, tries to jump on us, but Niklas holds him firmly by the collar.

"What are you doing here?"

"There was a problem with our booking. Would it be possible to stay here? I'll compensate you for the inconvenience."

Nik's jaw muscles tighten, he seems lost in thought. What is he thinking? What is he feeling?

Look at me...

My heart clenches in my chest as a powerful aura emanates from him. It's both frightening and captivating. I only want one thing: to be alone with him and explain myself about past events. It's not just the desire to talk to him that crosses my mind. This thought makes me ashamed and guilty. I'm with Rikard.

"I don't need your money. Come in."

His family being as rich as Croesus, Niklas can spend thousands of kroner without ever running out. His father built a legacy for several generations of Ekman through good investments, but also with his fraudulent businesses.

Before my boyfriend can reply to his refusal, I step in front of him.

"Thank you, we won't be a bother."

Niklas nods without giving me any more attention.

Look at me!

He lets us in and closes the door behind us. In an authoritative voice, he orders his dog to calm down, and it happily yaps. Apart from its bulky body, its fluffy head only asks for caresses.

"No one's here at night, you'll have to manage on your own. Alfrida will be here tomorrow morning."

The house feels so cold, with no lights on. Niklas retrieves a cigarette tucked behind his ear and walks away into the darkness. He heads toward the kitchen with his beast at his feet.

"Let's go to bed," Rikard intervenes.

It's not like him to stay silent for more than a minute. He must be really tired of this day to want to finish it quickly. I lead the way and head toward the stairs. Before going up, I cast a glance toward the library, shrouded in darkness, gloom and eerie. I shudder at the thought of knowing that it contained Hendrik's body just a few hours ago. I don't believe in ghosts, but if there were any, my stepfather's would be the first to haunt this place. He was too tough to get rid of for good.

Without further ado, I take Rikard to my room, where we each change in the bathroom. He in simple pajama pants, me in a black nightie with no underwear except for a small lace panties. For lingerie, it's him who chooses, he likes sexy outfits while I dream of soft and fluffy pajamas.

While I put away our things in my old wardrobe, Rik looks at the decorations of my room. Above my bed hangs a yellow fairy light, I wonder if it still works. Next to it, a bedside table that holds a picture frame of my mother and me when I was five. I was wearing a fairy costume and holding a glittery bucket full of candy. We were so happy when my father was still alive. His death changed our lives, a part of us died with him.

A little further away is my desk, where I spent long evenings doing my homework and studying for endless nights. My attention lingers on the huge calendar, expired for nine years. Underneath, I had engraved words in the wood that I'm dying to see again, but with Rikard a few feet from me, it's risky.

"Come to bed."

I turn off the light. Being in this room after so many years makes me feel like that rebellious and fiery teenager again. Except now I'm twenty-five years old and have a busy adult life.

With no curtains on the window, the view of the Northern Lights is breathtaking. I observe the play of light for a short moment, greenish-yellow in some areas and on blue in others. This magnificent sight moves me. I feel lucky to stay in the part of the country where this enchanting landscape offers me for a private dance that I admire with attention.

As I lie down in my bed, a flood of memories resurfaces. These sheets held my tears and my laughter, my anxieties, and fears. I've had pillow fights there, listened to music with Jonna for hours, sung, danced. This place saw me grow and evolve before seeing me leave, three years later.

Without wasting time, Rikard becomes assertive by slipping his hand under my nightie to caress my body. His fingers pass over my curves to my breast, which he massages with delight. He's an excellent lover, and when I'm cuddled in his arms while making love, I forget everything. In those moments, I rediscover the man he was at the beginning of our relationship.

After rather short foreplay, he takes off my panties and slides off his pajamas, under which he wears no boxers. I welcome him between my thighs where his hard and tense member penetrates me deeply. A sigh of pleasure escapes my half-opened mouth as I arch against him. His chest, hairless and finely muscled, presses against my exposed breast. The tips of my nipples are taut with budding arousal. I press my hips against his, giving him the opportunity to thrust deeply with each of his movements.

The exhaustion but also the emotional upheaval felt today make me forget to be discreet, and my moans echo throughout the walls and probably outside. Every movement of his hips releases my tension-filled body. My arousal drives Rikard to growl with pleasure as he speeds up his thrusts. A long shiver runs through my body. He kisses me, sliding his tongue into my mouth. Both dance and seek for each other as a wave of brutal pleasure overwhelms me at the same time as Rikard, who gives everything he has in one last thrust. My cry is muffled in his mouth with sweet notes of alcohol.

Out of breath, he pulls out and lies down next to me, leaving me panting and still burning with desire. My body twitches with delight a little longer before gradually finding a calming peace. Serenity washes over me. I take a few deep breaths in and out before finally getting up to clean myself in the bathroom. I take the opportunity to tie my hair into a side braid.

When I come back, Rikard is sound asleep; a snore escapes him and draws a smile from me. I find him adorable. If only he could be as vulnerable awake.

With a dry mouth and a parched throat, I venture into the hallway. Instinctively, my attention is drawn to Niklas' room, which is just a few feet away from me.

Shit, Nik... he must have heard me. Idiot!

I don't want him to witness my sexual escapades with Rik. Between our bedrooms, there's only my bathroom separating us. I know from experience that both of us can hear what's going on in the next room. I nervously bite my lip and curse myself for being so noisy. What does he think of what just happened? I'm mortified.

Stealthily, I decide to go downstairs in silence, or almost, because some steps of the stairs creak. I go to the kitchen, shrouded in darkness. Only the moon illuminates the place. Sounds of paws and claws scraping the floor approaches me, and Niklas' dog comes to lick my leg. His imposing posture scares me a little, but he remains gentle with me. I pet him, wondering how old he is, and what his name is. Nik has never really liked animals, except for his snake.

I pour myself a large glass of lemonade and gulp it down in several long swallows. The room is silent, just like the rest of the house. I can barely hear the wind rustling through the branches of the trees as their eerie shadows create unsettling shapes on the walls. Some leafless branches give the impression of sharp claws, ready to attack me.

As I go back upstairs to go to bed, I hear a door creak.

Niklas?

I freeze a few steps from my room and look toward his. I hold my breath as my body tenses, expecting to see his handsome face appear with his piercing gaze. Instead, it's a female figure with a slender body and long blonde hair presents itself to me. Jonna. Wear a far too large T-shirt that reaches down her buttocks, she approaches me with a mischievous smile.

"Jonna?" I murmur. "What are you doing here? I mean, I... You..."

No! I widen my eyes. My heart beats faster than my brain and feels like it's being squeezed in my chest. No, not this. No. Jo and Nik?

"Shush," she says, placing her index finger to her plump lips. "You'll wake up the boys."

With a complicit wink, she passes by me and heads downstairs, leaving me dumbfounded. Are they together? *What did you expect? He wasn't going to stay alone for you!* It's irrational and unfair of me, but I can't help but be angry with him. Why Jonna? There are billions of girls in the world, and he had to choose my best friend!

6

Niklas, 15 years old

She's tougher than I expected, I can't help but admire that quality. Standing her ground against everyone, at home and at school, she continues to defy me. I won't make her bend so easily, and I realize that as time passes, her presence becomes less burdensome to me. I continue to test her limits, waiting for her to crack. Or for me to get tired of it. But the second option won't happen; I'm having too much fun punishing her presence in my life.

***

This weekend with her is going to be more complicated than I had imagined. Not only do we have to share the same space, but on top of that, she makes me listen her getting fucked by her boyfriend! *Damn it!* It took all my strength to stop myself from bursting through her door to separate them. Her moans were torture to my ears. I'm in such a rage! Jonna didn't complain about my relentlessness on her body when we had sex. She even liked that rough and beastly side. Her ability to accept everything despite my behavior toward her will always surprise me. Often, the idea of rejecting her definitively crosses my mind, but the presence reminds me of a past and memories that I don't want to forget. She serves as a substitute for what I have lost.

"You're not eating anything?" asks Jo, sitting next to me.

The young woman is wearing a white nightgown that barely covers her thighs. The urge to take her on the table comes to me. She must feel the same way, because she keeps crossing and uncrossing her legs provocatively. As for me, I'm wearing only my midnight blue pajama pants.

"I'm not hungry."

My tone is harsher and colder than I wanted it to be. I don't care if she gets offended, she can leave if she doesn't like it.

Like every morning, Alfrida busies herself preparing lunch. She has been living on the property for several years, in a cottage built in her honor. She's been with us forever and doesn't seem to want to stop anytime soon.

She passes to my right and fills my cup coffee.

"You look a bit pale," she notes, placing a hand on my shoulder as her eyes scrutinize my pale face.

That's an understatement. I barely slept all night, tormented by my father's death and all that it implies. Lovisa's return also disturbed me. I never thought I'd see her show up here. Like a coward, I would have seen her pocket her inheritance from a distance.

The first steps of the stairs creak. *She's coming.* Immediately, Krigare, my dog, stands up behind me and whines.

"Don't move."

Lovisa, accompanied by her idiot boyfriend, enters through the glass door, the only separation between the kitchen and the hall. The sight of her freezes me for a moment. She's wearing tight jeans with a snug camel-colored sweater. Her beautiful curls cascade gracefully over her body, particularly over her breasts, which have grown significancy since our teenage years. *Still as beautiful.* A fiery desire fills my me before hatred replaces it when Rikard wraps his arms around her hips.

"The cries of a red fox disturbed my sleep," I growl, looking coldly at the couple.

The Iron House forest is teeming with these mammals for several years now. Anyone would think of these animals. But Lovisa feels targeted. My remark makes her blush with shame. She tugs at the sleeves of her sweater, chewing her lower lip. I recognize this gesture, having seen it a thousand times before: she's uncomfortable. If she thought I hadn't heard her, given the shameless moans she let out, she's dumber than I thought.

"Lovisa?" Alfrida is surprised. "What are you doing here?"

The housekeeper warmly kisses her cheek before inviting her to sit across from Jo and me. Without delay, she fills two cups with hot coffee and serves them breakfast.

"We had an issue with our hotel. They were all booked up."

"Really?"

I smirk wickedly and take a sip of my coffee; I like it black.

Yesterday, I acted impulsively, even though every fiber of my being revolts against her presence in my home. I wouldn't have been able to stand knowing she was so far away in the city. Now, I wonder if I made a mistake by pushing her to stay here. What do I expect from her? I attribute this error in judgment to the turmoil I felt at my father's sudden death. A heart attack. That's what killed the great Hendrik Ekman, respected and feared by all. His heart didn't care about his reputation as a shark and didn't hesitate to give up on him. His body tried to warn him several times, but he lived in opulence excess that eventually did him in.

I won't make the same mistake.

Around the table, the atmosphere is charged with a palpable tension. Rikard and Jonna eat without paying attention to what's happening around them. They discuss interesting things to do in town. The discomfort that I can almost feel on the tip of my tongue if I open my mouth comes from Lovisa.

My little Love, what makes you so anxious?

"It must feel strange to sleep here," Jonna says, eating her scrambled eggs.

The pretty redhead's gaze shifts from the blonde to me before quickly returning to her friend. Lovisa's beautiful irises darken for a moment before becoming as soft as those of a deer.

Soft and innocent.

Some things never change. Nevertheless, there's something different about her, but I don't know what yet.

To tease her, I lean toward Jonna and place a trail of kisses from her shoulder to her neck. My hand gently grabs the back of her neck, which I caress with my thumb. Jonna, receptive, slides a hand onto my leg and leans toward me, demanding more. Modesty is not in my vocabulary, and this kind of display is common. Alfrida no longer mind. She busies herself with the dishes while humming Swedish tune.

Lovisa follows this little show, stung with jealousy. She can't say anything; she neither has the right nor the courage. Rikard, by her side, savors this display of affection with shining eyes. His girlfriend doesn't satisfy him? I greatly appreciate Love's gaze, who can't help but moisten her lower lip as her gaze falls on my mouth, still against Jonna's skin.

It could have been you!

But it's not, and it never will be. Lovisa swallows hard, adverting her gaze. She clears her throat and mumbles reluctantly, "It's strange, yes, but deep down, it's like coming back from a long trip."

Nine years. Nine long and endless years. So much has happened. I'm no longer the teenager she knew, and she's no longer *my Love*.

I eventually separate from Jonna, and I casually go back to my coffee, while Jonna takes a moment to gather herself. She regains her beautiful smile.

"In any case, you didn't waste any time to inaugurate the place with your boyfriend," Jo quips mischievously.

I like her frankness. She always speaks her mind, even if it hurts people. She has a big mouth. When we were younger, it got her into some trouble. At seventeen, we went out drinking at a club where I had connections. Money can open all doors, no matter your age, especially if you find people who aren't too concerned about legality. A bunch of older guys, fueled by alcohol, had hit on her before one of them slapped her butt. Immediately, Jonna hurled the most vicious insults at him before resorting to blows. With the gang, we came to her rescue. I ended up with a black eye and a bloody fist.

"Sorry about last night, Lovisa doesn't know how to keep quiet," Rikard intervenes, pulling the young woman close to him.

"You must be good," Jo coos, giving them a wink.

"What do you think Lovisa?"

Lovisa blushes. Flustered, she stuffs a big piece of bread into her mouth and chews slowly.

"Are you keeping quiet because you're afraid I'll steal him?" Jonna teases.

"Or because he's a lousy lover," I taunt.

An awkward silence fills the room. Like Jo, I don't hold back, and my remark makes everyone uncomfortable. Rikard's pride takes a hit, and anger can be read on his face.

"That's not what Lovisa says every night, without fail," Rikard retorts, glaring at him.

"Every night, huh?" I ask.

"Exactly. We're having a great time."

"Rikard…" Lovisa starts, mortified at the thought of her sex life being aired out during our breakfast.

I can tell that Lovisa is mortified by the flush creeping up her neck and into her cheeks. She ducks her head to avoid my gaze and focuses intently on eating her breakfast. I smirk at her before standing up.

"Well, I have stuff to do. Love, Mr. Stallion," I say, holding myself back from laughing.

Without inviting Jonna to follow me, I leave the dining room. Before climbing the stairs, I hear Rikard say, "Why does he call you Love? You always forbade me to."

His question raises others within me. Indeed, why? For me? For us? Back then, I was the only one who called her Love, and I forbade her to be called that by anyone. Was this promise been kept after all these years? *Love…* Much more than a nickname, four little letters that mean many things, things that I haven't felt for a long time.

I slip away to take a shower, with Krigare on my heels. Business doesn't wait, and the cartel's *captains* don't care about my mourning. At twenty-seven, I'm now at the head of one of the biggest drug trafficking operations in Sweden, and I have to reassure my collaborators. For the past few years, I've been the intermediary between my father and most of his subordinates. I know the business inside out.

I'm the *sheriff* now.

I've always liked this title, a joke that only I find funny. Although immersed in criminal cases, we bear titles inspired by the world of justice. Me, the *sheriff*. The three *captains* who deal directly with me shared the country equally. Each manages a number of men, *lieutenants*, who bring cash to my *captains* and supply drugs to a *sergeant*, who themselves distribute the goods to *juniors*. The network, much more complex due to its security, transport, and above all production, is very vast and requires a lot of attention. No position can be neglected. With this new role, enormous responsibilities fall on me.

My phone has been ringing incessantly since I woke up. I answer every other time. Most of these calls are from people offering their condolences.

Bunch of ass-kissers.

I see in them as vultures waiting only two things from me: my death, to benefit from the fortune of the Ekmans, or my favors while I'm alive. Either way, they can all go to hell; I plan to piss them all off and handle business as I see fit.

"Have you showered yet?" Jonna asks.

This rhetorical question makes me smile. A shower with Jonna means guaranteed sex.

I fasten my watch while admiring the snowy landscape through the window. The young woman snuggles into my back, her arms around my waist.

"Don't you have something to do?" I ask her.

"I can stay more if you want?" she offers, slipping a hand under my sweater, where she caresses my tattoo on my ribs, on the left, which represents a grim reaper holding a sickle and a gun.

Naughty. I'd like to give in, but for now, I have other things on my mind. I turn around and lean my face toward hers. Wet locks frame my face.

"Another time. You should go, I'll be unavailable for the next few days. Maybe weeks."

My father's assets are extensive, and sorting everything out in order and putting it under my name should keep me pretty busy.

The young woman pouts before kissing me passionately. Her hands wander through my hair and grab it roughly. Her feeble attempt to rekindle desire in me normally works, but for now, it's a waste of time. I growl against her lips and grab her ass, squeezing it before releasing her.

"Go, it's better that way."

After tying up my hair, I put on my wolf head ring and slip my brass knuckles into the back pocket of my pants. A cigarette tucked behind my ear, I leave my room without looking at Jo, with Krigare following me like my shadow. My thoughts are already far away as I check my phone to sort out the importance of my missed phone calls.

At the bottom of the stairs, Oscar is waiting for me with a holster, which I put on. I slide in two black Golden Eagles, on the grip of which my initials are engraved. They've been with me for so long that the engraving is almost worn off.

Then, I head toward my father's old office, which is now mine.

"How long will they be here?" I ask, lighting my cigarette.

"An hour, sir. What do we do about Miss Granberg and her boyfriend?"

For a brief moment, I had forgotten their existence. I exhale the smoke while staring at the black-painted oak desk. More than once, to annoy my father, I came to snort lines of cocaine rails off it. My fingers graze the cigarette burns I left there. I was a brat. I probably deserved most of my father's beatings.

"Doesn't matter," I answer.

"Sir, that would be imprudent. Rikard Rapace seems unstable. It would be best if he stayed away from family business."

The manager of the Royal Ruby Hotel informed us of the scandal caused by Rikard. That jerk couldn't contain himself and almost came to blows with the poor receptionist. I've already figured out what kind of man he is. It's not difficult, I often meet this kind of guy.

"Ask Alfrida to take them to the farmer's market, it will keep them busy all morning."

Oscar promptly disappears.

Alone, I settle into the imposing leather armchair behind my desk and review the profiles of my captains. In all, there are three: Rodrigo Pérez, who handles the southern part between Gothenburg and Malmö. Erik Gustaf from Stockholm and surrounding cities like as Uppsala, Västeras, Örebro. As for Magnus Gyling, his territory is much larger, covering the entire north from Hudiksvall, as the population is not as dense as in the major cities. Each will come with their lieutenant. Only these men know my identity.

"It's done. They're leaving in ten minutes," Oscar says, placing three black suitcases on the desk.

Now, only Oscar, the two guards patrolling around the house, and I remain.

Not having Lovisa around will help me conduct my business, and more importantly, it will keep her safe from these thugs. She knows about the family business, but has always kept her distance. I don't intend to change that. I don't want her in this shit. At any moment, I could fall. I won't drag anyone down with me.

As I crush my cigarette, I reach into my phone and call one of my contacts. On the third ring, a sleepy voice answers.

"Gun? What the hell are you doing?"

"Shit," mutters my childhood friend. "I drank too much last night."

"Fuck, man, get over here or I'll put a bullet in your ass," I growl as I stand up.

I walk toward the large bay window, through which I see long mane of red hair by the bird feeders. Wearing a dark coat, Lovisa admires black-throated accentors feasting on the seeds of the birdhouse.

Damn, she's beautiful.

No matter how hard I try to deny it, I can't do anything against my heart racing at the sight of her. My feelings have never faded. Sensing my gaze on her, Lovisa twirls in my direction. Her face, so pale it would make the purest snow jealous, offers me a shy smile.

Don't. Smile. At. Me. Like. That.

How am I supposed to resist her if she keeps making my heart beat faster in her presence?

I just stare at her, running my hand through my beard. Without my being able to control it, an old memory resurfaces.

Twelve years ago

Five months have passed since Lovisa and her mother moved into Iron House. The war between her and me is still ongoing, and nothing seems to be able to ease this tension. Despite Hendrik and her mother, Sigrid, punishing us for the low blows we exchange, nothing changes. That's why they gave up and left us to fend for ourselves. I'm happy about it, now able to act without restraint. As for Lovisa, she laments this lack of authority and feels completely alone. At my mercy. My personal toy.

The holidays don't help. We're constantly fighting when I'm not with my friends. Today, I'm at the property, just like her. We're forbidden from entering the house, because my father is holding a meeting with his captains. I'll soon be sixteen, and I'll be able to learn the tricks of the business. Meanwhile, I live my teenage life and torment Lovisa whenever I get the chance.

Coming back from a bike ride, I turn left to go along the side of the house, where the bird feeders and a shed are located. As I approach the shed to store my bicycle, a man's voice reaches my ears. Silently, I unload my bike and frown when a second voice, Lovisa's, answers the stranger.

"I like taking care of them," Lovisa says, referring to the birds.

"And you? Who takes care of you?"

I spy on them, hidden behind the shed. Lovisa is with a man much older. In his thirties, probably. He's one of my dad's captains. A Spaniard with very short black hair and a beard of a few days. Rodrigo Pérez. He exudes a dark aura that, at thirteen, makes her uncomfortable. Her shoulders tense as he tries to touch her face.

"I... I have my mother, she must be waiting for me inside."

She tries to dodge him by heading toward the entrance through the kitchen, but he grabs her arm to turn her around. Her eyes widen. He immediately releases her, laughing.

"Easy there, I didn't mean to scare you. Stay, okay?"

Lovisa just nods. Her body is tense, she doesn't want to stay, but she also doesn't dare to run away. I feel a ball of anger ravaging my insides. Why such a reaction? I've been tormenting her for weeks, and yet, seeing her so disadvantaged against Rodrigo doesn't sit well with me. What does this bastard want from her? Shouldn't he be with my dad?

"You're beautiful," Pérez says, caressing her cheek. "So soft and innocent. You've never had a boyfriend, have you?"

It's too much for me to bear, I can't take it anymore. I come out of my hiding spot and rush at them. Seeing me, Rodrigo steps back, smiling.

"Niklas, my boy. Long time no see. I was just getting to know this charming young lady."

Without letting myself be fooled by his fake smile, I step between them and glare at the captain.

"Don't go near her," I hiss.

Rodrigo laughs at my hostile attitude. He's much taller than me and dominates the space between us. Nevertheless, I stand my ground and confront him.

"Don't be so defensive, we were just talking."

"I saw your hands on her."

Lovisa squirms behind me, uncomfortable being stuck in such a situation.

"So what? What are you going to do?" Rodrigo asks.

The lawless man raises an eyebrow, challenging me with his gaze. I try to contain myself while clenching my fists. My father would probably tell me to back down and not piss off his "employees" because it could harm his business. But being a rebellious teenager, I do as I please, and all the punishment in the world won't change that.

"For now, nothing but when I'll be at the head of this empire, believe me, I'll crush you."

The Spanish man starts to laugh again before abruptly stopping. All joy leaves his face as he roughly ruffles my hair.

"We'll see, kid."

He casts an envious glance at the girl behind me before walking away to go back into the house.

Alone, I turn to Lovisa and grab her by the shoulders.

"You never go near him again, understood?"

"I... Yes."

She nervously bites her lower lip.

"And stop doing that, you'll damage your skin."

Lovisa complies, blushing as she lowers her head. "Thank you."

Without me, who knows how far Pérez would have gone? She knows about Hendrik's business and his shady associates, but she doesn't know that, even though she's under my father's protection, he wouldn't lift a finger to help her if one of his men targeted her.

"I won't always be around, so don't be alone with him. Or anyone."

***

It was on that day I realize that, beyond my hatred, there was actually hiding a budding love for her.

Lovisa's beautiful smile fades when she notices the weapons strapped to my chest. The men she once feared as a child are now part of the past, and the one she loved seems to have become one of them. I can't do anything about it; it's my life now.

Lovisa is joined by her boyfriend and Alfrida. This distraction allows me to escape from her angelic image and focus on the meeting that is about to take place. I have to impose myself as a leader and assert my rights to the others. It's survival of the fittest, and I must be persuasive if I don't want them to betray me at the first opportunity.

The captains and their lieutenants almost all arrive at the same time. In front of my desk are three armchairs for Erik, Rodrigo, and Magnus. As for their followers, they position themselves behind their leader.

After cordial exchanges and the presentation of their condolences, the meeting can begin.

"I've gathered you here with the expectation that you'll show me the same loyalty that you had toward my father."

Magnus is about to speak, but I raise my hand to silence him.

"If you still intend to work with me, know that things are going to change. First, let's start with a more than generous gift to celebrate my ascent to this new position."

I open one of the three suitcases. It contains large wads of cash.

First, I call Marcus, Erik's lieutenant; I hand him the suitcase, and do the same with Jonas, who came with Magnus. When it's Artur's turn, I lock eyes with the young man.

"This suitcase is for you, if you agree to replace Rodrigo."

"What!" Rodrigo burst out, abruptly standing up. "What the hell is this?"

This announcement sends a chill through the room. The last time there was a change in the captain position was over fifteen years ago.

"Your sector isn't bringing in enough profit, you're not taking enough risks, and I need new blood."

"Niklas—"

"I'm not giving you a choice. If you contest my decision, I'll be happy to personally deal with you."

"It's not reasonable to put someone else in this position just as you've taken the reins," Magnus intervenes.

"Artur has been working by my side for many years; he knows how things works. Isn't that right?"

Artur nods. Deposing his boss probably wasn't part of his plans, but he knows that an opportunity like this may not come again for a long time.

"Power corrupts, kid," the Spanish man spits, angry.

"I always keep my promises," I whisper darkly.

A wicked smile spread across my face. One of my qualities is that I never forget anything. And the day I promised Rodrigo to get rid of him is etched in my memory.

"You're just a bastard. If you think my men will work for Artur without me around, you're wrong."

"I trust him, he'll know how to earn acceptance and respect. Now, get out before I take pleasure in getting rid of you," I threaten, tapping one of my guns.

Oscar returns in time. His imposing build doesn't make you want to fight him.

"Mr. Pérez, follow me."

"It's not over," Rodrigo threatens.

"This partnership is over. And so are you."

Fuming, he leaves the office, escorted by my head of security.

Far from being stupid, I know I'm taking a big risk with this move, but I believe in this change.

It's for the best.

"Are you sure you know what you're doing?" Magnus asks, breaking the silence.

"My father's reign died with him. I need to assert myself and change things."

"But firing Rodrigo—"

"Was necessary," I cut him off. "He was a weak link."

In my opinion, you have to be ruthless when the situation calls for it.

"Let's get back to our business."

With a nod, I gesture for Artur to take his suitcase, and he sits on Rodrigo's former seat.

"If you follow me, your profits will increase, and we can expand beyond Sweden."

"Do you want us to go international?" Magnus, the oldest of the three and the most reasonable, is surprised.

"Exactly. I'm tired of being satisfied with Swedish peanuts, we have a solid network, and so far, we've never been caught. We're ready."

I'm the youngest in the room, but also the most daring. I think big and want to prove that I can do better than my late father, who never wanted to extend his power beyond our borders.

"You've only just taken the throne, get your bearings before—" starts Artur.

"I've been in charge a lot longer than that. I know what I'm doing."

"I don't doubt that, but think carefully before making such a decision," Magnus calmly intervenes.

"I don't regret my new position, but with Rodrigo's Spanish origins, it would have brought us significant additional contacts to expand elsewhere," says Artur.

"I don't give a fuck about Rodrigo and his influence. He's not here anymore, we'll manage without him."

Isn't there one on my side?

I turn to Erik, a forty-year-old man with a military style. Close-shaven hair, pants tucked into large boots, with a fitted sweater that shows off his muscular build.

"And you? You have nothing to say?"

Erik caresses his gun, holstered at his belt. He inhales, exhales, before answering. "It's risky, but count me in. That's a fucking good idea."

If dollar bill could shine in his eyes, we wouldn't see his irises anymore, so delighted is he at the idea of earning money.

"In any field, change is scary. It brings its benefits, but also risks. I can't promise it'll be perfect at the beginning, but with our contact outside, it can work."

I lay out more arguments as I rise from my seat. I pace the room, and my audience listens to me attentively, as if I were a great orator. I speak clearly and fiercely when emphasizing certain words. I've always had the soul of a leader. Despite myself, I'm my father's legacy. He shaped who I am today.

At the end of the meeting, my captains are on my side. All points regarding drug trafficking have been addressed.

"You can go now. We'll stay in touch."

They all leave the room, guided by Oscar.

Now that things are clear, I can reign as I see fit.

***

Perched at the window in my bachelor apartment in the attic, I watch the sedan park in front of the villa while smoking a menthol cigarette. Lovisa, Rikard, and Alfrida get out of the vehicle, arms full of paper bags; the couple seem to be in deep conversation. After dropping off all the packages, they go up to the young woman's room. Their voices reach me, but not clearly enough for my liking, so I decide to go down, making the first steps creak. In the hallway, I lean against the doorframe of my gym and take a long drag of nicotine.

"Can you try to postpone the reading of the will?" Rikard asks.

"Impossible. It's not up to me."

"I don't like the idea of leaving you here alone," Rikard says

Leaving her alone? Is Rikard leaving? This news pleases me, though it shouldn't. If I could tear out my heart to feel nothing but a soothing emptiness, I would.

"You have to answer all my calls and text me as often as possible."

"Sometimes the reception is bad here, we're quite far from the city," Lovisa says.

"I don't care, do your best."

His tone is final and irritates me. Who does he think he is, talking to her like that?

"Wish her a good recovery from me," she says.

I deduce by myself that there's an injured person. They leave the room and go downstairs without noticing me. If he leaves Iron House, that changes everything. *Everything.* The desire to play with her again, to torture her and show her all that she has done to me in her absence gnaws at me. Oh yes, I'm going to have fun.

When Love is back in her room, I take the opportunity to join her. Stripped of her blouse and with her back to me, she gives me the opportunity to observe her skin, startlingly pale. On her right shoulder blade, the tattoo of a white wolf howling at the moon is drawn with a felt-tip pen effect. *It's for me.* It's obvious. I'm her white wolf, she's my red fox. My back represents what we have been, a red fox and a white wolf intertwined. This vision awakens in me far more emotions than I would like to admit. She doesn't make it easy for me.

"Nik… What are you doing here?"

Vision blurred by the feelings I'm trying to repress. I didn't see her turn around to face me. Blushing under my scrutinizing gaze, she grabs her sweater to cover her chest, whose fabric so thin and transparent leaving little to the imagination. I knew her with simpler underwear. This adult woman's body is foreign to me, and this harsh reality is much more painful than I thought. Consumed by a furious desire to hurt her in return, I grab her by the neck and pretend to tighten my grip on her tender flesh. Leaning toward her, I whisper, "You're mine now."

I brush her lips with mine and restrain myself from biting her. She has no idea of all the things I dream of doing to her.

I release her and step away with a smirk.

"Watch your back, Love, you'll need it."

7

Lovisa, 13 years old

For the first time in months, I glimpse his light. He's not just darkness as he tries to make me believe. Nik was kind to me by protecting me from Hendrik's henchman. To thank him, with mom's help, I set up his mother's old painting studio in an unoccupied room. I thought he would like the attention, but instead, he destroyed everything and ordered me never to touch his stuff again. I don't understand him. One day he's being nice, and the next day he's the same obnoxious teenager who welcomed me the first time. Mom says he suffer a lot from his own mother abandonment, who left without saying anything. I try to be understanding, but he doesn't make it easy for me.

***

I didn't expect to see foxes on the Ekman property. A whole family lives freely in the forest. Accustomed for years to being fed by humans, they are almost not afraid anymore. I never thought I would one day be able to get this close to these animals. With Alfrida's help, I found them easily. They have settled almost at the edge of the estate.

"Be careful, they're still wild animals," the housekeeper warned me.

I don't plan on rolling with them in the snow or playing with whoever submits to the other first. I'll keep my guard up. What I want is to be close enough to photograph them and entertain the idea of petting them if I detect no danger.

With my Nikon camera, I squat down and take some pictures of the fox cubs squabbling. This sight of innocent beings touches me.

They remind me of you, sweet and beautiful, words said a long time ago by Niklas.

Alfrida told me it was Nik's idea to bring foxes to Iron House.

It's for me, I thought immediately.

He promised me that one day he would give me these animals. My heart tightens, I bring a hand to my chest. It was Niklas who made me love these fiery-colored mammals.

Lost in thought, I don't immediately notice that a young fox is watching me, just few steps away. A smile lights up my face when I see him so close. I take a picture of him before extending my hand, palm up to gain his trust

"Don't be afraid. Come closer."

Seeming to understand me, he cautiously advances. His wet nose touches my fingers. I try to stroke his head, he runs away.

"No! I won't hurt you!" I exclaim, disappointed, as I stand up.

"He's lucky."

I startle and turn to the owner of the voice. Niklas stands behind me, hands in his pockets. He wears a simple sweater and jeans. No jacket or scarf despite the biting cold? He'll catch a cold.

At his feet, Krigare wags his tail vigorously when he sees the foxes fleeing our presence. Docile, he doesn't try to chase them.

"What are you doing here? I thought you were too busy avoiding me."

Since Rikard left yesterday, and his intrusion into my room while I was changing, Niklas has done everything possible to avoid crossing paths with me.

"It's my place, I go where I please," he says harshly.

"Well, I'll leave then."

I don't want to bother him anymore and make the situation more tense than necessary. After one last look at the foxes, I walk away toward the house. My steps crush the snow, and soon enough, I hear those of the Viking-like man behind me.

"What happened to you?"

"What are you talking about?" I ask without turning around.

He positions himself beside me, leaving a good foot between us, where his dog stands, tongue hanging out to the side.

"I knew you much more combative. You seem to be... extinguished."

His words hit me like a jolt of electricity. I stop abruptly and look at him, pale. Am I that transparent? How much have I changed? Sure, I'm no longer the teenager who dared to say no and who fought back when attacked, but isn't there still a last trace of that young girl in me?

"What? You lost your tongue?"

I open my mouth and then close it, which annoys Niklas, but I don't know why.

"You've changed. You lost that spark that—"

He interrupts himself, leaving me hanging. That what? What did he mean? A ball of frustration knots my stomach.

"I've grown up, that's all."

He chuckles, running his hand through his beard, where small ice crystals have formed. His lips are slightly blue, and his complexion pale. Couldn't he cover up like everyone else to go outside?

"If being an adult means being boring as hell, I'm glad I didn't grow up."

His words offend me. At least I know what he thinks of me. He has a low opinion of me, and it hurts me more than I would have wanted. Krigare licks my hand. Animals are sensitive and can feel the sadness of human. I thank him with a gentle look.

"Indeed," I finally let go, "I recognize the teenager that you were before."

I start walking again, a little faster to try to get ahead of him, but it's a waste of time. We both remain silent, and I think about the situation we find ourselves in. Soon, this torment will be over, and our paths will no longer cross. Suddenly, seeming to pick up on my thoughts, he gets angry next to me.

"You've got some nerve coming back for money. As if you didn't have enough when you ran away from here."

My escape… My banishment to be more precise. At the time, I was chased out of Iron House despite my protests. I didn't know get to say goodbye to Niklas. Worse, I was forced to write him a letter under Hendrik's instructions. My words, each crueler than the last, were said to prevent him from trying to find me. I nervously chew my lower lip as I quicken my pace.

I'm sorry, so sorry, and my heart bleeds every time I think of that fateful day.

My stepfather is dead, and yet, the truth can't seem to come out.

What's the point? The damage is done. I can never erase the past, and soon I'll be out of his life again. My desire to confess the truth evaporates.

Furious at getting no reaction from me, he roughly grabs my arm to force me to face him. His imposing and dominant stature always surprises me. He's grown so much!

"Answer me, for fuck's sake!"

Krigare barks nervously and circles around us. unperturbed, Nik glares at me and waits for an answer.

"I—"

The expression *saved by the bell* comes to mind when my phone rings. I managed to break free from his grip by placing my hand on his. This contact sends shiver down my spine, and a jolt tingles my fingers. Bewildered, Niklas lets go of me and strides away with his dog.

Nick…

Why does my tongue remain inert? My inner voice screams and knocks against the barriers that have risen between the rest of the world and me. I want to speak out, to shout, to strike without restraint. But I can't, I can't anymore. When did I change? I know when. Rikard. But realizing it changes nothing, because I let it happen, I could have said stop and told him to screw off. Instead, I let him take every piece of my being to make it his own and do what he wants. In fact, it's him calling me. I answer before the last ring.

"Rikard? Sorry, I'm out for a walk in the forest. Can you hear me okay?"

✱✱✱

Monday arrives, and Mr. Linderoth reads the will, seated in Niklas' chair. As for us, we're right across, awaiting the reading of Hendrik's final wishes. Oscar is among us, positioned near the entrance to be as discreet as possible. After listing the charities that the late Ekman decided to donate a considerable amount of money to comes the turn of the individuals present in the room.

"'To my son, Niklas Hendrik Ekman, I bequeath all my real estate properties as well as all my stocks and shares in the following companies…,'" Linderoth reads, listing the businesses. "'Iron House must stay in the family, and only a male descendant can be its owner.'"

The announcement of everything Niklas owns now is not surprising. He already knew it. I listen with a distracted ear to the rest of Hendrik's demands for his son. I'm in the grip by heightened anxiety. My hands nervously clutch my pants as my worried face stares at the lawyer. Hendrik never loved me; he found me too weak and fragile, and each of his punishments only confirmed what he thought of me.

"'To my daughter-in-law, Lovisa Granberg, I bequeath one hundred thousand kroner at the age of thirty-one, as well as the clothing store that I gave to her mother.'"

The lawyer slides an envelope toward me and adds, "He wanted to give you this letter."

I take it, squeezing it so tightly that the paper crumples.

Mr. Linderoth continues his monologue. I no longer listen, overcome by a feeling of anger, of betrayal. I was counting on the money to build myself a new life, but Hendrik decided otherwise. *Bastard!* Even after death, he continues to control me. I'm starting to get tired of the men around me dictating what I should do and how I should be. Tears of rage threaten to spill, but I hold them back until the end.

Despite the anger, a question remains. Why did he leave me this money? Does he regrets banishing me? Or maybe it's to continue to keep me away from Iron House? From Niklas? The answers must lie within this letter.

"Thank you, I'll schedule another meeting when you're finished with the paperwork," Niklas says, firmly shaking the lawyer's hand.

"Very well, Mr. Ekman. I'll do my best. Goodbye to you too, Miss Granberg."

I forget my manners and leave the room.

What am I going to do? This isn't what I had planned. I was counting on this money. At only thirty-one years old? The same age as my mother when she met him. And her boutique. What is he trying to tell me?

I escape into the garden, feverishly, tear open the envelope to read the few words he left for me.

Lovisa,

You've been loyal so far, and your efforts have been rewarded. I'm no longer here, but Mr. Linderoth will always look after my interests as well as those of my son. Keep staying away from him;

otherwise, the consequences could be terrible for you.
With all the affection I had for your mother,
H. Ekman

Tears blur my vision as I read his words, and I crumple the letter into a ball and throw it away.

While looking around for a solution, I let my tears stream down my face. I'm wearing only my sweater, and the cold immediately freezes my skin.

Bastard!

Bastard! Bastard! Bastard!!!

My breathing becomes shorter and more erratic, the fresh air stinging my nostrils unpleasantly. Dizzy, I lean forward, resting on my knees. A painful pressure tightens in the chest. I've been prone to these kinds of attacks for several years now. With blurred vision, I stare at a branch at my feet as I cry hot tears. Nothing seems to be able to stop me, and my anxiety only increases as the minutes go by.

A large, warm hand lands on my back.

"Lovisa…"

Unable to reply, stopping crying seems out of reach. My sobs mixed with my tears must reddening my skin. I probably look like a pitiful creature. Self-esteem, forget about it.

Taking deep breaths, I miraculously manage to calm myself down. Sniffling repeatedly, I rub my face with my sleeve and straighten up. For now, I don't care about being refined.

"Are you feeling better?"

"Not really."

I wipe the last of my teras from under my eyes with my index finger.

"What made you react like that? And don't try to tell me it's my father's death affecting you. You never cared for him."

That statement brings a weak smile to my tear-swollen face. I take a deep breath before lifting my emerald gaze to Nik.

"You wouldn't understand."

"You'd be surprised. Tell me," He demands.

Niklas is still the same. With just, nine years later, a body to die for and a fortune so vast he couldn't spend it all in one lifetime. He's physically stronger, but he also has an iron will. Not once have I seen him falter. He's my opposite.

"Is the money the problem? Rikard doesn't give you enough, is that it?" Nik asks.

"He gives me nothing, I provide for myself."

I'm not a kept woman, at least not entirely.

"Then what?"

"Leave me alone."

I try to go inside, but he blocks my way. I'm annoyed. It's a habit with him to constantly stand in my way.

"Let me in."

"Not until you explain to me what got you into this state. You want money? Haven't you had enough all these years?"

How does he know that I was receiving money?

"How do you know th—"

"I overheard my father talking to his accountant about it."

I could do without his judgmental gaze. He doesn't know the whole story.

"You really only came for the cash. You don't give a fuck about anything else!"

He takes his wallet out of his back pocket and throws a bill at my feet.

"Is that what you want?"

He throws a second bill.

"Stop."

"Want another one?"

He throws another, then another, and lets out a joyless laugh.

"Had enough or do want more? I've got plenty."

Another bill.

"Nik, stop…" I murmur, pleading.

He doesn't listen and throws all he has left.

"You're no different from Sigrid."

The mention of my mother fills me with anger. Without thinking, I slap him and shout, "I forbid you tarnish her memory! You don't know what you're talking about!"

Niklas has always had a fiery temper. Without hesitation, he grabs me by the neck and pins me against the wall of the house, so hard that he could have broken something. His eyes wild, he tightens his grip on my throat, just enough to show me that he's serious. It's a warning.

"Dare to raise your hand on me again and I swear you won't touch anything ever again," he hisses through gritted teeth.

I try to make him let go, but he's so strong that his hand doesn't move an inch. He's not the first to assault me, I'm used to it. However, his gesture affects me.

"Let go of me!"

My cries alert Alfrida, who rushes outside. Seeing us, she brings a scandalized hand to her mouth.

"Niklas! Let her go now!"

"Stay out of this, go back inside, you'll be cold."

The old lady descends the few steps and confronts the giant.

"I didn't raise you to strike women."

"Frida…"

My lips quiver with anger under the harsh words that I want to throw at him. I know what to say to get through to him. Several times, I open my mouth, but I can't seem to make a sound.

Damn it, speak!

"You…"

"You what, huh? Come on, speak!"

"You…"

"You, you, you," Niklas cruelly mocks.

My nostrils flare, I dig my nails into his hand to make him let me go.

"You're just like Hendrik," I spit out violently.

It's as if he just took a cold shower. His face turns pale, and in an instant, he releases me.

He steps back. I take advantage of this opening to flee inside.

"Niklas, what's wrong with you, my boy?" I hear Alfrida ask before I head to my room.

What's wrong with him indeed? He promised me a long time ago to take care of me, and his actions today have proved otherwise. His hatred toward me runs much deeper than I thought.

8

Niklas, 15 years old

She's so weak and fragile. She looks like a little bird that I could crush if I squeezed my hands too tight around her. I hate weakness, I get that from my father, and Lovisa represents everything he forbids me to be. He wants me to be tough, strict, and blunt. Or rather, cruel. For him, it's important to be a leader and make others to fear me. I apply his teaching to everyone except my friends and Lovisa. If I listen to my father, I weaken in front of pussy which isn't worth it. According to him, no woman deserves to make you weak. But is it weakness to feel compassion, or even tenderness, toward a person as cute and clumsy as her?

***

"Damn! What a hottie!" Gunkil exclaims as he watches Lovisa in front of the house.

She's waiting for the driver to bring the car. As she has no means of transport since Rikard left, I insisted that she use my black sedan.

"Check out at that little ass," continues my best friend, biting his fist. "Dude, your sis has gotten damn hot."

My childhood friend always pushes the boundaries; he's one of few people—along with Fredrik—that I'll never hurt. But when it comes to *my* Love, it's different. I let out a growl of annoyance. Drink in hand, I sit in front of the fireplace. "Shut up, she's not my sister."

I refuse to be called brother and sister, there's no blood relationship between us. If that were the case, I'd never love her and dream of doing all those things when I see her.

"Stop it, Gun, you know he's touchy when it comes to his chick," Fredrik intervenes, holding a half-empty glass of vodka.

Gunkil runs his tongue over his lower lip. Like a predator, he devours her with his icy gaze. She's off-limits. Always has been. As a teenager, he had nevertheless tried his luck. Few resisted him; his naturally tanned complexion and his black hair always styled in the latest fashion made all the girl crack. Lovisa was one of the few who resisted his charm. She called him a *perv* every time he made a move. His approach with girls back then was quite crude.

"How long is she staying?"

"I don't know, Gun. Who cares. I didn't bring you guys here to talk about her," I say impatiently as I refill my vodka glass.

When I'm in a bad mood, it's best not to provoke me.

My friends settle on the couches to my left and my right, ready to listen.

"I fired one of my guys, Rodrigo Pérez, a few days ago," I start, lighting a mint cigarette. "And since then, I've had problems."

It was to be expected. I knew I'd be faced with Rodrigo's fury, but not this soon.

"The bastard sold out several of my hideouts, worth millions, all gone, requisitioned by DEA. A dozen men were arrested; so far, they haven't said anything, but if we don't stop him, he'll destroy everything my father spent years building."

"The asshole," Fredrik swears, leaning forward to listen.

They've known about my family's business since their teenage years. In Kiruna, besides the two of them, nobody knows about it, yet everyone fears the Ekmans. An evil and dangerous energy has been emanating from us for generations. Feared and admired at the same time.

"He won't stop there this kind of man doesn't give up until the job's done."

"Why did you get rid of him? Don't tell me it's for Lovisa?" Gunkil asks.

Like me, he has a good memory, and that day he managed to reason with me because I was ready to turn Sweden upside down to find him. Even at fifteen, I was determined to go through with my ideas.

I exhale the white smoke in front of me before answering, "An old promise I had to respect."

"The word of an Ekman is sacred," Fredrik quotes, smiling.

I nod and get comfortable on the couch, my glass in hand with also my cigarette.

"What do you want from us?" he adds, already knowing the answer.

Gunkil and Fredrik are good trackers. They converted into bounty hunters after working in the police. Gunkil used to work in one of my bars, but he drank heavily and doing cocaine at all hours. I ended up firing him. If I hadn't, he'd probably be in the ground, killed by my hand.

"Find him and bring him to me."

"Alive?"

"Yes, I want to take care of him personally," I say grimly, drinking my glass in one gulp. "I need to make an example of him. I won't be taken seriously until I stop Rodrigo for fucking me."

My father had instilled a climate of terror. He was ruthless and wouldn't hesitate to get his hands dirty to teach a lesson to anyone who dared to defy his authority. More than once, I saw him draw blood. I went down to his basement, although it was a forbidden zone during my childhood, when I heard men screaming, begging him to stop. I witnessed the horrors Hendrik was capable of committing.

"We've just been given a case, but it can wait," Fredrik says, looking at his colleague.

Gunkil nods, suddenly gloomy. Of the three of us, he's the one who always laughs and doesn't take anything seriously. But work is work. He's found his calling and enjoy tracking down scum to put them in jail.

"You'll be compensated—"

"No need for that between us," Fredrik cuts in, waving his hand.

"Vodka for life in your bar will do," adds Gun.

I smile amused, I've access to all the alcohol I want for a few years now. Our favorite drink remains vodka, like most Swedes. We drank a lot of it in the past, which has often caused us to wake up with blackouts. For the past three years, I've drastically cut down on alcohol and adopted a healthier diet. I *had* to.

"I'm going to like this hunt a lot," Gunkil gloats, dimpling his cheeks and lighting a cigarette. "I'll make sure he can still walk."

"You're a really sicko," laughs Fredrik. "If we weren't friends, I'd take you for a psychopath."

It's not unusual for the criminals that Gun brings back to get beaten up. He always finds a good excuse to justify himself: he was trying to run away, he pulled a gun on him, he was being violent…

"You could work for me," I offer as my two friends joke around. "Full time, not just occasionally. I need men I can trust. Are you with me, my brothers?"

9

Lovisa, 14 years old

With delay, we celebrate my birthday. I'm living in a real fairy tale. For the occasion, Mom brought out the silver cutlery and chinas. We organized a party at Kiruna's large ice rink, and almost the entire school is there. I feel like a princess, all attention is on me, and most surprisingly, Niklas didn't make a fuss. He's having fun with his friends, but when it's time to dance, he outshines anyone who approaches me so we can dance together on the ice. The soft music, the play of blue and purple light makes this moment magical. Mom often talked to me about this feeling, butterflies in the stomach and the feeling of flying. Does she feel that with Hendrik? We never discussed it. My hands linked to Niklas', my eyes lock with his, I feel like if we're alone, that no one else exists except us. It's magic. He calls me Love, and the meaning of this nickname doesn't escape me. I don't know what to think about this, but I can't stop smiling. His Love.

***

My mother's shop is located on a small boulevard with upscale stores. The storefront of the store has a velvet red apothecary-style paint. On either side of the door, the illuminated windows display plastic mannequins dressed in sexy lingerie.

Hendrik you bastard.

Did he think it was funny when he decided to leave me a store that belonged to my mother? I never knew what to think of this place which didn't match her when she was alive.

But there's no way I'm keeping this store. I'll do anything to sell it, at any price. Then, I'll turn the page on my old life to go away from Kiruna and Stockholm. These cities have only brought me nothing but misery. After recovering from my emotions, I quickly realized that all was not completely lost. Sure, I won't have access to my inheritance for many years, but thanks to my mother's shop, nothing stop me from getting the money I need to leave.

"Miss?" calls the driver behind me, who is also an armed bodyguard.

"Wait for me in the car, I won't be long."

"Mr. Ekman specified that I shouldn't take my eyes off you."

I hold back a sigh and turn halfway toward him. I want to tell him that Niklas should do the dirty work, but this man is just doing his job and I'm not sure I prefer his boss's presence.

"I need to be alone. The car is in front, you'll see me."

Without waiting for his answer, I enter the shop. The interior is incredibly chic. Several lingerie displays showcase lace fabrics. Busts on the tables wear bras, corsets, bustiers, classics. There's everything for every taste. All highlight the woman's body. There are options for simple women wearing cotton underwear and covering their bodies, and also for those fully embracing their sensuality with lace and transparent materials. I'm in between. Rikard chooses what he likes, he believes it should please him, not me.

This store is not for me. I feel like an intruder who doesn't belong here. Yet, it belongs to me now. Including the two employees who work here.

After a quick scan, a saleswoman in her thirties approaches me. She wears a black suit with skirt that barely covers her buttocks. Is this the dress code imposed by Hendrik? With her endless legs, she has a confident step, one that makes me envious since I'm often clumsy.

"Hello, I'm Emila. Welcome. If I can help you with anything, please don't hesitate."

She takes me for a client, not for the owner of the place. Unfortunately, with a grease stain on the top of my blouse, it's true that I don't look credible. I regret having lunch without paying attention before showing up to this place that oozes luxury.

"Hello," I start, searching for words. "Actually, I'm—"

"Lovisa," growls a familiar voice behind me.

The saleswoman's eyes begin to glow with interest. Her body

leans forward to show herself off, and her slender fingers with painted nails run through her hair.

Come on.

I stop myself from rolling my eyes and turn toward Niklas. Even back then, he turned heads, and nothing has changed. His charm still works on everyone. Including me. This morning, I saw him with his two oldest friends, Gunkil and Fredrik. As teenagers, we were close; now, we barely exchange a word.

"Hello, Mr. Ekman," coos Emilia as she stands beside him.

"What are you doing here?" I ask, surprised by his arrival.

Is it a coincidence?

A palpable excitement emanates from the young saleswoman. If I wasn't here, she'd probably throw herself at him to lick every part of his Apollo-like body. I must admit that, despite my relationship, I still feel an attraction toward Nik. A desire that makes me blush and forces me to look away. A little voice inside me tells me to turn off this desire; Rikard would notice as soon as he returned.

"What can I do for you? The usual?"

What do you mean, the usual? *Has he been here before? Why? For whom?* My face heats up with jealousy that he might have bought fine lingerie for a woman. Yet, I have no right to feel this way. He can do whatever he wants.

"Yes."

"Fine, I'll select a few outfits and try them on," she says, mischief sparkling in her eyes.

What's going on here?

"Don't bother, take her size, she'll be the one trying today," Niklas says, wrapping his arm around my shoulders. "Right, Love?"

"Wh…what?"

"Don't be shy, sweetie, you'll look cute in these lingerie pieces."

What's wrong with him? I try to free myself from his grip, but he tightens his arm around my neck and lead us away, ordering the saleswoman to bring her most seductive pieces. My protests are in vain. He manages to take me to the back of the store, where there are large fitting rooms. Nik urges me to enter one of them. Fists and jaw clenched, I turn around and glare at him.

"What's wrong with you? *Sweeties*, seriously?"

"Don't get mad, it was to deceive her," he says.

"For what?"

The grease stain on my top doesn't make me credible, I could never claim to be the manager of such a glamorous and famous brand in Kiruna. But with this ridiculous acting, Niklas has just classified me in the category of *new high-class hooker* on his arm. I'm furious, everything inside me is boiling and I have a hard time containing myself. I have years of practice with Rikard, which is why the tone of my voice and my body seem almost normal.

"If you want to know how your employees work, you shouldn't reveal your true identity right away."

I then understand that this charade is meant to help me. My mood softens, but the dark cloud lingers over our heads.

"It was unnecessary; I want to sell this place and leave as soon as possible."

His beautiful blue eyes shoot terrifying sparks at me. He seems annoyed.

"Why are you so stubborn about wanting to leave at all costs? Do you miss your boyfriend that much?"

I sketch a wry smile before erasing it by turning my head away. Rikard, missing him? God, no. All I want is to run away from him, but Niklas wouldn't understand. This handsome Viking, big and strong, isn't afraid of anyone and deals with his problems face to face. So, what would he say to my plan of running away like a thief without facing my tormentor?

"It's complicated. You couldn't—"

"Understand? Is that it?" he finishes, approaching, forcing me to step back. "What do you know? You don't even try to talk to me; you dodge the conversation every time."

"That's not true. We're talking right now," I mutter, lowering my chin to my chest to avoid looking at him.

He growls in frustration at my ploy to divert his attention and walks away.

"Damn it!" he hisses.

The saleswoman returns with several pieces adorned with lace and black pearls. Without asking for my size, she selected a series of sets with a simple glance at my body.

"These are the latest models that have just arrived."

Her voice reminds me of a robot, she's much colder toward me than toward Nik. A palpable sexual tension hangs between them. *They slept together*. It's obvious. My gaze shifts from Emilia to Nik, our eyes meet, and a burning spark ignites my heart when I notice the intensity with which he's watching me.

Don't look at me like that.

"If you need me, I'm not far away."

None of us respond. Discomfort seizes me, and all I want is to leave this fitting room and flee this shop that oozes lust and decadence.

Once we're alone, Niklas runs his fingers over the black lace of a see-through bodysuit. He grabs it and throws it at me.

"Put it on," he orders.

"No way."

Again, he approaches and presses me against the wall. I'm aware of every part of his body against mine. Palpitations in the heart, stomach, but also in a much lower area, take me. His fingers graze my hip through my blouse, which suddenly feels tight and too small. He makes me hot, and the urge to take it off is itching me.

Why is he doing this?

I don't dare look at him, yet my head eventually lift timidly rising to confront him. He leans his chiseled, manly face toward mine and fills me with the scent of menthol cigarettes, but also a sweet fragrance that pleasantly makes my head spin. His lips teasingly brush against mine, exquisite in their touch. Chills once again twist my stomach, and my breath becomes short. My mouth slightly open, I dive my gaze into his icy stare.

"What are you playing at?" I whisper. "I'm in a relationship."

"That never stopped me. I even find it an additional reason to desire a woman. I don't like things that are easily acquired."

Things? I'm a human being and not an object. His way of speaking disgusts me. It's the kind of sentence could say Rikard, and yet I know deep down he's not like him.

I turn my head away and look through the still open curtain. From an external point of view, we could look like two lovers about to make love. But I'm in this fitting room with the wrong person. I place my hands on his chest to push him back.

"I'm not one of those women you play with."

As a teenager, I saw him far too often having fun with the girls, playing multiple games at once. He doesn't resist me and slowly back away.

"I made you a promise once. Do you remember?"

A promise? I search in my memory and widen my eyes when this memory comes back to me. I bite my lip as an unpleasant feeling knots my stomach. The promise to be my first kiss, first boyfriend, my first one. Unfortunately, this last step never happened.

"It's too late."

"Whose fault is it?"

Mine.

I know, I ruined everything, but did I have a choice? I was just a teenager facing a big man like Hendrik. I lower my eyes.

"Are you going to blame me for it forever?"

"You know me. I never forget anything."

Unfortunately. Damned memory.

10

Niklas, 16 years old

My dad didn't appreciate the little party in his office with my buddies. The cocaine from his stash spread out on the glass coffee table and beer bottles strewn all over the floor didn't amuse him. After chasing everyone away, he showed his anger with punches to my stomach and face. Sometimes he left the dirty work to his personal guard, Sören, an asshole who knew where to hit to make it hurt. After that, he took me to the basement, a place I'm rarely allowed to go to, especially when there are shady guys who get tortured there for mistakes he can't let go. I don't like going there; it reeks of fear, and I know what goes on there. Once again, he threw me on an old iron chair and doused me with cistern water, instantly chilling my body and destroyed all fighting spirit in me. When I went back up to my room, Lovisa came with something to heal me, and as she cleaned my split lip, I couldn't help but appreciate her delicate touch. It was so comforting, a little tenderness, no one had touched me like that since my moth

****

Damn. What the hell am I doing? I should leave her alone and let her go. Yet, something keeps me by her side, an attraction too strong to resist. She's always had this effect on me, which is why I've never been able to forget her. *Never.*

"If you won't do it for me, then do it for yourself. You have a sublime body. You should show it off."

Idiot. What kind of cheesy line is that? It's not like me to talk like that. I leave the fitting room and sit on a too small white leather couch. I always feel like a giant.

I pull out my phone and type a text to warn the driver—Malcolm— not to wait for Lovisa. I'll take care of her. He had warned me where they were going, and I couldn't resist cutting short the meeting with Gunkil and Fredrik to join them. I want to be near her, no matter where she is. And this shop is a good way to see what kind of woman she's become.

The rustle of the rings scraping the iron rod tells me that my little fox has pulled the curtain. I raise an eyebrow, looking in the direction of the dressing room. She obeyed me. I see her legs moving and her clothes falling to the floor. Immediately, a hot flush comes over me as I imagine her in her lingerie, her peachy skin exposed to the soft light of the spotlight above her. Her body is arousing. I got a glimpse of it when I barged into his room a few days ago. Her small breasts, raised to my view through her bra still haunt me. My gaze drift to her slender legs. The curtain stops above her calves, giving me a taste. I don't know her adult silhouette. She piques my curiosity. Putting away my phone, I get up and walk slowly over to the red fabric that contrasts with the rest of the immaculate white room.

My little Love, show me what's rightfully mine.

She must be mine. Body and soul. I was supposed to be her first and that place was stolen from me. By whom? When did she do it? Did she like it? Did she think of me that day? many regrets and bitterness consume me when I think of all that we missed together. Her return might be a sign. It's not that stupid Rikard Rapace who will stop me.

You have better things to do than run after her.

That's true. I have to deal with cartel problems and take care of all the assets now in my possession. But Lovisa also belongs to me, no matter who has had her first. I'll erase every kiss, every caress, every thrust until she swears by my presence alone. And then, I'll break her heart, just like she broke mine. Because I partly owe her for the cold man that I am today.

With the curtain partly open, I can see Lovisa fastens her garter belts to the black lace bustier. *Goodness.* This vision, both erotic and angelic, makes me hard instantly. I force myself not to enter this cramped space to fuck her. She's so enticing. Seeing her inspires me various ideas that I find hard to restrain. I've seen plenty of attractive women, but Love is different. *Unique.* A sublime creature from the send from the underworld to tempt anyone who lays eyes on her.

Her long red hair caresses the fabric as well as her skin, which

I imagine to be as soft as a baby's. I want to grab them and feel them. Closing my eyes, I almost sense a fragrance of delicate flowers tickling my sense. I take a deep breath and watch her. She admires herself in the mirror with a shy smile that tugs at my heartstrings my heart. She's so adorable.

Don't mess this up, Nik.

A throat clearing brings me back to reality. I barely glance behind me to find Emilia, holding a tray with two steaming cups adorned with golden patterns.

"Would you like a coffee?"

When I turn around, her seductive gaze devours me. This greedy woman, with whom I've already slept, doesn't care if I'm in a relationship. That's not that kind of detail that stops her. I see myself in her.

I decline her offer.

If I don't want to do something stupid, I have to get out of here.

"I'm leaving. Give her whatever she wants, I want her to leave with multiple outfits. Treat her as if you were serving me."

I look in the direction of Lovisa. *I know you're watching me.* I can feel it. This thought makes me harder, and I have to resist the urge to join her. I step out, adjusting my leather jacket.

I pull a cigarette from my pack and light it. It's bad for me, I know. Like junkies know drugs screw them up. I can't help it. Thank you, Gunkil.

I inhale and exhale the smoke toward the boutique window. I'm not interested in the lingerie models. My gaze goes beyond. Images of Lovisa undressing take root in my mind. I shake my head. *Stop thinking with your dick.*

My phone rings. Oscar. I take another minty puff and pick up.

"Sir, there's news about Rodrigo."

OK, spill it. My silence prompts him to continue.

"Several of his men turned against Artur, they refused his authority and left."

This was to be expected. Loyalty can't be bought, it must be earned. Artur hasn't yet proven himself as a captain, he needs to earn the trust of his men if he doesn't want to end up with a bullet between his eyes.

"Where are they now?"

"I don't know yet, we're working on it. They must have joined Rodrigo."

"I think so, too. Inform Gun and Fredrik and give them men if they need them."

I pause when I see Lovisa at the cash register. She takes out her wallet as Emilia place a red shiny paper bag. Immediately, I toss my cigarette aside and go back into the store.

"Put that away," I scold as I approach Love.

With a quick move, I give my credit card to Emilia.

"No, please, I want to pay."

"Don't argue, it's on me."

A stern look in her direction is enough to silence her. Docile and obedient. *God, since when are you like this?*

"Wait for me outside. I'll be right there."

Her peach complexion turns red on her cheeks. She bites her lip in an adorable manner and grabs the bag.

"Thank you."

Adorable. fragile. *Weak.* I shake my head slightly and let the saleswoman charge me.

"Hire reliable men to protect the property," I instruct Oscar as I bring the phone back to my ear. "You still have contacts with veterans who aren't too picky about their boss's business?"

"Yes, I know a few."

"Do what you have to do, have them free up as soon as possible."

As I get my card back, I hang up while nodding to Emilia. Through the window, I see Lovisa, who waits patiently for me. Her angelic vision is overshadowed by a hooded figure watching her on the opposite sidewalk. My senses on alert, I rush outside and abruptly pull the young woman behind me, slipping a hand behind my back where a gun is tucked.

"What's going on?" she asks, her voice troubled by panic.

My instinct rarely deceives me, and I don't trust this man. With his face in shadow, I know he's watching us.

If he thinks I'm going to stand by and do nothing.

I order Lovisa not to move and cross the street. The cars to my left brake urgently, honking in displeasure. I don't give a fuck; let them yell, let them get out of their vehicle, I'll be waiting. I take another step when Lovisa screams, "Watch out!"

I stop just in time. A truck passes by quickly. *Fuck!* That was close. After its passes, I quickly look at the opposite sidewalk. Empty. The man is no longer there. Fuck it. I return to Lovisa and start walking with her without further delay, placing a hand in the small of her back.

"You're crazy! You could have been run over! Or worse."

I smirk mockingly. Crossing a busy street isn't the most dangerous thing I've ever done.

"Don't worry, I'll die long before a simple accident happens."

"What do you mean?"

Oh, no, my little Love, I don't intend to tell you my secrets so easily.

I stop her in front of my car. As I open her door, her stomach growls. Parked right next to a square where about a dozen food trucks are parked, I decide to stop before we leave.

"Are you hungry?"

"A little," she admits, embarrassed.

I take her bag, which I place on the back seat, and lead her toward the food truck.

A working fountain sits in the middle of the square; several people are sitting on the edge, chatting with each other. Winter flower beds are symmetrically arranged around the water basin. Their warm colors contrast with the gray of the ground. The old double streetlamps diffuse a yellowish light in the evening. Wooden benches with iron frames sit in different places of the square. This place hasn't changed in over twenty years. I used to hang out here with my friends when I was in high school.

The different food trucks are lined up all around the square. The smells of grilled meat, smoked fish, fried food, and hot treats makes my mouth water and awaken my stomach.

"What do you want to eat?"

Her emerald gaze flickers toward the trucks we stroll by slowly, allowing her time to go over the menus. Whatever she chooses, I'll like it. Being by her side after all these years of separation feels surreal. This moment, simple and uncomplicated, gives me a glimpse of what we missed during our time apart.

Living with regret is pointless. *Think about something else. Say something.*

"What do you think of your mother's boutique?"

My question surprises her, as she looks at me with astonishment.

"I… It's not me. It's too… too…"

Too what? Glamour? Sexy? Alluring? Provocative? *You could be all of that, Love. If you loose a bit, you'd have potential.* A body as gorgeous as hers with a subdued personality just doesn't match. The two don't go together.

"In the long term, you would profit more by keeping it than selling it. The numbers speak for themselves. Profits only keep climbing every year."

What are you doing? Shut up, asshole. I want her presence, but also her destruction, two opposites.

"Online sales would be a huge step forward, now's the time to expand your business."

"It's not my business. I don't want it."

"You don't know what you're talking about. Selling it would be stupid."

Don't sell. Don't leave.

She would be foolish not to take advantage of such a business. If she plays her cards right, she could win a lot. She needs to see the bigger picture.

I don't insist, but my mind is working on a business plan while she chooses a truck selling herring burgers. *Mmm, good choice.*

In the line, I observe her profile. A small, straight nose with freckles that spreads across her high cheekbones. A detail that drives me crazy in a woman. Her long, coppery, curved eyelashes widen her eyes. Her lips, plump, with almost the same thickness, are naturally tinted a light pink. A beautiful goddess descended to earth. Her body tenses slightly under my inquisitive gaze, and she blushes. God she's such a prude. Innocent. Does Rikard have the same effect on her? I'd rather not think about it. That jerk is far away, and it's better that way.

This man doesn't deserve her. No man deserves her.

Not even me.

But that won't stop me from taking everything from him.

One step, two steps, three steps. It's our turn to be served.

"Two, please. Something to drink?" I ask.

She shakes her head and closes her jacket up to her neck. It's chilly. I slip an arm around her and pull her to me. She tries vainly to free herself, but when I tighten my grip, she completely surrenders to me. I enjoy this closeness between us, and I almost feel… normal. I don't date women. I just sleep with them without bothering with outings. When they come with me, they know what to expect. As for Lovisa, I don't know what she's thinking. She made it clear she's in a relationship. So why does she let herself go with another man? If she were my girlfriend, I would never allow it.

"When is he coming back?"

I don't need to say his name, she knows who I'm talking about.

"On Friday, he wants us to leave and that I handle everything remotely."

He wants to keep her away from me. I would do the same in his place. Nevertheless, this idea doesn't thrill me. If I want to make her suffer, I'll need more than two days. I'm good at executing my plans, but not that good.

"And you, what do you want?"

My question makes her smile. A soft and beautiful smile while her eyes seem sad. Interesting contrast. She's hiding something from me, and I'm going to find out.

"It's funny that you ask me that question."

"Why is that?"

The food truck guy hails us to take our orders. She moves away, her smile fading like a pretty flower in winter. More and more intriguing. We walk away while enjoying our meal. A true delight.

I take her to a bench where we sit down. Our thighs touching. Feeling her so close to me takes me back to another time. Hand in hand, smiles on our faces, presses against each other as we make out until our lips go numb. The carefree days of two teenagers in love. A bygone era.

11

Lovisa, 14 years old

Iron House is protected by a wall that surrounds the vast property; it's monitored by cameras, but also by the security team guarding the gate. However, on the other side of the lake, there's a door that leads to the outside, long forgotten. We take it whenever we want to go out at night. Tonight, at the beginning of the summer vacation, we're going to celebrate with the gang the end of the school year. At the same time, my first year in Kiruna. One year already. So many things have happened, and although Niklas and I are no longer at war, we are still looking for what binds us without ever taking the plunge. Yet it's not for lack of wanting it, but if I agree to be with him and things go wrong, will I be able to bear it? Living under the same roof makes the situation even more difficult.

***

The violin has always been more than a passion. I live to play it, alone or accompanied, I love this instrument that transport me with each of its sweet notes. I play in all circumstances: when I'm sad, scared, happy, melancholic, or even lost. Like today. I have one of those days where I feel all these emotions at once. I call it the *Nik effect*. In his presence, you never stay unaffected. It's impossible to orbit around him without being influenced by his dominating aura.

He has this gift of making others feel their emotions a hundredfold. We don't live halfway with him. He encourages us to open up; it's hard to hide anything from him. He can also make us do things that we don't normally do. When I was sixteen, he had dared me to steal the keys from

Mr. Stenbock, our math teacher. The craziest thing is, that one day, I had my first driving lesson with Nik, while I was sitting on his lap. I will remember all my life the adrenaline pumping through every part of my body, and my heart threatening to burst from the fear I felt when I almost collided with another.

Stop.

Replaying the past will only torment me more.

I close my eyes and press my musical instrument against my cheek. Bow in hand, I caress the strings from which emerges a melancholic sound spreading through the Iron house forest. The music scares away the timid birds and attracts the bravest ones who chirp while ruffling their feathers. This morning, a case and its violin were waiting for me on the lunch table with a note:

I love hearing you play.
N.

This is no ordinary violin. It's the instrument that accompanied me from my early youth until I left Iron House.

Its sentimental value is priceless. I never thought I'd see it again.

This gesture touches me. I like to think maybe he's moved on, that he's forgiven me. Two days ago, when we ate a burger together, the ice between us seemed to have melted a bit. He talked to me and even dared to give me smiles that made my heart race. *My God, his smile…* I'd give anything to see it more often. He melted my walls up every time his cold gaze fell on me, every time he dared to touch my hand while chatting. His deep, smooth voice sent shivers down my spine.

God, what am I doing? I can't deny what he makes me feel, but I'm ashamed of these feelings because I'm with Rikard, a man I love and hate at the same time. I'm not that kind of girl. This isn't me.

I'm completely lost.

All that should matter to me is my escape and rebuild myself elsewhere. Far from the violence that my boyfriend has brought in my life, turning it into a banal act of everyday life. This isn't normal. What he does is not fair or justified. I know it, and yet here I am, still with him. I'm close to the goal, but will I be able to do it?

Several tears fall, and I abruptly stop playing. I throw the violin and bow to the ground and bury my face in my hands.

Shitty situation!

I scream into my palms.

When did I lose control of my life? When did I let go? I was a fighter, I used to live my life to the fullest. I had friends, activities, passions, my freedom. It's all gone.

I need to get my life back, to reclaim it.

"Love."

Before I can turn around, two strong arms wrap around me, pulling me close to a firm chest. I'm never really alone. Niklas is always there, somewhere waiting for the right moment to catch me or talk to me. I don't have a minute of respite. One day he avoids me, the next he does everything to be with me.

I try to break free, but he easily turns me around, then grabs my chin.

"Let me go," I beg, grimacing.

Why does he insist on touching me? His skin constantly ignites mine and I know he feels the same; His body tenses against mine, and his thumb caresses my cheek. It's torture. I close my eyes, biting my lips.

"I give you a violin. And this is how you treat it?"

My body starts trembling uncontrollably. I've been in this kind of situation far too often to know that playing smart is pointless. He looks like Rikard in many ways, but I know he won't hit me. Whether it's instinct or naivety, deep down, I know he's very different.

"I… I'm sorry," I murmur, refusing to look at him.

I feel his breath hit my face. His beard rubs against my cheek, this unpleasant caress goes down my neck. *What*— I grimace as I feel him bite my flesh. Again, I try to pull away. I don't know what sick game he's playing, but I don't want to be part of it.

"You're hurting me."

He releases suddenly. Without waiting, I hurry toward the house. Too bad for the violin; one of his men will go get it.

Behind me, Niklas follows me closely and leads me once we've crossed the kitchen threshold. There's no one there, but a delicious smell of roast chicken lingers all around us. A business dinner is organized. I'm surprised he's not doing this in a fancy restaurant, but since the shareholders have been friends with Hendrik for about thirty years, he finds it more appropriate to do this at the property.

"I don't understand you," Niklas starts. "You inherit a sum of money and a shop. You're with a guy who's loaded, and you're a talented violinist, far surpassing all those assholes in the orchestra. So, what's got you all worked up?"

Money, it's the only thing on his mind. Like his father. It's all about money. Without my presence which seemed to make him more human nine years ago, he has now become like Hendrik. Under his thumb, he could only obey him. What would I have become if I had also grown up at Iron House? I'll never know.

As for my career as a musician, I find myself talented, but I'm stuck in an orchestra. Even if I like playing with my colleagues, I wish to spread my wings and fly on my own, to go solo. A question gnaws at me about this.

I turn to him, stopping in doorway between the kitchen and the hallway.

"How… What makes you say that I'm better than the others?" I ask, chewing my lip nervously, then add, "Have you ever heard one of our concerts?"

Niklas stiffens and adopt a thoughtful look. Is he searching for words? If he's seen me play before, it means he's already watched me, perhaps even searched for me on the internet. Maybe I'm not the only one who's been following the other's life these past few years.

You've been watching me all this time?

"Frida must have put it on the TV, and I probably came across it," he explains, casually shrugging.

Not so casual. He's not telling me the truth. I can tell by the way his body is under tension. Have I unmasked you, handsome Viking? The idea flatters me and please me a lot. I like the idea of having occupied his thoughts after I left, just as he occupied mine.

"What do you think?" I ask.

What should do I care?

A part of me wants his approval. I play for myself, for my mother's memory, but also for him. He always loved to hear me play; he'd spent hours listening to me when I was practicing. I loved those moments. *Our* moments. Nothing mattered except us. It always ended with kisses and caresses until the excitement pushed us away from each other. Two years separated us, but at our ages, it made a big difference and he wanted to wait for the right moment.

Which never happened. Hendrik stole this moment from us like so many others.

"You're good. Yeah, it's cool."

He won't say more about it. He just advises me to look presentable for dinner. Unexpectedly, he didn't dismiss me to my room for the evening.

I want to be pretty, I don't feel obliged to, as has happened many times with Rikard. Since he left, almost a week ago, I've given him rundown of my days, but it's never enough. My boyfriend demands more texts, more phone calls, and more photos. The distance makes him even more jealous and possessive than usual. I can't stand the pressure anymore and find myself neglecting my phone more and more.

He's going to make me pay for it.

That's for sure. I know he's going to make me regret my lack of cooperation. No one upsets Rikard Rapace. Raised as a prince with all the privileges that go with it, he can't stand it when things don't go as he decided.

I shake my head, forcing myself not to think about it, at the risk of holing up in my room when a nice party is about to take place.

After a nice hot shower and my routine for forming beautiful curls in my hair, I put on a black lace dress that reaches my mid-thigh. The fabric over my arms is transparent with embroidered flowers and stops at the elbows. The fitted bodice and the flared bottom are separated by a thin dark belt.

A quick glance at the clock in my room tells me I still have time before the evening with the guests begins. Wanting to soak up the atmosphere, I go downstair, wearing my heels, and meet Alfrida at the bottom of the stairs. In her hands, a freshly ironed and folded white shirt. This woman is versatile and doesn't hesitate to work very late for the smooth running of the house, even if it means doing the work of others.

"Oh, you look gorgeous, darling," she compliments as I reach her. "Very pretty. You're a woman now."

I giggle as I kiss her on the cheek.

"Thank you, Alfrida. Do you need help?" I ask, glancing at the garment.

"You'd be an angel if you could take this to Niklas."

She hands me the shirt and gives me a friendly tap on the cheek before slipping away into the kitchen, limping slightly. The soft and still warm fabric is in my hands, I make my way up to his room. I can't help but glance at my outfit, wondering what he'll think.

I knock on his door.

No answer.

I try again, but only silence answers me. I listen more carefully. The sound of water reaches me. He's taking a shower. Just like me, he has his own bathroom.

Alfrida asked me for a favor, I'll go in, drop the shirt, and turn around. I won't linger to hope to see him naked. This thought makes me blush as all sorts of images come to me. My mind tries to build his male body, without success. As teenagers, we had already found ourselves in underwear against each other, but never without.

As I enter, the smell of mint cigarettes hits me. Near the window, I immediately spot an ashtray overflowing with cigarette butts.

The room has changed a lot since then. There are no longer his sports trophy on the wall with his medals. Nor the posters of women with big boobs which, by the way, made me blush the first time I came across them. The textbooks on his desk have disappeared, replaced neatly arranged liquor bottles and several large black folders. The room is more sober and serious. Only his bed hasn't changed, the Scottish-style green plaid is the same as I remember.

The bed.

I approach it and put the shirt down. My hand caresses the cover. The softness of the familiar fabric brings back memories in my mind. I sigh and step away immediately. When I turn around, Niklas is standing between the door and me.

Oh.

My.

God.

Goodness gracious.

I remain speechless at the sight before me. Freshly out of the shower and still wet, his body is covered only by a white towel around his waist. His broad, yet not too bulky chest reveals muscles worthy of a magazine. His pecs and abs are enticing. Are they as firm as they look? His arms could crush me effortlessly. My gaze is hypnotized by the water drops cascading down his skin and flowing down to his waist. I imagine my tongue against his skin, tracing the path of the water droplets, tasting the flavor of his body.

He's very arousing.

The thought makes me blush as my mind continues to imagine my mouth on him. Using my teeth, I could even untie his towel and make it fall.

I also notice a grim reaper tattooed on his ribs. This tattoo bothers me because of its sinister meaning. Why this design? There are so many more beautiful ones.

Nik's gaze burns with desire. His wet hair frames his face perfectly, giving him a wild look. He's the one who's half-naked; yet, he makes me feel like I'm the one wearing nothing. His blue eyes scrutinize at me with such intensity that I forget to breathe.

"Love," he growls, in his voice husky, giving me shivers. "What are you doing here?"

I look him in the eyes and get lost in their depth. I feel like I'm being drawn into icy waters. I'm breathless and unable to move. He approaches slowly, like a predator enticing his prey before throwing himself on it. I'm captivated by his overpowering aura that pins me in place.

"Love…"

His voice, low and almost dark, gives me goosebumps.

Keep talking, please, just keep talking to me.

Instead, he wraps one of his strong arms around my waist and pulls me roughly against him. By reflex, I place my hands on his chest, but I quickly realize that I don't want to escape from his touch. Automatically, my fingers caress his damp skin. Thanks to my heels, I'm almost at his height, with my face very close to his.

We devour each other with our eyes as the tension between us builds. It scares me. I've never felt such a connection with someone. Not even when we were teenagers. Somehow, I manage to articulate, slowly and in a whisper, "I came to bring you your shirt… Alfrida asked me to."

He smirks and tilts his head slightly toward mine. His wet locks tickle my skin, it might mess up my makeup, *but I don't care.*

"I hope I didn't wrinkle it, otherwise you'll look bad for dinner," I articulate with difficulty.

"We can keep talking about clothes or we can engage in a much more interesting activity."

I gasp in surprise, instinctively looking at his mouth, the ultimate temptation. I remember the softness of his lips, their skill, their taste. At the mention of this memory, a sudden urge overwhelms me. Like a drug addict deprived for years, I rush toward them. Responding, Niklas places his hand on the back of my neck and immediately forces my lips to part to welcome his tongue.

Oh my God!

His tongue explores every corner of my mouth, dances with mine, tease it, rediscovers it. I can't help but moan as he presses me against the wall. My body stuck under his, I feel a beginning of an erection against my thigh. The towel suddenly feels too much and I'm dying to rip it off.

I plunge my hands into his hair and pull, trying to control in this wild kiss. He tries to dominate me, to subject me to his desire as he rubs his cock against me, eliciting another moan from me. My reactions drive him crazy, he growls into our kiss and carries me to his desk, where the bottles clink under our roughness.

"Wait," I say as he sits me on top of the desk.

Everything is happening so fast. I can't think clearly about the situation and his kisses make me lose my mind.

He lays me down, pushing away the bottles that threaten to fall, and dive back on my mouth, which he takes full possession. Naturally, I wrap my legs around his hips.

In that moment, I forget everything. I forget Rikard and his violence, my mother's death, the years away from Nik, my work worries, and especially my escape plan. He makes me forget *everything*.

The towel and my panties are the only obstacles to what could happen. I'm dying to take it everything off, but the kiss totally captures my attention and I'm unable to do anything else at the same time.

I feel feverish and full of desire. This moment is much more intense than anything I've felt with Rikard so far. The memory of our embrace is nothing compared to what we're sharing today. It's a thousand times better.

Nik attacks my neck, kissing it, nibbling it, and licking it in places. I'm at his mercy. My body doesn't resist him, on the contrary, it craves more as I rock my hips against him.

Make love to me... Fuck me!

I'm dying for it and I don't know how to tell him. It's not like me, I'm a reserved person who would never seek sexual favors. But Nik is different, his ability to make me do anything is still there.

Skillful with his hands, he caresses the sensitive areas of my body, the ones that have always turned me on. The inside of my thighs, my small of my back, or even the base of my neck. He knows how to drive me crazy and uses these places to make me lose my mind.

I'm about to crack and reveal the thoughts in my mind so that this torture stops. He finally deigns to take me when an object hits the wall above our heads brutally. We both startle, Niklas ready to pounce on the intruder. At the door stands Jonna, furious. She sports the same shade as her dress: crimson red. Her murderous gaze pushes me to sit up quickly, lowering my dress.

"What the hell is going on?"

Niklas, relaxed, chuckles and lifts his chin toward the young woman, not at all impressed by her anger.

"I didn't expect to see you so soon, you're early."

"Thank goodness for that! One more minute and I would've found you two having sex."

"Possible," he says, smirking.

He walks away, grabbing a small white and green package from which he takes out a lighter and a cigarette, which he quickly lights. He glances at the shirt and sits down on the bed. His evident erection lifts the towel, which doesn't escape my or gaze Jo's gaze, who fumes seeing this.

What have I done? Overwhelmed with shame, I stand up, running my hand through my hair and over my face. I'm glad I didn't wear lipstick given our passionate exchange.

"You should be ashamed," Jonna attacks me. "You're cheating on your boyfriend with mine, it's disgusting."

"We're not together," Nik intervenes, nonchalant and seemingly unwilling to defense me.

He doesn't help by making her even angrier. Jonna has always been a hot temper, she's not afraid of confrontations, and if it came to blows, she wouldn't hesitate. I'm the calmer one between us, and it's not in my interest to stock her anger.

"I'm sorry, I—"

I stop myself. What can I say? No justification will appease her. I know my behavior is shameful, because I'm in a relationship and, even if I wasn't, Jonna is with him. Sort of. I've always been aware of her feelings for Niklas, even back then. Yet, it didn't stop me from dating him. What bound us was stronger than my new friendship with her. It didn't stop us from becoming best friends afterwards. Was our relationship sincere? From what I remember, it was natural and without resentment. Those days are over. Today, she wants to reclaim what slipped away from her in the past.

"When Rikard finds out, he'll be very disappointed."

"No!" I shout, despite myself.

My sharp reaction makes her smile. Shit, I know what's going to happen. She approaches me, like a predator thirsty for blood, and glares at me.

"Please, don't tell him anything. It was a mistake, a moment of weakness."

"You've put your tongue where it shouldn't be, my dear. You're going to regret it."

You have no idea how much.

When Rikard finds out, I won't be able to stand up anymore, and who knows what will happen to me next. I shiver and tremble immediately. I plead Niklas with my eyes, whose smile disappears as he scrutinizes me curiously.

He finally stands up and interposes himself between us, exposing me his perfect back where an immense tattoo leaves me speechless. It represents a white wolf and a red fox intertwined. I'm awestruck. The drawing is beautiful and must have taken hours of suffering.

Nik exhales his smoke on the side before speaking, "That's enough," he says harshly. "Leave her alone."

"But—"

"Get out. Wait for me downstairs."

His tone is final. Anyone would understand to shut up and comply. Jonna is still upset, but obeys. Nik blocks my view; I only hear my friend's heels clacking toward the exit.

When he turns back to me, all desire has vanished from his face. His swollen, red lips are the last evidence of what just happened.

The handsome Viking runs his hand through my hair and then along my jawline. My body tenses, craving more from him. But nothing. He lets his arm fall and takes a long drag on his cigarette. How does he manage to suppress all emotion from his face and look so indifferent when I'm still reeling from our kiss?

So hard… So cold.

He's no longer my Viking. I'm no longer his Love.

I see it now. We'll never be who we were again, and chasing after our past is a waste of time. I've long made peace with what we could have been together, but I still feel a twinge of sadness.

"Get out, you too," he says more gently. "Guests will be arriving soon."

I'm unable to say anything.

After leaving his room, I slip into mine to touch up my makeup and fix my hair.

As I walk into the dining room, I wonder why I'm putting myself through this evening when I could be under my covers reminiscing about Nik's lips on my skin. I don't feel like I belong, and all the eyes on me make me uncomfortable. A quick scan of the room makes me aware of the people present: Jonna is standing next to Niklas, chatting with a man in his forties. He's wearing the shirt I brought him with a navy-blue suit that suits him perfectly. I almost regret this fabric covering him a little too much for my taste.

A few feet away, three gray-haired men are having a drink while giving me interested looks.

Disgusting.

Their attention on me makes me feel dirty, and I itch to take a scalding hot shower.

Niklas breaks away from Jo and takes a step toward me, extending his hand to invite me closer.

"Let me introduce you to Lovisa Granberg."

"Sigrid's little one?" asks one of the men in a classy suit.

He's wearing rectangular glasses behind which thick eyebrows bloom. His salt and pepper hair is combed to the side. He seems to know me; I don't recognize him.

"Not so little anymore," says the man in his forties who was chatting with Nik a moments ago.

He's a foreigner. Swedish isn't his native language. His accent gave him away. His blond hair and tanned complexion suggest he lives under a very hot sun. Or he's a sunbed enthusiast. His tanned skin brings out his blue eyes. He undoubtedly possesses a charisma that appeals to women. His gray suit hugs his body, demonstrating a slender and elegant build.

He steps forward, extending his hand. I take it and allow him to place a chaste kiss on it.

"John Gray."

"Lovisa," I introduce myself once again.

"Please to meet you. Dinner is going to be more interesting than I thought."

What a charmer!

I can't help but glance toward Niklas. He stares back, hiding his emotions. But I'm not fooled; even if he's good at this game, his eyes full of lightning betray him. Jealous? It would be audacious of him, considering he has Jonna on his arm.

If I have to endure this evening, I might as well do it by sympathizing with this man. I don't yet understand my presence at this dinner, but something tells me that I'm a pretty ornament to make the evening more enjoyable and the associates more inclined to accept Nik's proposals. I overheard him talking with Oscar. The idea of being exploited like this bother me a little. I don't intend to play along with this sick little game and will only do what please me.

"If you'll excuses us, we'll have dinner."

At the table, Nik is at the head. To his right are two men, with Jonna between them, and to his left is the third man, then me and John. I suspect our host strategically chose these seats. Jo and I are entertainment for these gentlemen. I'm not sure know if I should feel flattered or insulted to be reduced to a mere object of amusement for his business.

The first part of the meal remains formal. The men talk business and focus on the negotiations Niklas is trying to impose. I discover a new facet of his personality: that of a businessman. He exudes such confidence that he could sell a pair of glasses to a blind man.

Unlike Jonna, who laughs heartily and entertains the room whenever she gets the chance, I focus on what Nik is saying to understand what's going on. Each man runs a company in which my stepbrother has shares. The one with glasses is named Ivan Petrén; he owns a large fish distribution chain. Joel Rosell, a stout man with gold teeth that shine a bit too much, owns shopping centers in Kiruna, Stockholm, and Copenhagen. Stig Boberg manages prestigious hotels that compete with the Ekmans'. As for John Gray, the Australian, he was hired to manage the handsome Viking's stock portfolio. He's been in Sweden for a short time and has already made him a lot of money. Hence this meeting tonight.

"I hope we're not boring you," John whispers in my ear.

"No, not at all."

I can't help but smile at his concern.

"It's a big responsibility you have here," I remark. "A bad investment and your clients can lose everything."

"It's a risk, indeed, but that's what makes it exciting."

When he says his last word, I detect a double meaning. I don't know if it's due to the alcohol clouding my judgment.

"The stakes are huge, but I've never been wrong so far. I know how to satisfy my clients."

Another innuendo? I think so. He's charming, and his company is pleasant. But he's not Nik. I feel him constantly watching me, even though I don't dare look in his direction at the moment; I'm afraid to meet his disapproving gaze. I feel like I'm sinning, even though he's the one who threw me into the arms of these men to satisfy his interests.

"What made you want to pursue this profession?" I ask, picking at the vegetables on my plate.

He sets down his glass of red wine and ponders the question, running his thumb over his lower lip, a gesture I don't miss.

"Having control over someone's finances is to control them, to control their life. The most powerful men are at my mercy with just money; it's a feeling I'll never tire of."

Money rules the world; it has been that way since the dawn of time. Money and power. It's also because of this that man is the cruelest of species; he inflicts suffering on his fellow human beings for his own ends. Sometimes I envy the carefree nature of animals. It's much simpler with them.

We continue to exchange words, with many hidden—or thinly veiled—hints from John. He doesn't say things directly, but I manage to understand. I don't accept them, though. I almost slept with Nik earlier despite being with Rikard. This is not me.

The second part of the meal is much more festive.

Nik managed to persuade Mr. Rosell to sell him his shopping center in Kiruna for a very large sum. Mr. Petrén agreed to give him exclusivity on his sales of fish and shellfish. Mr. Boberg, on the other hand, is more difficult to convince to give him more shares in his business. He doesn't know the shark he's dealing with, who seems fiercer in business than his late father.

Throughout the evening, we're served by two employees who clear away our dishes and refill our glasses. The alcohol flows freely.

The men are all hanging on Jonna's every word, who relishes being the center of attention. She doesn't care how old they are. She dances with them and doesn't hesitate to be provocative. Her lover watches the scene with an approving eye; things are going in his way, and he has no intention of intervening.

On my side, I stopped the formality with John; we're talking openly, standing by the gentle warmth of the fireplace.

"If I take one more sip, I'm going to collapse," I chuckle, my eyes half-closed. I'm exhausted by this evening, my body longs my cozy bed, but Mr. Gray doesn't seem to agree and just keeps me by his side.

"Don't worry, sweetheart, I'll be there to catch you," he whispers in my ear, placing an arm on my waist to emphasize his words.

"What a smooth talker!" I laugh, holding my empty glass against me. His touch disturbs me but my body refuses to move, and my mind suppresses the warning signals telling me to be careful.

"I can do more than that. Is there a place where we could be alone?"

His proposition is enough to bring me back to reality. It only means one thing: sex. That's not what I want.

I smile, tapping his chest. "I think I'm going to bed."

I step aside and almost stumble. John catches me as promised, causing a nervous laugh from me.

"I've had too much drink."

"I think so too. Where's your room? I'll take you there."

"No need, I'll do it," Nik intervenes, taking me by the elbow to pull me away.

He glares at my drinking companion and announces to everyone, "Gentlemen, thank you for this evening. A limousine is waiting for you at the entrance; your cars will be brought back to you tomorrow morning."

The guests grumble but maintain their good mood as they leave. They regret having to leave Jonna behind. They think they have a chance with her, but she's playing a role.

My head is spinning, and my heavy body fails me. I'm subject to a blackout during which I go from the dining room to upstairs. Where is John? I was talking to him just a moment ago. My feet don't touch the ground. I'm being carried.

"What a silly idea to drink so much," Nik scolds me as he enters his room.

"The cocktails were sweet, I got tricked." My voice escapes my lips without me realizing it. It feels like someone else is speaking for me.

"You never been able to handle alcohol."

That's true. Even the simple beers we used to drink with the gang gave me a headache. Here, I've far exceeded my tolerance limit.

He slowly lays me down, but that doesn't relieve the dizziness that overwhelms me.

"I… I'm going to throw up," I grimace.

With agility, he picks me up and carries me to the bathroom. Barely in front of the toilet, I vomit up my meal as well as the alcohol ingested.

Niklas pulls my hair back to keep it from getting dirty. I mumble apologies and ask him to leave, but he stands behind me and waits until I'm done. He gives me a glass of water to rinse my mouth and tries again to lay me down on the bed.

"I'm sorry," I repeat for the umpteenth time.

"Stop apologizing. Sleep, I'll watch you over."

"Leave her. Let her do her own thing. If she wants to play grown-up, she should do it all the way, says Jo's who came in my room.

Jo's venom reaches me. Even in this moment of weakness, she strikes where it hurts. She approaches me, waving her phone. Victorious.

"I took some pictures from the party, which I shared on my Instagram account. Rikard seemed very interested in the one where you're in the arms of handsome John."

My blood runs cold and freezes my entire body. I widen my eyes as I look at her and sit up on my elbows in attempt to get up, but Nik stops me. I look at her, completely lost.

"No… please tell me you didn't do that!"

"I sure did. He'll see what kind of slut you are."

"You—" Nik begins, getting up.

Without hesitation, he rushes toward Jonna and grabs her by the shoulders. pinning her against the wall near the door. He squeezes so hard that she grimaces in pain. Helpless due to my drunkenness, I can only witness the scene.

"You had no right to do that!" shout Niklas.

"Why? What do you give a fuck? She abandoned you, remember!"

He's furious, his anger palpable. I wouldn't want to be in Jonna's shoes.

"It wasn't up to you do it! I was in control of everything!"

What was in control of? I'm lost and unable of holding a serious conversation. I slump onto the bed as they argue.

Another blackout.

When I look around me, Nik is lying next to me. I don't know how much time has passed, but he's sleeping beside me. His serene expression makes me want to stroke his hair to continue looking at his peaceful face.

I turn back to the dresser where my phone is. I don't know how it ended up there; I don't remember putting it here. Unlocking it, I notice missed calls and texts from Rikard.

Oh my God.

His texts are aggressive and full of hostility. I don't dare listen to the voicemails. In writing, he informs me that he'll be there much earlier than planned and that we'll have a discussion. A ball of anxiety knots my stomach as I look at the man next to me.

What am I going to do?

12

Niklas, 16 years old

The more time passes, the more I fall in love with her. She's like a puppy; she's sweet, affectionate, and full of life. She's the new attraction that was missing in my busy life. Everything opposes us, our parents, my reputation... Lovisa refuses even to sleep with me. I must be crazy to love this forbidden fruit. She constantly pushes me away, but I feel her defenses weakening week after week. I'll eventually get what I want. And then what? What will happen? I'll probably just discard her like all the others, but part of me wishes it could be different with her. I don't want to hurt her. If I explained this to my friends, they'd laugh at me. Niklas Ekman has feelings for a girl! That would be a first.

***

Focus, damn it.

A cigarette stuck between my index and my middle finger, I analyze my father's documents regarding an old building that he tried to renovate without success. His project was repeatedly rejected because the council deciding on it was led by Samuel Agardh, an old enemy Hendrik. Their conflict dated back to their childhood, and they tried to get in each other's way whenever they could. Now that he's dead, won't have trouble doing whatever I want with this building. Unless Agardh decides to come after me.

That's just a detail. For now, I need to decide what I want to do with it. This place has potential; it's an old hotel that hasn't been in use for almost a hundred years. Samuel could piss me off by classifying this building as a historical monument. I need to play it smart.

A groan behind me interrupts my train of thought and forces me to look in her direction.

God.

Is she doing this on purpose or what?

Lying in my bed, Lovisa expose me her cute, round little ass. Her skin is very soft here; I couldn't help but caress her while helping her take off her dress to put on one of my T-shirts.

I spent the night watching her, afraid that she would choke on her own vomit if she felt sick again. Luckily, she only slept restlessly. Several times, I went to calm her down. When I held her in my arms, she seemed so small and fragile that I was afraid to hold her too tightly. Beside, her body is marked by bruises, mainly on the thighs and ribs. What does she do to hurt herself so much? My fingers made her skin shiver when I touched her there; even in her sleep, she didn't appreciate it.

Big pervert, you took advantage of the fact that she's asleep to touch her.

I'm just a selfish bastard. Waiting for her to wake up is taking too long. I only caress the superficial parts of her body and yet, I feel like I've crossed the line.

Screw it. It's done.

At least I got a taste of her goddess body.

Another moan escapes her lips and prompts me to close the file. I stub out my cigarette, which has burned itself out, and get up, stretching. I would have like to continue sleeping with her, but this scene is too strange for me. I dreamed about it for a long time, and now that she's here, in my bed, I can't sleep with her.

Not without fucking her.

Never has a woman slept with me unless it was to fuck just before. Their presence in my life serves no other purpose than to offer me the warmth they have between the thighs. Usually, they leave without looking back. Jonna is one of those who cling to me. She's become a regular, but yesterday, she crossed the line. Her jealousy messed up my plans, and it pissed me off. Rikard will be here soon, he'll probably be here today. Without meaning to, Jonna got involved in my revenge.

Idiot.

The positive thing is that he'll break up with my little Love, and that she'll suffer from that abandonment. It'd be well deserved.

For now, I feel like playing a little.

It's wrong, don't do it.

The little voice in my head tells me it's a dangerous game and that Lovisa won't be the only loser. I have no willpower when I'm faced with a female body, especially with hers.

I slip in behind her. She presses her hips against mine with a sigh. The naughty girl. Is she having an erotic dream? I wonder if I'm in it. I caress her thigh with my fingertips and move my hand up to her hip. She arches her back.

Oh, babe, you're so sexy.

Does she realize how sexy she is? She drives me crazy.

And fuck. I have a hard-on. It was inevitable. And not just a little. It's becoming painful as the space between our bodies narrows. I've already experienced this scene with her countless times. But today is different. We're adults, and we can fuck.

A sick idea comes to my mind. Fuck her and ditch her. But also… make love to her and cuddle her. Shit. What do I want?

Lovisa moves again, she turns around, and her face is almost against mine. I watch her closely; her serene look makes me envious. She seems so peaceful, without any problem. My gaze falls on what she's wearing: a black T-shirt with a golden eagle printed on it. I'd like to take it off her to feel the warmth of her skin against mine. I'm wearing simple pants that are becoming too tight at the crotch.

I start caressing her skin, directing my hand to her back. The sun filters through the window and dazzles her angelic silhouette. She grumbles as she snuggles up against me and places an arm on my hips. Her mouth meets mine.

Holy shit!

She's seducing me in her sleep.

I run a hand through her messy hair and press more my lips against her. She lets out an adorable moan that urges me to roll her on her back and pull myself on top of her.

Stop it!

I'm taking advantage of her trust and her sleep for a sick game that only I can understand. She might wake up scared or screaming. That's not what I want; I'm not that kind of guy.

It's time to stop.

I want to pull back, but against all odds, Lovisa welcomes me between her thighs and wraps her arms around me. I nearly lose my mind feeling the warmth of her pussy against my stomach. She's so hot that I can feel her arousal. Her moans, her twisting body, and the heat in her panties make it clear that she is having an erotic dream.

"Nik…" she whispers.

Oh my God!

What's more arousing than a woman whispering your name like that? I'd like to get inside her head and see what she's seeing to share this moment with her.

I first kiss her lips, then move down to her chin and along her jawline, nibbling on it.

Another moan.

My mouth moves to under her ear, which I kiss before teasing her earlobe with my tongue.

A sigh this time.

"It would be much more interesting if you woke up, my beauty," I whisper.

My words resonate within her. Love moves beneath me and finally opens her tired eyes. Those deep green hypnotizes me. I look at her with desire and lick her lower lip. It doesn't take her long to come to her sense and widen her eyes, realizing the situation.

"Nick?" she whispers, unsure.

"You're not dreaming, my beauty, and before you get mad, I want to clarify that it was you who started this."

And God knows I want to be inside her right now.

This thought sends me shivers of desire and increases my erection. One word from her, and I won't hesitate for a moment.

Say yes, Love. Come on.

"I… but I was sleeping," she justifies herself.

She suddenly covers her mouth with her hands. Her voice is hoarse and weak, but it only adds to her charm.

I smile at her embarrassed expression and prop myself up on one arm while the other one moves down to her hip, which I caress.

"You're awake now. Say no, and I'll stop."

It's not what I want, but I'd do it.

A reddish lock falls carelessly across her forehead. I brush it away with my nose and take the opportunity to enjoy her fruity shampoo smell. Everything about her drives me crazy. Her skin as soft as a peach, her sweet smell, her emerald doe eyes, her curves where they should be. Her smile… in my memories, it used to light up the room wherever she was. Now, I only see shadows on her face.

Smile for me, Love.

With the tips of my lips, I kiss the skin of her face down to her full, inviting lips. My teeth catch her lower lip and suck on it. Her reaction is immediate. Eyes half-closed, she lets out a little sigh as her body tenses.

That's what I was waiting for.

I slip a hand under her T-shirt and grab her round, firm breast, massaging it through her bra. Under my touch, I feel her nipple harden and stiffen.

"Please… stop."

"Are you sure? Your body seems to want the opposite."

She blushes and turns her head away.

Oh, no, babe, embrace your desires.

I force her to face me. Her gaze is puzzling, there's desire, but also fear. Do I scare her? This thought pleases me and annoys me. If I have to scare her, it's certainly won't be in the bed. She opens her lovely little mouth to retort, but she's interrupted by her phone, vibrating nearby. Before she can grab it, I grab it, rising to my knees, Lovisa trapped between my legs.

"Give it to me!" she exclaims, trying to free herself.

The screen indicates the recipient of the incoming call: Rikard. The bastard is always around. Soon, he won't be a problem anymore, and I'll have Lovisa all to myself. No man has been an obstacle when I desired to have a woman, and this snob prick won't be the first.

Rikard done trying to contact my Love, the screen changes, and I catch a glimpse that she has missed several calls and dozen messages. All from Rikard. He must be furious not being able to reach her. She going to take a lot.

I want revenge, so why does this thought make me so angry?

I give her the phone back when it stops vibrating. I'll deal with her later.

"The petty snob is trying to reach you."

I leave the bed, open the window, and light a cigarette. The cool morning air makes me shiver. I like this cold sensation unique to Sweden. I've been immersed in it since I was born, and I wouldn't trade a single day to be in a warm country.

The calm of the property and the beauty of the snow-covered forest bring me an inner peace that I can't find anywhere else. There was a time when I hated being here, because of Hendrik's grip. When I took control of my life, I finally found my place and saw what this place could offer me.

Weakness takes hold of my body, forcing me to close my eyes to avoid faltering. I take a breath and throw my half-burned cigarette out the window. I pull myself away from the view of the lake, which is beginning to thaw in shallower area, and glance at the redhead. Still on my bed, she looks even paler, her features are taut with anxiety. She's on her knees, floating in my T-shirt which literally engulfing her body.

I don't know what Rikard wrote to her, but it can't be pleasant. What does he say her? She looks like she's about to throw up. I wish I could snatch her phone away so she'd stops worrying about that asshole.

He doesn't deserve her attention.

"Tell him to screw off," I advise, leaning on the window ledge.

She abruptly gets up and leaves the room without bothering to reply.

Damn. I don't know what he said to her, but it's effective, she's completely shaken. He seems to have a strong grip her. I wonder how much. They've been a couple for a few years, that must count for something. I've never experienced that, I'm all about one-night stands. It's less complicated and you don't have to pretend to be interested in the other person.

Sex. That's all that matters between a man and a woman.

I press the intercom button near my door. Oscar's deep voice—whose device is in his own office—answers me.

"Sir?"

"I need to go to Ogs, have the car ready and contact my captains for a video conference at one o'clock. And see if Gunkil and Fredrik have any updates."

"Understood. Anything else, sir?"

"No… Actually yes, let me know when Lovisa's boyfriend gets here. I don't know when he'll show up."

"Is he going to be a problem?"

"I don't know."

I end the call.

My instinct tells me to watch out for this asshole. Any guy would freak out seeing his girlfriend in someone else's arms. Jonna took advantage of Lovisa's clumsiness to make it look like she was falling for another guy behind her boyfriend's back.

An idiot. But a sneaky idiot.

I've always admired that devious side of her. Jo knows what she wants. She's smart, daring, and resourceful. But she's also impatient, possessive, unpredictable, and immature. Her flaws make her someone unstable and untrustworthy. She knows what my family is involved in, she's part of the gang, and that detail push me to keep an eye on her.

Half an hour later, I step out of my room, ready to start the day. In the hallway, Alfrida comes out of the next room, where Lovisa stays. A tray with an untouched fruit juice.

"Frida? Can you have Alma clean up?"

The floor is strewn with clothes, including Lovisa's dress, which will end up in the trash. I walk away, but the housekeeper calls out to me.

"It's about Lovisa, I don't know if I should be worried," she begins.

"What are you talking about?"

I hate it when someone doesn't get to the point and makes me ask for the rest, but Alfrida is like a second mother to me, and I respect her too much to make the remark.

"Mr. Rapace called the house phone and asked to speak to Lovisa; I called her while she was in her bath. When I wanted to drain the water, I was surprised to find the water cold."

"So what?"

The housekeeper bites her lips.

"The water was really very cold, Niklas. It reminded me… it reminded me—"

"I get it," I cut her off harshly.

I haven't thought about that in a long time. I got over what Hendrik did to us years ago and, when he saw that it didn't affect me anymore, he stopped that little torture.

"What should we do?"

"Nothing. I'll take care of it," I reassure her, affectionately squeezing her shoulder.

If Lovisa continues *this punishment*, only I can make her stop. We share the same experience. After all this time away from Hendrik, she still punishes herself. Why? What does she have to blame herself for?

That's the last thing I needed.

I tighten my holster to my shoulders. It contains replacement weapons; my Golden will have to be analyzed by Ogs. I quickly go downstairs. I'm greeted by Krigare, whom I have neglected a lot lately. Usually, I take him everywhere with me. Thank God, he has Alfrida to take care of him.

Looking to my left, I see my office door open, where Oscar is waiting for me. To my right I hear Lovisa's voice in the living room. I approach her with my dog and find her in a bathrobe in front of the phone. Her long red hair always looks darker when it's wet.

For now, she seems frightened; her body curls up on itself. She's trembles. She's terrified of her boyfriend. There's something fishy about their relationship.

When she hangs up, I leap in her direction as she turns around. Her big green eyes widen in surprise.

"What's going on with you?"

I lock my eyes in hers.

"You took an ice bath."

"What?"

My statement freezes her. She bites her lip so hard that the underside turns whitens. I move closer to her.

"Why?" I ask. "Why do you do this on yourself?"

"I… It's complicated."

Complicated! What the hell is she hiding from me? This girl is a real enigma. There was a time when I could read her like a book. Now she's nothing but a stranger.

Hendrik threw us in the shower; the freezing water jet chilled us to the bone. It was a punishment whenever one of us misbehaved. Most of the time I managed to take Lovisa's place, when my father was in a merciful mood, but I couldn't always protect her. And when that wasn't enough, he would force us into ice baths with large ice cubes and take us out when we were completely livid. He was a cruel man who wanted to make us obedient, and he had no shortage of ingenious methods to make us pay for our behavior. Bastard. I hated him so much!

"I have to go get dressed, Rikard will be here soon."

"You're not going anywhere. We need to sort all this shit out first."

She avoids me too often for my taste.

A little honestly, babe, just a little.

Lovisa reminds me of a mouse scared by a big cat. She shakes as soon as I raise my voice and shrinks in place when I approach. I like to have that effect on men; they should fear me, but not women. And seeing that terrified look in her eyes completely turns me inside out.

"Sir, the car is ready, Ogs is waiting for us."

I take a deep breath, closing my eyes. Ogs can't wait; his time is precious, and mine too. Lovisa needs me, even if she won't admit it. I can't afford to leave her alone, but I need to hurry if I don't want to miss the meeting with my men.

"I'll help Lovisa get dressed, wait for us in the car."

I forbid her from answering me with a simple look and take her upstairs. Against all odds, she lets me lead her to her room.

When I open her wardrobe, I notice that she has almost nothing. She must have only planned to stay for a few days, but it's been a week since she got here.

"Wait for me."

I come back a few moments later with a white woolen dress with a large turtleneck.

"This should fit you."

"Whose is it?"

She looks at the fabric in her hands and asks me to turn around. I type on my phone and answer in a distracted voice, "No idea. A woman must have forgotten it."

"Am I wearing the dress of one of your booty calls?"

I smirk and glance over my shoulder. She pulls the dress down to mid-thigh and puts on black stockings. It's still very chilly in this early spring. The snow is melting little by little; the lake is still frozen but weakened by the milder temperatures.

"You're the same size," I say, facing her.

"Great, thrilled to hear that," she grumbles while slipping on her boots, which come just above her knee.

Damn. She's so beautiful!

Her hair is already curling around her angelic face. She wears a natural expression. Her eyes reflect a deep sadness that still escapes me.

Her attention shifts to my weapons. I place a reassuring hand on them.

"You're safe."

"You used to hate guns so much. You loathed touching them."

That time is over; many years have passed. I shrug casually, but her remark still irks me. Her image constantly reminds me of the person I used to be.

"Everyone evolves; only the fools remain stuck on their ways without seeing what the changes can bring to their lives."

"There are different ways to evolve, and not all of them are good."

"Who judges what's good or bad? You maybe? Do you think you've always made good decisions in your life?"

She seems to understand where I'm going with this and lowers her gaze to her hands, which zip up her boots. She stands up and ties her hair in a high ponytail.

"There are some things I regret that I can never take back," she whispers.

An awkward silence surrounds us. Shit. I hate this.

Come on, pull yourself together, damn it!

"I'm going to be late, let's go."

After putting on our coats, we get into my sedan. Oscar, sitting next to the driver, stares at the road.

"Where are we going?" Lovisa asks, clutching the edge of her dress.

"The gun shop in town."

My red fox pales and nervously bites her lip as she looks out the window. She's terrified of guns ever since t one was pointed at her head one night. I could have spared her this stop, but I need to know she's by my side.

Are you getting sentimental, Ekman?

That's not my style. Yet, I can't help but worry about her. Only about her.

Ogs' shop is located at the entrance of town, in a quiet corner where we easily park. Inside, there are a lot of weapons displayed behind the counter, locked up, but also in showcases. To contain so many dangerous objects, this place is highly secure. The old Ogs even has a security guard at the entrance.

"Mr. Ekman," the manager greets.

He comes around the counter, shakes my hand before looking at the young woman next to me with his decades-old eyes.

"My stepsister, Lovisa Granberg."

Calling her that makes me want to vomit. I refrain from making an expression of disgust. Ogs takes her hand, and shakes it warmly.

"It's rare to see such a pretty face in my shop."

She blushes like an idiot, and I get annoyed. She's never received a compliment or what? I can give her a lot of compliments if that's it takes to please her. Beautiful eyes, a mouth to die for, hair that smells like fruit, perky little breasts, even though I've only seen them through her bra. Skin as soft as silk, smelling like morning dew. A damn fine ass. Hell, just imagining it in my hands gets me excited.

Think of something else before you get a hard-on in front of everyone.

"I need you to take another look at my Goldens, they make a weird noise when I shoot," I intervene, pulling Lovisa back a bit.

Oscar puts a suitcase on the counter before leaving the shop to watch the street. The seller opens it to take a look.

"They're really old; don't you prefer new ones?"

"No. When can I get them back?"

I approach the counter, which also serves as a display case, and linger over some automatic guns. A replica of a silver Walther PPK 9 mm with a pink grip catches my eye.

"I'd like to see this model," I say.

"Really? It's a gun for a woman," remarks Ogs, but under my murderous gaze, he complies.

The gun is small and light, perfect for Lovisa's slender hands. I turn to her and hand it to her. She immediately back away, which makes me smile.

"You can touch it. It won't bite you."

I know of something else she could touch without getting bitten.

"I'd rather not," she answers.

"Come on, go ahead, see what it feels like."

I take her hand and guide it to the grip. She resists a little before giving in and taking it timidly.

Go on, babe, play with it.

Lovisa looks like she's holding a bomb, she doesn't dare make any movement and her breathing seems to be caught.

"Don't be afraid, it's not loaded."

This information changes everything. She slowly turns the gun over and examines it from every angle. I find her very sexy with that gun in her hands.

"Does she have a gun permit?"

"Put it in my name," I say.

I place myself behind Lovisa and put my hands on hers. She startles and turns her face toward mine. Her full lips are close to mine.

"What are you doing?"

"Let me show you how to hold it."

With skilled hands, I properly position the gun in her hands and raise her arms in front of her. A target is a little further away, untouched because it's not meant for shooting. I spread her legs with my foot. Like a good student, she complies without saying anything. Her behavior surprises me, but in a good way. She has always hated my world, yet she slips into my shoes for a moment. I whisper in her ear. Her lobe gently brushes my lips and makes me want to nibble on it.

"Small and light, but with real power. It's not something to handle lightly. You can kill someone with it."

She whispers softly, "Lord…"

I'm so comfortable with guns, and Lovisa is so intimidated and scared at the mere thought of touching them that this contrast strikes me. We're so different. She's the day, I'm the night. She's the sun, I'm the moon. She's fire, I'm ice. These elements that can't live without each other but which can never be together.

Never. I'm harmful to her, and she would be my weakness.

I step back and say to Ogs, "Put it on my account," I demand as I take back the gun from her. "And I want my guns ASAP."

The basement of the villa has an arsenal that would keep me safe for years, but my Goldens are the first guns I ever shot. There's sentimental value to them. It's easier and less of a headache to appreciate objects than people.

As I'm about to pay, Oscar bursts into the shop and whispers to me, "Sir, we're being watched. We need to go back home."

Shit. Who is it? No time for questions. I glance at Lovisa, who is standing back. Her attention is fixed on shotguns.

"Let's go out."

"I'll prepare your order as quickly as possible," Ogs assures, handing me a bag with the box containing the gun for Lovisa.

I grab my pretty redhead by the waist and follow Oscar outside. I don't like shooting without my favorite guns, but I'll have to content myself with the replacement ones in my holster.

Outside, the atmosphere changes. There's a palpable tension all around us. Quietly, as we head toward the car, Oscar points me to the corner of the street. Where there's a pet supply store. First, I don't see anything, then a man whose hood obscures his face leans in to watch us.

Him again.

The first time, he got away from me, I don't want to make that mistake again.

I push Lovisa into the car and order her not to move.

"Sir?"

"We're going to get that son of a bitch."

"Is it wise? We don't know who we're dealing with."

Doesn't matter. I won't allow anyone to spy on me freely. I knew that by taking over my father's business, his enemies would become mine. It didn't take long for them to come after me.

"Let's go. Vanni, Lovisa is your responsibility. If anything happens to her, you'll pay for it," I say to my driver, slamming the door.

Confusion is written on Love's face. I don't have time to explain to her. I walk away with Oscar and signal him to go around the corner while I head straight to him. The stranger leans over again, and when he sees me coming in his direction, he bolts immediately. I run after him without difficulty. This motherfucker runs fast, but I'm faster. I run every morning, in any weather and on any ground: snowy, muddy, rocky, steep. He won't escape me. I redouble my efforts, closing the distance between us as he turns into a dead-end street. He ducks and jumps over the fence, starting to climb it. I see Oscar on the other side, pointing his gun at him, but the prospect of getting shot doesn't seem to stop him.

"Don't shoot!" I shout as I leap onto the climbing stranger.

I grab him roughly and slam him to the ground, almost ripping off his hood. Underneath it's a man in his twenties with blond hair. He's skin and bones with a waxen complexion. His eyes seem about to pop out of their sockets. A junkie.

"Don't hurt me!"

"That depends on your answer. Who sent you?"

"No one!"

He tries to escape, but I pin him down under my knee. I feel his alarming thinness under my kneecap. A little more pressure from me and I'll break his ribs.

"Don't play that with me."

I search the pockets of his hoodie and find a flip phone with a piece of paper containing a number. The pockets of his jeans are empty, only an almost finished bag of cocaine is there. His weakness.

"No! No! Give it back!" the junkie shouts, almost hysterical.

"Tell me what I want to know. Who sent you? What do you want from me?"

The drug addict scream under my knee before calming down, exhausted. His breathing becomes difficult and erratic. A pitiful whimper escapes his mouth before he starts talking, "I don't know who he is, he paid me a thousand kroner to follow you."

"I want more details. What did he look like?"

He shakes his head and closes his eyes, whimpering. I lift him up and pin him against the fence, Oscar points his gun at his neck.

"Can you feel this? He won't hesitate to put a hole in your if you don't speak. What did the guy who hired you look like?"

"I… I don't know! R… red hair, very short on the sides and curly on top. He was tall," he mumbles, shaking his head. "I just had to watch you, man, okay? I swear I don't know anything else."

This junkie is just a pawn, a subcontractor. Someone doesn't want to reveal himself right away.

"Do you have to contact him on this phone?"

He nods. I slip the phone into my pocket. It might come handy.

"Were you the one watching us last time?"

This time, he shakes his head vigorously. If it wasn't him, then it means he's not the only one involved. How many of them are stalking me? This is a mess.

I release him and toss the bag of drugs on the ground. He rushes to it.

"I don't want to see you again. If I catch you following me again, I'll be less merciful."

He leaves quickly as he can.

"Was it wise to let him go?"

"He's just a junkie, he's harmless. It's not him that I'm worried about."

Oscar holsters his gun, the furrows on his forehead prompt me ask him what's bothering him.

"Rodrigo," he says, looking around us.

It's a possibility. I expect revenge from him. I can't wait to take care of him.

"Let's go home."

When we get back to the car, I immediately feel that something is wrong. Vanni is waiting for me outside, nervous.

"Sir, I did everything to stop her."

I look at the back of the car and then turn sharply to my driver.

"Where is she?"

"She got a call and left the car suddenly. Before I could reach her, she was in a cab."

"Fuck!"

What was she thinking doing that? I angrily run my hand over my face and open the back door.

"Oscar, her number! Let's go home. Hopefully, she's at the villa."

On the way, I'm saving her number, my father's funeral has its benefits, we had all the guests' numbers. I immediately send her a message.

[Where are you?]

[Who is it?]

[Nik, damn it. Tell me where you are!]

[Rikard is at Iron House, I have to join him.]

Rikard. He didn't take long to come back. I understand better her eagerness to get back. I throw my phone onto the seat next to me and catch Vanni's gaze in his rearview mirror.

"Speed up. I need to get there as soon as possible."

13

Lovisa, 14 years old

As we head back to school, Niklas and I are closer than ever. We spent our summer vacation with our parents in Spain. This warm and magical country transported us to another world. Outside our usual context, our respective barriers are lifted, and even with Hendrik and my mother on our backs, we manage to stay close. While my head says me no, my heart beats faster in his presence, especially when we touch. I wish we could have stayed there; he was so different from the one he is in Kiruna. But I'm not giving up; I'll bring out the good in him here, even if it means taking the plunge and revealing my feelings for him. It may be arrogant of me, but I'm sure I can change him.

***

The taxi drives away, leaving me on the porch, full of anxiety. I don't want to step inside, I know Rikard is waiting for me. I could still turn around and hide until he leaves, but he would eventually find me. Tenacity is one of his qualities. With a shaky hand, I open the door. The gentle warmth of the fireplace envelops me like a velvet cloak. My skin tingles, but it's nothing compared to the nervousness twisting my insides. I close the door without making a sound. One of Niklas' men spots me and greets me. I forgot that the gatekeepers alert when someone enters Iron House.

I take off my coat and soaked boots while being alert to any noise. The voices of my boyfriend and Alfrida reach me from the kitchen. At first glance, he seems calm and laughs with the housekeeper. I approach slowly toward my source of fear.

Rikard is sitting on a stool at the kitchen counter. In his hands is a steaming cup of coffee. When he sees me, a radiant smile lights up his face.

"Lovisa, darling."

Approaching, he kisses me firmly before taking me into his arms and holding me close to him. He adds, "I missed you."

"Rick, I—"

"Later."

He urges me to sit down beside him and accept Alfrida's tea. Behind the door, outside, Nik's dog barks and scratches the window to come in. Rik has always hated dogs. Their instinct tells them to be wary of him, and rightly so.

His almost *normal* behavior doesn't help me calm down. If there's one thing I've learned from our relationship, it's that the angrier Rikard gets, the calmer he appears. Here, he's like a peaceful lake, with no ripples disturbing the surface. What should I expect? I struggle to swallow my tea.

"How's your mother doing?"

"She's much better, thank you," Rikard replies. "That's why I came to pick up Lovisa, so she can come back with me on my family's private jet."

Alfrida smiles at him and places a plate of cookies in front of him. She answers, "It will be much more pleasant than having all these people packed together like sardines in a can."

A deadly can of sardines.

I can't participate in the conversation. The air feels thin in the room, and I can't help but feel anxious about being alone with him. His presence here seems incongruous, unsuitable.

He doesn't belong here.

I realize that since he left, I've felt better, less oppressed, and freer in my movements.

In no time, I find myself climbing the stairs alongside Rikard. How? I don't know; I must have had a lapse while my mind was elsewhere.

Please, I want him to stay calm.

"If you need anything, I'll be in the kitchen," Alfrida reminds us.

We don't bother to reply, my boyfriend's hand insistent on my back, forcing me to pick up the pace.

One.

My temperature rises under the fear.

Rikard closes the door behind me; I don't dare to turn around.

Two.

My heart is pounding harder.

The floor creaks under his weight. I close my eyes and bite my lips.

Three.

Inhale, exh—

My body is suddenly manhandled. Rikard forces me to turn around to face him. Without waiting, he slaps me hard, throwing my head back.

"You slut," he hisses, his face red with anger.

"It's not what you think," I murmur, swallowing back a sob.

I try to suppress my trembling, but it's a waste of time.

"Shut up! Save your lies for someone else, your viper tongues can only speak lies. You're just a greedy whore who's nothing without me. I gave you everything, and this is how you thanks me."

My blood runs cold. He's right. He made me dependent on him, on this life we've been living for four years. Even if he doesn't know it yet, it's over. I'll soon say goodbye to my past to rebuild myself elsewhere.

"When I think I was taking care of my injured mother while *Madame* was fooling around elsewhere."

"I… didn't… cheat on you."

My voice, stronger this time, rings in the room like a challenge, a revolt from me.

Unable to contain himself any longer, he punches me in the stomach, then again when I try to escape. Breathless, I fall to my knees, struggling with all my might to contain my cries of pain. I don't want to give him the satisfaction of hearing me scream for him. The pain twists my body, and the tears that I struggle to hold back stream down my cheeks. I end up curling up on the floor as he walks away to lock himself in the bathroom.

I don't dare to move. At the slightest movement, I fear that he'll appear again to hurt me. I'm miserable. I must look like a scared animal whose master has just given a beating. Pathetic. I disgust myself. I don't want to be this insignificant woman who allows herself to be dominated.

A few minutes later, Rikard comes back, calmer, more relaxed, and with slightly wet hair. A few rebellious locks fall across his forehead. He's handsome. A dark beauty rarely seen. Unlike Nik, who has a wild beauty, almost reassuring when you know him. By his side, I feel protected. He also has his share of darkness, but it's less oppressive than the man who is in this room with me.

"Get up and pack your bags; we're leaving."

No way. Fuck him.

"I don't want to go with you," I whisper, staying huddled.

"What? What did you say?"

He grabs me by the ponytail and lifts me up. My feet leave the ground for a moment before landing heavily. A groan of pain escapes me as I try to make him let go.

"Say that again."

His face inches from mine, his coffee breath crashes against my skin. The smell makes me nauseous.

"I said that—"

"Shut up!" Rikard thunders, releasing my hair to grab my cheeks with one hand, his fingers painfully digging into my flesh. "You're going back home with me, whether you like it or not."

He throws me on the bed and leans dangerously over me. Heart pounding, I can't make a sound as he slips a hand under my dress.

"I'm going to show you that you'll never have a better lover."

His hand roughly caresses my thigh, freezing my blood. With a sudden movement, he tears my stocking. I shiver, but not from desire. A mix of darker feelings brews inside me, threatening to explode.

"Don't do this…"

Beatings are part of my daily life, but is he ready to go as far as rape to teach me a lesson? He never gone that far.

"You'll soon forget that asshole who hugged you."

He talks about John Gray. No matter how much I plead my case, Rikard won't listen to me. I'm just a liar in his eyes. An unfaithful woman he must set back on the right path.

When his hand reaches the now forbidden zone for him, my body is filled with an electric shock. Courage and strength I didn't known I had takes over me. I curl my legs against my chest, pushing him away with my arms and pressing my feet against his abdomen to throw him backward. My action surprises both of us. I never rebelled. Before he recovers, I stand up and run to the door.

"Come back here!"

I leave and rush to the stairs, almost stumbling. Behind me, Rikard's heavy step indicate he's chasing me. The strong, rapid beating of my heart prevents me from hearing anything else. To my right, the sound of the front door slamming catches my attention. Niklas, followed by Oscar, looks at me strangely. My tousled hair and torn tights must make me look like a tramp. A hand lands on my shoulder. I don't need to turn around to know that Rikard has caught up with me.

"Let's go back up."

I don't move, my heavy body no longer obeys me. My breath becomes short and rapid, I gasp at the mere thought of what will happen to me if I go back up with him.

My gaze meets that of the handsome Viking. We lock eyes for a long moment. Through this simple contact, I hope that he senses all my distress and my fear.

Help me.

I want to say it out loud, but I'm incapable of it.

Rikard pulls me back, grabs my arm, and forces me up to step onto the first stair. I try to resist, but my feeble efforts are in vain.

"A moment."

A long shiver runs down my spine when I hear the deep tone of his voice. As one, we turn back toward Niklas.

My heart almost leaps for joy. This connection I thought was lost between us is still there.

Rikard tenses beside me and tightens his grip on me.

"I advise you to let her go."

"It's none of your business. It only concerns Lovisa and me."

Nik approaches us until there're three feet left. A powerful force emanates from him, both from his stature as from the weapon revealed, strapped on his chest.

"Everything concerning Lovisa concerns me."

"She's my girlfriend!"

To emphasize his words, he tightens his grips on my arm and pulls me toward him. I try to pull away, but he's much stronger.

"Is this how you treat your girlfriend? By hurting her?"

Nik's voice is filled with anger. He looks down at my torn tights. He recoils, his lips parting before snapping shut. Without hesitation, he throws himself on my boyfriend, causing us to tumble down the stairs. Surprised, Rikard lets go of me, I take the opportunity to push myself to the side and get up.

"You little shit!" Niklas curses as he crushes his fist on Rikard's jaw.

A fight I didn't expect breaks out between the two men. Fists and feet are used to injure each other. Nik has the upper hand on Rik, and that's what scares me. If he keeps going, he'll end up killing him.

"Stop," I murmur, my voice so weak it can't barely be heard.

The blows continue. Blood starts to run down their hands and faces. I look toward Oscar.

"Do something!"

He puts his hand on his earpiece and calls for backup. Meanwhile, Oscar pulls his boss back and tries to restrain him. As for me, I rush to Rikard and help him up.

"What the hell are you doing?" Niklas snap at me, glaring at me.

"I'm stopping you from doing something stupid," I dare to say.

Rikard is disfigured, with a split lip and left eyebrow, a red and swollen cheek. There're traces of blood everywhere. Nik is also looking bad, but he's faring better. It hurt me to see him injured. I'd like to heal his wounds, but right now, I have to keep Rik away.

Two henchmen enter the house, but Oscar promptly sends them away, their help is no longer needed. I watch Nik rub his bloodied lip with the back of his hand. I can feel his anger from here. He's a powerful man, but so is Rikard, and his family has a lot of influence in Sweden. If anything were to happen to him, they would do everything to destroy the culprit. I refuse to let that happen to him. He shouldn't be involved in my problems.

Without a word, I accompany my boyfriend—or ex-boyfriend?— to the bathroom in my bedroom. Niklas tries to follow us, but I stop him, and I can see that he's not pleased at all. What must he be thinking? Upstairs, I keep my distance from Rikard, preferring to maintain a safe distance between him and me. Besides, the bedroom door remains open; I refuse to be in a closed room with him again. He angrily washes his face. His ego took a hit. No one has ever dared to lay a hand on him like Niklas did.

"We're leaving now," he demands, examining his face in the mirror.

After what has just happened, he's still fixated on the idea of me going back with him to Stockholm. I shake my head and cross my arms against me, awakening the pain in my stomach. He hurt me. Again. He'll never stop. I believed in his sweet words for too long. From the beginning, he knew how to charm me, to manipulate me. The first few times, when he raised his hand against me, I was convinced that I deserved it, that it was my fault. Years passed, and I realized that I wasn't the problem. It's all in his head, and no matter what I do to please him, he'll always find an excuse to hit me or belittle me.

I take a deep breath, hoping to give myself the courage to speak up.

"I'm not coming with you. It's over."

"It'll be when I say it's over."

He exits the bathroom and approaches me. Like opposing magnets, I recoil and raise a hand toward him. My gesture surprises him and has the desired effect. He stops.

"I wish you a safe trip back. It's better if we break up."

Once again, I feel like crying, but I stay strong. My lip trembles slightly, I choke back a sob, and leave before he can reply. Now that things are clear about our situation and that he's not too hurt, I need to know what's going on with Niklas. In the hall, Alfrida comes out of the living room with a first aid kit. Her worried look knots my stomach. When she notices me, her face tenses even more.

"Honey, why didn't you tell me about your situation?"

She knows it's not the first time he's laid a hand on me. How does she know? A mother senses these things. She's been one in a way since Mom's passing. I bite my lip and lower my eyes, ashamed.

"I just couldn't…"

Alfrida wraps me in her arms. I lean into her and hug her as if she were a lifeline. She smells of sweet biscuits, but also herbal tea, plunges me into old happy memories with her. I miss those simple and mostly happy time terribly. She pats my back, gives me an affectionate kiss on my cheek, and scrutinizes me as she releases me.

"You'll need to put some ice on that cheek before it bruises."

"I will. How is he doing?"

My gaze shifts to the living room, where no noise is coming out.

"He's been through worse. Go see him, he's worried about you."

He's worried about me, even though he got hit because of me? I approach silently and find him, standing in front of the bay window overlooking the driveway, a glass of alcohol in his hand. His right profile bears a cut on his cheekbone, and a bruise is starting to turn his skin blue.

His hair, usually tied in a tight bun, is loose and tousled, accentuating his wild beauty. A true Viking. My heart tightens, and a volcano begins to simmer in the hollow of my stomach at the sight of this warrior, fallen straight from Valhalla. His voice interrupts my thoughts.

"I rarely feel hatred," Niklas begins, still staring outside. "I've hit people to defend someone, to defend myself, or to assert my superiority within the cartel, I've fought for the pleasure of brawl, but hitting out of hatred is very rare."

He turns around, leaning against the window. His steel eyes lock on mine, freezing me in place. He seems relaxed, but his face remains closed.

"When I saw the state he put you in, I wanted to kill him. Knowing that a man like Rikard Rapace can hit you with impunity drives me mad. Scum like him deserves no mercy. I've killed for less than that."

He puts down his glass next to his guns and glares at me. His voice hardens and becomes accusatory.

"But I don't know what's more unbearable. The fact that you stopped me from finishing him off or the fact that you went back upstairs with him. Explain to me what the hell are you playing at? You like taking hits, is that it?"

I open my mouth then close it. If I did it, it was for him, to protect him from troubles he couldn't handle. I step into the room, crossing my arms over my chest. I'm cold. Standing by the fireplace, I watch the flames dance, lick, and consumes the wood.

A crack is created in me, specifically on the wall that I've built for years to protect myself from others, but mostly to protect all my secrets. Today, in front of Niklas, I finally feel the need to explain myself. About my relationship with Rikard, but also about how I got there. About what triggered this new life: my sudden departure nine years ago. This departure that Niklas still seems to blame me. I didn't plan to bring it up again, but now it seems necessary. He talks about the hatred he feels toward my ex-boyfriend, but what I mostly perceive, as he uses such harsh words toward me, is his hatred toward me. Toward the teenager who left him with nothing but a filthy letter. I don't want those to be the images he has of me. Neither that of the sixteen-year-old Lovisa who abandoned him without a backward glance nor that of the twenty-five-year-old Lovisa who accepts her boyfriend's violence without protest. I want him to know who I truly am.

"I didn't leave of my own free will," I confess, tense. "Your father... Hendrik forced me to leave."

I expect him to interrupt me, but he doesn't. I continue, "I lived in a boarding school where there were music classes, at least he granted me that. I was alone, terribly lonely despite the friends I had made. Something was missing…"

You.

"Year went by; I took odd jobs after my studies and joined an orchestra. During one of our concerts, I met Rikard."

A smile stretches my lips at the thought of our first dates.

"He was very kind and attentive. He always came to see me. I felt good, he managed to fill the void that I had inside. We started dating quickly, and before I knew it, I had moved with him."

The downfall. I was so stupid. Everything went to hell from that moment. I often regret going too fast with him. I relied so much in our sweet and beautiful romance that I didn't see who he really was.

"At first, it was jealousy fits; I thought it was cute that he cared about me so much. Then he started slapping me, apologizing each time promising never to do it again, but he never kept his promise."

I bite my lip and turn around. Seeing Nik so close to me makes me jump slightly; I hadn't heard him approach. The flames illuminate his face with golden hues, his hair looks lighter with these blonde highlights on either side. I breathe in to give myself the courage to continue my monologue.

"I loved him, but his blows became more and more violent and regular. I gave him a second chance every time, hoping he would change. And then… I was so scared. Scared of the consequences if I dared to suggest leaving him. He said he'd rather kill me than let me go, and I believed him. I still do."

A relief like no other before takes hold of me. The weight I carry on my shoulders evaporates in an instant. This toxic relationship has been suffocating me for too long and slowly poisoning me. It can't go on like this anymore. Feeling ashamed of exposing myself to him, I lower my head and stare at his black shoes. I suddenly find myself fascinated by them, but mostly, by the size of his feet. I prefer to think about that rather than face Niklas's judgment.

In front of me, the young heir to the Ekman fortune steps forward, reducing the distance between us to almost nothing. His arms draw me against him and trap me against his chest. His fingers slide into my hair. He removes my hair tie and then releases it. Through his sweater, his heart is pounding. Does mine beat the same way? I feel it pounding against my chest, happy to be nestled against the one it's been waiting for all this time. I eventually lift my head. His gaze is softer, almost apologetic.

"I don't need your pity," I say immediately.

"You inspire many things in me, but not pity. I didn't know it was my dad who kicked you out. The bastard! And the fact that Rikard was beating you…"

Unable to say more for fear of giving in to anger, he falls silent.

I shake my head and raise a hand to his cheek. I've dreamed of making this gesture countless times. Slowly, I stroke his beard, which is surprisingly soft despite appearances.

"Don't dwell on it, it's in the past."

"I hated you so much," he admits, pulling me closer to him. "I hated you for leaving without me. Back then you were all that mattered to me, and when I woke up and read your letter—"

"Hendrik made me write it, those weren't my words," I interrupt. "All these horrors didn't come from me."

He nods and seems lost in thoughts. What is he thinking about? Unlike me, he's difficult to read. His mind is as closed as a double-locked door. I decide to break the silence between us.

"If you decide not to see me anymore, given what happened with Rikard, I'll understand. We come into your life and cause trouble, and I can see that my presence here is causing you trouble."

He stifles a discreet chuckle and lifts me up a little slightly, my feet leaving the ground. This position forces me to wrap my arms around his neck to avoid falling.

"I won't let you go. I want you to stay here if that's what you want."

Is he asking me to live here? That wasn't in my plans. All I wanted was to collect my inheritance and rebuild myself elsewhere. His proposition troubles me. I know he's not Rikard, but a part of me fears reliving that situation with someone else. I nervously bite my lip.

"I'm not forcing you to do anything, it'll still be your decision, but if you stay here, nothing bad will ever happen to you."

I wish I could believe him, be confident, and close my eyes to let myself go to a life by his side, but Rik's imprint is still very present on my body. It's still too fresh.

He set me back on my feet, I take the opportunity to put some distance between us. I'm too hot and I don't know if it's because of the fireplace or this brief close contact with the handsome Viking.

"I need to go check if he's ready to go," I mutter unsure.

I won't be able to think clearly around him, I need to get away.

As I barely take a few steps, Niklas strides over me and turns me around. I don't have time to ask him what's going on when his mouth presses against mine. He kisses me as if it was vital, as if he needed it to live a few extra minutes. This kiss is passionate and deliciously flavored with honey whiskey. The taste is pleasant and makes it even more delicious. Lost in an avalanche of emotions and physical sensations, I surrender in his arms and caress his tongue with mine, my hands gripping his hair. My heart threatens to explode and my brain disconnects. I think of nothing else but this passionate moment.

This exchange is so good that I forget all decorum as I let him grab my butt. He sucks on my lower lip before releasing it under the shouts behind us.

"You slut!" Rikard insults from the entrance hall. "You're just a whore, you disgust me!"

I recoil from Niklas so violently that I almost fall backwards. The latter turns toward to my ex-boyfriend and is about to jump on him when Oscar and a second guard intervene to force Rik out.

"Let me take care of him," Nik says angrily as he's held back by Oscar.

"He's not worth it, sir. Don't give him that satisfaction."

Through the window, I see Rikard storming toward his rental car. Before climbing into the driver's seat, he looks in my direction. His eyes are filled with anger and resentment. Unable to meet his gaze, I flee into my room. The last image he'll have of me is of a woman being groped by another guy five minutes after our breakup. Despite everything he's done to me, this thought is unbearable. Niklas calls out to me as I lock the door of my bedroom.

My skin itches as it always does when guilt gnaws at me. A furious urge to take a cold shower overwhelms me. *I have sinned. I must be punished.* Hendrik taught me that lesson well. I rush into the bathroom, where I turn on the rain-effect shower. The transparent walls of the shower don't fog up because the water is freezing. Without hesitation, I step underneath the streams of water. The low temperature of the water takes my breath away before quickly making it jagged. You might think that after all these years of practice I'd be used to it, but every time, it's a thermal shock, and it takes me a moment before I can breathe normally without shivering without uncontrollably. With my eyes closed, I fold my arms around myself. I go over what I've done wrong, as I do after every argument with Rikard. I ended our relationship, which wasn't a bad thing, but then I kissed Niklas, just minutes after our breakup.

I shouldn't have, but I don't regret it. That kiss…

My lips still taste of his, and I run a cold finger over them, remembering our exchange.

My dress, heavy and soaked with water, clings to my body like a second skin. I hate this sensation, yet I don't shed it.

A little further, someone starts banging on my bedroom door. Niklas's voice rises, demanding me to open the door.

Leave me alone! I want to scream.

I crouch down and wrap my arms around my legs, my face buried against my knees.

It's over with Rikard. For good? Will I fall back into his arms fearing change?

I have to be strong. I must not let myself be walked over me anymore. He's done dictating my life and forbidding me from being who I want to be.

A crash behind me makes me jump. The hurried steps of someone running in my direction and opening the shower door makes me lift my head.

"Lovisa!"

The shower, excessively large, easily accommodates both of us. He squats in front of me.

"What the fuck are you doing?"

The water pounds our faces, slightly blurring my vision when I look at him. His powerful hands grab me to lift me up. His angry gaze amplifies my shivers.

"You're going to get sick."

With a trembling lip, I retort, "It wouldn't be the first time. Right?"

He snorts and pulls me out of the shower after turning off the water.

"You're right, but enough of this bullshit. He's not here anymore."

I don't know if he's talking about Rikard or Hendrik. More than once, we got sick when he forced us to take a cold shower or bath, or even plunge into the lake on the estate when it comes to Niklas.

"Take off your clothes," he orders as he himself taking off his sweater and long-sleeved shirt.

Seeing that I don't move, he grunts and turns away. I remove my dress and my tights, ending up in underwear. I grab a towel and wrap myself in it. Niklas's back tenses when I touch his tattoo of the white wolf intertwined with a red fox. He faces me and assesses me with a softer look this time. With a silent command, he brings me to my bed. On the way, I see the door frame of my door, which is almost torn off when he forced it open.

"You're completely crazy."

I pull the blanket and slide into my bed. My wet hair soaks my pillow. With a shrug, he pull the blanket over me and cuddles me like a mother would with her child. This image brings a weak smile to my face.

"You didn't open the door. I imagined the worst."

The prospect of my suicide sends shivers down my spine and a tightens my throat. I'd be lying if I said that idea hasn't crossed my mind during my short existence. But I never dared to act on it.

"I'm fine. You can go."

He lets out a silent, bitter laugh.

"You're not fooling me, I thought that all that was behind us. But you still do it?"

My silence answers his question.

"I hated when he did this to you. And if there was one positive thing about you leaving, it's that he couldn't punish you anymore."

Niklas sits on the edge of the bed. Hesitantly, I put my hand over his. He doesn't hesitate to squeeze my fingers.

"I'm sad to think he kept punishing you to shape you to his liking," I say, biting my lips together.

His gaze hardens at the memory of his past. He sketches a joyless smile.

"He knew how to be very inventive on his good days. Once, I rebelled and it all stopped. Hendrik is dead and Rikard will soon be far from Kiruna, you have nothing to fear anymore, and you must stop punishing yourself for I don't know what fault. They were assholes."

He plunges his beautiful blue irises into mine.

"Be strong. Don't let anyone step on you."

The depth of his eyes and his words make the muscle in my stomach contract, and my fingers tighten around his. He had often said these words to me when I was younger, and I had always lived up to them, but over time, they had been forgotten.

With a nod, I end our conversation without letting go of his hand. I don't want him to leave. This desire reactivates the itching in my body, and I have to bite the inside of my cheek to keep from diving into the icy lake of Iron House. *No more bullshit, my dear.* It has to stop now.

I.

Am.

Strong.

14

Niklas, 16 years old

She is attracted to me. She finally admitted it to me. I won. All I have to do is go for it, but I can't. Something is holding me back. We're playing and teasing with each other constantly. I love this cat-and-mouse game. We're changing and everyone notices it. Including our parents. My father promised me a hydrotherapy session to calm me down. That's what he calls the ice-cold showers he forces me to take or the jumps into the lake. I hate these punishments, most of them are unfounded and cruel. As for Sigrid, she threatened to cut off my balls if I touched a single hair of her princess. In short, none of them want us to fool around under their roof. Let them talk. I won't let them dictate my behavior. They can threaten me with anything, but they won't decide for me.

* * *

Three years ago

Always running faster, farther. In sport, I can escape and dream of another life, simpler, less complicated. Without Henrik. He makes my days very dark when he wants to. In those moments, I put on sportwear, plug my headphones into my ears, and run until the air burns my lungs. In all weather, I go out. My body heats up so much that I don't feel the polar cold of this part of the country where temperatures are very low.

Under a light snowfall, I've been running for an hour. My limbs are painful, and my body frozen from the inside, every breath is torture. I'm exhausted. Drained of my energy, I turn back to return to Iron House. On the way, my phone rings.

Gunkil.

I pick up, my breath ragged and loud. "Hey, man. What's up?"

His voice comes directly through my headphones.

"Hey, what's that noise? Are you still running?"

Gunkil isn't the type to do sport, and it baffles him that I'm so addicted to the adrenaline it gives me. I do climbing, crossfit, hiking, rafting in the summer. This last activity is the only one that Gunkil shares with me. Fredrik, on the other hand, accompanies me on almost all my adventures.

"What do you want?" I ask between ragged breaths.

"Jonna is having her birthday party at the Red Mill next week. Since the manager is a very good friend, we thought he'd close the bar for one night."

I've owned the bar for two years. The previous owner turned it into one of the trendiest places in Kiruna. I love going there, so when he decided to sell, I didn't hesitate. Since then, my friends have been enjoying free drinks. More than once, Gunkil got kicked out of the Red Mill. I put him in charge of my business, but he proved to be unreliable. Our collaboration didn't last long, but this incident didn't change our friendship.

"Okay. But if you break anything, it's on you."

I cough and clear my throat. A heavy fatigue overwhelms me and crushes my head and shoulders; I gave too much during this jogging session.

"You're awesome! I'll let Jo know, you'll make her day."

This idea elicits no emotion in me. Jonna is a very good friend whom I occasionally sleep with, but I have no feelings for her. I'm aware of what she feels for me, and many times she's had jealous outbursts. I don't know why I still bother with this relationship.

The gates of Iron House loom in the distance.

Finally.

I'm out of breath, and my body screams at me to stop. I've used all my reserves.

"Sort it out with Bethenny and don't take the opportunity to hit on her. My employees are off-limits."

"I can't promise anything, you know I can't resist a pretty face."

"Gun…"

I pause, unable to say more. I stop short, leaning on my knees, and taking deep breaths of fresh air. A sharp pain shoot through my chest;

my heart is beating so hard it feels like it might explode. My ears are ringing, and my vision blurs.

"Nik, dude? You okay?"

"I—"

My voice is barely a whisper, I can't seem to raise it. A wave of heat washes over me before the world fall beneath my feet. I collapse into the snow, Gunkil shooting in my ears.

****

At the end of the second floor, facing the lake and the forest of the property, there's a gym equipped with everything needed for weightlifting, as well a treadmill, a bike, and a punching bag for boxing. I need light, and the view from the window is very captivating. I no longer use the gym located in the basement, not far from the shooting range. It's too gloomy and cold.

Lying on a bench, I lift weight under the watchful eye of Micaël, a personal trainer I hired three years ago. He comes several times a week and puts me through a controlled program that he insists I follow precisely. It's for my own good. Most of the time, when I run, he's by my side, but I much prefer being alone.

"Take it easy," Micaël advises, standing near my head.

No breaks. I lift my bar, again and again. Micaël watches for any weakness sign on my part. He sighs for the umpteenth time when I refuse his help when the weight proves challenging. Damn, I've done worse, but today my body is failing me. My arms are shaking, and I have to give up. I sit up and wipe a towel over my neck. My body is drenched in sweat, as if I've just run a marathon.

"You're not in good shape today," says Micaël, writing in his notebook. "Are you taking your treatment properly?"

"Are you my mother or what?" I scoff, grabbing my water bottle taking big gulps.

Micaël packs up his things. He's of averaged height, slim build, and the only one who can beat me in a race. His short black hair and his hazel eyes seduced Lucia, an old high school friend who comes to the property to take care of the red foxes. As she grew up, she became passionate about animals, and she studied to become a veterinarian.

She takes care of my animals. Lucia comes a little too often; I suspect she's coming for Micaël. They're looking at each other without anyone making the first move.

"Come on, I wasn't that bad, look what I just lifted."

"You're all red, you pushed too hard, and you're sweating," Micaël worries, swinging his bag over his shoulder. "If you don't listen to me, we'd better stop everything."

He exaggerates, I listen to him more than I'd like. I get up and fist bump him before he leaves. I get this threat at least once a month.

After he leaves, I wrap my hands in wraps and hit the punching bag. Lovisa will be there soon. After the incident with Rikard, a week ago now, I started training her so she can defend herself at least in case of an attack. She needs to toughen up and assert herself. I want to see the fighter inside her. My fox learn fast, and while her moves are still soft and clumsy, the will to learn is there. The sight of her body covered in bruises clouds my mind for a moment. After that bastard Rikard left, I demanded the whole truth and when she showed me the bruises, a wild rage took over me. The urge to go to Stockholm and beat the shit out of him, but I promised Lovisa I wouldn't do anything. And I never break a promise.

At the same time, I've been rethinking my own actions toward her. I didn't hit her, but several time, I roughed her up by grabbing her by the throat or speaking to her harshly and authoritatively. The thought that she might one day see similarities between us makes me question myself, but how do you change such a deep-rooted nature, instilled by a father's violence? Isn't it difficult not to reproduce the same pattern?

Lovisa eventually shows up, her hair tied up in a high ponytail, dressed in black and neon yellow leggings and a matching bra. She's adorable. This outfit highlights the abuse she suffered, but it doesn't take away from her beauty. Her bruises are slowly turning from purple to brownish-yellow. Soon she won't have any lasting mark.

"Ready, babe?"

She blushes at my nickname. Since Rikard's left, I've been rediscovering Lovisa in a new light. She's more relaxed, smiling, almost radiant. Like in our adolescence, we're constantly searching for each other. We flirt like two kids. I'm getting to know her kisses, her touches, her sometimes clumsy hugs under her shyness. We haven't gone all the way yet. I don't think she's ready, and I think after such a breakup, she'll probably need some time before moving on completely. But that doesn't stop me from trying by teasing her erogenous zones like her neck or the base of her ears.

"What are we doing today?"

Her gaze slides over my chest, and the way she bites her lower lip raises my tension. Does she realize the effect she has on me? Sweating, I take off my T-shirt and throw it in the corner of the room.

"Do you like the view?"

"What? I wasn't looking at you!" she justifies, turning her head away.

I chuckle and step away to grab some clean wraps. She can lie to me, but her body will always tell me the truth.

She extends her hands, which I bandage carefully.

"Your tattoo is huge. It must have hurt."

On my eighteenth birthday, I got this tattoo that covers my entire back. A white wolf intertwined with a fiery red fox. It's us. The vision I had back then. I'm a white wolf, cold and terrifying, and she's a red fox, soft and harmless. I often forget it existences, until someone brought up to me. In those moments, Lovisa occupies all my thoughts. Now I don't need it anymore to remember her. She's back.

"Just like yours."

I turn her around and run my fingers over her right shoulder blade where a wolf's head seems to have been drawn with a marker. I touch it lightly, her skin shivers.

"I'm jealous," I admit, placing a kiss on her shoulder. "This tattoo is embedded in you, you have it in your skin for life. I envy its place."

I loosen her ponytail and place another kiss on her neck. Her body reacts to my touch, driving me even crazier about her. Her back leans against me, she tilts her head to the side, offering me her slender neck.

"It's just lifeless ink, without personality, without feeling. You're much more than a simple tattoo to me."

Her words swell my heart with pleasure. My head reminds me to be careful, that all this is too good to be true. Even though she left me the first time because of Hendrik, there's no guarantee she won't do it again on her own. Knowing that, I can't help but want everything from her, everything with her.

I kiss her under the ear and gently push her toward the punching bag.

"Let's get to work. I won't let you go until you know how to defend yourself."

She positions herself in front of the bag and starts hitting it. At first, I let her do it, then I stand behind her. I tap her elbows to lower them.

"Too high. Keep them close to you when you strike, your ribs aren't protected. When you throw a direct punch, you have to do it like this."

I move her to the side and hit the bag with strong, quick punches. My elbows rise a bit, but quickly come back against me after each attack. She mimics my movements, her eyebrows furrowed with concentration. The more she trains, the more precise her movements become.

"Great. You're a good student."

"I must say I have a good teacher."

"Flattering. If you're trying to score points, you'll need more than that," I tease with a playful glance.

She laughs and gives me a friendly punch on the shoulder.

For the next part, I teach her self-defense moves by simulating different attacks, how to free herself from a hold, whether she gets caught by the wrist, throat, or body. She doesn't block any of the attacks and often finds herself on the mat, with me on top of her. At the end of the tenth takedown, she gives up, lying down.

"I give up. I'll never get it."

"Don't give up. It's normal not to get it right the first time. Thanks to me, you'll know how to disarm any guy who dares to attack you."

I lie down next to her and pull her close. Her frail, sweaty body snuggled into my arms. Her red hair scattered around her face, barely held in place by the elastic band.

"It all seems so easy for you."

I smile at her words. We don't have the same physical condition, and it took me years to master everything.

"You'll get there," I repeat. "Rushing into things only makes them poorly done. Every art has its discipline, its eases, and its difficulties. You have to train and push beyond your limits, not give up, and stop only when your body threatens to break."

Hendrik was a bastard, but some of his values have served me well in becoming the man I am today.

We get up just as my phone rings. Jonna. Damn it. Again. Since I kicked her out of my house, I haven't seen her, and she keeps calling me. Didn't she get the message? This has to stop.

"Hello!"

"Nick! Oh, Nik, finally! I'm sorry. Listen, I screwed up. Okay? It won't happen again."

I sigh. Barely a few seconds on the phone with her and her voice annoys me. How did I put up with her until now?

"You need to stop trying to reach me. It's over, got it? Coming to the gates, pissing off my men, and calling the house phone won't change anything."

I try to speak as calmly as possible. A little further away, Lovisa drinks her water while looking at me, bewildered. I shake my head and turn my back to her.

"We had fun, but it's over now, we have to move on. Find yourself a good guy, marry him, and have kids. I'm not the one for you."

A sniffle on the phone tells me she's crying. Not this. I hate making a woman cry. I'm harsh with my words, but I'm direct, I don't like beating around the bush.

"You're such a heartless jerk. I hate you. You'll pay for this, and so will she!" she screams, damaging my eardrum in the process. "It's because of Lovisa, isn't it? She shows up and you dump me! I won't give up! She'll regret it."

"Listen," I snap, "if you touch any of her hair, I swear you'll deal with me. Got it? So now, get out of my life and don't come back!"

After hanging up, I take a deep breath and turn back to Lovisa. Seeing my furious expression, she tightens her grip on her water bottle, hesitating.

"Are you okay?" she asks.

Her expression softens me. I don't like the fear I see on her face, especially if it's caused by me. I approach and embrace her shoulders.

"Don't worry, just a thorn in the foot that I finally removed."

She nods, unconvinced by my vague explanation.

"By the way, do you have any news from Rikard?"

"No. He didn't try to reach me, and I saw that he blocked me everywhere on social media. That's official."

A hint of sadness crosses her emerald eyes. Saying goodbye to a four-year relationship, chaotic as it may be, can't be easy.

I put on a black hoodie as Oscar bursts into the room, informing me of Gunkil and Fredrik's presence.

"How are they doing?" Lovisa asks as we leave the gym together.

"They're on their own, bounty hunters."

She laughs as she walks down the hallway. I love that sound. Seeing her happy is much more pleasant than the troubled look she had in the first few days.

"I think this profession suits them very well."

I agree. They've always had this crazy side that doesn't fit into any box. When they announced they were joining the police force, I was shocked. What were those cops thinking, hiring two crazies like them? Anyway, they found their true calling, and they're much better as bounty hunters.

When I enter the living room, Fredrik greets me, while Gunkil helps himself to a drink. When the latter turns around, his eyes light up at the sight of the young woman by my side. But upon noticing the bruises on her abdomen, his eyebrows furrow; he silently questions me, I signal him not to say anything.

"Hello," Lovisa greets, shyly.

She's adorable.

She hasn't seen them in many years. Yet, this scene is familiar to me. Back in the day, our gang used to gather in my bachelor pad.

"Hello, stranger!" Gunkil exclaims as he approaches.

He tries to hug her, but I put my arm around his shoulders to stop him and move him away from her. My intervention makes him laugh; he says over his shoulder, "Are you back for good? Everyone missed you, especially Nik, right, buddy?"

"Shut up," I growl.

I don't know if she's going to stay; we haven't really discussed it, and I don't want to. If she has to leave, I'd rather know it the day of her departure. Burring my head in the sand won't help, but I'll make sure she doesn't want to leave me again. The idea of revenge I wanted to inflict on her vanished the day she told me the truth about her sudden departure.

I invite her to join me on the couch, while my friends settle into individual armchairs on either side of the coffee table.

"If you're here, it means there's new about Rodrigo, right?"

This name catches Lovisa's attention. Her delicate eyebrows

furrow as do Fredrik's to my right.

"Does she know?"

"No, but you can speak freely in front of her."

They exchange a long look between them, which annoys me. I don't need their opinion on the matter. Damn it, they don't have to question my orders. Frustrated, I sigh.

"So?"

Fredrik immediately continues, "A man, quite close to him, gave us one of his hideouts in Mölnadal. We went to look for him."

"How do you know that man told the truth?"

"Considering the beating we gave him, I highly doubt he lied to us," Gunkil boasts. "And we saw Rodrigo heading there."

What? I pretend to look around then give them a murderous look.

"Alright, so where is he? Why didn't you bring him back?"

"He was surrounded by five heavily armed men, and they didn't leave his side. We didn't stand a chance. We followed him to a warehouse near the docks in the Långedrag neighborhoods, where he had chat with the captain of a container ship— Are you okay, man?"

"The name of the ship."

Fredrik searches through a notebook and finds the desired page.

"The *Black Eagle*."

What expression is on my face? I can't control my features. Internally, the mechanisms in my brain stopped at this name. I know it, I know it too well. My dad talked me about it. It's thanks to him that his illegal business is thriving. A business that is now mine. And the fact I wasn't informed about this meeting, even though the captain has been generously paid by my family for a long time, doesn't bode well.

This is a mess.

"Are you okay?" Lovisa asks me.

"Nick?" Gunkil adds.

I stand up, a little too quickly; I'm dizzy, but I quickly shake it off. This is not the time to falter. I pace around the room, deep in thought, not bothering to answer their questions.

If Rodrigo takes control of my means of importation, I'm screwed. A shipment is supposed to arrive in two days, and distribution takes place the day after. He must not get his hands of it.

"Fredrik, go get Oscar, I need him. Gunkil, contact Patrik Hallgreen, he's the captain of The *Black Eagle*. Make arrangements to see him and ensure his loyalty."

Gunkil has radical persuasion methods; this mission is perfect for him. Patrik is a corrupt sailor who accepts envelopes slipped under the table. He receives one from us every month.

"Oscar will give you his number and what you need. If he's too greedy, show him we don't negotiate with an Ekman."

"With pleasure, boss," he replies as he heads into the hall.

Fredrik slips away to inform Oscar. I take out the pack of cigarettes I keep in a drawer in the living room. I quickly light one and take a long drag. As I exhale, I pinch the bridge of my nose, closing my eyes. What will I look like if I screw everything up, barely having the business in my hands? My father would turn in his grave.

Lovisa approaches silently and slips her hand into mine. This gesture surprises me; it's so intimate, so *couple-like* when nothing has been defined between us yet. I look at her and place a kiss on her lips. From her grimace, I know the smell of cigarettes bothers her. I crush my cigarette and pull Lovisa close to me.

"You have serious problems, don't you?"

"Nothing that I can't deal with, I assure you. You don't have to worry about me."

"You constantly do it for me, so why can't I do the same?"

Adorable. I run my hand through her hair and then on her cheek. I feel the need to touch her quite often. I see her in front of me, I feel her warmth when our bodies are close, but sometimes, my mind plays tricks on me and tells me it's not real.

In the entrance, Gunkil is getting to leave. For once, he's thoughtful enough to keep his mouth shut. On the contrary, he winks at me with a smile; I can almost read his thoughts. When we were younger, we were like Siamese twins. Without that bond of brotherhood between us, I'd have kicked his ass long time ago and chased him out of my life.

"Sir?"

Oscar enters the room and appears before me.

"Set up a meeting with everyone. Today. Send them the jet."

"It's a short notice, I doubt that—"

"I know," I cut him off. "It's urgent, it can't wait."

Rodrigo wastes no time to mess with my business; I can't afford to wait any longer. Gunkil goes with him to his office after receiving my instructions. Fredrik awaits his new instructions, his notebook close to him. He loves to note down absolutely everything; he's diligent and meticulous in his work. He's the brain and Gun is the muscle.

"Continue researching Rodrigo, he must not escape me."

As long as he's not in my hands, he'll remain in my mind. With me, things can turn into obsession; I never give up until I have what I want.

A pain stabs through my head, followed by a nosebleed. I pinch my nostrils and tilt my head back.

"Damn, not again,"

"Don't move, I'll get you a tissue," she says.

Lovisa hurries into the kitchen. I sit down on the couch, facing the fireplace, and rest my neck on the backrest.

"You look pale," Fredrik observes.

I chuckle.

"Like most of us. Besides, I can't go around naked outside in this snow to get a tan."

"You know what I mean."

I keep my cheerful demeanor and glance at him sideways. Fredrik is perceptive, observant. A quality and a flaw, because he meddles in things that don't concerns him.

"My blood pressure is high," I say casually. "No wonder with all I have to deal with."

He falls silent for a moment before sighing and moving closer the flames to soak up the warmth.

"I wouldn't take your place for anything in the world."

"You're right. Between the paperwork, the estate fees, the complaints from hotel clients, and also from tenants, Rodrigo starting to piss me off, and Jonna who doesn't leave me alone, I need a break. The only positive point is the immense fortune, but it comes at a price; if I don't manage all this shit properly, I can quickly lose everything."

A poisonous gift.

Lovisa returns with a tissue. She sits in the chair, her face gnawed with worry. I don't like to make people feel that way, I don't need their empathy. This kind of attention annoys me more than anything and tends to irritate me.

"You should go take a shower. I've booked a table tonight in a nice restaurant."

"I'll do that. But if you're not feeling well or you have too much… work, we can reschedule."

I shake my head and steal a kiss from her. Another natural yet new gesture. Her lips are so soft that it's hard for me to stop at just one kiss. It's almost electrifying.

Her way of avoiding the subject amuses me; she doesn't like what I do and rejects drugs like the plague. She's not wrong to avoid this aspect of my life, but if she wants to stay by my side, she has to accept that I'm not like everyone else.

"Not an option. I want to go out with you. I'll manage. You should find something to wear in your room; I have brought over several dresses."

Her eyes light up with excitement. Before she disappears, she says to Fredrik, "I 'm leaving him to you."

As Lovisa leaves, my friend purses his lips.

"I think she's reserved, something different."

He's right; her past is too deeply rooted in her to be forgotten with a snap of fingers. When she had a little too much to drink at my party a week ago, her guard was down, she was talking, smiling and laughing at stupid jokes. Tonight, the alcohol will flow freely.

"When all this is behind us, it'd be nice to get the whole gang back together, like the old days."

"Good idea," I agree.

Now that my nose has stopped bleeding, I get up and light a new cigarette. As cancerous as it is, this menthol stick helps me relax. For a brief moment, my mind travels back years, and a smile spreads across my face.

"Do you remember the very first pack of cigarettes Gunkil stole?"

"Vaguely. Was it at Big Raoul's?"

"That's right. Gun was about thirteen at the time. He was short and skinny back then. This old pig used to grope his butt every time he passed by. Gun always said he'd make him pay back. One day, he showed up with a baseball bat, beat the crap out him, and trashed his shop. And he left with just a pack of cigarettes."

I laugh as I exhale the white smoke, which curls above me. There's hasn't been a moment when I haven't had fun with him. He's been there in all the good and bad times of my life.

"He's fearless."

"Is that why you're sending him to Patrik Hallgreen?"

I see in his eyes that he doesn't like my decision. Being relegated to office work is the best choice for him, he's not like us. That's what I liked about him. His slightly more serious side. He doesn't hesitate to canalize us when we go overboard and, even if he knows how to have fun, he's the one who drives us home at the end of the night.

"You're not cut out for this mission. Don't take it personally; you're much better with your computer than your fists."

"If you're referring to the fight at the Red Mill, I was drunk, I wasn't in full control of my faculties."

"Fred…" I sigh, looking at him. "It's not a flaw to not know how to fight; we all have different abilities, and yours is important. Come on, don't compare yourself to that idiot, you have more brain cell than him, that should make you happy, right?"

I make him laugh. It's better. When he's sulking, he's not productive. And I need him with all his operational capabilities.

"I hope you're not talking about me!" Gunkil intervenes, slipping an envelope into the inner pocket of his jacket as he joins us.

Oscar follows him.

"Of course we are," I chuckle. "Are you ready to go?"

He nods.

"You can take the jet. It's almost noon, you'll have time to see Patrik. Give me your report as soon as possible."

The pilot will have time to drop him off and pick up his other passengers. A simple nod from Oscar tells me that everything is okay. I see problems as a ball of knots. As I make decisions and take action, the knots gradually untangle. The rope around my neck loosens, allowing me to live another day.

"Everyone knows what they have to do."

It's the signal to leave.

Alone with Oscar, I exhale as I crush my cigarette. I run my hands through my hair and pull it back, then let my shoulders slump.

"I'm going upstairs," I tell Oscar. "If you have any updates, let me know."

I need a shower and to relax under the hot water.

I feel a little better. It's just a low blood pressure, nothing else. I can't afford for it to be more; I have too much shit to deal with to let my health betray me.

I climb the stairs four at a time and walk along the pale gray hallway to Lovisa's room. The soft sound of running water reaches me.

She's still in the shower. A flush of excitement rises in me at the image of her wet body. I undress as I walk like a predator into her room and open the bathroom door. The air is warm and heavy, my skin quickly becomes moist. I remove the last fabric on my body, my underwear, and find myself completely naked.

"Is there room for me?"

I try to respect her personal space so as not to rush her, but the temptation to slip into the shower is too strong to resist.

Lovisa turns around and look at me with a smile after wiping the steam off the glass door. The shower can fit two, or even three people. It's fully glass, just like half of the wall opposite, overlooking the property.

It was my mother's idea when she was still living here. Back then, she asked to have walls replaced with bay windows. She wanted the forest to be part of the villa. Her memory clouds my mind and pinches my heart. A mixture of hatred, sadness, and anger leaves a bitter taste in my mouth. I push her out of my thoughts and concentrate on the beautiful young woman in front of me, whose sight makes me burn with desire.

In response and to my surprise, Lovisa opens the shower door and steps back. The water jet deliciously pounds her plump breasts. Aphrodite can step aside; the sight of this woman with the fiery hair would make any goddess pale.

I close the door behind me. Instantly, the water drenches me completely. Its warmth pleasantly massages my sore muscles and relaxes every nerve, reducing the tension in my body. I close my eyes, and tilt my head back, pushing my hair off my face as her eager hands come to brush my chest with soap. She first rubs my pectorals in a circular motion, which makes me chuckle.

"I should be the one caressing you like this, not the other way around."

I glance at her with a playful smile on my lips. She returns my smile and moves down to my left ribs, her fingers grazing my tattoo of the Grim Reaper holding a sickle and a gun.

"It's such a dark design. Why did you choose to get something so grim inked on your skin?"

"It represents the path I chose to take."

"The one you were forced to follow," Lovisa corrects, frowning. "You didn't want to walk in your father's footsteps. You aspired to simpler project. To a more honest life.”

“With you, but you weren’t there.”

I place my index finger to her lips as she starts to speak.

“I know what you’re going to say. It doesn’t change the facts. If I’m here today, it’s because things had to happen this way. Fate is a bastard sometimes, but look, it brought us back together.”

Lovisa giggles and starts rubbing my chest again. I give her a questioning look.

“I didn’t know you were into *we don’t choose our fate, it chooses us* thing.”

I press my lips together and take her hands, sliding them around my neck. I pull her close, one arm around her hips and the other on her butt.

“I’ve learned the hard way that we’re not always in control of our lives. You can be the strongest, the most beautiful, or the richest, but if life has decided to fuck you, it will.”

Intrigued, she narrows her eyes and waits for more. I don’t want to dwell on the subject, she doesn’t need to know. Not yet.

“My turn. Turn around,” I demand.

She does it. I take her hands and place them on the wall. I whisper in her ear, “Don’t move.”

I squeeze the bottle of shower gel into my hand. The clear liquid has a floral scent that fills the room. I’ve smelled it on her before, a delicate fragrance that makes me want to bite her.

Palms together, I spread the gel and start on her thin, delicate shoulders. I remember her violin resting on one of them, as notes flowed out to form music. I slide my hands down her arms and intertwine our fingers. Her body tenses as I press her back, making me smile.

“Where do you want me to touch you?”

I nibble her ear and lick it. She lets out an adorable little cry, encouraging me to do it again. My hands move to her hips, which I knead slowly as I work my way to her stomach.

“I’m listening,” I say in her ear. “Tell me… Where?”

“I—”

She bites her lower lip. She turns her head slightly, and I’m not sure if it’s the hot water, but I notice her cheeks are a bit flushed. Maybe she’s not used to a man asking her what she wants?

As my growing erection presses against her butt, my hands move to the next step and travel up to her chest. I grab her breasts and massage them with extremely slowness, making sure to pinch her nipples. She arches, pressing back against me as her nipples harden. My temperature rises, and I have to hold myself back from fucking her hardly in this shower. "You drive me crazy. You know that?"

"Sorry."

"Don't apologize, I love it," I say.

Once again, she half-turn her face toward me and smiles.

"You're a masochist… oh!" she finishes with a moan.

I just more grabbed her chest firmly and dive into her neck to kiss it. I chuckle against her skin and rub my cock against her.

"My delicious little Love, who doesn't realize the power she has over me."

I lower one hand and cover her pussy, my fingers starting to caress her most intimate parts. Soft, warm, and wet. Perfection.

Lovisa shifts forward a little and puts an arm behind her. Her fingers wrap around my cock. She starts moving up and down.

Holy shit.

I've had this kind of favor before, but it's different because it's her.

"Love, stop."

She freezes and pull her hand away. Lovisa turns to look at me, even redder, if that's possible.

"I'm doing it wrong, aren't I?"

"Not at all," I reply, kissing her. "I want to take care of you. Let yourself be taken care of."

I gently push her against one of the glass walls, imagining her butt pressed it. This vision alone makes my erection painful. I spread her legs by sliding a thigh between them and take her sex hostage. Slowly, I explore her body. My fingers caress each external part. I'm discovering her for the first time. It was once a fantasy, now it's reality. Inner lips, outer lips, clitoris. I tease the latter, finding what makes her vibrate the most.

"Relax," I whisper.

Her legs become less rigid. She lets herself go into my hand. Eyes half-closed, she clings to me. Her breathing quickens as this small piece of flesh swells with her desire. Continuing this gentle torture, I insert a finger inside her. The moan comes quickly. She presses her chest against me and throws her head back. The water sprays over us and run between us, giving me a much more erotic vision of what could be streaming down her body. I kiss her passionately, slipping past her lips to caress her tongue. Our breaths mingle and quicken.

I want more. "I want to taste you."

Swallowing hard, she watches me turn off the water and get on my knees. Her eyes widen, and she puts a hand to her mouth.

"You've never had that before?"

"I have, but… I never really liked it."

Contrary to what I might have thought, knowing another man has gone down on her doesn't bother me. She never enjoyed it. I'm going to be the one to change her mind.

"Let me do it, if you're okay with that."

I grab one of her thighs and lift it over my shoulder. Then, I raise her other leg to wrap around me.

"Hold on tight."

She squeezes her legs around my head and grips the top of the glass wall with her hands.

"It's a very acrobatic position, are you sure it's safe?"

"Do you trust me?"

"I think so."

I smile, amused, easing her anxiety. Her worried expression fades away a little.

Enough jokes. I grab her butt, lifting her up a little more. My lips linger on the delicate skin inside her thighs. I kiss and nibble. I love this part of a woman's body. The skin is soft and tender here, while just bit higher, sex is a formidable weapon that can brings any man to his knees.

The closer I get to the coveted area, the more Lovisa squirms under my lips. A glance in her direction shows me two little green eyes watching me intently.

Watch, Love, you're going to love this.

My mouth reaches her pussy. I close my eyes, taking in her scent. She fidgets a little, uncomfortable. I pinch her ass to make her stop.

"Don't move if you don't want to fall."

I hear her whimper, but that sound turns into a moan when I start nibbling and licking her sex. I savor this moment, a shared pleasure that she expresses through her sounds, through her body reacting to my every move. If she didn't like it before, I'm now certain I'll make her addicted.

My tongue slide deeper in her and slips in and out several times. Her moans guide my path. I torture her inside, teasing her clitoris, her lips, and the entrance to all her desires.

Do it, babe, let go.

Her hips undulate with pleasure. Her mouth lets out all kinds of sensual sounds, driving me crazy. I speed up the pace until her body starts to tremble.

Almost there.

I give the final blow by torturing her clitoris, pushing her over the edge into orgasm. Her body arches sharply, and her legs clamp around my head. She moans so loudly that the guards at the gate probably heard her.

I let her calm down and set her feet back on the ground. She can barely stand and collapses against me when I stand up.

"Verdict?" I ask, lifting her flushed face.

"It was fabulous!"

"Fabulous?" I chuckle.

Lovisa slap my shoulder, pressing herself tightly against my chest. "Oh, shut up! Don't make fun of me."

"I loved to make you come," I confess, still hard. "Can you feel it?"

She nods and step back to look at my cock. I have no shame standing before her like this.

Without a word, she kneels down.

Angelic vision.

I never imagined such a sight could be so arousing. Her hand grabs my throbbing cock. Aching with excitement, it begs for relief.

"What are you going to do now?"

Her mouth approaches my tip, timidly sucking it before starting her movement.

God's goodness.

I devour her with my eyes, watching her mouth move on the tips of my dick as if it were a treat that she's savoring. My heart races and my breathing quickens.

Her lips move over my sex as far as her mouth can tolerate. The inside of her mouth, warm and wet, tightens and moves back and forth.

"Fuck, that feels so good."

I place my hand behind her head, watching this incredibly arousing sight. Her lips tighten, and the occasional scrape of her teeth makes me moan.

She's good at his.

With my hand in her hair, I guide her movements. As she speeds up, my cock swells with increasing pleasure and reaches its full size.

It's coming. I feel the orgasm approaching faster than I expected. With a grunt, I cum between her lips. She keeps moving on my cock before letting go.

"Damn it, Lovisa, I didn't expect that."

She stands up, wiping her mouth. Her smile brings out mine. Her power over me is grows every day. This isn't just a relationship based on sex; it's different. I haven't made love to her yet, and strangely, I'm not frustrated. Not completely. All the others were just one-night stands.

"There was no reason for me to be the only one taking pleasure."

"I was taking it while taking care of you."

I kiss her then turn on the water back to clean myself one last time. Lovisa does the same, soaping herself up and provocatively rubbing her chest. Behind her angel look hides a wild side waiting to be free.

I can't wait to see all her facets. I'm going to peel away every layer of her shell to uncover the real Lovisa.

15

Lovisa, 14 years old

To avoid complicating things, we decide not to reveal our relationship to Hendrik and my mother. We live under the same roof, and adults would refuse to legitimize our relationship. That's why we use high school as an opportunity to stick together. We rarely get to spend time together at Iron House. We steal hurried kisses, exchange caresses in the shadows of trees, and share loving smile whenever we see each other. Our secret romance strengthens our feelings. A part of me can't help but feel guilty about betraying my mother, who doesn't think I'm capable of lying to her face. But do I have a choice? I don't want to deceive her, but I don't want to break up with Niklas either.

***

Asleep on my bed, I'm haunted by Rikard's presence. My sleeping mind tortures me with vision of him coming back to finish the job. My body lies on the floor in a pool of water and blood. I don't move as he hits me again and again. He insults me, humiliates me, and promises slow and painful death. I don't cry anymore; my body is too dry to produce tears

With a jolt, I wake from this nightmare and, unsurprisingly, find my cheeks are wet. I often woke up in tears when I was with my ex-boyfriend, and it seems my body is stuck with that habit.

A glance at the clock on my dresser shows it's past eight o'clock in the evening. Looks like Niklas hasn't finished his meeting. He hasn't come to see me since the shower.

I get up slowly and drag my body to the bathroom, where I wipe off the makeup that runs down my face. Among the dresses Nik chose, I opted for a deep red outfit that reaches above my knee. My left shoulder is bare while the other is covered by a pleated fabric that hook at the back near the waist. It's stunning and highlights my pale complexion and my red hair. I know almost nothing about the adult Niklas, but when it comes to clothing, he has excellent taste.

He's a stranger to me.

This realization depresses me. How can I still love a man I don't know? As I return to my room, I list what I know about him. He's the heir to Hendrik's immense fortune and the last of the Ekmans. He's had more women in his bed than there are days in a year. Thank you, Alfrida, for that detail. He had an affair with Jonna, which ended badly. He loves sports and eats his steak rare, which I find revolting. If he could bite directly into the thigh of a cow, he would. Among other details about his life, the most disturbing is that he's a drug trafficker.

Drugs.

I feel betrayed, even though he owes me nothing. I want him to stop trafficking, even though I've just come back into his life.

I have no right.

What if he becomes like Hendrik? Just as cruel and insensitive? I had a taste of his darkness when he fought with Rikard, but through his fascination with guns. And the way he spoke to Jonna earlier sent chills down my spine. I shake my head, refusing to think the worst. He'll never be like his father and doesn't look like Rikard. He's different.

His good sides replace the bad. He's caring, gentle, patient, and he helps me stand up for myself. I feel good being by his side, but I must not get too comfortable in the luxury he offers, being dependent on another man without being able to escape. I couldn't bear it if things between us are not working.

He'll end up abandoning you, like everyone else.

No! I tug on my hair with a groan and sit on my bed.

Stop being stupid, Lovisa. Pull yourself together!

I can't give him everything, he'll dump me away immediately. There's only one thing he didn't get from me. If I don't sleep with him, he'll continue wanting me and won't leave me. Unless he gets tired of this cat-and-mousse game? No. He loves playing. He teases me, provokes me, and tries to break through my defenses. In high school, as soon as he got what he wanted, he left the girl and never talked to her again. What if he does the same with me? Uncertainty and doubt consume me to the point that I don't hear Niklas enter my room.

"Love?"

That nickname makes me shiver with pleasure, completely banishing my worries when I look at him.

He's wearing fitted black pants that, even without seeing them, must mold perfectly his butt, with a white shirt whose top buttons are open, revealing his prominent collarbones and the start of his muscles. His hair is pulled back in a bun, with a few strands framing his face.

A wild desire rises in me, my hands itch to touch him, to feel his hard, firm skin. I lick my lips and hold my breath as he approaches me.

I manage to say, "Are you done?"

He stops a few inches from me. My face is right in front of his crotch. I only need to raise my hand to touch that zone of all my fantasies. I can still feel his taste and the sensation of having him in my mouth.

I stand up to chase away this erotic vision from my mind and focus on his light-colored eyes.

His teasing smile makes me believe he can read my thoughts. He caresses my cheek and admires my dress.

"Sorry to keep you waiting. Rodrigo is trying to destroy me, to destroy everything my father built. I had to act immediately."

Lips pressed together; I turn my back to him to hide my displeasure. My change of mood doesn't escape him. His hands come to grip my shoulder. In front of me, the window reflects our image against the pitch-black night. He's watching me.

"Tell me what's on your mind."

I take a deep breath to muster the courage.

"I don't like what you're doing. Drugs are… wrong, destructive. It's dangerous and illegal. How can you take over such a horrible business? My mother died of an overdose because of your father!"

There, I've said it.

I brace for his reaction.

His hands tighten on my shoulders. He spins me around and lock his gaze onto mine. Frowning and looking upset, he speaks in a harsh voice, "My business doesn't concern you. I make my living as I see fit and I'm not going to stop just because your mother couldn't keep her nose out of the powder. Everyone makes their own choices, no one forced her. Yes, it's illegal and dangerous, but this market has such immense potential that you can't imagine the money it brings in."

He pauses for a moment to pull me against him.

"I'll take care of you, you'll never lack for anything, and I'll protect you from any danger. You don't need to worry about anything; I won't let anyone lay a hand on you ever again."

How can he be so harsh and insensitive and then follow up with something that melts my heart? I don't know how to react. Torn between anger and being flattered.

"Take back what you said about my mother."

"Why? It's the truth. She was weak."

What? He didn't dare! My lower lip tremble and my eyes tingle.

"I… you're fucking unbelievable," I snap, pushing him away. "How can you disrespect my mother like that? She loved you; she was a good person, unlike your bastard father. You're nothing but… You're nothing but…"

"But what?" He encourages me to continue undisturbed by my accusations.

"A jerk!" I explode. "A fucking asshole! A piece of trash. You think you can get away with anything because of your dirty money, but without it, you're nothing! You're nothing!"

He starts to smile and tries to touch me, but I push his hands away.

"You're finally rebelling."

"Don't touch me! You'll never lay a hand on me again!"

Wait… what?

I blink several times and stare at him, stunned, before instantly calming down. My last words weren't meant for him. They were for Rikard. Words I never had the chance to throw in his face. I open my mouth to speak, but Nik place a finger on it before hugging me.

"I know. You don't need to explain."

He kisses my forehead and keeps holding me close. I finally give in and snuggle into his comforting embrace. With my head nested under his chin. I smell his scent, which tickles my nostrils. I get intoxicated by his soothing fragrance.

"I'm sorry," I murmur against his skin.

The wound Rikard left is still raw and bleeding. I'll probably live with regret of never telling him everything I thought of him. I could write him a letter. An email? A text? Would he even read it?

"You'll overcome your past," Nik reassures me, pulling back to look at me. "There's no challenge I don't think you can't overcome."

He pauses to kiss my fingers.

"I have a surprise for you."

Without further explanation, he takes me downstairs, where we put on our coats. A long white fur coat for me, a black leather jacket lined with sheepskin for Niklas. Then we step outside.

"What's my surprise?"

"See for yourself."

I follow his gaze.

Next to his electric blue Chevrolet Corvette Stingray, a vehicle that wasn't there before catches my eyes. Before my eyes, a much more modest car with new paint shines under the spotlights. Not just any car.

An olive-green Peugeot 604.

No way...

I look at Niklas, speechless. He watches me with a smile, waiting for my reaction.

"It's her? Is it really *her*?"

"With many improvements, but yes, it's her."

My sight blurs as tears fill my eyes. I struggle to hold them back and step down the porch.

With a feverish hand, I lightly touch the hood and move to the passenger side window. The same brown leather seats, at least in appearance, because these are new.

"I could never get rid of her, and I knew she meant a lot to you. After all, it's all you have left of your father."

I swallow hard and wipe the corner of my eyes. A faint smile stretches across my lips.

"I thought Hendrik destroyed her after I left."

Niklas put himself behind me and wraps his arms around me. His chin rest on my shoulder.

"Are you happy?"

I nod as I turn to him. My fingers, cold from the night air, touch his bearded cheeks.

"You couldn't have made me happier. Thank you, so much."

I place several tender kisses on his lips.

This gift is the kindest thing anyone has ever done for me. In four years of being with Rikard, he never made a gesture as meaningful as what Niklas did tonight.

We came in this car with my mother to get to Kiruna. She was terrified of flying. I still remember complaining the entire trip about how uncomfortable the car was. Once at Iron House, Hendrik decided that this car shouldn't be driven anymore and gave my mother a new one. He wanted to get rid of it, but its sentimental value was too big, my mother and I didn't allow it.

"Can I drive it?" I ask, sniffling, still emotional.

"It's up to standard. Starting tomorrow, you can use it. The key is in my office."

In one last embrace, we part and head to his luxury car. The comfortable, heated seats are a delight for the body.

The car swiftly navigates the estate before leaving it.

As he drives smoothly and quickly, I still marvel at how we went from fighting to making up in a minute, ending with such a wonderful gift. When I argued with Rikard, it could last for days. It was endless.

"Of the three, this dress was my favorite," Niklas suddenly says, bringing my hand to his lips. "You look stunning."

His compliment touches me.

"Then why did you offer me several option?"

"I didn't want to impose my choice on you, not completely."

He places my hand on his thigh. Through his pants, I feel the warmth of his body heating my palm. This simple yet intimate gesture pleases me.

"Are you hungry?"

"I'm starving! Where are you taking us?"

"It's a surprise, but I promise you the experience will be worth it."

Experience? What is he talking about? The little information he provides doesn't help me figure out where we're going. I don't know what to expect. But given our elegance, it must be a fancy place.

"Do you go there often?" I try to find out.

"Once a month. Meals are a quite an affair, and they rarely open their doors."

I don't know more about it. This intrigues me.

"Who have you gone there with before?"

He smirks. Women, obviously. A pang of jealousy pierces my heart. I know he wasn't celibate during my absence and owes me nothing, but the thought of going to the same restaurant as his booty calls doesn't sit well with me. He glances at me, squeezing my hand.

"It's only you now. No one else matters."

How many times has he used that line to get these women into his bed?

A call gets transferred from his phone to the car. The name Bethenny appears on the screen. I blush immediately and tense up in my seat. Who is she? He answers after two rings.

"Hello."

"Good evening, Nik," says the voice of a young woman, her voice barely covering the rhythmic music playing in the background. "I'm sorry to bother you, but you need to come. Jason stole again. This time, a whole crate of vodka bottles. Bob from security is keeping him in his office because he tried to run. We have all the evidence recorded."

Niklas checks the time on his watch, frowning.

"I'll be right there. There hasn't been any commotion, right?"

"No, the night is in full swing. Everything's going well. See you soon."

After he hangs up, I look at him insistently, wanting to know what's going on. Bethenny, stolen bottles, music. Bethenny?

"I own a bar that turns into a nightclub at night. One of my employees has been stealing from me repeatedly. I let it slide because he needed the money, but he did it again. Little shit is taking advantage of my kindness."

"Are you going to turn him over to the police?"

He chuckles, pushing a stray lock of hair back.

"I'll handle it internally."

I swallow hard. Is he going to…?

Seeing my pale face, he reassures me, "Hey, don't make that face, I'm not going to kill him, but he deserves a lesson before I fire him."

Why do I get so worked up over everything he says? I often can't tell if he's joking or serious. I don't always understand his reactions or actions. He's unpredictable. It's both scaring and exciting because I never know what to expect with him.

"Just relax, we're going to have a good night. I'll take care of this, and then we'll go to dinner."

The car roars as Nik accelerates, burning more fuel to increase speed. Despite the speedometer showing a much higher speed than allowed, I feel safe with him and even manage to enjoy the adrenaline rush this illicit speed gives me.

When we arrive, red neon lights spell out the bar's name: *Red Mill*. A name full of lust and promises of guaranteed night of debauchery.

"I'm not surprised," I comment as I get out of the car.

"By what?"

I shake my head and take the arm he offers me.

We pass a small line of people. The bouncer lets us in and greets Nik respectfully. He's someone important, and not just in this bar. Everyone seems to know him. People want to greet him, talk to him.

I linger on the clients' fashion choices. There's a lot of leather, half-open shirts for the men, and thigh-high slit dresses for the women. They exude glamour and sex. They all seem on the hunt for a partner to end the night with. I feel overdressed, and the sensation of being watched like a fairground animal makes my neck tingle.

This place is a reflection of him. There's a large dance floor surrounded by high iron tables with surface as clean as the floor. Along the walls, booths with black, studded, cushioned benches and table are occupied by customers. The dim red and yellow lighting gives the place an intimate feel. To our left, a neon-lit bar. Where three bartenders behind the counter serving customers while playing with shakers. Behind them, the wall is lined with liquor bottles, which they grab by climbing a fluorescent ladder. My eyes gradually get used to the lighting. Loud music and the crowd are overwhelming, but Niklas's presence, whose arm around my hips are holding me close, feels like a lifeline in an ocean.

"Stay close to me," he shouts in my ear.

Niklas is very tall. He's taller than most people. This giant impresses with his size, but also with his reputation. He has no trouble moving forward, like Moses parting the Red Sea. Customers step aside, pausing their dancing or chat.

Near the bar, a woman with long, curly brown hair stares at us, smiling. She's wearing a short flesh-colored dress with rhinestones. Her tanned skin contrasts with the fabric. Large gold hoops earrings dangle from her ears. She's stunning. Generous breasts, curvy butt, and a captivating face, she fits fits the décor perfectly.

We head toward her. Still clinging to my lifeline, I realize this is Bethenny.

"There you are!" she addresses Niklas before turning her gaze to me, her radiant smile prompting mine.

"This is Lovisa."

The way he says my name, which almost slips between his lips, makes me want to kiss him. I share a heated look with him. Under this light, he seems even more mysterious and attractive than ever. Is that possible? Every time I look at him, I find him even more handsome than the moment before.

"Nice to meet you, Lovisa, I'm Bethenny."

"Let's get this thing over with," Nik cuts in, stopping me from answering the young woman. "Lead the way, I'll follow you."

As his employee heads toward a black door marked *Staff Only*, Nik leads me to an empty seat at the bar.

"Order yourself a drink while you wait; I won't be long." He kisses me just below the ear. "I recommend the Love drink; you'll like it."

Could it be a cocktail named after me? Before he leaves, he lets the bartenders know I'm with him, so I don't have to pay. I watch him cross the crowd and disappear behind the door. I wish I could be a fly on the wall to see what happen back there even though a small voice inside tells me there's going to be blood. Does his life always have to be ruled by violence? Isn't the world already ugly enough?

I catch the attention of one of the bartenders, a blonde with a bob cut. She's wearing low-rise leather pants that reveal her thong, and her top is so cropped I can almost see her breasts from underneath. Vulgar but sexy. A requirement from the big boss?

"A Love, please" I order to Blondie.

She performs a little dance with the shaker. The blonde mixes vodka with cane sugar. Then, she fills the bottom of a glass with strawberry syrup, adds ice, and pours the shaker's contents. The impact of the red, transparent liquid creates a beautiful pink hue. My fascinated gaze doesn't leave her as she finishes by sugaring the rim of the glass and adding a big strawberry and a straw. She places a coaster with the club's logo and my drink in front of me.

"Enjoy."

She gives me a flirty wink before walking away. With her energy and seductive skills, she must end the night with pockets overflowing with tips. I myself am under her spell.

If there's one thing I've learned going out with my orchestra friends, it's always to keep a hand over the top of my drink to prevent any creep from slipping something illicit into it. Being here with Niklas doesn't eliminate all the dangers.

Let's taste this.

The first sip goes down hard. The taste of the vodka is strong, making my throat contract against the burning sensation. Then comes the pleasant flavor of cane sugar and strawberry. I end up licking the sugar off the corner of my lips.

At first, this drink is strong; then it turns sweet and indulgent. Is that how Nik sees me? I take another sip and then another. It's delicious and quickly goes to my head. Drinking with an empty stomach isn't a good idea. Around me, the evening takes on a different turn. Or is my mind playing tricks on me? The atmosphere, charged with pheromones from all these people, envelops me and transports me into the mood.

The more my glass empties, the dizzier I get, and my eyelids grow heavy. I need to pull myself together. I ask Blondie where the restrooms are and get up.

Whoa. The room is spinning!

I focus on my goal and venture out into the crowd. I get shoved, touched, yelled at, and even have my butt groped. Who did that? I can't find the culprit. I quicken my pace toward the restrooms. Like the rest of the Red Mill, this place is clean. The floor isn't wet, no dirty shoe marks, no stray toilet paper. No urine smell or suspicious stains. This room exudes luxury! There are five toilet stalls; the red walls aren't covered in graffiti like I've seen elsewhere. Across from them are several sinks with mirrors on a black wall. Niklas spared no expenses. Everything is spotless.

I take off my coat; it's way too hot. The cold water on my cheeks and my forehead soothes my burning skin. Using a paper towel, I dab my face.

I'm hot. I don't know what the temperature is, but it's too high for me. Or maybe it's the alcohol heating up my body? When we'll go to eat, I'll feel better. Maybe he's finished and looking for me? I walk out trying not to stumble, my heels seem more dangerous than ever.

My head is spinning, and my vision blurs several times. My drink was so sweet that I drank it as quickly as if it were lemonade, and now I'm paying the price.

If you don't know how to drink, don't do it. Damn conscience.

A group of young people sweeps me along. I lose my coat. I

don't have the reflex to hold onto it, and I curse these young people for preventing me from turning back. Do they realize they've dragged a stranger with them? I try to slip between two girls to get free, but it's useless. They stop in front of a bouncer as he's tall.

Who's this gorilla? Behind him, an entrance with a curtain of black chains seems under his protection and piques my curiosity. The young people show a stamp mark on the inside of their wrist. It's a dog's head, specifically a boxer. This must be a pass to access whatever is happening behind the chain curtain.

When my turn comes, I stare at the gorilla, dazed. In a booming voice, he says to me, "If you don't have authorization, sweetheart, move along."

I try to peek around him as he blocks the door completely. "What's back there? An organ trafficking ring?" I joke.

Oops, I shouldn't have said that. He doesn't look like he's in the mood to laugh. I lower my head, ashamed, bracing some harsh words to put me in my place when I realize this isn't Rikard standing before me. Plus, I'm with Niklas; surely, I have the right to go wherever I want.

"Can I go through?" I squeak.

"No."

His tone is final; nevertheless, I persist.

"You know, I'm here with the big boss. Your boss. So, I have the right to pass."

He chuckles and waves me away dismissively.

"Go on, kid, get out of here before I throw you out."

Kid? I'm a woman!

He doesn't believe me, too bad, I'll come back with Nik and shut him up. Well, as soon as I find him. As I start to walk away, an arm lands heavily on my shoulders, pulling me against a male body.

"It's okay, Oz, she's with me."

"Azerty! Are you fighting tonight?"

The gorilla called Oz—probably a nickname—softens and even smiles.

"Well, that depends on how the evening goes," he says with a funny accent.

Where is he from? And what kind of name is Azerty? This closeness makes me uncomfortable. I don't know him, and he's touching me like we're friends.

Oz steps aside, and the man next to me pulls me through the chains.

"Watch out, there's a staircase."

Six feet ahead, stairs appear, the edge dimly lit as we descent almost in the dark pressed against each other. Who the hell is this guy?

"I don't know what you want from me, but you'd better let me go. I'm not alone."

He chuckles behind me and eventually releases me. I can't go back up; he's behind me and determined to keep going down.

Anxiety churns in my gut as we move away from the music. What have I gotten myself into? My mind is screaming to turn back, but my body doesn't obey. I'm like a robot, feeling my way along the walls as we walk a dark corridor. The walls are soundproofed so well that the noise from upstairs fades, replaced by a raw, powerful rock music.

"Where are we going? If you hurt me, I swear I'll—"

"I won't do anything," the stranger interrupts. "You wanted to come down, I helped you."

An act of kindness, with no string attached, in a nightclub? Did I meet a good Samaritan? Nothing is free, I've learned that the hard way. I glance at him suspiciously while taking the opportunity to get a good looks at him.

Azerty has a square face with curly hair styled to the side. He's wearing jeans and a navy, or maybe black, long-sleeved T-shirt. A gold necklace adorns his neck, and a piercing grace his left eyebrow. He looks quite handsome in his own way.

My analysis ends as a blinding light hits me when the corridor opens into a room. The spotlight moves away from me and center on the room. The contrast between the warm colors upstairs and the cold concrete of the basement is stark. The floor and walls are made of concrete too. The music blares from speakers hung in the four corners of the room. An unfamiliar rock band blasts my eardrums.

To my right, a large screen displays names and numbers i. A scoreboard? What's going on here?

The atmosphere is different. A mix of animalistic excitement, nervousness, and sweat fills the air around us. I figure out pretty quickly what's going on when a man in the center with a blond mustache raises his arms to calm the crowd. He's dressed like a cowboy, with pointy shoes and a black bolo tie, whose claps glisten under the spotlight. His hat is firmly in place, revealing shoulder-length blond hair.

"That was a great fight. Blackie is in the lead tonight. I don't know what you had for breakfast but keep it up!"

Laughter follows. He quiets them again by raising his hands and walks, tracing the circle the crowd has formed around the about thirteen feet in diameter stage.

"Tonight's prize exceeds all sums from the month. It's a big bet you don't want to miss! Please give a big cheer for our next two challengers. I present Half-Pint and Osius!"

The crowd cheers the two fighters in a mix of shouts and growls. A shiver runs down my spine. There's a powerful energy from all these people that overwhelms me. A rumble shakes my feet and travels up through my body. I'm quickly caught up in the excitement of the situation. Although, I'm against fighting and violence, I can't pull myself away from this energy. I look around, and Azerty is gone. I don't know anyone, and no one knows where I am. My dress attracts a few looks before everyone's attention shifts to the fight that is starting.

Half-Pint, who is actually a six-foot-five giant, charges heavily toward his opponent, a much smaller and nimbler opponent. Osius, a bald man in his thirties, slams his fists into the ribs of the hulking brute. Half-Pint laughs and punches him in the jaw. Osius spits blood and sends a tooth flying toward a couple who scream as they try to catch it.

Caught in the crowd, I can't tear myself away from the spectacle.

The attacks keep coming, the blood flows more and more. The bones crack, skin splits and tears at the cheekbones, lips. The adrenaline pumping through my veins heats me up with newfound excitement. I project myself into the fight and imagine myself delivering the blows and using the attack techniques Niklas taught me. I find myself joining the shouts of the other spectators, cheering for Osius. Something tells me not to underestimate his small size. He's much stronger than he looks.

Osius manages to bring Half-Pint down. He climbs onto his sturdy body and smashes his face with his battered fist. Acting like an animal, he yells and growls at his opponent with every punch. The crowd is in a frenzy, demanding more. More blood, more violence.

He's going to kill him!

A shiver runs through me at the ferocity of the scene. Half-Pint's face is swollen and smeared with blood; I can't see his eyes anymore.

But there's something else.

Someone is watching me.

I manage to take my eyes off the fight and start scanning the crowd. They're all moving, jumping, shouting; some are kissing; others, aroused at the sight of blood, are ready to have sex in front of everyone.

That's when I see her. Beyond the stage, directly across from me, two dark eyes framed by blonde hair are staring at me.

Jonna.

Her fiery gaze never leaves me. She doesn't care about the fight. How long has she been watching me? Is it a coincidence that we're in the same place? I should go see her, explain myself to her. I never wanted her to suffer, and even though it was Nik's decision to break up with her, I feel guilty. I'm responsible for her pain.

A man manages to slip beside her. Azerty. My face tingles with unease. Did he know who I was? Did Jonna ask him to bring me down? Away from Niklas. An invisible vice seems to grip me. The pressure of the crowd around me is nothing compared to the internal oppression I feel at the thought of being completely alone with Jo and her accomplice.

The fight ends.

Osius is declared the winner, and Half-Pint lies unconscious on the floor, covered in both fresh and dried blood. Many must have bled tonight.

I couldn't care less. I barely hear the cowboy's comments.

Jonna leans toward Azerty and whispers something in his ear. Whatever she says makes him smile as he glances in my direction. A new shiver runs downs my spine. Unpleasant and disturbing. I'm the subject of their conversation, likely their mockery and his lies. I want to hide away, far from here, far from them.

All trace of friendship between us have vanished. The best friends we once were have become strangers, and eventually end up becoming enemies. The young girls we used to be would never have believed this possible. We have grown up since then and followed very different paths.

After Jo's last words, Azerty moves to the right and takes a step in my direction. Even though the ring separates us, I quickly step back and bump into a broad chest. Two arms in a white shirt wrap around me and turn me around roughly.

Nick!

The relief I feel is so overwhelming that I throw my arm around his neck. He hugs me tightly and kisses me hard. His face is tense with worry and anger.

"Damn it, Lovisa! What the hell are you doing here? I told you to wait for me at the bar!" he scolds.

I'm so relieved to see him that his gruff tone doesn't bother me.

"It happened so fast. I was in the bathroom and the next second I was here. Nik, did you know there are illegal fights happening here?"

Of course he does, idiot, it's beneath his bar!

He doesn't need to answer me; the evidence is obvious.

"This is not a place for you. Let's go back up."

His arm possessively tightens around me. We turn to leave, but a familiar voice calls out to us. Jonna and Azerty have caught up with us. Beside me, Niklas tenses, ready to fight.

"Good evening, Nick!" she says, smiling. "I was hoping to see you."

"Well, saw me. Now get lost with your lapdog," Niklas barks.

Jonna's face tightens, her hazel eyes darken, and her cheeks flush.

"Don't talk to her like that, asshole," Azerty growls, stepping forward.

Niklas pushes me behind him and step forward. The two men stare at each other down. Azerty is a few inches shorter than Nik, but it doesn't stop him from standing up his ground.

"Are you her new purse?" Nik taunts. "Does she carry you around like her toy? Azer, I thought you were smarter than that."

Around us, people begin to quiet and step back. Everyone knows the manager of the Red Mill.

"Fuck you," Azerty spits, shoving him roughly.

Niklas stumbles back a few steps, bumping into me. He growls and raises his fist in Azerty's direction.

"Stop!" I plead.

I grab Niklas arm and force him to turn toward me. I clutch his face and press several urgent kisses on his lips.

"Please, no, don't fight him. Let's get out of here, okay? We don't have to stay."

"Yeah, listen to your girl," Azerty sneers, backing away. He spins around to address everyone. "Who wants to see the great Niklas Ekman get his ass kicked? He makes so much money off our backs, it's time he paid up! Don't you agree?"

Immediately, shouts erupt from all sides. They demand a fight. Encouraged by the crowd, Azerty feels stronger. He riles them up, making them chant his nickname.

His little game doesn't escape me. He's trapping Niklas by making everyone watch. Either he fights and has a fifty-fifty chance of winning, or he refuses and looks like a coward in front of everyone. He'll never back down.

When he turns to me, I see his decision written on his face. As he unbuttons his shirt, the women around us go wild. My heart is pounding so hard it feels like it might jump out of my throat.

"Don't fight," I whisper.

He takes off his shirt and watch and hands them to me. His muscular, tattooed chest draws whistles and lewd comments, stoking my jealousy. I remind myself that he's mine, and all the others can only dream of touching him. Tonight, he'll leave with me on his arm. He leans in to kiss me.

"Don't worry, babe, I'm not going to lose."

His words don't reassure me.

He approaches a man near a sound system I hadn't noticed and speaks in his ear. The guy cuts the music, drawing protests from customers. They don't wait long before the speakers blare again playing "Let the Sparks Fly" by Thousand Foot Krutch. This music gives me chills and my mind flashes back to years ago. It's Nik's favorite song.

Niklas position himself in the center, facing Azerty, who's also shirtless. He's not as bulky as my man, but that doesn't comfort me. Half-Pint was much bigger than Osius, yet he ended up on the mat, probably missing an eye. What if it that happens to Nik? I'd never forgive myself. And I wouldn't forgive him either.

Oh, Nik, you and your damn pride!

16

Niklas, 17 years old

I can't stand it anymore. Lovisa drives me crazy. We've been dating for a year, and she's making me lose my mind. I love every moment with her; we have fun, but damn, I really want to sleep with her! She wants to wait until she's sixteen and see if I really care about her. I hate this ultimatum, but I love a challenge. I channel all this frustration into the shooting practice my dad insists me to do. If at first, I hated it, now holding the black Golden Eagles he gave me is a real pleasure. The power I feel using them is greater than the rush I get from fighting. For now, I shoot at targets in the basement, and at night I use a silencer and shoot at glass bottles on a log on the ground. Lovisa hates coming into the forest with me, or rather, she hates that I use these guns, but she always comes.

* * *

My heart pounds as loudly as the crowd's screams, and the lyrics of "Let the Sparks Fly" pierce my eardrums. They're as wild as my fists slamming into Azerty. This French bastard is as agile as a cat, dodging my attacks far too often for my liking.

Blood trickles from my eyebrow. A moment of inattention cost me this injury, but I didn't wait for his next strike, I drove my knuckles in his shoulder. The pain was so intense that he lost his composure for a moment.

He's agile.

I'm stronger.

More ferocious.

Lovisa stares at me intently, her face entering my field of vision as I check to make sure she's still there. Her worried expression has completely vanished, replaced by a primal desire on her face, making me want to stop the fight and rip off her dress, to fuck her on the counter of my bar.

Even though I'm taking blows, she's what matters.

I was so worried when I noticed she was missing. I imagined the worst. I have too many enemies to leave her unguarded. That's a mistake I won't make again. She's far too important to me to lose her so stupidly.

The meeting with my captains about Rodrigo was productive. They're setting everything in motion to catch him. Artur, his former right-hand man, knows him well, and his help will be invaluable. My mood has lightened, but I'm still on edge and alert. The threat is still there.

I need to be vigilant.

"Is that all you've got, Ekman?" Azerty taunts, spitting saliva mixed with the blood onto the floor. "I thought you were tougher!"

Shut up, asshole.

You don't know what I'm capable of.

This fight is a show of strength for him. For me, it's a chance to shut him up. I've known Azerty for a few months; he's a regular at the Red Mill and a suitor of Jonna. He's been chasing her for so long it's pathetic. She must have twisted him mind to make him come after me.

She's got a filthy mouth.

Azerty babbles to the crowd, hopping from one foot to foot and flaunting his weaknesses. He's more about attacking than defending.

I've weakened his shoulder. I need to exploit that to bring him down.

I let him hit me in the stomach. His predictable attack gave me time to brace myself for the impact. I smirk and strike with all my strength between his left collarbone and shoulder. He groans in pain and curl up. His face, twisted and red, shows me the path to victory.

"Giving up, Azer? I won't blame you if you bow out," I sneer.

I approach while massaging my hands. I'm not afraid of confrontation and I rise to every challenge. It's not this stupid Parisian, lost in Sweden, that will make me back down. This is my home, he's on my land, and I'm going to show him who controls this place.

As I prepare another attack, he quickly raises his hand.

"Wait!"

I stop.

"You're giving up?"

Less than three feet separates us. Azerty is hunched over, hands on his knees. He's trying to suppress his pain.

"I…"

He falls silent. I frown, waiting for him to continue, but he doesn't. What's going on with him?

West steps into the circle, adjusting his hat. I half-turn toward him.

"We've got a forfeit, it seems," I spit.

Disappointing, I expected more. At least it's over. Lovisa, out of breath, smiles at me. She hasn't missed a moment of the fight, and her relief is palpable. Eyes shining, I devour her with my gaze. Sexier than ever and aroused by the fight, she seems ready to completely abandon herself to me. A thrill of excitement runs through me at the thought of undressing her and covering her body with kisses.

Is it all the things I imagine doing to her that has made me less vigilant? I don't know, but as Lovisa's scream warns me of danger, the blow to my neck is too quick for me to block. I collapse to the ground, with the vision of my lovely redhead, furious, trying to come to my rescue but being held back by a man.

Get your hands off my girl!

I curse at this guy and groan as I lay flat out. I quickly roll onto my back.

The crowd, booing Azerty's low blow, hisses and cries out in scandal. Azerty throw himself at me and punches me in the jaw.

"You think I'm going to let be humiliated without doing anything?"

He hits me again and then forces me to look at Lovisa. My beautiful, sweet Love is struggling like a tigress in the arms of this stranger. She keeps screaming my name. This sight tears my heart apart and sends adrenaline pumping through my body.

She needs me.

Azerty leans in close to my ear.

"I know what you're up to, Jo told me everything. One day it will end badly, and when it does, I'll take your girlfriend under my wing."

A cold fury washes over me. Jonna betrayed me. I should have seen it coming. A scorned woman would do anything to hurt you, but

I thought she had more sense. She'll pay for this. Her action won't go unpunished.

His threat against Lovisa is what pisses me off the most. Every cell in my body demands retribution.

I growl fiercely as I grab him by the neck. I squeeze just hard enough to make him step back as I rise to my feet. My fist slams into his abdomen, knocking the wind out of him. I throw him away. He rolls on the ground, crashing into the legs of the spectators who erupt in renewed excitement.

"Never dare touch her if you value your life!" I roar, turning to the crowd. "No one is allowed to lay a hand on her!"

This message is especially for the guy holding her around her waist. He lets go of her immediately. Back on her feet, Lovisa rushes to me. I catch her and bury my face in her hair; her scent instantly calms and soothes me. Feeling her against me comforts me and momentarily eases the pains from the fight.

"You're okay?" she asks me.

She examines me, worried, running her hand over my cheek, her fingers tangling in my beard. I nod briefly and see over my shoulder Azerty trying to catch his breath.

"Throw that piece of trash out of my club," I order.

Two bouncers weave through the crowd to carry out my command.

Lovisa in my arms, I have no reason to stay here any longer. I put on my shirt and my watch, and we head upstairs in silence. The music and the warmth of the club envelop us, urging us to blend into the crowd to dance, drink, and have fun. But my stubborn mind refuses these distractions and wants only one thing: to leave. Although I love my club and used to spend all my nights here before my father's death, things have changed. My current obligations force me to neglect certain aspects of my life. Before stepping out, I get my jacket and wrap it around Lovisa. It's very cold tonight.

Once outside, I take a deep breath. The temperature has dropped, giving me goosebumps.

"Let's get in the car. I owe you a meal."

She giggles and snuggles against me.

"After everything that just happened, I don't know if I'm still hungry."

As soon as she says those words her stomach starts rumbling. Our laughter fills the air and lightens our moods.

"Your body has spoken."

She smiles tenderly at me while stroking my beard. A dark shadow crossed her green eyes.

"I was so scared when you were fighting. Then, when I saw you collapse, I thought I was going to lose it, I wouldn't have been able to handle it if something had happened to you."

Adorable.

I wrap my arms around her hips.

"And I couldn't bear to lose you. I couldn't find you. I feared the worst. It drove me crazy to see you nowhere. When they told me that you had gone downstairs, it made me feel even worse."

The bond that once united us is still there. Stronger. With adult feelings. We're no longer kids afraid to love each other. That's behind us.

Now, we're free to do whatever we want.

Free.

Such a small word that carries great importance and meaning. But even though we're together and free to do everything together, external factors can interfere and shatter this feeling of freedom, of security. By my side, she risks her life at any moment. Can I make her run such a risk? I'd like to be selfish, to keep her with me, even if it means putting her in danger, but that would be crazy of me. Yet, I feel that I won't be able to do otherwise.

Without delay, we get into the car. Heat on and blasting music, I drive as if I was doing the last race of my life. The adrenaline flowing through my veins from by the fight fuels this excitement that grips me. Lovisa feels the same way, I can tell. In an adventurous mood, her hand softly massages the inside of my thigh, dangerously close to my member, and a slight erection starts.

"I should fight more often," I say, covering her hand with mine.

"Out of the question. I refuse to let anyone damage your body."

She bites her lip, lowering her eyes to our intertwined fingers.

"I'll be careful for you."

Her body relaxes into her seat.

"You're much wiser than you used to be. I feel like I know you inside out, yet there's a part of you that eludes me, the part I don't know yet. Sometimes it scares me because I don't know if you'll like the person I am today."

I share her concern. I'm everything she's always hated, yet she's still here. Out of despair? Because she has no other choice?

I'm not good at reassuring people, but with Lovisa, it seems easier, more natural.

I bring her hand to my lips and kiss it tenderly. Her skin is so soft, I want to devour every inch of it.

"I can't promise you everything will be perfect between us. There will time you hate me, I'll piss you off, I'll make you doubt, and you'll probably want to kill me," I say, laughing. "But I can promise you that you'll never be bored with me. I'll take you on the wildest adventures, I'll make love to you until you can't take it anymore, you'll beg me to stop. And most importantly, I will never abandon you."

No filters, no barriers. I didn't think about my words, just let my heart speak. I believe every syllable I utter, and I'm ready to say more to convince her not to be afraid to open up to me.

"I love you," she suddenly blurts out.

My foot slams on the brake. Before Lovisa can lurch forward, I press my hand on her chest to keep her in her seat. I quickly pull myself together and resume a more moderate speed.

"Sorry," I mumble, confused.

"It's me who should apologize. I don't know what I'm saying, it's probably too soon. We haven't even slept together yet."

I shake my head and put my hand back on the wheel, focusing on the road. The reflection of the moon in the snow naturally lights the road, complementing my headlights. Yet, I can't see anything. My mind is simply replaying Lovisa's lips whispering words that so many women have said to me, words that never meant anything to me before.

We've loved each other for so long that if she had said it the moment she came back, I wouldn't have thought it was too soon.

"Say it again."

She fidgets in her seat, making me wait for a moment before she adorably squeaks, "I love you."

How can three little words move me so deeply? Words that are both simple and complex, filled with promises and a future together?

A gentle warmth fills my heart, and tingling sensation flood my mind as endorphins are released giving me a sense of well-being. I feel like a pimply teenager who just got his first kiss. Lovisa makes me feel foolish, possessive, and passionate.

In love.

I've never stopped being in love with her. This feeling has always been part of me; I just buried it so deep that I thought I didn't love her anymore.

I've stopped fooling myself, even when she came back into my life and all I wanted was to destroy her. A part of me knew what my true feelings for her were.

Smiling, I place her hand back on my thigh and focus on the road.

An immense hangar stands before us as I park in a lot guarded by a watchman, Stewart. The surroundings are dimly lit and deserted. The place seems abandoned, with no restaurant in sight. It's so quiet than even a single breath would echo in the distance.

"Are you sure we're in the right place?"

"Don't you trust me?"

My question seems to shock her. She stiffens. What's going on with her? I wish I could access her thoughts to know what she took the wrong way.

I get out and walk around the car to help Lovisa out. On the way, I greet Stewart and head toward a black door guarded by another man in a black suit and heavy coat, equipped with an earpiece. My pretty redhead's heels click sharply, piercing the air with their sound. The ground is littered with puddles water and half-melted snow. Spring is struggling to take hold; the weather in Kiruna is much colder than elsewhere in the country.

"Ekman, I have a reservation."

The guard puts a hand on his earpiece and announces us. A few seconds later, he opens the door for us.

Unlike the outside, the corridor we walk through is completely renovated. For more privacy and discretion, the windows have been covered with plasterboard and painted in anthracite blue. Recessed ceiling lights provide dim lighting. There are no decorations, no signs. Nothing to indicate where we are.

"I don't understand," she says. Her timid voice prompts me to look at her and pull her closer to me.

The first time, anyone feels lost and bewildered. Even I didn't know what to expect, and the experience made me want to come back every time they organized these dinners.

"You'll understand soon enough," I whisper in her ear, giving it a kiss.

At the end of the hallway, a receptionist awaits us. She checks our names off on her tablet and set it aside. Our tardiness doesn't matter given the amount I paid for a spot tonight.

With a polite smile and a formal demeanor, the young woman hands us two bracelets.

"Good evening and welcome to the Ephemeral. These are your bracelets to open your lockers as well as your room. They have an emergency button in case of any issues. The meal will be served as soon as you signal via the room's intercom. What is your preference? Male or female?"

Lovisa questions me with her eyes. I answer, "Female."

"Any allergies or physical conditions we should be aware of?"

"None."

I tighten my hold on Lovisa, she squirms a bit. I can see a hundred questions racing through her mind.

The receptionist guides us to a private dressing room. I close the door behind us. The room is small and dimly lit, with the ceiling lights that barely illuminate the space. This immediately sets a different mood. The black-painted walls also cover two lockers where we can store our clothes. The room is furnished with a table containing various accessories. At the back, there's a sink along with clean towels and toiletries.

Facing us is a rolling wardrobe, displaying two outfits: a white silk nightie with angel wings and fishnet stockings, and a leather boxer held by straps to be worn over the shoulders. On the table beside it are devil horns to stick to the forehead and a whip with leather straps.

Lovisa turns to me, her face showing complete confusion.

"What does all this mean?"

I slip my hands over her shoulders and squeeze them while looking into her eyes. I smile, trying to reassure her.

"It's a special kind of dinner. I picked outfits for us that shouldn't make you too uncomfortable."

She glances at them again.

"Are we going to eat in these outfits?"

"We won't just eat," I growl, suddenly kissing her.

Just the thought of her in that nightie makes me hard. She as an angel, me as a demon. It's perfect. White will bring out her purity, innocence, and fragility. But also her fiery red hair, a color I've always loved. It represents a blazing fire, passion, and desire.

I step back, unbuttoning my shirt under Love's gaze, my lips swollen from her kiss. I strip off all my clothes and take off my boxers. My erection stands proudly, showing her all my desire. At this moment, holding back from pinning her against the table feels insurmountable. With a superhuman effort, I manage to grab the leather boxers short, which I put on slowly. Teasing her, showing her what could be hers, is a game that I enjoy with pleasure.

"Your turn."

She takes a few steps back, giving me a full view of what's to come. Her red dress hugs her enticing curves perfectly.

I hit the mark.

She slowly slides her strap down her arm and removes it.

The naughty girl, she's turning me on.

My burning gaze doesn't miss a single detail of the show.

Her dress caresses her skin as she lets it fall to the floor. Her underwear takes my breath away. She does a little spin, biting her lower lip provocatively.

Not so sweet and innocent, after all.

What an erotic sight. Divine!

Her red lace thong is connected to garter straps without stockings; delicate bands of embroidered fabric circle her thighs. The top is as transparent as the bottom and leaves little to the imagination.

My breathing quickens, my boxers become way too tight.

Damn it, Lovisa!

"You're so sexy."

Half-naked, I growl and approach her like a predator on its prey. My hands seem huge as I place them on her arms. I caress her skin, slowly moving up to her shoulders and then down to her breast. Under my fingers, her nipples harden and strain against the lace.

I hold my breath for a moment, overwhelmed by my excitement. Dinner hasn't even started yet, and I'm acting like a young virgin excited by a playboy magazine.

My fingers tease her erect flesh, gently pinching and rubbing. Her body arches toward me. She closes her eyes and runs her hands over my chest, digging her nails into my skin.

"I should take you right now. I don't know how I managed to hold back all week. Every time I see you, touch you, you ignite a fire so intense, so burning, that it consumes and frustrates me to no end."

Her green eyes lock onto mine.

"I didn't know you wanted me so much. I don't understand, you saw the marks. They're hideous."

I shake my head and run my hands around her back to unhook her bra.

"They'll fade. I don't want you to worry about them anymore. I'll erase every trace he left on you. I'll eclipse every sensation he made you feel in bed, I'll wash away his scent, his and the others'. I'll regret for the rest of my life not being your first."

A regret that leaves a bitter taste on my tongue. She promised me that I would be her first, but when she disappeared, I knew that promise would never be kept. A hint of jealousy gnaws at me thinking about the pleasure she might have had with other men. How many? Did she enjoy it? Will I be better? I'm a skilled lover, all my partners have told me so. But sleeping with Lovisa is different, there's the pressure of the years we've been apart. I know it will be fantastic. I'll have the time of my life and fulfill an old fantasy. But what if the reality falls short? How will I react? And how Love will react?

Damn. I sound like a green.

Don't overthinking, man, you'll never know if you think too much.

I remove her bra, freeing her breasts from its confines. Her small breasts bounce, standing proudly, urging me to kiss them. I run my lips over her rosy nipples, eliciting shiver and sigh from her. With no protest from her, I slide my hand over one of them and tease it while cupping my hand over her other breast. I suck on her nipple greedily before releasing it to move to the other. She moans under my assault and presses my head against her chest.

"Nick…"

Hearing her moan my name makes my cock even harder against the leather.

Without any gentleness, I pin her against the cold locker, making her arch her back. Her hips undulate against mine, rubbing our sexes together.

I growl against her breast and raise my head to capture her mouth. I breach the barrier of her lips with my tongue. Lovisa welcomes me with joy. Her warm, wet tongue caresses mine, they intertwine, dance together. The desire between us rises quickly.

I'm hot.

I grab her ass.

"If you keep turning me on like this, I won't last long," I growl into her mouth.

She laughs and, with a small jump she wraps her legs around my hips. The heat of her thighs and her pussy against my belly is driving me wild. Her mouth caresses my ear. She whispers, "I don't want you to stop."

Holy shit!

Did I hear that right? Do I have the green light?

I catch her gaze to be sure I have her consent. All I see is a want and an intense desire to proceed.

Kissing her passionately, I move us toward the table. With a sweep of my hand, I knock everything off and lay her down. Like a belly dancer, she lets her body undulate against mine.

Enchanting.

I kiss her neck and move down to her breast, then her stomach, where bruises mar her perfect skin. My hands slide under the elastic of her thong and pull it down her hips and then her pubis.

"Your skin is so soft and delicate. And your scent…" I finish with a growl. "I don't think I'll ever get tired of it."

She laughs, wiggling a bit to prop herself up on her elbows.

"Good idea. Stay in that position." I demand. I quickly pull down my boxers, releasing my sex for that's been restrained too long. It stands erect, and I sigh in relief.

"Damn, that feels good," I confess, running my hand over it.

Her lustful gaze pleases me. She seems freed from her chains, her complexes, and her shyness. I love the woman I see. Is it the place that's responsible of this sudden change in personality? For answer, her thighs part to welcome me.

God's goodness. My goddess is so exciting in this position.

I quickly open my locker and take out a condom. I have one requirement at the Ephemeral: there must always be condoms available. I take no risks. I don't want a stranger showing up ten years later with a kid and demanding money.

I tear the wrapper with my teeth and spit the plastic out the side. Carefully, I roll the condom onto my cock.

"They might hear us," Lovisa notes, looking at the door behind me.

"Probably."

"And that doesn't bother you?"

"That they'll hear how much I'm going to make you moan? Don't care. Let them listen if they want," I chuckle.

I position myself between her thighs. The heat emanating from her cunt and her wetness prove she's ready to welcome me.

Breathing short, I penetrate her with my tip. We moan in unison. We've waited a long time for this moment. Too long. I go in a little more, slowly, not all at once. The sadistic pleasure I feel is worth the torture of not fucking her fast and deep.

Her moan, a sweet melody to my ears, makes me smile like an idiot. She closes her eyes.

"Look at me, babe. Look at me."

She obeys. Her beautiful emerald eyes lock onto mine as I penetrate her a bit more. Her walls tighten around my member, enveloping it in a warm, soft caress.

Damn, she's so tight.

I breathe in and decide to enter her fully.

Lovisa arches.

"Mmm! Yes. Don't stop…"

I smile. She's breathtaking. I almost pull out of her and thrust back in fully, faster, deeper. She moans. I'm in ecstasy.

"Like this? Is this what you like?"

Her face flushes. Her body turns red, looking less pale. She nods, biting her gorgeous lips.

I repeat these long thrust several times. As she becomes wetter, my excitement grows, making me even harder. I speed up, bending her legs and spreading them wider to avoid any hindrance.

I've never experienced anything like this. My pleasure is magnified, satisfying a physical desire as well as a psychological desire. My body sings Lovisa's praises, and my head threatens to explode with the emotions raging inside.

She fulfills me in every way.

Oh, sweet Lovisa.

Where have you been hiding all this time?

"Niklas," she moans, her body undulating.

A sheen of sweat makes her skin shine. The room is small, too small, and the heat from our bodies makes us feverish.

At the peak of my pleasure, my thrusts become faster, plunging deeply into her. Our moans blend and fill the air.

To hell with those who might hearing us, they don't matter.

We climax together, my roan rough and masculine, hers feminine and exciting to the ears.

I collapse against her. Our damp, trembling skins is the last vestiges of our passionate encounter. I kiss her lips and nestle my face against her breast, my breath caressing her pink nipples.

We remain silent for a few minutes, savoring the lingering pulses from our bodies.

When I pull out of her warmth, a profound emptiness fills me, prompting me to quickly wash up my sex and put on my leather boxers. Meanwhile, Lovisa also cleans herself up, puts on her angel outfit, and puts on the heels that go with it. She puts our things in the lockers and waits for me, leaning against the table.

This outfit makes her adorable and innocent again with a sexy touch.

"Are you ready for what's next?"

"If it's anything like what just happened, I can't wait for dinner," she murmurs, nibbling her lip.

I fasten the bracelet that unlocks our quarters on our wrist, put on mine, then run my hand through her red curls, pulling her toward the exit.

"It's going to be beyond anything you imagine."

17

Lovisa, 15 years old

The brightest light that illuminates my life has just gone out. Today is the second darkest day I've experienced. Mom is dead. She's dead... I can't seem to wrap my mind around information. I'm devastated. She was my anchor, my confidant, the one I loved more than anything despite our differences. I want to hate Hendrik. It's his cocaine that caused her overdose, but I have to face the reality: if it hadn't happened here, it would have been at home, in Gothenburg. My heart is shattered, and nothing can fix it. There are so many things I regret, and it's too late to turn back or to tell her everything I wished she knew. I hope she's happy and waiting for me with my father, that they've found each other, and that she's no longer suffering.

***

He doesn't tell me anything about what's going to happen.

Nothing.

I'm completely lost. And in a nightie. I shiver from the biting cold of the hallway we're walking through. Ahead of us, a woman named Marissa, wearing a black latex catsuit that perfectly hugs her curves, guides us to our room. Her thick, long brown hair is tightly braided, swaying from side to side as her heels pound the floor. I feel like I'm in an SM movie, and I wouldn't be surprised to find a table adorned with whips, leather straps, and other gadgets my narrow mind can't even imagine.

I half-turn to Niklas walking beside me. He seems different. A bestial aura emanates from him, dark and seductive, craving to feast on my flesh. A new shiver invades me, but this time, it's a mix of apprehension and excitement. His blue eyes almost turn black in the dim hallway, giving him a harsh and cold look, but the softness of his features when he looks at me proves that underneath this appearance, he's the same person I once knew.

My handsome warrior.

To everyone else, he's a strong and powerful man, but to me, he's Niklas, the teenager who stole my heart when I first stepped into his icy world.

When I returned to Iron House for his father's funeral, all the pieces of my broken heart came together again as soon as I laid eyes on him. Despite his cold and distant demeanor toward me, I couldn't help but feel my heat beat stronger in his presence.

I didn't think I was ready to move on, to forget Rikard, but today changed my mind. We reached a new milestone. *And what a milestone it was*! What happened in the shower was so sudden and so good that I blush at the mere thought of his head between my thighs. Our first time on the table wasn't as romantic as I imagined, but I loved it. More than that. Sex with him promises to be explosive, surprising, and acrobatic.

"What are you thinking about?"

My smile intrigues him.

"I was wondering what you were up to here."

The woman in latex stops in front of a black door and places a magnetic card on the box to her left. She steps away from the room where a minimalistic, seductive music is playing. Dim red neon lights illuminate the place.

"Ring me when you want your entrees," Marissa whispers in her honeyed voice.

"Serve us the champagne," Niklas orders as he guides me inside.

In the center of the room are two black Baroque-style chairs around a round table, with an unlit candle holder waiting for us on top. Right next to it, a bottle sits in an ice bucket.

While our host attends to our drinks, my eyes adjust to the darkness. I thought this place was bare of all objects, but it's quite the opposite. To my right, there's a leather swing; the chains adorned with white feathers attract me.

"I used to love swinging, but I'm not a kid anymore and I'm starving."

Niklas' chuckle as he approaches me prompts me to question him with my eyes. His hands rest on my hips, urging me to sit on the mobile seat. He then lifts two chains with leather loops hanging for them. I immediately understand what they are for. Thankfully, it's dark; otherwise, he would see my face flushed with embarrassment at my naivety.

"If you're good girl," he growls, titling his face toward mine, "I'll show you everything we can do."

I bite my lip and lift my head to meet his gaze. He's so bold, and I'm so prim; it's almost ridiculous. Tonight, fueled by alcohol and still under the influence of our exchange in the locker room, I want to let go and let out the femme fatale hiding in each of us.

"I'd rather show you the naughty girl that I am. You've got the wrong costume," I retort as I stand up. "Tonight, I won't be an angel."

I walk away to continue exploring the premises under Niklas' interested gaze.

On the wall, supports like bars and chains hang at different heights. It reminds me of the shower rog I clung to while Nik explored my intimacy with his tongue. This memory makes my lower belly tighten and creates palpitations in my clitoris.

A large dark wardrobe beckons to me. I open the doors with eager curiosity. My eyes fall on three whips: the first with fabric straps, the second with a single large feather, and the third with a thin rope. There are also several pairs of handcuffs, lubricant, condoms, ribbons, probably for tying up or blindfolding. And…

"I won't be wearing this," I say.

I turn back to him and wave my find, amused: a studded dog collar.

"Is this what you like?"

Sexual preferences and games of all kinds haven't been discussed between us, and I don't know what he enjoys.

Niklas joins me with two glasses of champagne. The hostess is gone, and the door is closed. We are alone.

"It's quite exciting, but it's not my favorite."

He hands me a glass, and toast, looking into each other's eyes.

"To us. May we never be separated again," he says in his deep, sensual voice.

"Never again."

As we drink our champagne, we exchange burning looks into each other's eyes.

Never again do I want to be apart from him.

He was the missing piece in my life to be happy.

"If I have another drop of alcohol on an empty stomach, I'm going to be sick and sprain my ankle with these heels."

We laugh. Without waiting, he heads to the intercom near the door and presses the button. A red light activates.

"Bring the appetizer."

I roll my eyes at his authoritative tone and put my drink on the table.

"Don't you know how to do anything than give orders? Do this, do that. You demand so much with such a harsh tone!"

How does his staff put up with him? Does money make them forget his rude and cold tone?

"*Please* and *thank you* are free. I promise you won't choke on them when you say them," I tease, smiling.

"Miss Granberg, you're quite spirited all of a sudden," he chuckles, amused.

He comes back to me, setting aside his glass to push me back against the wall.

"You should review the basics of politeness, Mr. Ekman," I advise, breathless from our proximity, his bare chest inches from my face.

"Your impertinence deserves punishment."

Desire light up his eyes.

He turns me around and presses my hands against the wall. His fingers trail down my neck and along my spine. My body arches, accentuating my buttocks where his hand grazes my skin through my nightie.

"A spanking is in order."

He lifts the fabric and caresses me slowly, too slowly. I bite my lip, anticipating the slap that doesn't come. His fingers glide over the string of my thong, tracing the lace and then descending again.

"You make me so hard. I'm getting hard just by seeing you in this position."

He grasps my flesh, kneading it before releasing it.

A few moments later, his hand smacks my right buttock. My skin tingles and warms. It's a bit painful, but the context makes this bite exciting. I don't feel assaulted or mistreated, but rather safe and secure. He won't harm me.

My lack of reaction alerts him; his warm body presses against my back, radiating heat onto my skin. He envelops me with his serenity and nestles his face into my hair.

"I'm an idiot, I didn't think about—" he interrupts himself. "Are you okay? I can stop if it's too much for you."

"Don't worry, I liked it. Really, I'm fine."

His concern touches me.

After making sure of my well-being, he steps back and blushes my buttocks again. Each slap sends a wave of pleasure that gnaws at every part of my body. A mixture of little cries of surprise, as well as embarrassed moans and giggles, escape my mouth as he intensifies his punishment, going a little harder each time.

When my raw skin can't take it anymore, he stops to squat down and place kisses on it. The softness of his mouth is a gentle contrast to his iron hand. I turn around, his lips divert to my pussy hidden under my thong. He smiles against it and slowly trails his kisses up, lifting my dress to nibble on my belly until he reaches my chest where he teases one of my nipples through my bra. It hardens just as quickly and strains toward his divine mouth.

"Personally, I'm already savoring my appetizer."

I laugh and guide his face toward mine to kiss him. Sweet and prickly. His beard doesn't bother me. It's part of his charisma.

Marissa knocks on the door and waits for Niklas's permission to enter, carrying a large tray with two plates under a cloche. With a seductive walk, she sways her hips to the table where we sit.

She lift the cloche and announces, "Fricassee of porcini mushrooms in ravioli on its bed of parsley mousse."

The plate, refined and very simple, is an art that only great chefs possess. The presentation is perfect, and it would almost be a sacrilegious to eat this dish. The lack of light doesn't prevent me from admiring my appetizer.

Using my cutlery, I cut into the ravioli and take a generous bite. My taste buds awaken. Different flavors, both mild and strong, explode in my mouth. I salivate, and my hunger drives me to finish my appetizer quickly. Too quickly. I'm still hungry, and this small plate would barely satisfy a child.

Across from me, Niklas watches me with a small amused smile.

"Do you have any idea the price of the meal? You just devoured a certain amount without even savoring it."

"I would have been happy with the first burger I came across."

"The local food truck doesn't have the best chef or a room where anything is possible," he points out, putting down his cutlery.

Two wine glasses are placed in front of us, he takes white wine bottle and fills them.

"Nor does it have this nectar."

I pick up my glass and take a sip. It's smooth, with a good mouthfeel, and sweet. It's not sparkling and doesn't attack the throat.

"Delicious," I comment, taking another sip.

"It comes from my vineyard in Italy."

His vineyard!

I almost choke and struggle to swallow the wine.

"You own… your own wine? You amaze me."

This man does it all. He's filled with ambition, it's in his genes. He gets that from his father. When will he stop? Will he ever be satisfied with what he has?

"I partnered with a family that cultivates their land and proposed a partnership because banks refused to grant them a loan."

"But you, you believed in it."

"I tasted this wine when I went on vacation to Italy. I knew it had potential. That was seven years ago. Today, we distribute our wine in several countries, including Sweden."

Talking about his business lights up his face with happiness. It's something he loves to do. I don't see that spark when it comes to his illegal activities. Can't he stop if it doesn't make him happy?

"I never thought you were a wine enthusiast. Since I've been here, I've seen you down liters of vodka and whiskey, but no wine."

"There are many things about me thar might surprise you."

"Like what?"

He thinks, leaning against his chair. One arm rests on the armrest, and he brings his hand to his chin to support it. His relaxed demeanor and muscular body give me palpitations. The leather molds around his resting sex and makes me want to rub myself against him to awaken the beast within him.

"If I didn't have all this, this wealth, these responsibilities, I would have pursed another career. I love rock climbing, scaling the highest mountains, exploring untouched nature, unspoiled by man. I probably would have bought a cottage deep in the forest where I would live with a pretty woman, preferably a red-haired with big green eyes to keep me warm at night."

I listen to him, amazed by the beautiful images unfolding before my eyes. This simple life is totally the opposite of what he's currently living.

"It's like a dream. It's always possible, you know. We could drop everything and run away, far away, with no one to bother us or hurt us."

Being a drug dealer is far from peaceful and comes with many risks we could escape if he stops.

"Too many people rely on me; it would be chaos if I left. Besides, my health doesn't allow it."

His face suddenly closes off. He straightens in his chair and takes a long sip of wine.

"Your health? What are you talking about?" I ask, worried.

I didn't know he had a health issue. He never told me. What else is he hiding from me?

"It's nothing important. Nothing to worry about."

"I want to know."

I'm not going to let go. His health is my concerns, he's part of my life. Losing him would be unbearable.

"A blood pressure problem," he says, waving his hand. "Nothing serious, but with the altitude, it's risky."

His far too casual tone makes me believe he's trying to hide something bigger.

"Since when?"

He narrows his eyes, looking at me for long moment before sighing.

"Three years."

"Is it dangerous? Are you at risk?"

Second sigh; he seems exasperated. "No. That's enough now."

He avoids the subject. There's something fishy, and I'll find out what he's hiding from me.

Niklas stands up and heads to the cabinet. He grabs the whip with the feather and the white fur handcuffs. He gives me a mischievous look.

"I's rather have fun and give you a good time."

"Are you distracting me with sex?" That's exactly what he's doing.

He comes back to me and kisses me, lifting me up. I'm intoxicated by the kiss, but not enough to forget he's hiding something. If I don't find out now, I'll find out later.

He squeezes my hand in his and guides me to the wall behind me. "Do you trust me?"

I look at him, perplexed. That question again. I glance at the handcuffs and purse my lips before nodding. The first time he asked me this question, I was surprised. I thought it was clear after what had just happened in the shower. I don't do that with just anyone, especially not cunnilingus, which has always seemed very intimate to me. I feel vulnerable and stripped of all protection, so submissive to his mouth, and yet, the hesitation I felt quickly dissipated.

"If it's too tight or if you're uncomfortable, I'll stop," he reassures me while fastening my arms above my head. "We need a safe word. How about *black*? It's simple but effective."

"*Black* is fine, but I find the whole code thing ridiculous. Why not just say stop?"

He smiles and tightens the cuffs just enough to keep my wrists from slipping out. The fur brushes against my skin, thrilling me. My body tenses, anticipating what's next. I was used to classic sex with Rikard; he stuck to the bed, and that was fine with me. But I have to admit, what Niklas offers me is more exciting.

His gaze admires me as he steps back.

"You might say stop or no in the heat of the moment without really meaning it, just to moan. But saying a color or a word out of context it gives it all its meaning; it's clear and remind me to stop."

"Okay, but why not red? It's the color of danger."

Using the feather, he caresses the bottom of my leg, slowly moving up.

"Red is the color of desire, of passion, of your skin when you're aroused. Red represents too many pleasurable things to be associated with stopping our activity."

"Could I say red when I want more?" I suggest with a seductive smile.

A shiver starts from the sole of my left foot and travels up my leg as the feather moves.

"Please do. Don't hesitate to tell me when you want more."

This little game, barely begun, already pleases me. The softness of the feather alerts the nerve endings in my skin and intensifies around sensitive areas like the inside of my thighs, which I instinctively spread to let him in.

Alcohol numbs my mind and relaxes my body, making me more inclined to new experiences.

Since returning to Iron House, I feel so alive and aware of the strength and potential of my body. I'm reclaiming my life back and it's just… amazing.

Niklas takes his time caressing every part of my body. He eventually lifts my nightie, tucking it behind my head, exposing me almost entirely. My lace underwear is so thin and transparent that it hides little. Niklas pushes the cups of my bra aside to free my breasts.

"You're stunning." He teases my nipples, eliciting a small squeak of frustration from me.

"It kills me to see how good you are."

"Wait until you see the what's next," he says.

"I can't imagine how many women you've charmed," I can't help but say.

His feather lingers on my collarbones, tracing them from point to point before he looks me in the eyes.

"I won't lie and say I waited for you all these years. We both have our past. It drives me crazy knowing other men have touched you, but I deal with it because we can't change the past." He places a tender kiss on my lips. A kiss so gentle that it gives me shiver. I lean into him, my restraints preventing me from moving away from the wall. He slides his hand to my neck, his fingers squeezing my throat, but not enough to stop me from breathing.

"Now you belong to me, body and soul, and anyone who touches you again will have to answer to me," he growls, giving me a wild kiss.

My body vibrates with this beautiful promise, and my heart burst with joy. Rikard has said these words to me before, but as a threat, whereas here, it's something else. The context is different, and so is Niklas.

With my consent, he takes the whip with the rope strands and the contact delights my skin, which reddens in places. These micro-pains awaken my senses and introduce me to a side of sex that I didn't know. It's pleasant and exciting; I want to feel him against me and inside me, but he refuses my request torturing me over and over, using the whip as well as his expert lips.

The game ends when my stomach growls again, makes us both laugh.

When he unties me, I throw myself at him, kissing him has I take off myself from my dress. I nearly fall with my heels, so I take them off. I wrap my legs around his hips as he moves toward the door. My lips migrate down his neck, kissing, nibbling, and tasting him with my tongue.

"Bring the main course," he says, pressing the intercom.

I'm consumed by two hungers. For food and for sex. And I don't know which is stronger. Nik decides for me and sits down on his chair, holding me against him. With a firm hand, he grabs my hair and pulls me back to devour my lips.

Authoritative and direct.

For some aspects of life, like right now, these qualities are highly appreciated.

My hands explore his firm, muscular body, his soft skin covered by a thin line of hair on his belly, leading down into his boxers. This detail drives me even crazier for him. I find it incredibly sexy on a man. I place my palms against his pecs and pull my face back to admire him.

"Do you remember how back then, we only exchanged kisses without ever never going to the next level? Look at us now."

"It's not for lack of trying!"

He laughs and resumes, "Now you're straddling me, half-naked and horny."

Observant. It's obvious; I touch him and kiss him as if it were the last time this would happen.

"Wait until the passion fades after a few years," I chuckle, teasing him.

"I'll never let such a thing happen."

"Promise?"

He grabs my neck and presses his forehead against mine, looking into my eyes. The intensity of his gaze unsettles me, just as it does every time he gets deep and serious. He completely makes me upside down and makes me lose my footing. How does he do that? Does he realize the power he has over me? The attraction between us is so strong that it sometimes suffocates me, but I wouldn't want it to stop for anything in the world.

Three knocks on the door, it's Marissa bringing the dish. A flank steak with small vegetables. A real treat. Between each bite, we talk about our lives; the subject of my job comes up, and he makes a surprising revelation. I put down my fork and lean back in my chair, speechless.

"It was you every time?" I ask, running my hand over my nightie, which I put on to eat.

He nods, smiling.

"I looked up all the concerts you were playing and made sure that you received the biggest bouquet of flowers."

"Orange roses?"

"The most beautiful in Sweden. I would have given them to you in person, but it was… too difficult."

My heart tightens, hearing a hint of sadness in his voice. I wish I could erase the pain of the past nine years, but it's impossible.

Life has given us a second chance, and we must seize it to forget our past.

Now that I know who the true author of this gift is, the gears in my brain freeze for a moment before restarting. The motherfucker!

"What a little shit," I say, grabbing my glass of wine. "He lied to me."

"What are you talking about?"

My sudden change in mood catches his attention and makes him suddenly tense.

I sigh. Too late to stay quiet, I have to spill it.

"I met Rikard a few months after joining the orchestra; we were in Stockholm for a month. Already at that time, you were sending me the flowers. When he approached me at the end of our first week, he told me that he came every day. Naturally, I thought he was the sender of the roses, and he didn't contradict me."

A real manipulator. From our first meeting, he didn't play fair and didn't hesitate to lie to me to lure me in. I was so stupid and naive.

"I found it adorable and romantic, and I hate to admit it, but it was this gesture at each of my concerts that pushed me into his arms."

I swallow. Why did I confess that? It's as if I'm telling him to his face that it's because of him I got together with Rikard. I bite my lip, waiting for Nik's outburst of anger. But nothing. Instead, he says in a cold voice, "And you didn't question when the bouquets kept being delivered while you were together?"

I shake my head.

"He kept making me believe they came from him. Sometimes he would get angry and throw the flowers, but I blamed that on his impulsive nature."

On the surface, Niklas's body, tense as a bow express nothing else, he seems to be containing himself from exploding.

"I lived with blinders on. I didn't see what he really was."

A part of my life leaves me with a bitter taste due to this deception. I wouldn't be surprised to discover more deceit from Rikard. What a fraud!

Niklas' silence is more devastating than his anger. I hate it. It makes me feel bad and stupid for buying such a lie.

"Please say something. Are you mad at me?" I whisper.

"If there's one person who has nothing to reproach herself for, it's you. Rikard who's responsible and he's the one who should be ashamed."

His icy irises pin me in place and take my breath away. My insides twist and all hunger disappear.

"He turned, tarnished my gift with his lies, which pushed you into his arms. While I imagined a part of me by your side, it turned out that wasn't the case. That bastard didn't have enough balls to win you over fairly." His voice vibrates with anger while his body remains frozen, only his lips and his clenched fist on the table move. I want to nestle in his arms, but I don't know what would be his reaction.

We remain silent for what seems like an eternity before he breaks the silence with his weary, distant voice.

"I came to listen to you play once. I was sitting in the third row, I didn't want you to see me, but I wanted to be close enough to admire you."

I listen to him carefully. My heart pounds against my ribcage and threatens to burst out and crash onto the table. This revelation leaves me speechless. What would have been my reaction if I had seen him?

"I didn't take my eyes off you for a moment, and when you had your solo, I became the teenager who listened to you practice at home again. My… heart was so painful as memories with you came back. It felt like someone was piercing me with ice spikes. I couldn't bear it. I didn't want to stay, but my legs wouldn't obey me. I stayed until the end promising myself never to come see you again."

My eyes are burning, and tears are clouding my vision. I let them flow without any embarrassment and stand up, trembling slightly. I share his pain, and when I sit on his lap to hug him, my body tries to suck all the sadness from his. His vulnerability hits me in the face. He who always shows himself so strong and uncompromising lets me glimpse deep pain.

His arms close around me, and his face nestles into my neck. His warm breath tickles my skin. My fingers run through his tied-up hair and wander over his broad neck. The vulnerability of this giant touches me deeply. I realize that 'm not the only one who has suffered all these years. Besides, he had to live with the lie I told him before I left.

I lower my face close to his ear and whisper, "I'll never leave you again. Never, do you hear me? I'll stay as long as you want me."

This promise, I make it for him and for me. I don't want to be away from him anymore.

He's my strength.

My weakness.

My pillar.

My Achilles' heel.

We are one.

18

Niklas, 17 years old

Since Sigrid's death, Lovisa has lost that sparkle in her eyes, and even though I can still make her smile, it's not the same. Things don't stay the same as they do in movies. In reality, a single moment can turn your life upside down. I'd do anything to make her happy, but my father keeps putting her down whenever he gets the chance, especially now that her mom isn't around to protect her. I try to stand up for her, but the more I defend her, the more he targets her. My interest in Lovisa puts her in danger; he uses this weakness to make me to do what he wants. Anyone else would dump her to be free, but I won't let him win. Hendrik won't have the upper hand. I won't leave her.

***

Never I had opened up about my feelings. Hendrik always told me to appear tough and strong, to leave emotions to the weak. Deep down, I knew he was wrong, that loving, laughing, crying, and having fun were normal.

Feelings aren't for the weak. You have to be strong to embrace them and live with them. My father was too weak to deal with them.

After dinner and long conversations about our lives, we change in the locker room. As I get dressed, I devour her with my eyes. Lovisa does the same. This evening took an unexpected turn; I didn't show her all the room's potential. Instead, we talked until our mouths went numb and our throats dried out despite the endless wine. Lovisa staggers slightly but maintain her composure.

Remarkable

She amazes me.

As she pointed out, she rarely drinks, but I find her resilience impressive given everything she's drunk tonight.

I place my jacket over her shoulders and give her dress a long look.

"This color looks stunning on you. You should wear red more often."

"I will," she promises, biting her lip.

I love it when she does that. I'd love to nibble and lick her, but we're interrupted by the door opening to let Oscar in.

"Oscar, what are you doing here?"

My mood darkens when I see his serious expression.

Shit. What's happening now?

His gaze shifts from Lovisa to me.

"Love," I start, kissing her lips. "Wait for me here, I'll be back in a minute."

I step out and close the door behind me. The hallway is empty and silent. Too silent. The sudden quietness unnerves me.

"Tell me."

"There's been another intrusion."

My body tenses, and my anger flares immediately.

"Fuck!" I growl, punching the wall opposite the door. "This is the second time this week. Why am I even paying you?"

I can't let this new mistake pass. Heads will roll. I curse again, exhaling loudly.

"Did you see his face?"

"There was a problem. None of the cameras were activated, it seems that there was a power outage."

"Back-up generator?"

"Out of service."

I'll be damned! How is this possible? I growl, holding back from punching the wall again, and glare at my head of security.

"This generator is not *supposed* to be down. What the hell happened?"

"And that's not all," he says, looking grim.

Oscar usually has a serious demeanor and appears confident, but tonight, the fine lines around his eyes are more pronounced.

"We didn't see the intruder, but we saw what he did. When Roger was making his rounds, he found dead foxes all around the villa. All of them were gutted. I'm almost sure they're all dead. One was hanging on the porch.

My blood runs cold as horrifying images form in my mind. If Oscar is touched by this, it must be hard to face. Who would attack these animals?

After the shock of the news, rage floods me, warming every part of my body. I hate the idea of an intruder sneaking into my place without anyone stopping him. And now, he's targeting living creatures!

"I want that bastard found. Review the camera footage, go back as far as needed to spot any suspicious presence during the day."

"Our technician is already on site, working to get everything back online. Someone knew how to hack our defenses; this has never happened before."

Oscar glance at the door where Lovisa is.

"Should I wait for you?"

"No. Go."

He nods and slips away, walking down the dark hallway before disappearing behind a door.

As for me, I stay alone a long minute.

Breathe in and out.

The problems keep piling up without fully resolving.

Brad, the one who designed Iron House's security, is skilled in his field—one of the best, even. I can't believe someone managed to breach the firewalls he set up. Who could be talented enough to beat him? And crazy enough to target me? Brad better provides me some answers.

Behind the door, Lovisa waits for me, looking worried. You don't have to be a genius to figured out she heard everything.

"You have nothing to worry about," I start before she can speaks. "The situation is under control."

Is it really? I feel like things are starting to get out of hand, and I hate that.

She bites her lips, hugging her arms.

"If you say so… Nik, those poor foxes… What an awful death."

"I know, it's terrible. Whoever did this is will pay, I promise."

I kiss her before leading her outside. The evening has been eventful, and all I want now is to sleep with the woman I love.

"We should go to the hotel or leave the city," Lovisa suggests.

We're in the car, warmed by the heater and with music in the background, "My Demons" by Starset. I've had a thing for American music since my teenage years.

I snort and shake my head, keeping my eyes on the road.

"No one will make me run away from my own home. I'm not afraid; let them come, ten or a hundred, I'll take them down."

"We're not running away, we're taking shelter."

"It's the same for me. We'll review the security system and it'll be fine. If I need to hire more men, I will. More weapons? No problem, I'll get them."

She fidgets in her seat, uneasy. This isn't her world; she doesn't belong in the midst of all this violence, these plots, and these bloody acts, like the death of red foxes. But what can I do? I can't let her leave me again. It would be like sticking a dagger through my heart. I'd rather die than endure the pain of losing her.

When I park in front of the villa, a cleaning team is hastily scrubbing the porch stained with dried blood. A bit further away, a wheelbarrow containing the animals' corpses gives us an idea of the savagery of the attack. Lovisa, not being able to bear this morbid sight, immediately goes upstairs to take refuge. I walk over to the foxes and observe them for a moment. It could have been one of my men, or me. *Or worse*, Love. This thought reignites my anger. When did things start to go wrong? Oh, right! My father's gift: his cursed legacy.

"Doctor Karlsson will be saddened by this news," says Oscar, descending down the porch to join me.

I nod, taking the cigarette he offers and lighting it immediately. I'm no longer a secret to him.

"Lucia loved them."

She often came to see and took care of them.

"Any updates?" I ask.

"The backup generator empty; someone completely drained it, that's why it didn't start. The cameras aren't operational yet, but Brad is working on it. Sir, I've been thinking, and I don't believe this is an attack from Rodrigo. It's way too personal. Could it be from one of your love affairs?"

I've considered this possibility as well. During the drive, my mind went through all the people I've crossed, and Jonna's name kept coming up. She's the one I hurt the most; she has every reason in the world to be mad at me. She knows a skilled IT, Azerty. But did they have time to do their show at the Red Mill and then come and slaughter the foxes on my property? Besides, Jonna is crazy, but she wouldn't get her hands dirty. Unless she's even more unpredictable than I think she is?

"Anything is possible. You don't get my status without making some enemies along the way."

It was my father who raised my family to this rank, but I've contributed to our notoriety and made quite a few enemies.

I scratch my beard before smoothing it out. The cigarette burns between my fingers without me taking a single puff.

"First thing tomorrow morning, I want all the files of our employees. What happened tonight is unacceptable. I need to trust the men who protect me, and that's not the case."

"I'll take care of it. A police patrol was alerted by an anonymous call; they wanted to inspect the house, but I managed to dissuade them."

I frown and look at the forest around us. Is the author of this act still on the property?

If there's an inspection, I'll end up in jail. In the basement, there are unregistered weapons and cocaine, not to mention the detailed account in my office.

Suddenly, a detail jumps out at me. I look around me. "What about Alfrida and Krigare?"

"They're safe. A man is watching the house, and she took Krigare for the night."

Relieved, I sigh. For the past few years, the housekeeper has been living on the Iron House property. I had the shed in the forest demolished to build her a small house. Since she had no family, she liked the idea. It's not unusual for her to take my dog when I'm busy. Lately, my dog is often been with her.

"A thorough cleaning is in order," I say, pinching the bridge of my nose. "We'll talk about it tomorrow. Make sure everything is cleaned up. I don't want to see a drop of blood on the wood or even in the snow."

I take a drag from my cigarette before tossing it away.

As I enter the house, the unsettling feeling that my territory has been invaded lingers. Sure, they didn't get inside, but it feels like it. A quick look around the living room shows nothing out of place.

But it feels different.

I feel watched. Besides the hidden cameras inside that only Oscar and I know about, there's something else. Is it just a feeling? There are so many people outside; that's probably it. I shake my head and go upstairs.

My bedroom is empty, as is my bathroom. She must be in hers. Through the slightly open door, repaired since my forced entry a week ago, I see her moving around, wearing a long black T-shirt. Mine. A white wolf print on the chest, howling under the full moon. It suits her better than me. Her long legs are bare, the fabric stopping just below her round butt. It's a much more pleasant view than the one outside.

I push open the creaking door, making her jump.

"You scared me."

She puts a hand to her heart and sighs.

"You're already ready for bed," I say, closing the door behind me.

Lovisa's steps are unsteady as she flops onto the bed. Alcohol still soaks her body and will be with her for the rest of the night; it will take hours to digest everything.

"I'm exhausted, but I don't think I can sleep with those awful images running through my head."

She shivers and shakes her head, lying down on top of the blanket.

"Your world is cruel."

I take off my shoes and start undressing while reflecting on her words.

"The world is cruel," I correct. "My life is the result of a series of internal and external factors. I didn't choose the life I have, just like you didn't choose yours."

She smiles wistfully as she stared at the ceiling. The T-shirt has ridden up to the bottom of her belly, and revealing her red lace thong.

"My life wasn't perfect before my mom met your dad, but I liked it. It was just the two of us, and that was enough for me. Then, all the darkness from your family tainted us."

Her smile fades. A shadow crosses her face.

"I'm repeating the same mistakes my mother made."

Wearing only my boxers, I slide in beside her and lean over her.

"I'm not my father, and you're not your mother. The two of us, aren't a mistake, we're a certainty, a necessity. Our destiny. We can't live without each other, and you know that. Love isn't just happiness. Sometimes we suffer, but that doesn't mean we should give up."

Our eyes meet, and I see doubt in hers. I brush my fingertips along her cheek, down to her jawline, then to her collarbones.

"When I've sorted out these problems, I'll show you that life with me is worth it."

"Despite the chaos, I can't leave. My weakness scares me. I'm willing to let you destroy me just to stay by your side."

Her lower lip quivers slightly, and her eyes glisten with tears. I wrap my arms around her and hug her tightly. Seeing her move breaks my heart. How deeply has life scarred her? How much did Rikard's behavior affect her?

"The day I make you unhappy, when our relationship becomes toxic, I'll put a bullet in my head so you won't have to go through that again."

The warmth of her body against mine soothes me. Her presence helps me put aside what's happening downstairs. I wish I could stay in her arms forever, locking ourselves in this room. We would live off sex, kisses, and caresses.

"I'll never let you die for me," she mumbles, letting herself be won over little by little by sleep.

"If I have to die, let it be in your arms after an orgasm," I smile, pulling the blanket over us. "That would be the most beautiful way to go."

Lovisa rubs her cold nose against my chest.

"Let's not talk about death anymore, please…"

"Sleep, my Love, sleep."

The night brings advice and erases troubles.

Our tangled limbs take me back to an old memory, the last one we share. The fateful night when everything changed. Automatically, I rub my right temple, where an old scar lies…

Nine years ago

My bachelor pad has changed a lot since Lovisa arrived. It's now occupied only by the gang. No other girls come here, except for Lucia and Jonna from my group. I'm going to prove to Lovisa that she's the only one who matters now.

"Are you sure about this?" I ask.

"I feel ready," she answers.

I dreamed of this moment for a long time. I patiently waited for her to agree to be willing to move beyond kisses and caresses.

I will be her first.

Me and no one else.

A privilege she's giving me. She won't regret it.

We are lying next to each other on the beige fabric couch. A thin wool blanket covers us. For her, I've cleaned up everything and lit some candles. She loves candles, especially the ones with nice scents. The setting is quite romantic if we ignore the foosball table and the huge TV with my console and my video games.

"Do you have what we need?"

She's talking about condoms. I glance at the coffee table where they're stored.

"Don't worry, I never take any risks."

I like having sex, but I always make sure to protect myself.

She gives me a tense smile.

"Relax, it's going to be fine."

The tension of her body in her underwear against mine makes me a little nervous. I've done this dozens of times. So why am I so anxious about having sex with her?

Maybe because she's not just a one-night stand?

I'm already horny, my cock is hard against one of her thighs. That must be intimidating for her, having never experienced this.

The pressure.

That's what I feel. I need to show her how amazing sex can be. I've never slept with a virgin before.

"It's going to be okay," I repeat, more for myself than for her.

I smile back at her and kiss her, positioning my body between her and the back of the couch. Her lips and skin are the softest things I've ever touched. My hands keep caressing her, moving dangerously toward the inside of her thighs.

Slowly, she relaxes against me and surrenders to the passion of our embrace. So close to the goal, yet still far away. I don't want to rush her. I'll go as gently as possible. Everything will be perfect. She'll remember this night forever.

"Well, well, what do we have here?"

We jump at the sound of intruders entering the room. The attic stairs have been creaking for years, but I hadn't heard a thing. In the doorway, my father and one of his men, an asshole named Sören, look at us with a sick smile.

I immediately lose my temper, covering Lovisa with the blanket.

"Get out!"

"I'm in my home. I go wherever I want."

Hendrik step closer, his heavy footsteps echoing. My instinct tells me to stand up and block him from getting to Lovisa. Being in boxers doesn't stop me from confronting him with all the dignity I can muster.

He stops in front of me, with Sören standing behind him.

"What do you think you're doing under my roof, kid?" asks my father.

He glances at Lovisa with interest, licking his lower lip.

"We're not doing anything wrong."

He turns his attention back to me, his cold eyes, identical to mine, scrutinizing me.

"You want to deflower your sister? The law calls that incest."

I clench my fist and hold his gaze, pouring all my hatred for him into my stare.

"She's not my sister, and you know it. This is none of your business. Leave us alone."

I seem to amuse him, he starts to laugh and glancing at his men.

"Do you hear that, Sören? The kid wants us to leave him to his business."

Sören chuckles, showing his large teeth that look like they could bite your arm off. I hate him; he's a bastard who thinks he can do anything.

"It's not up to little boys to handle these things. To become a real woman, she needs a real man to show her how it's done," says my father.

My blood stops pulsing in my face and my heart skip a beat.

What the fuck is he talking about?

I risk a glance at Lovisa, now sitting on the couch wrapped in the blanket. She understands what's happening. So do I.

"You're not going to touch her!"

"She's not to my type. But Sören here likes them young and tender."

Sören giggles again behind his master.

Hendrik steps aside, glancing around.

"You've put in a lot of effort for tonight, she must mean something to you. Sören will be gentle if she behaves. Right, Sören?"

"I'll try, boss."

His words reek of lies. He looks at her with desire, making me shiver with disgust.

I won't let him do it. Without hesitation, I throw myself on him, hitting him in the face with all my strength. Taken by surprise, he lets me touch him several times before blocking my punches and pushing me away. I fall, hitting the side of my head on the wooden arm of the couch. Lovisa's scream makes me look at her, but a violent kick to my stomach knocks the wind out of me, forcing me to curl up.

Hendrik leans down, grabbing my hair to lift my head. Warm, thick blood runs down my temple, the pain soon overshadows the ache in my stomach.

"Don't worry, son, we'll take good care of her."

He punches me in the face, sending me into unconsciousness. The last sound I hear is the heartbreaking cry of Lovisa calling my name.

****

I jolt back to reality.

In the dark, I don't know how much time has passed, but the house is silent, and Lovisa sleeps soundly in my arms.

I've often thought back to that moment. Many times, I've rewritten the scene in my head, becoming the hero who takes down my father and Sören. Then, I'd grab Lovisa by the waist and we'd escape from Iron House. But that was just a fantasy. Reality was much different. Two days later, she disappeared from my life, leaving me a goodbye letter. Mad with rage and pride, I never tried to find out the real reason for her departure, even though her letter seemed off. Back then, I preferred to believe she had abandoned me cowardly. That night, she wasn't raped like I had feared, but my fury toward her didn't diminish.

I was foolish but mostly heartbroken at losing the only person, besides Alfrida, who genuinely cared about me. Losing her felt like losing my mother, who also fled because of my father.

This place has housed so much suffering, but it's over now.

Everything is going to change.

19

Lovisa, 16 years old

Niklas,

I'm tired of pretending and lying. I don't love you, I never have. I've been playing with you.

I've always hated you, but after my mother's death, I didn't want to be thrown out on the street, so I pretended to love you to convince your father to keep me. But it's too hard. You disgust me, your presence is unbearable. Kissing you, touching you, or even breathing the same air as you has become too painful.

Hendrik understands my situation, he loves me like a daughter, and our relationship isn't right. I asked him to send me somewhere else, far from you, to receive the best education in the country. He's thinking about my well-being, and I'd like you to do the same, so never try to contact me, it's better this way.

Take care and make your father proud.

***

A week has passed since the murder of the red foxes on the property. Several days during which Nik has been on edge and often in a terrible mood. I try to give him as much space as possible, spending time with Alfrida and his dog Krigare—this ball of fur has adopted me—or in town, getting to know my mother's shop better. The idea of selling it never left me. I know the store belonged to her, but she never really cared about it. So why would I? Niklas no longer bothers me about it or pushes me to keep it. He's confessed that his insistence was because he thought the store would keep me close to him.

While he juggles phones meetings and appointments in his office and outside the estates, I talk to various potential buyers interested in an ad posted online. I show them around the shop, accompanied by a bodyguard that Niklas insists I have with me at all times, and by also accompanied by John Gray. The latter manages Nik's investment portfolio and is the best person to advise me.

John and I discussed the evening when, drunk, I stumbled on him. He admitted that after that event, Niklas strictly forbade him from seeing me again. Now, Nik has changed his mind, deeming him no longer a threat and able to help me get rid of my property. In a light tone, Niklas announced that if John behaved inappropriately, he might mysteriously disappear. This thinly veiled threat made us only half-laugh. Each of us knows he's capable of it and has the means to carry out his threat.

"Another waste of time," John exclaims, closing a leather briefcase containing the applications of potential buyers.

Two men just left. Obsessed with the details, all they did was point out the flaws to lower the price as much as possible, which annoyed John.

"We'll find someone who's interested. We have one more appointment, then we can go home."

It's getting late. The night has already fallen over the city. The streetlights are on, and we can see the businesses closing one by one. We're the last ones. Outside, the rain is pouring down and doesn't seem to want to stop.

Exhausted, I collapse on the stool behind the counter. I'm wearing high, black patent leather heels that are killing me.

All my belongings are in Rikard's apartment in Stockholm, and I'll never see them again. That's why I had to redo my wardrobe. I have to admit, I enjoy buying new clothes, choosing what I wanted instead of what I was expected to wear. So, in the spirit of trying new things, I ended up with these too-high heels that are ruining my toes. I dream of throwing them in the trash. Only my skinny jeans and my white blouse with black polka dots please me. I'm comfortable, and the silk of my top feels delightful against my skin. It's nice to wear.

"I'm tired," I groan, massaging my ankles. "I didn't think it would be this exhausting to show the shop and repeat the same pitch over and over."

"Selling a property isn't that easy. It often takes weeks, even months, for a transaction to go through."

I sigh dramatically, raising my hands in the air. Months? I can't stand it. All I want is to get back to playing music in the orchestra and going tour. The only downside is that I'll be far from Nik. I doubt he'll comes with me everywhere. He has too many responsibilities here. I'll visit him as often as I can because now, he's my home.

"I can take care of it if you want," John offers, serving us two cups of tea.

I turn my stool toward him and shake my head.

"It's my responsibility. I have to do it."

I blow on the surface of my drink and take a sip, warming my hands around the cup. Glancing out the window, I see my bodyguard, Vanni, in the car. He's not just a driver. He's a former military who switched to private protection it pays better.

"I'd like to ask him to come in."

At that moment, Vanni looks in our direction and nods at me. I do the same, and before I can signal him to come in, the door opens.

A tall redhead appears. He shakes his head. Droplets fall and water the floor of the shop. He's dressed all in black, making his hair stands out like lava flowing from a volcano. He reminds me of myself, except his eyes are dark.

"Good evening, I'm here for the visit," he says with a calm, steady voice. A deep voice that sends chills down our spine. He approaches us with a confident stride. I don't know this guy, but he seems comfortable in his boots.

"Good evening. Mr. Larsson? We were expecting you," John says as he moves around the counter. "May I offer you something to drink?"

"No need, I'm in a hurry."

His gaze shift from John to me, then scans the surroundings.

My right-hand man starts his usual spiel as he walks through the store. I know every word he's going to say before he says it, which makes me smile. I'm glad he's with me; he knows how to talk to people. He's a good salesman. But this time, his listener isn't paying attention. His eyes keep meeting mine. He's scrutinizing me, analyzing me. It feels like he's trying to read me.

He's unsettling.

I cross my arms over my chest and close myself off the conversation happening between the two men. The old Lovisa, fearful and fragile, tries to resurface for protecting myself. But I stop her. I've become stronger lately, more assertive, and I will never go back. I uncross my arms, letting them hang by my sides, straighten my posture, and hold the redhead's gaze when he looks at me for the umpteenth time.

"I have all the information I need. Thank you for your time, I'll be in touch."

After he leaves, the atmosphere in the shop lightens. I relax.

"I have a good feeling about him. We might have found a buyer," John says enthusiastically.

"Didn't he seem strange to you?" He looks at me quizzically while he puts away our still-full cups. "I don't know, he was weird," I continue, shrugging my shoulders as I put on my coat.

John cracks his knuckles and yawns loudly.

"Whatever, we're done for the night. Let's go home and review the applications on our own."

I nod in agreement and turn off the lights with him, then lock the shop. He waves goodbye to me as my driver opens the car door. I slide into the leather seats and fasten my seatbelt.

"Where are we going?" asks Vanni.

"Home."

Home. It feels strange to use that word to refer to Iron House, but that's what the property has become. Again. I've come back home for good. This time, there's no mother, no Hendrik. Just *him* and me.

Niklas.

This past week, he's been distant, even during my shooting or self-defense lessons. He's consumed by his many troubles. So much to deal with. The murder of the red foxes remains unsolved, and not knowing who broke into the property pisses him off. He hates not having his life under control.

The car's purr and the warm interior lull me into a half-sleep. A soothing calm fills the air. Staring out the window, I already imagine being wrapped in the arms of my handsome Viking, kissing him to distract him from his worries. His soft, full lips make me want to bite them every time they touch mine.

The city gradually gives way to a dense forest of spiky pine trees. The rain has stopped, and the Northern Lights illuminate the dark sky. Every night, I watch them before falling asleep.

The car slows down in front of the Iron House's gates. This sight always makes me shiver. The thought of becoming the scared girl who discovered these gates a decade ago terrifies me. Will I ever get used to it?

After getting permission to enter the property, we drive straight to the villa.

He parks next to a light gray vehicle. A car I don't recognize.

Once out of the sedan, I glance inside the unknow car, trying to find a clue about its owner. I have no idea who it belongs to, but this car is worth a lot of money. Having dated a guy whose parents specialize in luxury cars, I immediately recognize quality.

I climb the stairs to the door. Instinctively, or perhaps out of wariness that happiness is never fully perfect, I sense something is off as I step inside. I take off my coat and hang it on the coat rack, then head straight for the voices coming from Niklas's office. I stop near the stairs. Oscar comes out, accompanied by a man.

"He has to stop. If it continues, it will be more serious next time."

The man in the suit holds a typical doctor's briefcase, with a stethoscope peeking out. With his free hand, he hands a paper to Oscar.

"He needs to come to my clinic. This is no longer a suggestion, but an order."

Oscar sighs. "I'll see what I can do."

I step forward, interrupting their conversation. Oscar looks half-surprised; my arrival is never a secret—once I pass the gates, the guards notify their chief.

"Keep me informed of any changes," the doctor says, shaking Oscar's hand.

"I will."

They walk past me. I don't wait another moment and rush into the office. On the floor, documents are scattered, along with a glass of alcohol that has soaked most of the papers. To my right, Niklas is lying on the couch. His complexion is waxy, his forehead sweaty, and a few strands of hair are plastered to his face. My heart tightens.

"God, Nick."

I rush to him and fall to my knees. I take his face in my hands, looking at him worried.

"What's wrong? What's happening? I saw a doctor. Why did you need a doctor?"

His exhausted eyes meet mine, and he tries to reassure me with a smile as he places his hands over mine.

"Love, calm down. I'm fine."

"Usually, when a doctor comes, something is wrong."

He sits up and positions me between his legs. His fully unbuttoned shirt reveals his muscular build and his reaper tattoo.

"I'm overworked right now. I'm not eating enough and I'm not staying hydrated. The doc gave me something to help. I'll be better in a few days."

Why do I feel like he's lying to me? His mouth says one thing, but his eyes say another. What is he trying to hide?

I press my lips together and place my hands on his thighs, squeezing them affectionately.

"If you had something serious, you would tell me, right?"

Niklas doesn't answer immediately. He's usually straightforward, quick to answer, so this brief silence sets off alarms. Or am I just imagining things? His isolation in recent days makes me doubt everything he says. He's trying to protect me from whatever he's plotting, and his illegal activities don't reassure me.

"I… we should take a break for a while, get away from all the chaos and go somewhere, just the two of us. What do you think?"

With apparent ease, he lifts me onto his lap. His hand slips into my hair, lingering there with soothing strokes.

"You know I'd love that, really, but it might make things worse. The problems won't disappear if we bury our heads in the sand. I promise, once Rodrigo is six feet under, we'll take a long trip."

A shiver of fear runs through me. He talks about death so casually that it sends chills down my spine.

I press my body against his and run my hands along his neck, gently stroking it. Eye to eye, we stare at each other intensely.

"I often forget the darkness inside you; you hide it so easily."

"There's a dark side in all of us, Love, even in you. But you're one of the purest people I know, and I'll do everything to preserve that."

His gaze is burning, full of desire. All signs of his discomfort have vanished. His large hands caress my hips, massaging them slowly. However, this gentle hug doesn't stop the alarm bells ringing in my head, signaling that he's trying to distract me. I'm really worried about him, and the thought of losing him crosses my mind as his lips capture mine to give me a fiery kiss.

I don't want to lose him.

Ever.

His tongue teases the tips of my lips, asking for entry, which I willingly grant. A warm, wet kiss full of passion plunges us into a whirlwind of love, joy, but also fear that it might end one day. I will never get tired of his mouth, his hands, his body against mine. This strong, virile man who seems made of stone is all mine, and nothing will change that.

A throat-clearing brings us back to the present moment. I groan in frustration and see Oscar standing a few feet away, holding a kraft paper envelope.

"Sorry to interrupt," begins the head of security, "but I received some photos that might interest you."

Niklas doesn't seem in the mood to talk about work; his arms tighten authoritatively around me when I try to pull away.

"Can't it wait?"

"I am afraid not, sir."

His serious tone convinces Nik to accept his request. In one swift motion, we get up. My handsome Viking wobbles a little before steadying himself and taking the envelope. He pulls out several snapshots.

"It appears Miss Norell was approached by Rodrigo's men."

In the photos, Jonna is standing in front of two men in black and gray suits. At first glance, nothing seems suspicious. They're in her mother's restaurant in Kiruna.

"Do we know what he wants from her?"

"Not yet, we haven't been able to catch them. Her family has a lot of resources and influence. Besides, Jonna knows a lot about you."

Could she be hurt enough to team up with mafiosos and go after Niklas? She's changed so much since we were teenagers; I no longer know what she's capable of.

I press my lips together and turn to the man beside me.

"Could she hurt you?"

Again, that frustrating silence. So, she can hurt him! A wave of heat sweeps over me. I'm powerless against a gangster like Rodrigo, but Jonna is within my reach, and if there's anything I can do to dissuade her from attacking the one I love, I'll do it.

"What do you think we should do?" asks Niklas.

"We need to review everything she knows about you, everything that could be used against you, to be ready."

Ready for what? A vise grips my insides as I imagine armed men, with Jonna and Rodrigo by their side, coming to attack us. I shift from one leg to the other and then move away, wrapping my arms around myself. My steps lead me to the window, scene unfolds before me. The leafless trees, illuminated by the moon, cast eerie shadows on the ground and in my direction. Their sharp branches, like claws, are shaken by an icy wind and seem ready to shred anything that comes close. This estate, beautiful during the day, terrifies me at night and gives me goosebumps. But I can't let fear take over.

I turn to the two men. "I'm going to talk to her. To Jonna."

I raise my hand to silence Niklas as he's about to speak.

"She's targeting you because of me. We need to have a discussion; one we should have had a long time ago."

"It's not your job to handle this," Niklas says authoritatively, handing the photos back to Oscar.

Oscar intervenes. "It might not be a bad idea. Maybe she'd come to her senses."

Niklas' dark gaze pins Oscar in place. He nods and leaves immediately. Oscar is twice Niklas's age, yet he respects his boss's authority and always makes sure not to overstep.

Once we're alone, I move back to Nik.

"Don't be so stubborn; this could solve some of your problems. Let me handle it."

"No way. Why do you always want to help me? It's my mess, not yours."

"Because I love you, idiot! And if I can help you, I will. Stop pushing me away, I can't stand it."

I can't stand it *anymore*.

We're too distant for my liking. I need to feel that connection between us, that gravity that keeps us from never stay far from each other.

"If you keep this up... then I might as well leave."

He pushes me to bluff.

I pretend to move toward the door, but he's quicker than me. His large hand slams the door shut, and he presses me against it. His cold, fierce gaze seems to pierce my whole being, paralyzing me. He leans his face close to mine and growls near my lips.

"And I… It's because I love you that I don't want you involved in this mess. Do you understand?"

Time seems to stand still as my mind erases everything else and clings to the three little words my heart has been waiting to hear. I can't help but smile.

I murmur, "Say it again."

Sharp-witted, he immediately understands what I mean. His body presses against mine, and his hand slides partly over my cheek and jaw. Under his warm, rough palm, tingles spread across my skin. His voice becomes deeper, more sensual and intense.

"I love you. I've always loved you, and that will never change."

My body relaxes, sinking into a comfort filled with love, while my mind, fogged by the joy and affection, forgets everything else.

"Nick…"

He growls and firmly presses his lips to mine before lifting me.

"I want you to say it again, but moaning while I take you on my desk."

I laugh and kiss him, clinging to him. My butt hits the oak wood. With a sweep of his hand, he clears anything on the desk. His urgency ignites mine. My desire for him is insatiable. Feverishly, I take off his shirt. My hands explore his muscular chest, lingering on his firm pecs. I lean toward one and flick my tongue over his nipple, making it harden. I tease it before moving to the other. His hand tangles gently in my hair.

"You know how to drive me crazy."

I smile against his skin and lift my face to his for a kiss. My hands, a not wasting a moment, unbuckle his belt and remove it, then unbutton and unzip his pants. My fingers slide under the elastic of his boxers, grasping his already erect cock. I free it to admire every inch. I whisper, biting my lip, "Hello, you."

Niklas thrusts his hips forward, giving me full access. One hand rests on my shoulder, while the other unbuttons my blouse to reach my chest. He pushes aside one cup of my bra and takes hold of my breast. Having him like this, at my mercy, makes my desire skyrocket. I love giving him pleasure, and the thought that only I have this power over him now excites me. I bring my hand to my lips, licking it while looking him in the eye.

"You…" he growls, knowing what's coming next.

I place my moistened hand back on his cock, beginning slow, long strokes. Instantly, he opens his lips, taking a deep breath. My fingers are both firm and gentle, applying the pressure he loves. As I stroke him, he massages my breast, teasing and pinching my nipple. I imagine his mouth on it, kissing, licking, and sucking until I lose my mind.

Niklas grips my shoulder more tightly as his pleasure climbs. His cock swells and grows between my fingers. He moves his hips, resembling a Greek statue come to life before my eyes. So big and beautiful. Perfection.

"I want you so much," I whisper.

I pull him toward me and kiss him deeply. Everything about him is intoxicating. He is temptation itself.

Sensing my arousal, he quickly strips me of my pants and almost tears off my panties. I laugh and invite him between my thighs. His cock presses against to my warm and wet pussy. He groans, feeling my wetness, and rubs against it, heating us both up. Several moans escape my lips as my body arches under his.

"Do you want me to make love to you?"

This sweet term sounds in his mouth like an invitation to every imaginable pleasure. I nod vigorously, biting my lip.

"Yes. I want it so much."

My plaintive, almost begging tone drives him crazy. With a powerful thrust, he penetrates me deeply, burying himself to the hilt. I arch, throwing my head back, and moan. I don't care if anyone can hear me, though I doubt anyone is still in the villa. At night, we're completely alone; the staff disappears until morning.

As his hips move back and forth, gripping mine firmly. My legs, wrapped around him, tighten each time he thrust fully inside me. The waves of pleasure that wash over my body are divine. My sex clenches around his hard, hot sex. Without a condom, it's feels even better, and having confirmed we were both disease-free after getting tested, we decided to go without. Plus, I've been on the pill for years.

It feels so good; I'll never get enough. I end up lying back on his desk, surrendering to the pleasure he gives me. He parts my blouse and pushes up my bra, exposing my breasts to his feverish gaze. He makes me feel beautiful and desired, his eyes devouring me with such intensity that it feels like he's seeing beyond the physical, into my heart, into my soul.

"You're so damn sexy. Do you realize that?"

He lifts me onto his hips and carry me to the wall, right beside the door, where he resumes his thrusts into me deliciously. My hips move in perfect sync with his. Our bodies fit together beautifully. I crash into his full lips and kiss him, gripping his hair. Gentle sex with him is wonderful, it's like eating a treat you love. But rough, intense sex is like witnessing a spectacular, colorful fireworks display. My head is full of stars, and I feel like I'm exploding from the inside. I feel so alive with him that sometimes, for a brief moment, I fear waking up in Rikard's apartment.

All that is behind you, move on.

His hard cock continues to thrust into me, eliciting moans each time. His mouth nibbles my neck and moves down to my breast. I arch my back, pushing my breasts toward his lips and shivering as he sucks one nipple, then the other. He alternates several times before ending with gentle bites.

"Mmm! My God…"

He chuckles against my skin and continues his sweet tortures. My nipples, erect and hard, become painfully sensitive under his assault.

"You're going to kill me!"

"Dying of pleasure, that's a beautiful death," he coos, pulling out of me several times only to thrust back in quickly and forcefully.

I arch my back as much as possible and tug on his hair. It's soft and thick. Just like his beard that my fingers love to caress when I'm in his arms.

Niklas continues pleasuring me for a long time until his body shakes with spasms, and he tenses against my body, climaxing deep inside me. I moan with him, holding him tightly with my arms and legs. My inside contract around his sex, pulsing with waves of pleasure.

"Fuck!"

He arches a bit more before relaxing against me, his forehead resting on my shoulder. Breathing heavily and slightly sweaty, he gradually calms down. A blissful smile spreads across my face as I rest the back of my head against the wall.

Drawing on his last strength, he leads us to the couch, where he sits down. His cock still inside me, my body finishing its final contractions. He holds me close and buries his face in my neck. Inhaling my scent, he says, "You're the cure for all my problems."

Not all of them, unfortunately.

If I could fix everything wrong in his life, I would. I stroke his hair and plant a kiss there.

"Sex isn't the answer to everything, but it helps to lighten difficult days."

"And right now, you could definitely say they're tough as hell."

"I want to help you."

He raises his head and looks at me. His complexion is rosier than when I came in, and his eyes are brighter.

"Just being by my side already make a huge difference."

It's not enough, but he doesn't understand that.

We eventually getting dressed again. Leaving the warmth of his body is torture. Nik's office feels cold away from him. As I button my shirt, I watch him put on his clothes carefully, which doesn't escape him. He smiles.

"Want a second round?"

"Not right now. Can you tell me about your scars?"

Whenever I get the chance, I admire the curves of his body and scrutinize his tattoos. His skin isn't perfect, it bears many long-healed wounds, and until now, I've let it be.

"Which ones? There are so many."

"It's sad that you have so many."

Niklas walks around his desk and opens the top drawer, pulling out a pack of menthol cigarettes with a large silver lighter. He waits to take a first puff of smoke before answering me.

"They've shaped me, but it's all in the past. What do you want to know?"

Despite my aversion to the smell of cigarettes, I approach him and lift his shirt at his back. My fingers brush over his left side where the skin is slightly blistered several inches long and about a centimeter wide.

"A fall while rock climbing, it wasn't very high, but I landed on a sharp rock."

He must have suffered, but knowing him, it didn't stop him from trying again. I lift the shirt a little bit higher and brush another scar along the spine. It's tiny.

"Another fall, but I was a teenager. It was at the skate park."

Sport is really his thing. He tried everything.

"You're quite a daredevil."

I walk around to face him and don't flinch as I pass through the nicotine smoke. I look up at his right temple, where an old scar reminds me of a painful memory.

"I remember this one," I murmur, brushing the top of his head.

He grabs my hand and kisses it.

"It was for a good cause."

I shake my head and frown, pulling my hand away.

"No cause is worth getting hit for."

I press my lips together and look at his left arm. I try to roll up his sleeve, but he stops me. Inside, three circular scars are deeply embedded in his flesh. One night, while I was taking his arm off my shoulders to get a drink, those scars caught my eye.

"Those are burns, aren't they?" I whisper, almost ashamed to ask. "Did you do them yourself?"

I can recognize cigarette burns from seeing them on my roommates at the boarding school where Hendrik sent me.

My question unsettles him for a moment, and he shuts down. A taboo subject? I place my hands on his chest and smile affectionately.

"It's okay, we don't have to talk about it."

"It's not that. It was just a stupid thing I did as a troubled teenager. I feel dumb for doing this."

I shake my head and wrap my arms around his waist. On tiptoe, I plant a kiss on his lips.

"One pain for another? I think we've all been there."

"Did you hurt yourself too?" he asks me, raising a thick eyebrow.

"Not physically."

Except for the cold showers, I was too scared to hurt my body— or maybe it was a strength? My torture was mostly internal. For a long time, I blame myself for not being a good girl to my mother, for not being kinder and more grateful for what she did for me. I also regretted that horrible letter I wrote to Nik after my hasty departure; I hated myself for a long time. At boarding school, I constantly isolated myself, thinking that I didn't deserve the happiness and friendship the other girls could offer me. Later, when I was with Rikard, there were times when I thought I deserved what he was doing to me.

"We've all done things we regret or find ridiculous in hindsight. The important thing is to realize it."

Niklas crushes his cigarette butt in the ashtray and exhales the smoke to the side to spare me.

"Let's go take a shower, then I'll show you just how much I've realized that life should be lived to the fullest and without regrets."

On those words, we leave the office to climb the stairs to his room. The villa is so peaceful and quiet that every step echoes, and our breathing seems too loud.

"I'll join you. I just need to grab something to change into my room."

"We're always in mine; you should bring all your stuff here."

"I'll take care of it tomorrow."

In a way, I still feel like we're those two teenagers sneaking from one room to the other. Yet now, as adults, we're not afraid to be seen together. Hendrik's death played a big part in that.

After grabbing cotton pajamas set, I head back to our cozy nest. For some reason, my eyes land on the desk where there are two bottles of medication with labels that look familiar. There are some in Nik's bathroom too. I pick up the plastic bottles and read at the names. I frown.

"Seloken," I murmur, turning the bottles over to see what they're for.

The terms are unfamiliar. One of them, *antianginal*, puzzles me. What could they be for? Lost in thought, I put the bottles back on the desk and join Niklas in the bathroom where he's relaxing under a stream of hot water. What is he hiding from me? And why? I undress, my mind swirling with a thousand questions about the secrets he must be keeping. Our eyes meet, and he smiles as if everything is fine, making me wonder if he's always honest with me.

"I'm almost done."

I open the shower door and slip in beside him. The hot water envelops me while the spray washes away the last traces of our previous wild encounter. I run my hands over his soapy chest and caress him, then move them up to his face, cupping it. His wet, soft beard forms a barrier between his skin and mine. I look into his eyes, putting all the intensity and sincerity of which I am capable. He stops moving, giving me his full attention.

"Nik, you know I love you? I love you so much that I would die if anything happened to you. I don't want to lose you."

Come on, react, tell me what I want to hear!

All I get is a smile and a kiss on the forehead.

"What's gotten into you all of a sudden? I told you everything's fine."

I give him a chance to tell me the truth, but he chooses to lie. I tense up and step back, leaving the shower in anger.

"Hey, baby, what's wrong? Come back!"

I grab a towel and dry off as I exit the bathroom. My movements are sharp and brisk, making my skin redden, but I don't care right now. I hear his heavy steps coming back into the room. He's drenched, with a towel around his hips. His hair frames his face wildly, and there's still soap on his perfect chest. Under different circumstances, the sight would have been a major turn-on and I wouldn't have waited to jump on him. I look away, too angry to face him.

"You're nothing but a liar. I know something's up, and I don't know what it is, but if you won't tell me, it must be serious. Prove me if I'm wrong!" I challenge him.

He closes the remaining distance between us and grabs me by the shoulders. Realizing I'm naked, I wrap the towel around myself and pull away from his grip.

"Talk to me."

"You already know everything there is to—"

"No!" I cut him off, shouting. "I don't want to hear any of your bullshit. Either you tell me what's going on or it's… it's over."

Niklas pale and takes a step back. His steel-blue eyes widen before hardening. Wow, what a quick change!

"You can't be serious?"

"We'll find out soon enough if you don't talk to me."

I lift my chin and give him a defiant look. If he thinks I'm going to back down, he's dead wrong. He taught me to say no, to stand up for myself, and to demand what I want. If we're clashing today, it's thanks to his lessons. He raises a thick eyebrow and crosses his muscular arms against his pecs, staying silent. Again, not the reaction I was expecting. He must not be taking me seriously. With a disdainful pout, I size him up for a moment before storming out, slamming his door behind me.

Ok, maybe that wasn't necessary, but it feels good.

I rush to my room and take my suitcase out from under my bed. With angry gestures, I throw my clothes into it without bothering to fold them. My vision blurs with burning tears that I struggle to wipe away. Is he really so stubborn that he'll let me leave? Is his secret worth it?

I pull too hard on the drawer of my dresser, and it crashes to the floor. I groan and kneel to pick up my underwear. The floor creaks behind me, and before I can turn around, a hand grabs me and pull me up roughly. Surprised, I yank my arm back and my elbow the intruder in the stomach.

Niklas' groan is immediate, followed by a curse.

"Damn it, Lovisa!"

He rubs his belly, grimacing.

"You scared me! Why did you pop up like that behind my back?"

"If you were more aware to your surroundings, you would've heard me coming."

I frown and cross my arms over my chest, glaring at him. "What do you want? I need to pack my bags."

"Don't be ridiculous, you're not going anywhere."

I scoff and roll my eyes. If he thinks I going to listen to him. I turn my back and close my suitcase. Niklas shoves me aside, grabs my suitcase, and throws it across the room.

"Are you crazy?" I scream, pushing him. "Are you completely insane? What's wrong with you?"

"What's wrong with me?" Niklas growls, glaring at me.

He runs a hand through his hair, letting out a bitter laugh. He shifts from one foot to the other, licking his lower lip. Then, without warning, he throws himself on me and kisses me like his life depends on it. His tongue forces its ways past my lips to taste me. I'm way too mad with him to let him do this, and he won't make me forget our fight with sex. His hands tug at my towel, which I hold tightly against me.

"Stop!" I manage to demand against his lips.

I gesticulate in all directions. He ends up releasing me abruptly. I almost fall over.

What the hell is that?

Niklas let out another joyless laugh and steps away, punching my door and sending it slamming against the wall. With a wild look in his eyes, he turns sharply toward me and points a finger.

"I forbid you to leave me! If you don't love me anymore, it's okay, I'll have enough love for both of us, but you're not leaving here."

What is he talking about? This has nothing to do with my feelings for him. He's mixing everything up. I love him to death, but I can't stand lies.

"Sometimes, you remind me of Rikard, and I didn't leave one monster just to find another."

My comment hits him like a cold shower. His face pales. He steps back, and all aggression disappears. I don't want to hurt him, but I can't stay quiet about how he makes me feel when he's violent.

"You don't really mean that…" he murmurs, not daring to look me in the eye.

I press my lips together and take a step in his direction.

"Tell me what I want to know. Tell me what you're hiding from me."

A few strands of hair fall across his face, making him look wilder and more dangerous. He reminds me of a trapped animal baring its teeth to ward off an enemy. I know he would never hurt me despite his harsh words and sometimes rough actions. That's why I approach him slowly. "I need to know."

He remains silent for a moment. His shoulders slump, and he lowers his head before raising it to meet my gaze.

"I have heart failure for about four years. It's not hereditary, but my father had it too, and it's what killed him."

My brain freezes, and no more information gets through, except for what he just told me. Heart failure? What is that? Of course, I've heard these terms before, but I've never really looked into it. This disease affects the heart, a vital organ. I bring my hand to my mouth. It's exactly what I thought; he was hiding something serious from me.

"Are you going to die?" I manage to articulate.

"What? No, Love, I'm not going to die if I'm careful."

He sighs before pulling me into his arms. I press my cheek against his chest, my ear level with his heart.

Thump. Thump. Thump.

Rapid and steady heartbeats. Hearing them soothes me and reassures me. He's alive, but for how long?

"It wasn't just a simple fainting spell, was it?"

"Sometimes my heart acts up when my lifestyle is less than ideal or when I don't take my medication."

I lift my head and look at him.

"Smoking?"

"And alcohol. It doesn't help, but I can't live without nicotine."

"Even to save your life?"

His hand caresses my cheek, then my hair, finally resting in the small of my back.

"I have the best doctor who takes care of me. He'll know how to get me back on my feet if things get bad."

He's probably talking about the doctor I saw leaving earlier. Who knows about his condition? Oscar, undoubtedly. He's his head of security; he probably knows everything about Nik. Alfrida? She's been in his life forever, so she must be aware of something this serious. She never mentioned anything to me in her letters about him, tough. Then again, I never asked.

"What could happen in the long term?" I ask, not sure if I want to hear the answer, afraid it might upset me.

"I could have heart attack after heart attack if not properly treated. I've already had a few, but each time the doc was there for me. At that point, I would need surgery to put a device that help my heartbeat normally when it acts up. I can't remember the exact term."

I swallow and tighten my grip on his arms at the thought of someone opening up his chest, exposing him to danger and making him vulnerable. But if that's the solution…

"Why haven't you already had the surgery?"

"I don't want that thing in my body; as long as I can avoid it, I will."

It's reckless of him to think that way. I give him a light punch on the chest. Immediately, he bends in two, his face contorted in pain.

Oh, no! What have I done?

I rush to support him, panicking.

"Nick! Oh, I'm sorry! Are you hurt? Is it your heart?"

His body sakes with sudden laughter. Realizing I've been fooled, I punch him in the arm.

"Idiot! Don't ever do that again!"

How can he laugh about something so serious? He has no right to scare me like that. I push him, but his laughter only grows louder. He grabs me, and we fall onto my bed.

"Stop it. Let go of me, you idiot!"

I try to wriggle free, but his strong hold prevents it. I give in and relax against him. His laughter reverberates through my body, making me laugh as well. It feels good and eases my worries about him. He seems fine, and now that I know about his condition, I'll do everything to keep him healthy.

"Why didn't you want to tell me?" I ask after we've calmed down.

We are now in his room, him in navy blue boxers and me in my cotton pajamas.

"Because I know you. You're gonna make a big deal out of it and treat me like a child. You're my girlfriend, I don't want you acting like my mother. Alfrida already does that, and my doctor is enougt on my back."

He slips under the covers with me, pulling me into his arm. I look at him, biting my lip. His girlfriend? It's the first time he's used that word to describe what we have.

"So, I'm your girlfriend?"

Niklas smiles and caresses my cheek.

"Of course, you're even more than that. We're a couple."

I blush and snuggle closer to him. His girlfriend, I love that.

"I want you to treat me the same as always, don't change anything," he continues about his illness.

"You can't ask me that."

Niklas growls and forces me to look at him. The room is dark, but the moonlight filtering in allows me to see him.

"That's not an option, Love."

I decide not to argue and let him believe I'll listen to him. He's too stubborn to accept help, and I'm too stubborn to let him do whatever he wants.

With a final kiss, we seal the end of the day, our minds filled with new information.

20

Niklas, 18 years old

She left me.

Lovisa is gone. Gone…

All I got was a letter full of lies as an explanation. Because that's what it is, right? I can't believe she never loved me. It's impossible.

It's been weeks since she's been gone, and yet the pain in my heart doesn't stop tormenting me. When I'm high on alcohol or cocaine, it's almost bearable. Everyone tells me to forget her, but how? I feel her presence everywhere around me and within me. She occupies all my thought and guides my every step. Yet, with each passing day, my resentment toward her image grows. Since the end of high school, my father monopolizes all my time, dragging me along on all his trips. What I do, what he forces me do to those men when they need to be punished, hardens me and makes me cruel. The pain Lovisa causes me will gradually fade, replaced by a gaping void of darkness. I'll owe this change to my father.

***

When I wake up, Lovisa's warm and comforting body is no longer in my arms. Sound asleep, I didn't hear her leave. Glancing at my phone, I realize my alarm didn't ring. Or maybe it did? Either way, I wake up an hour late.

Shit.

I groan as I stand up, massaging my neck. First thing in the morning, I light a cigarette and take a drag as I head to the bathroom. A painful, dry cough seizes me. Those are the worst. When it calms down,

I fill a glass with water and take big gulps. I hate mornings like this. Every time I faint, I can be sure I'll still suffer the next day.

But this time, it's different—more painful, and intense.

My hand goes to my chest, over my heart. How can I have such a weak organ? I have an empire to run; I can't afford any missteps. Yet, there are things I can't control.

Actually, you can, but you refuse to.

I shake my head to silence that voice of reason and get dressed, wedging my cigarette between my lips.

My thoughts drift back to the events of the previous day. Lovisa finally knows about my condition. Part of me is relieved; the lie was weighing on me, and I know she would have been deeply hurt if something serious had happened to me and she didn't know. As for my behavior toward her… The violence I displayed yesterday, and the weeks before, makes me question myself. Am I really like Rikard? That vile man who breaks a woman when things don't go his way? This thought disgusts me. I'd hate to become like him, for Lovisa to see me as a violent man who could hurt her. I need to change; I don't want to become the monster of her nightmares—Rikard already haunts them enough.

My phone vibrates on the nightstand. I check my messages. Oscar informs me that the meeting went well. Today, he's briefing his team at the watchtower at the entrance of the estate. He doesn't need me for that; they're his men, even if I pay them.

The first thing I notice as I go downstairs is the quiet. If there's one thing that's not normal during the day, it's silence. And for good reason, Krigare usually greets me with joyful barks when I reach the ground floor. But this time, not a sound.

"Krigare? Come here, big guy."

No sound of paw scratching on the wooden floor. Where the hell is he? The smell of hot coffee tickles my nose, leading me to the kitchen. No one. A note awaits me near the coffee maker.

I went for a walk with Krigare.
The coffee is ready, and your breakfast is under a cloche.
Alfrida

So that's the reason for the silence. Is Lovisa with her? She's clearly not in the house. I call her while pouring myself a large mug of black coffee. As I finish my cigarette, I open the window above the kitchen sink and stub it out in the ashtray on the windowsill. I take a moment to listen and hear my dog barking in the distance. The glass is so thick that his yelps fade away as I close the window.

"Hello—"

"Babe, where are you?" I ask as I sit down at the table.

"This is Lovisa, I'm not available right now, but leave me a message."

Her voicemail. Her *fucking* voicemail. I hate it when she doesn't answer right away, especially when I don't know where she is. Before I let myself get angry, I remember my new resolution. I take a deep breath.

"Lovisa, it's me. Where are you? Call me back, please."

Controlling myself is much harder than I thought, but I can do it.

I put my phone on the table and slump into one of the chairs. Every morning, I have breakfast with her, and today, being alone, I realize just how much I miss her presence. Being dependent on someone is a bad thing. When they're gone, nothing else matters, and you don't know how to move forward alone.

I've been in this situation before.

I'm in big trouble. I've always been independent, even emotionally, and seeing the grip she has on me grow day by day terrifies me.

I lift the cloche from my plate and notice, without much surprise, that my meal consists of sliced cheese, toast, and a salad. Next to my plate, the local newspaper. I spread butter on my bread and place a slice of cheese on it, devouring it quickly while reading the news, about the damage several stores have suffered. Kiruna is a big city, and my family has ruled the region for decades. We've been untouchable for so long that I've never had to worry about the safety of my people. But things always change. I've provoked Rodrigo's anger by removing him from his position, and now he wants revenge. I haven't been hit by an attack on one of my properties in Kiruna yet, but for how long?

I should have killed him. He wouldn't be the first on my list.

Alfrida interrupts my thought as she walks through the kitchen door. Krigare barks joyfully when he sees me. The old housekeeper wipes his paws and lets him go. She no longer has her old strength, and the dog gives her a hard time. Krigare runs to me and gives me affectionate licks to the hand I extend to him. I scratch his back and then pat his side to shoo him away. Happy, he runs to his water bowl.

"Niklas," she greets me, coming over to kiss my forehead. "I hope the coffee was still hot when you came down."

"It was."

I give her an affectionate look and take a sip of my black coffee. I don't know what I'd do without her. Alfrida is not just a staff. She's the closest thing to a mother. She takes off her coat and her scarf and step out to hang them up in the hallway. When she returns, I question her immediately.

"Have you seen Lovisa? She wasn't there when I woke up."

She purses her lips so tightly they turn into a thin line. She glances at the clock and then back at me.

"Lovisa left early this morning to talk to Jonna and sort things out."

I slam my cup down on the table, spilling hot coffee on my hand. I get up, pushing the chair against the wall. The sudden commotion in the kitchen makes Krigare anxious, and barks at me, wagging his tail.

"You've got to be kidding me!"

I grab the towel Alfrida hands me and wipe my hand.

"Why wasn't I informed?"

Unimpressed by my outburst, Alfrida responds calmly, "She wanted you to rest and have a good breakfast, and you know what? I agree with her, you need to take care of yourself."

I almost regret telling her about my illness. I shouldn't have told her about this heart problem; now she's going to treat me like a baby and take care of me like a poor sick person.

I won't let her do that.

A pain interrupts my momentum as I consider grabbing my keys to join Lovisa. I lean against the table and close my eyes. *My heart.* Acting up again.

I breathe in and out deeply. I feel Alfrida touch my arm, then my forehead. The coolness of her fingers soothes me slightly. Krigare calms down and comes to sit next to me.

"Did you take your medication?"

I shake my head. I forgot, as usual. Alfrida disappears upstairs to get them. I can't wait for her. Lovisa won't be able to do anything except stir up Jonna's fury against us even more.

I put on my jacket and my shoes and head straight for my car. On the way, I notice the Peugeot 604 is gone.

The driveway to the gate is narrow, but that doesn't stop me from speeding. I know every turn like the back of my hand, having driven them thousands of times.

Just like this forest holds no secrets for me.

When I see the gates, I honk to alert the guards to open them. I don't want to stop. They do it quickly, and I speed through without giving them a glance.

A few moments later, my head of security calls me.

"Sir, is everything okay?" asks Oscar.

"Lovisa went to meet Jonna behind my back."

"I thought you knew."

If I had been, I wouldn't have allowed her to leave the villa. I pinch the bridge of my nose to ease the pain piercing my chest.

"No. Is the tracker on her car?"

"I'll send you where she is right away," he says, anticipating my next request.

I know it's wrong, spying on her goes against the man I'm trying to become. But her safety matters so much to me that I'm willing to make a few exceptions. Besides, it's not to stalk her day and night, but to help her in situations like this.

I wait less than a minute before he sends me the location, which matches with Jonna's building. It will take me half an hour to get there, less if I exceed the speed limit. I see my reflection in the rearview mirror; my sweaty forehead and pale skin make me look like a walking corpse. I catch my reflection in the rearview mirror; my sweaty forehead and pale skin make me look like a walking corpse. I wipe it with my jacket and press the accelerator deeper.

Faster.

Come on.

I grit my teeth and focus on the road, whose edges become blurred from the speed. I love driving fast, but now it's vital, necessary. It's not a want, but a need.

I try calling Lovisa, but it goes straight to voicemail. Again. I growl in frustration and pound the steering wheel.

Minutes and miles fly by, my engine roaring louder until I finally reach the city.

Finally.

I reduce my speed and navigate the streets until I arrive at a luxurious apartment building. I park, braking abruptly behind Lovisa's car, and get out of my vehicle.

The wind whips my face, giving me goosebumps, and the sweat on my forehead freezes, chilling me to the bones.

I glance around and spot the two young women in the grove of trees at the edge of the park, across from the building. They're standing some distance apart, engaged in what appears to be a heated conversation, judging by their animated gestures. I stop in my tracks, suddenly nauseous.

I take a deep breath before walking toward them again; now is not the time to vomit on my shoes.

"You always thought everything was yours," I hear Jonna says.

"Are you kidding me?" says Lovisa.

My arrival interrupts their conversation. Lovisa looks at me, surprised, while Jonna shoots me a murderous glare, which I gladly return.

"Nik, are you okay?" ask Lovisa.

"Let's go," I growl, grabbing Lovisa by the wrist. "I'll deal with this later."

With no time or patience for their argument, I just want to get out of here.

There are more urgent matters.

"I told you I'd take care of it," Lovisa protests.

"And I told you to stay out of it!"

Resisting the urge to drag her to my car, I let her walk at her own pace. Surprisingly, Jonna lets us leave without a word. What is she up to? As I cast a final glance in her direction, I catch a sly smile on her lips.

In front of the car, I put my hand on the roof and close my eyes. My breathing is erratic. Am I… out of breath? For so little? Dr. Söderholm's words echo in my mind. Could it be—?

"You're driving," I declare, handing the keys to Lovisa.

"What? But why?"

I force her into the driver's seat and settle into the passenger side. I groan as my back hits the seat, arching slightly.

"Just do what I say, damn it!"

She fastens her seatbelt, giving me a worried look. Unfamiliar with my car, she revs the engine a bit too loudly as she starts it.

"You don't look well. Is it your heart?"

A bead of sweat runs down my temple and gets lost in my beard. I struggle to tap on the car's touchscreen and press to contact Oscar.

"If I'm not mistaken, I'm having a heart attack." Saying it out loud makes the situation more real and terrifying.

I'm scared.

I'm fucking scared!

I never get scared.

Lovisa stares at me, her jaw almost dropping in shock. I can't bear to look at her any longer without feeling a sense of panic about what's happening to me.

The pain in my chest is constant and seems unwilling to let go.

He picks up after two rings, not giving my pretty redhead a chance to respond.

"Did you find her?"

"She's with me. Oscar, let Söderholm know I'm coming. I need him urgently."

My voice is weak and uncertain.

Damn, I'm really not doing well.

I take a deep breath before continuing for Lovisa, "Follow the GPS, and you'll be fine."

I search for the address and select it. The pain rises in my head, making it hard to think clearly. I feel the faintness coming. My body starts to relax in my seat.

Beside me, Lovisa drives at high speed, making sharp movements with the steering wheel. Driving a car she's not familiar with in worrying circumstances makes her clumsy in her actions.

Easy, Love...

My mouth refuses to obey me; I can't tell her to calm down.

I hear her voice telling me that everything will be okay, that the doctor will get me back on my feet, but I'm unable to answer her.

"Stay with me," she begs me. "Stay with m—"

***

Why do people insist on choosing for me?

Lovisa, Oscar, and Dr. Söderholm have teamed up to stand against the terror that I seem to embody in their eyes.

I growl for the umpteenth time and try to get out of this damn hospital bed, but my current weakness doesn't help me push away Oscar's arms, which keep me lying down. I glare at him and spit in his face, "I swear, if you don't let go of me immediately, you're fired!"

"Nik, calm down, it's for your own good," Lovisa says, placing her hand on my shoulder.

I try to suppress my rage, but it's difficult.

"You had a heart attack, Mr. Ekman, it could have been fatal if you hadn't been brought to my clinic in time," Dr. Söderholm intervenes. "Your condition is getting worse. Your health is not the same as it was four years ago."

I know what he's getting at, and this idea pisses me off.

"If my chest is going to be opened up, it'll be to remove a bullet, not to put in a damn box."

"A cardiac defibrillator," the doctor corrects me, "and it's not open-heart surgery. It could fix everything, and your symptoms will disappear. You could live longer if you take the necessary step to preserve your health."

I've heard his spiel several times before. Every time I've ended up between these walls.

Oscar lets go of me when I finally give in. I tug at the ridiculous hospital gown they put on when I was unconscious and look at the doctor.

"Give me a year," I request.

"No. That will be too late."

I sigh and roll my eyes. "Then give me six months. I can't be weakened right now. I need to be at the top of my game."

The doctor places my medical file on the bedside table and looks at me sternly.

"You pay me a lot, perhaps too much, to take care of you, but you refuse everything I suggest, and you only half-listen to my advice. If you continue down this path, only death will await you at the end of the road."

Death.

I've always known I'd die young.

In a shootout because of drug trafficking, from falling off the top of a mountain, in a car accident. At twenty-seven, I've already had so many experiences that could have killed me, but I'm still here, and I don't plan on leaving anytime soon.

I shake my head and wave my hand in front of him.

"A few more months won't change anything."

"You're mistaken. It could change everything. I'll keep you until tomorrow morning. You have a few hours to decide."

I'm not thrilled about having to stay overnight here, but if it's the price to pay to avoid immediate surgery, then so be it.

Dr. Söderholm leaves, taking my medical file with him. I squint as I watch him go, then turn to Oscar.

"Don't do that again," I scold.

He nods and adjusts his suit.

"If you don't need me anymore, I'll leave."

Oscar exits after the doctor.

Now that I'm alone with Lovisa, she explodes.

"You're completely insane! Do you realize how scared I was? Driving without knowing if you were still alive beside me!"

Her face flushed with anger, but also with pain at the thought of losing me, gives me a glimpse of her fury. Her beautiful green eyes glare at me.

She hits my shoulder.

"Calm down."

"Stop telling me to calm down! Stop telling me that everything's fine, because it's not! You almost died today next to me, and I couldn't do anything. You selfish bastard!"

Seeing her get angry and insult me is something exciting. The tigress inside her is unleashed to throw more insults at me. I can't help but smile as she jumps in place while continuing to talk. I feel myself hardening, my blood pulsing in my lower abdomen and speeding up my heartbeat.

The pain… Shit, it's happening again.

"Are you listening to me?"

"Half listening. I almost died, come into my arms instead."

She lets out a furious cry and stomps her foot. I try to grab her, but she moves away toward the window overlooking the clinic's park.

"You don't take anything seriously," she grumbles. "I wonder if deep down you're hoping to die, given the little effort you make."

Bullshit!

I value life as much as anyone else.

She doesn't know what she's talking about.

My days are a series of efforts to stay alive. Exercise, healthy food, no more cocaine in my body, just in the pockets. I smoke and drink often, but I never get wasted. And she dares to say I'm not making an effort?

I get up. I wobble from one foot to the other to test my balance.

Before joining her, I take off this robe; underneath, I'm still in pants with a bare chest.

She's angry because she's scared. I understand that feeling; it drove me when I lost her at the Red Mill, I had feared the worst when she was nowhere to be found.

I put my hands on her shoulders and squeeze them.

"I had no right to leave you with the responsibility of my weakness. I should have gone straight to the clinic instead of coming to get you."

Her shoulders tense up, and she sighs loudly before facing me. Her face, usually soft and smooth, wears a troubled pout.

"I don't blame you for scaring me, but for taking an unreasonable risk. You should have gone to the clinic as soon as you started feeling unwell because you needed to, not to avoid inconveniencing me."

She bites her lips and locks her gaze with mine. "When it comes to you, to your health, you can ask me anything you want, it will never bother me."

The tone of her voice has calmed down, even though she seems to be on her guard.

I nod and kiss her forehead, hugging her. "I'm used to handling things on my own; I never ask for help."

"That's exactly your problem," Lovisa mutters, resting her cheek against my chest.

I run my hand through her red curls and bring one to my lips. The scent of her floral shampoo teases my senses. I absorb it, closing my eyes. I never want to forget her fragrance.

We stay like that for a while until someone knocks on the door, breaking the silence of the room.

"Sorry to disturb you, I'm bringing the form for the surgery."

A young nurse approaches with a paper and places it on the table, in front of the bed.

"I said that—"

"Thanks, we'll take a look," Lovisa interrupts.

"My colleague will be here shortly with your medication."

Lovisa leaves my arms and grabs the document as the nurse exits. The clinic staff's uniforms are different from those in a basic hospital. Here, women wear white coats with matching caps. Dr. Söderholm is attached to the old-fashioned uniforms. Only the medical equipment is state-of-the-art; there's nothing better within a thousand miles. Hendrik found it ridiculous that I put so much money into this place, but for me it's vital. I want to be treated by the best and always be a priority. Even though I rarely come here, I have a reserved room, which is why the modern and minimalist decor of this room resembles the Iron House villa.

"Tell me you're going to do it."

I grab a bottle of water from the table and glance at the paper. Damn document, reminding me of my infirmity.

I take a long sip before answering, "I'll do it, but not right away."

I won't change my mind. The subject is closed for me, and I won't go over it again.

Lovisa is the one I love, and she has a say in my life decisions, but there are some issues where only my opinion matters.

"I know what I'm doing. I'll be more vigilant, and I won't have any more problems before the surgery."

Looking unconvinced. I realize I need more arguments to reassure her, as well as to reassure myself. I hate what I can't control, and this illness has been ruining my life for four years. The time has come to remedy that. I just need a few more months.

Now that this is settled, another issue comes to mind. An issue just as thorny as my heart problems.

"I explicitly asked you not to go see Jonna, yet I found you with her today."

I don't want to control her; but for this, I need to set boundaries because she's dealing with Jonna, a devious snake who won't hesitate to strike if Lovisa isn't careful.

Ashamed, she bites her lip and tucks a lock of her hair behind her ear.

"I know, but no matter what you say, it's not just your problem. I had to try to do something. Talking to her was necessary."

I don't know what frustrates me more, the timid and subdued Lovisa or the Lovisa with a hero complex who ignores my warnings and does whatever she wants.

"What am I going to do with you?" I sigh, smiling.

Part of me can't help but feel proud of her changing character. She's asserting herself.

"So, what's the result of your conversation?"

"You were right, it was pointless. I even tried to apologize, but it only made her angrier because she thinks I'm pitying her and that she's above that, above me."

Jonna has always had an ego problem.

She's like me.

She always needs to prove that she's the best and that no one can surpass her. That's why I understand her feeling of failure, the fact that she refuses to accept losing to someone like Lovisa. Someone insignificant in her eyes, but who means everything to me.

Lovisa meant well, I know that. Still, I wonder if her intervention might make things worse.

But could it really get any shittier?

"Well, it's done, we can't turn back time. Thanks for trying, but let me handle it now."

She nods and looks away at the door.

"I hate hospitals," she confesses, crossing her arms. "They mean sickness and death, and when someone close to me is in one, I hate them even more."

She's not wrong, but they also symbolize hope and life. It's here that the gravely ill are healed, and newborns come into the world, the new generation set to walk the earth.

"You don't have to stay. Go home, you'll be more comfortable."

"No. I want to stay with you, especially after what happened. It's still there." Lovisa taps her temple.

"Don't think about it anymore. Come rest with me."

I take her hand and lie down on the bed, holding her close.

Out of habit, I reach for the bedside table, but realize my pack of cigarettes isn't there. Damn habit.

Lovisa snuggles against me, pulling the sheet over us. Her fingers caress the Grim Reaper tattoo on my chest.

"This drawing is a bad omen, a prediction engraved in your skin, as if you knew what would happen to you soon."

"We all die someday, and it can happen in any way."

"May we live as long as possible."

I nod.

That's what I want too, to spend my life with her by my side.

Overcome with fatigue, I fall asleep quickly.

I wake up several times throughout the day, each time falling back asleep with the vision of Lovisa either in my arms or out of bed. Meanwhile, Oscar came by to check on me. Around 6 p.m., he's sitting by my bed and brings unexpected news as Lovisa has gone to get us some coffee.

"Torston was captured by Gunkil and Fredrik."

"Rodrigo's right-hand man?"

He nods and shows me a photo on his phone.

"He got caught visiting a prostitute at a club he frequents often."

Caught because he couldn't keep his cock in his pants. I laugh to myself at the thought of his disappointment at not being able to fuck his girlfriend, on top of being caught by the enemy of his boss.

Rodrigo is going to lose it when he finds out we have him. He's going to panic. The noose is tightening around him. We're finding more and more of his hideouts and the places he frequents.

We're close to the endgame.

Soon he'll be in my hands.

"I sent the jet to pick up Gunkil and Fredrik. They're bringing Torston. I've already got everything set up for the interrogation in the basement."

Interrogation isn't my favorite part. Killing someone cleanly and quickly is more my style. I get no pleasure from inflicting pain, even if it's sometimes necessary.

"What did the doctor say? Will you be okay for tomorrow?"

By this, he wants to know if I'll be able handle it and get the answers we need.

I sit up and look at him sternly. Even in a hospital bed, I'm still his superior, and I'm just as fierce and ruthless when it's needed.

"Don't worry about me. Just make sure he stays alive until tomorrow morning."

21

Lovisa, 16 years old

A small lie can have big consequences. The only comfort I find in this boarding school for girls in the depths of Sweden countryside, where I've been sent, is music. Hendrik, against all odds, kept his promise by allowing me this pleasure.

Yet, a part of me can't be fully satisfied with this life. I wish I could go back, return to Iron House, but if I do, Hendrik promised that he'd let Sören take care of me and make Niklas's life a living hell. By staying away, I ensure his safety, at least partly, because I know Hendricks has to give him a hard time every day to turn Niklas into a monster. Like him. This place is my penance for loving him. It was forbidden, and we did as we pleased anyway.

***

We can finally leave.

Even though this clinic feels more like a rest center than a hospital, it still smells like one.

I practically run outside to get to Niklas's car. In the rush yesterday, I parked in the middle of the parking lot, but later Oscar move it to a place reserved for patients.

How did you feel about driving it?" Niklas asks me as we leav the parking lot.

"I couldn't really enjoy it, given the circumstances, but it's powerful. I felt strong behind the wheel."

That's exactly what it felt like.

The car, light and fast, drives silently and rumbles when needed.

Behind the wheel, you feel invincible, like you could drive for days without ever getting tired.

"I need to get my car back."

Yesterday, my father's car was left in front of Jonna's building, and I must admit that I'm not reassured to know it's there. Jo knows its sentimental value, and I fear what might happen to it if she wanted to use it to get to me.

"Don't worry, Oscar will take care of it."

Niklas taps on his phone and sends a text. Then he turns his attention back to me. His serious expression tells me that the conversation is about to get serious.

"It would be best if you weren't at the house for the next few hours. Maybe you could go into town with Alfrida to relax?"

My stomach knots up when I think about our conversation from last night. The idea of closing my eyes and ears and being miles away crosses my mind, but honestly, I'd rather stay at the estate.

"I'll play the violin in the forest. I need to practice, and it has been too long since I put it aside."

The absence has been noticeable for some time now. I need music in my life, and since my return to Iron House, my career has been put on hold. My colleagues often check in on me. My solo has been taken over by a friend who plays very well, and I have no doubt about her success, but I can't wait to reclaim my place. Since I was a teenager, I've aspired to be the best. I've had the most talented teachers, and I practiced every day. I don't want to lose my place, which is why I would like to come back to the group once things calm down here.

"Play loudly so I can hear you. I love listening to you."

And I love playing for you.

These moments, unique and intense, offered by the sounds emanating from my instrument, awaken so many emotions in me that I often shed a tear. The violin is for me the most beautiful instrument ever created, and sharing that with Niklas is a pure joy. A joy that could be short-lived if he continues to refuse the surgery suggested by Dr. Söderholm. It's not definitive, just postponed, but it scares me because even if he thinks he can last another six months, it's not certain. He's playing with his life like playing Russian roulette, counting on the luck not to hit the wrong turn.

So reckless, so stupid, sometimes.

I sigh inwardly and focus on the road the rest of the way.

Nik barely gets out of the car when Oscar greets him, looking serious. Today promises to be very dark due to yesterday's events, but also because of what will follow. Niklas briefly kisses me on the lips and leaves me in the hall to immediately disappear into the basement.

As for me, I give Krigare a few strokes before going upstairs to get my violin. When I come back down, I linger in front of the basement door, guarded by a security guard. I can't help but hold my breath, waiting for any alarming noise. But this place, more than the rest of the house, is perfectly isolated, and I hear no noise, no scream or moan that would give me a glimpse of the horrors that must be taking place inside.

"Come, Krigare."

I pass through the kitchen hoping to see Alfrida, but the old lady isn't there. I step out into the garden and head to the frozen lake, wrapped in my coat, even though today's the temperatures are around 35°degrees Fahrenheit, which is much better than last week.

Some parts of the lake have started to crack, water seeping through in places. Walking on it would be madness, the surface could give way under my weight. This beautiful place also holds many bad memories, but Hendrik's death seems to have erased all traces of darkness from this splendid scenery.

"It's beautiful, isn't it?"

That voice, coming out of nowhere, nearly gives me a heart attack. Krigare rushes behind me, barking. As I turn around, I see Oscar crouching down to pet the dog. A bit farther away, a man stands tall, a gun strapped to his waist.

"Did I scare you?" Oscar gets up, I can almost hear his knees crack under the weight of his fifty years. As Oscar approaches, the dog leaves us to throw himself on a dead tree trunk.

"It's okay," I say with a pause, lips pursed, before continuing, "Why aren't with Nik?"

He's his head of security, his right-hand man, who's watched over him forever. Oscar is like his shadow.

"I came to make sure, at his request, that you're doing okay. Tomas will stay with you."

I glance over his shoulder. The man, who must be around my age, is as impassive as a statue, his gaze so serious it's almost comical.

I highly doubt anyone would suddenly appear to attack us in broad daylight.

"Shouldn't you be focusing your units on more important area?"

He smiles, his eyes sparkling, catching mine.

"Wherever you are, that place becomes the most important area to protect."

I blush and lower my head, clutching my violin case against me. "You've always been very kind to me."

Taking a deep breath that freezes my lungs, I turn back to the lake and admire its frozen surface.

"I remember after my mother's death, I took refuge in the property's mausoleum. I know she's not buried there, since she wasn't married to Hendrik, but at least there, no one came looking for me. I think this place has always scared them, Nik and his father."

I never knew why. I suppose coming to the place that would be their final resting place must have frightened them.

"But you, you came. You told me that death isn't the end, but the beginning of a new life, that one day, I'll join her, and my sorrow will diminish over time."

Oscar stifles a small laugh and shoves his hands into his coat pockets. "How could I forget such sappy words?"

I smile and shake my head slightly. "It helped me a lot. I don't know if I believe in life after death, but it helped me better cope with my grief. I never thanked you for that."

"You don't have to. I only did—"

"Your job?" I interrupt. "Your job to take care of Hendrik's security, and now Niklas's."

Krigare come back to us, seeking for our attention. In his mouth, a piece of bark half-eaten and dripping with saliva. He can forget about me throwing it for him. I pick up another thin branch and toss it. The dog happily runs to fetch it. His naivety makes me jealous. For him, life is simple, it's just about eating, sleeping, and playing.

"Don't you aspire to peace? To stop everything and start a new life?"

"I've always lived to serve. First in the army, then for the Ekman family. *That's* my life. I can't see myself doing anything else."

I don't know whether to applaud his courage for dedicating his life to protecting people or feel sorry that his life is all about that.

I just smile. Who am I to judge his choices? I haven't made any better ones in my life.

"I leave you under the protection of Tomas," Oscar tells me, smiling at me. "It was nice talking to you."

"Likewise."

I watch him walk away toward Tomas to give him an order.

Once he's out of sight, I do what I came here to do.

I place my case on the ground and take out my violin. With gloves on, I grab my bow and start playing the first notes, which immediately transport me.

The presence of Tomas doesn't bother me; I'm used to performing in front of hundreds of spectators.

Music is a universal language that touches everyone in many ways. No matter where you are, there's always music, whether it's from a TV, a radio, an instrument, or even your own voice. There's also the melody of nature, animals, insects. The whole universe sings every day; you just have to listen to enjoy it.

Krigare barks joyfully and runs around me. I can't help but laugh at his antics.

Suddenly, an idea crosses my mind.

I take out my phone and prop it against my case. From there, I activate the camera and livestream the video on my Instagram. The view is stunning, to my left the frozen lake, behind it the vast forest with its skeletal trees, the ground covered in snow, and Krigare running everywhere, his black and white fur with a big brown spot on his muzzle contrasting with the ground. As for me, I stand in the middle, playing the violin for people watching me. A virtual audience, but they're really there.

I rub the strings of my instrument, again and again, producing melodies that I know by heart. The echo of sounds reverberates off every stone, every tree stumps all the way to the villa. Part of me wishes that the music reaches Niklas and soften his heart and what he's doing.

Exhausted in my arms, but mostly in my fingers, I decide to stop and wave to all those who followed me. I end the live and put away my instrument.

My heart is lighter and the urge to laugh and dance with Krigare comes over me. I end up falling into the snow and lie there, contemplating the blue sky and its vastness. My wet clothes bother me, but not enough for me to immediately go warm up inside. I take a deep breath, breathing in the fresh air and the scent of damp wood that covers on the ground nearby. The quiet is so soothing. Living away from the city has its advantages. We are far from everything, there is only nature and us.

"Do you know a better place to live, Krigare?"

The dog barks and ends up lying down a little further away. In my pocket, my phone vibrates and the sound of a notification gently rings out. I turn on my screen and almost drop it when I see *Rikard Rapace wants to send you a message* displayed.

Rik!

What does he want from me?

Since our breakup, he has never tried to contact me. Until now. I could delete his message and continue to admire the sky. But if I do that, I'll never know what he wants to tell me.

Nervously, I click on his message, biting my lip.

A link to a photo. I open it. The image of a violin in a black case with a red silk interior. *My* violin. I go back upon hearing a second notification and see that Rikard has just written to me.

[If you don't come to pick it up,

I'll throw it in the trash.]

"No!" I shout as I stand up.

Behind me, Tomas rushes in my direction.

"Is everything okay, miss?" he asks, his gun in hand, scanning the area, ready to shoot.

"Yes, yes, excuse me," I say, turning my back to him and focusing on my phone.

Rikard knows how important this instrument is to me. It has accompanied me to every one of my concerts; I never play with any other instrument on stage. This violin is my lucky charm, the one I practiced with for thousands of hours while my mother's violin remained at Iron House.

My fingers quickly type on my phone.

[Please don't do this.]

[Beg me, I love it.]

You bastard, he's playing with me.

[I owe you nothing, quite the opposite.

If you don't come get it,

I'll smash it into a thousand pieces.]

I can't let him do that. I hate that he's manipulating me again, but if I don't go along with him, he might put his threats into action.

> [I'll come.
> I don't know when,
> but I'll do it as soon as possible.]

"Krigare, let's go home."

I put away my phone, pick up my violin and head straight for the villa, with Tomas right behind me.

The cold from my wet clothes no longer bother me; I'm warm from head to toe, and all I want to do is get back inside and tell Niklas about the situation.

As I walk, I'm already visualizing the continuation of events. He wouldn't be opposed to lending me his jet to go to Stockholm. He probably wouldn't let me go alone, and the idea of him accompanying me wouldn't displease me. I want to get him away from Kiruna, and this would be a good opportunity.

I pass through the kitchen again. Krigare has dirtied the floor and left his prints everywhere; the cleaning lady won't be pleased. I take off my coat and place my violin on the table. Without waiting, I leave the kitchen and turn directly to the right, where the basement door is. A man, Gregor, blocks my way.

"Excuse me, miss, you can't go down there," he says.

Tomas stands beside him, looking at his colleague, bewildered.

"I don't know what's going on," Tomas says.

"It's important. I need to talk to him," I insist.

Gregor looks over his shoulder at the closed door, then nods.

"Wait here, I'll inform him. You can join Max up front, Tomas."

I step back, thanking him, and watch him disappear behind the door while the other man slips out through the front door.

Exhausted, Krigare has also disappeared.

Once again, curiosity grips me when I hear a whimper behind the half-open door.

Don't open it.

I stare at the handle, which seems to call out to me.

I know I shouldn't, just like with Rikard's message, but it's stronger than me. I put my hand on the iron and open the door. I pull it slowly. The stairs are dimly lit.

Don't go down.

My legs don't listen to my reason and descend the concrete steps. Down, I see Gregor passing through a door in the distance. I follow the same direction, crossing an old shooting range and a deserted boxing ring a bit further. I'm not interested in the rest of the scenery and quicken my pace until I reach the second door.

Behind it, I hear Nik's voice, slightly out of breath.

"Speak, and I'll stop. Tell me where I can find Rodrigo."

The stranger swallows. I guess the loud spit I hear is coming from him.

"Go fuck yourself, you fucking asshole!"

"You're tough, aren't you? But I highly doubt you'll keep that courage when I rip out all your teeth."

I pale and take a step back. What the hell is going on?

Don't act shocked; you knew what was happening here.

No! Not this, not like this. I knew he'd probably rough him up, even though I avoided thinking about it, but torture him? Is Nik really capable of that? I don't know if it's the first time he's resorted to these methods, but it's a dangerous slope that's hard to turn back from.

Hand shaking, I slowly push open the door, holding my breath.

"Oh my God!" I exclaim, bringing my hand to my mouth.

22

Niklas, 19 years old

Tonight, I puked my guts outs. And even when my stomach was completely emptied, I kept spewing bile until I collapsed to the ground. The cause? The blade cutting into the flesh of a man who had betrayed my father. I hated it. Yet, my hand continued to carve into the thin, translucent skin under my father's lecherous gaze. This son of a bitch gets off of seeing me on seeing me descent into Hell. This initiation ritual is my open door and the finish line to my new destiny. I'm now an official member of his cartel. I can't escape anymore. I belong to Hendrik until my death.

***

Torston, Rodrigo's right-hand man, shows a much greater tolerance for pain than I had hoped. He doesn't flatter under my fists, whose knuckles are as bruised as his face. He's just a bastard trying to get me dow his boss, but he deserves credit for being loyal to Rodrigo, and I can't take that away from him. But every man has his limits, and   break through his courage.

"You'll talk eventually."

He sneers and spits his warm, viscous blood mixed with his saliva in my face.

The bastard.

The acrid smell of blood fills my nostrils. A familiar smell that no longer fazes me over time.

I punch him in the nose. It cracks under my fingers, and a spray of blood drips onto his swollen mouth and his already soaked clothes, soaked with icy water and sweat. I suspect he's pissed himself, given the wafting odor.

Gunkil started the interrogation by hitting him in the abdomen and throwing buckets of icy water at him from a tank a little further into the room. I know how cold it can be, having experienced it with Hendrik when I disobeyed him. This familiar place sticks to my skin like the dirt that surrounds us. This place reeks of humidity and dust.

"Maybe we should move on to something stronger," Oscar suggests, unfolding his arsenal of tools.

He grabs a pair of pliers.

Understanding what he intends to do, Torston pukes his guts to the side and coughs his lungs out. He then raises his head and gives us a look full of terror and hatred.

"Tear out my tongue, because you won't get anything from me. I'd rather die than suffer Rodrigo's wrath!"

Is he that terrible? Can he do worse than what Torston is currently enduring? I grab the pair of pliers and approach him. His dislocated body is a mixture of mutilated flesh and bones. Even if he gets out of here, he'll never be the same and won't walk properly again. I broke one of his kneecaps with a baseball bat. The sound of his bone shattering nearly made Fredrik faint, unused to such violence.

And the worst part is, Torston hasn't spilled a single piece of information yet. He's tough. Could I have held on if I were him?

I hadn't displayed such violence in a long time. I hate resorting to this kind of practice, which always pushes me further into darkness. The possibility of any redemption fades away. My existence is ruled by brutality and the men I break under my will. By accepting my inheritance, I must deal with all aspects of my new status.

Gregor enters the room, momentarily distracting me. He murmurs something to Oscar.

"Got to hell, motherfucker!" Torston bellows, pushing me to turn my attention back to him.

His one remaining eye looks at the pliers near his face. He groans and tries to pull back, but the chair is firmly bolted to the floor. He has no way out.

"You're tough, aren't you? But I highly doubt you'll keep that courage when I rip out all your teeth."

I grab him by the jaw and force him to open his mouth. It's an excruciating pain to have a tooth ripped out without anesthesia. He'll crack, there's no other way. Otherwise, I'll be forced to kill him without getting any information.

Sweat runs down my temples. My body is boiling from the efforts put forth during this interrogation. I wouldn't mind a little break, but he's on the verge of breaking despite his stubborn refusal to talk. Just a little more and—

"Oh, my God!"

As one, we all turn toward the door. Oscar and Gregor draw their weapon, but just as quickly, they holster them when they realize it's Lovisa. Her horrified expression reflects the scene with horror.

Holy shit!

What the hell must be going through her mind right now? I can't imagine what image we must be presenting.

"What the hell are you doing here? Go back upstairs right now," I order, tossing the pliers on the table, which clatter against the other tools.

I don't want to frighten her any more than necessary, but she can't stay here. I want to shield her as much as possible from the horrors that are going on here.

I approach, but she immediately takes a step back, eyes widening. I half-turn toward a dirty mirror above the sink and understand why I'm so horrifying to her. Splatters of blood stain my sweater and face. My injured hands are a mix of bright and dark red. I look like something out of a horror movie.

I soften and give her a compassionate look.

"Lovisa, you shouldn't be here."

"I just—I…," stammers Lovisa, searching for her words.

She turns on her heels and bolts, slamming the door behind her. I want to follow her, but I can't leave without having finished my job. I need to put myself back into the role of the ruthless cartel leader to continue this grim task.

"Nik," Gunkil starts behind me, "We can take over if you want."

I shake my head, come back to the table, and grab the pliers with renewed determination.

"Gregor, go upstairs and make sure Lovisa hasn't run off."

I roughly grab Torston's jaw, force his mouth open, and manage to rip a canine tooth out of him. He groans in pain and spits blood. With a shudder, he passes out. His body has been abused for far too long.

"Let's take a break. We'll continue when he wakes up."

The sound of the tooth being torn from its gum, nerves ripping out with it, is a nauseating noise that turns my stomach. I throw the pliers with the tooth onto the table and rush to the sink. Leaning against the grimy edges, I inhale and exhale deeply. The smell of iron, vomit on the floor, and my own unwellness makes me feel queasy. I don't really enjoy torturing, but over the years, I've learned to control myself. I must still be weak from my heart attack the night before.

Fuck, get it together.

No one in the room dares to say anything. They better not, I don't want their pity. I chuckle and shake my head. What must I look like, Niklas Ekman, sensitive to a little vomit and the smell of blood? I was never like this, so weak, so incapable. I grunt and splash my face with cold water.

I give myself one more minute to gather my thoughts before straightening up at the first groan from Torston.

"Our dear friend is back with us," I say, turning to him with a smile. "Well, where were we?"

****

I wash my hands, scrubbing away all traces of blood. Behind me, Gunkil and Fredrik are wrapping up Torston's body. He finally spilled the beans after losing a few teeth and getting a beating from Gun.

"We don't have much time, if we want to make it in time, we need to leave as soon as possible," Oscar advises, watching the two men secure the tarp around the corpse.

The smell of raw meat fills the room, reminding me of an old butcher shop in Kiruna that closed down years ago.

The smell of death.

"I'm going to talk to Lovisa. Meanwhile, get everything ready for our departure."

He nods and leaves the room. I wipe my hands and check the damage to my knuckles. I have several open wounds and bruises on some fingers, the last evidence of the brutality with which I struck Torston.

"You guys okay?" I ask my friends who are lifting the body.

"Yeah. We're going to go through the tunnel; a buddy of mine works at the funeral home, he knows we're coming," Fredrik informs me.

In the main basement room, there's a hidden entrance leading to a long tunnel that ends in a room with the backup generator. From there, an exit opens into the woods on the property.

"Don't get caught."

As Gunkil walks past me, I grab his pack of cigarettes from the back pocket and light one up immediately.

"Give me one," Gunkil says.

I stuck the one I just lit between his lips and light myself another.

"Hurry up and come back; you're coming with us," I say.

Gunkil's face lights up as if I've just told him he won a million kroner.

"A trip to Stockholm, awesome!" he exclaims, holding the cigarette between his lips.

"We're not going there to have fun."

"Nothing's stopping us from mixing work and pleasure."

He'll never change, and honestly, it's for the best. Behind his emancipated adult façade is the teenager who loves to have a good time and party. Sometimes a bit too much. With him around, you never get bored.

I follow them and cross the first room to a cabinet with sport equipment. It's about thirty feet from the entrance to the house, along the same wall. I slide the cabinet, its wheels hidden behind a metal edge, and open the door to the tunnel. I switch on the lights, which cast a very faint white glow in the passage.

I close the door behind them. Before going upstairs, I take off my sweater and roll it into a ball. The cold of the basement gives me goosebumps as I find myself in a simple short-sleeved T-shirt.

I take few more drags on my cigarette, finish it, and toss the butt behind me. I climb the stairs and arrive in the silent hall.

Way too quiet.

At the foot of the stairs, Gregor is standing guard.

"Where is she?"

"Upstairs, sir. She refused to let me follow her."

Thank goodness. No man except me or Oscar, whom I trust completely, is allowed to be alone in a room with Lovisa. It happened once when we were in the attic. That day, when I woke up and she wasn't on the couch anymore, I feared the worst. But thankfully, Hendrik and Sören just laugh after knocking me out and forced Lovisa back to her room, leaving me alone.

My father has done so much harm, to Lovisa, to Sigrid, and to me. Even my mother. She left and abandoned me, but did she have a choice? Looking back, I understand that she didn't; he would never have allowed her to leave with his only heir. Despite that, I never made up my mind to look for her.

Upstairs, I habitually head to my room and find Lovisa there. Sitting in the middle of the bed, she seems to be waiting for me, Krigare lying beside her. He lazily lifts his head toward me before resting it back on the lap of my pretty redhead.

"Are done?"

Her tone carries no reproach, no fear nor anger. I expected to find her furious, ready to leave me. But nothing. Lovisa is surprising, she always acts the opposite of what I imagine.

"I got the info I needed," I say, heading to my wardrobe to take out a black, form-fitting sweater. I take the opportunity to remove my jeans and put on slightly dressier pants.

"What are you going to do with him?"

"Do you really want to know?"

The bed creaks, indicating she's getting up and approaching me. I turn to face her.

"I want the truth."

"He's dead and far from here. He's no longer a problem."

Her complexion is paler than usual, and her eyes reveal the doubt creeping in. She needs to be reassured. I toss my sweater over my shoulder and place my hands on her upper arms.

"Did you kill him?"

This detail worries her.

I could lie, but I don't want to deceive her about who I really am. "Yes."

Lovisa stays silent, her eyebrows furrowing slightly and her lips thinning. What is she thinking? If she runs away, I could hold her back and force her to stay, but she'd never see me the same way again.

Her beautiful green eyes meet mine.

That intensity…

We're connected, I can't deny it. Hypnotized by her emerald eyes,

I can't look away. This powerful attraction, I'm sure, will never fade.

"Are you in pain?" she asks, taking my battered hands.

"Yes, but that's nothing compared to what I've been through. With ice and some meds, it will be fine."

She examines my hands and eventually lifts them to her face. Gently, she kisses my fingers where there are no wounds and looks at me.

"I have to accept all aspects of your life. It's not going to be easy because what you do goes against my morals, but I love you, and I won't let these dark spots push me away of you. If I seem distant to you, when it's too much for me, don't hold it against me."

Her words touch and anger me because I don't want her to change for me or feel bad about what I do. I pull her close and hold her in my arms.

"In time, you'll have the life you deserve."

She nods and kisses me before looking up at my hair with a grimace.

"You still have blood in your hair. You need a shower."

Lovisa steps back to analyze me. Even though I cleaned up in the basement, there must still be traces of blood. I head to the bathroom with Lovisa following me. I undress and turn on the water in the shower.

"I'm heading for Stockholm tonight. Rodrigo's right-hand man told us about a gathering at a club with his future partners. It's the perfect time to catch him."

I step into the shower, letting the steaming water hit my skin. My hands hurt, the water stinging my fresh wounds and washing away the newly formed scabs. Lovisa sits on the sink, watching me intently.

"I want to come with you."

I chuckle and raise an eyebrow at her. I open the shower door to get a better look at her, the steam clinging to the walls.

"It will be dangerous. There's no way you're coming."

"ll the more reason for me to be there. With your unstable health, I'd rather be with you."

My health? Is she seriusly going to keep bugging me about that? I growl and shake my head while I shampoo my hair.

"I'll be heavily armed, and so will the men with me, but for you, who barely knows how to handle a gun, it's too dangerous."

"I don't give a fuck! I want to come with you. Initiate me into your world."

"Into my what?" I choke out. "It's not for you."

Lovisa storms out of the bathroom.

She wants to come with me, to a place where there will be a bloodbath and dead bodies? This girl is completely crazy.

And yet…

If she's close by, you can keep an eye on her.

As I dry off, I consider this perspective. It might not be such a bad idea after all. She could stay safe in the car while I deal with Rodrigo.

I head back to the bedroom to put on a pair of boxers and the rest of my clothes. Lovisa is sitting on my bed, watching me with a closed-off expression. I resist the urge to smile; her attitude amuses me. I sit next to her and put on my shoes.

"You can come, but I want you to stay in the car and you'll have to take your gun. I'm not taking you along without any protection."

"Okay, I'll take the gun, but I want to come inside with you. I can defend myself."

"It's not even up for negotiation. You won't stand a chance against these guys."

Lovisa gets up and stands in front of me, raising her skinny fists. I chuckle, raising an eyebrow.

"I know how to defend myself, you taught me."

I stand up, towering over her with my height and broad shoulders.

"Higher with your fists," I advise her, adjusting her stance. "Even if you know the basics, you won't be able to do anything. These guys don't fight with their hands; they use guns that can blow your brains out in seconds if you're not careful."

Her determined expression makes me proud, but I wish she'd listen for her own good.

"By the way, why did you come downstairs to join me?"

Her thin eyebrows furrow, and her hesitant look worries me.

"I got a message from Rikard. He's threatening to throw away my violin. I know it's sound silly, but it has great sentimental value. I'd like to get it back, and since you're going to Stockholm."

Rikard? Why is he always in our lives? I exhale loudly.

"Lovisa, this isn't the time to make a detour to your ex's place. We have more urgent matters."

"I know and I completely understand the situation. I promise you it will be quick."

She steps closer, wrapping her arms around my neck.

"Come with me if it makes you feel better. Before or after Rodrigo, it doesn't matter. I'll wait."

It's not a bad idea for me to go. I could take my revenge and make him pay for all the suffering he caused her.

"Alright. I can't promise anything, but we'll see tomorrow if we have time to swing by. Go change and dress in dark colors preferably."

She smiled, dropping her arms.

"A dress?"

"It doesn't matter, No one will see it anyway because you're staying in the car."

The mischievous look on her face makes me suspect she'll do as she pleases. I half regret agreeing to let her come with us. She leaves, calling for Krigare, who quickly follow her. Since she's been there, that dog only has eyes for her and completely ignores me.

Twenty minutes later, we're all ready to go. The men are already in the cars, waiting for Lovisa and me. I've swapped my sweater for a black shirt, slightly unbuttoned, and a leather jacket that conceals my Goldens well.

Standing at the bottom of the stairs, I glance at my watch, growling.

"Lovisa, hurry up!"

The hallway floor creaks under her light steps. Soon, I see her at the top of the stairs, and her outfit makes my jaw drops.

"Damn, baby, what are you wearing?"

My beautiful redhead descends, holding onto the banister. Her long legs are clad in black faux leather pants with leather boots that stop just above her ankles. Her top, if you can call it that, is made of black lace that barely covers her chest. Over it, a leather jacket that seems custom-made for her. She's carrying a small black bag.

"You don't like it?" she asks, with a mock pout.

She steps down the last few stairs. Her hair is tied to one side, and her dark eye makeup highlights her stunning green eyes.

"I love it, you look sexy, but everyone's going to see your breasts. What is that top?"

"A bodysuit it's trendy."

"Where? In a strip club?"

She rolls her eyes and sighs. Lovisa is so hot I could take her right there on the stairs.

"Don't be old fashioned. Alfrida told me about all the women who walked here, and most of them didn't even know what underwear was."

I chuckle. She got me.

I kiss her and tug a little on her jacket.

"Okay, but zip it up. I don't want my men ogling you on the plane."

She gives me an adorable smile and zips it up. From her right pocket, the pink grip of her gun peeks out. A woman with a gun is so sexy! I check that the safety is on and clip the button on her pocket to ensure it doesn't fall out.

"If you behave, I'll do what you asked me to do the other day."

My cock immediately swells in my boxers. I growl, pulling her sharply against me.

"Show yourself as much as you want, because tonight, it's me who will go home with you."

She laughs heartily.

Alfrida appears, Krigare at her feet. The worried look on her face reminds me of all the times she comforted me after a beating from my father. I give her a reassuring glance to show that everything will be fine. She nods and turns to Lovisa, hugging her.

"Be careful, darling."

"I will, Frida," answers Lovisa.

"Come back to me quickly."

She doesn't know what's going to happen or what happened in the basement, but she senses that something dark is brewing and that there will be no turning back.

We leave Iron House and head to my sedan where Tomas will drive us to the jet. He's new and still has to prove himself, which is why he's not accompanying us.

Tonight, will determine the future. Tonight, could mark the end of Rodrigo's reign. Or mine. But if Torston didn't lie, we're finally going to take him down.

"You can still change your mind."

"Never. I'm coming with you. You won't get rid of me that easily."

I hope she's right, because tonight, anything is possible, and I know how things never go as planned.

23

Lovisa, 17 years old

A year has passed since I left Iron House. My time there seems so far away now, though it's only been twelve months. The anxiety, fear, and pain of being chased away has faded over the months, but he still lingers in my mind. Niklas. I desperately want to reach out to him, but Hendrik's threat still hangs over our heads, preventing me from doing so. The boarding school isn't that bad. My friends take my mind off things and push me to break the rules. I find myself enjoying it, defying the forbidden. It reminds me of the moments I spent with him. I like playing the rebel, a little too much sometimes, because it gets me in trouble. But it's so good to feel alive!

***

Several private rental cars are waiting for us as we get off the jet. I could have been impressed by all the logistics put in place whenever Niklas goes somewhere, but I got used to this lifestyle with Rikard. He, too, can afford anything. The difference with my handsome Viking is that he's not pretentious; he doesn't throw a fit and send a car back if something isn't to his liking.

The contrast with Kiruna striking because of the climate. Here, it's less cold, and there's much less snow than at the estate. Snow plows and trucks turn the snow into a dark slush, and make it lose its charm at this end of winter, which seems eternal in Niklas's hometown.

I feel a little apprehensive about being in Stockholm. It's a big city, and I know it's unlikely I'll run into anyone from Rikard's circle, but the possibility lingers in my mind. Having to justify myself to his friends is not something I want to do.

Despite this fear, I wouldn't have let Niklas go alone, especially if it was the last night we'd spend together. I know it's dangerous and I'm taking so many risks, but if I can't fight for the one I love, then who can I fight for?

We landed in the early evening, the night covering the city, and the lights of bars, fast-food places, and nightclubs dazzled us. I miss this nightlife a lot; it reminds me of all the drinks I had with my orchestra friends after rehearsals. Life in Iron House is calmer, if we overlook the constant threat from Niklas's illegal activities.

The club where Rodrigo is supposed to show up is called the Charm. The place is massive and already packed. A line of about ten people blocks the entrance, watched over by two bouncers and a receptionist who lets people in with just an interested glance. Basically, the unattractive ones stay out, and the good-looking ones get in. Not very nice.

"Shouldn't be a problem to get in," Gunkil says, crushing his cigarette on the ground.

The young bounty hunter can't keep still; he seems very agitated tonight. Is it the excitement of another massacre that has him so riled up? Niklas has noticed his behavior too and grabs him by the neck, bringing his face close to his.

"You're high, damn it," he growls, letting him go. "How much did you take?"

"Don't worry, man, I've got this, it's just to give me a boost."

Niklas shoots Fredrik a stern look, and Fredrik shrugs.

"Don't look at me like that, he must have done it in the airplane bathroom."

"I'm telling you, it's fine," Gunkil exclaims, hopping from one foot to the other before calming down. "We should split up and search separately."

My boyfriend pinches the bridge of his nose and sighs.

"You guys go first. Then I'll come in with Lovisa."

Well, I'm not staying in the car anymore?

"Oscar!" calls Niklas turning around. "Post men around the club and enter with the extra ones."

He nods and signal behind him. A dozen henchmen accompany us, all dressed in civilian clothes to blend in with the other patrons.

Before Gunkil walks away, Niklas grabs him again and presses his forehead against his, looking him in the eyes.

"Don't do anything stupid, brother."

"You know me," he says with a mocking smile.

"Exactly, I don't want to bury you."

A strong bond connects them. They've known each other for so long that they consider themselves family. I envy this complicity they share. I've never experienced anything like it. The two bounty hunters leave and walk pass everyone in line. They're both striking men, Gunkil with his tan complexion, slicked-back black hair, and dimples when he smiles, and Fredrik with his air of a well-bred boy, casually styled light brown hair, and brown eyes that could melt the coldest heart. To give themselves a boost, even though they don't really need it, they slip an extra bill into the receptionist's pocket.

"It's going to be our turn," Niklas informs me, taking my hand.

He glances at my outfit. When I got out of the car, I left my purse on the back seat and opened my jacket to reveal my bodysuit.

"You're really looking for trouble," Niklas whispers, wrapping a possessive arm around my hips.

I just give him a flirtatious smile and snuggle up to him, glad he gave up on the idea of leaving me in the car. I slip my hand into the back pocket of his pants.

"I still think it's a bad idea for you to come in with me."

"Unless you tied me up in the car, I would have ended up joining you."

"Don't tempt me, that can still be arranged."

I chuckle and kiss his cheek before we reach the receptionist.

"Please wait in line," he tells us, allowing two young women to enter.

Judging by their youthful faces, they probably aren't old enough to be in this club. These girls don't realize the danger they're in by entering a nightclub filled with men ready to pounce as soon as they start to falter under the influence of alcohol.

"I'm sure we work something out."

Niklas pulls out a wad of cash equivalent to a week's worth of tips for the club's waitresses. The receptionist must have done the math, as he quickly collects the money and lets us in after stamping the image of a profile silhouette of a woman on the back of our hand. Behind us, the customers grumble and hurl insults.

We pass through a door and a curtain of satin black beads. I stay close to Niklas as I survey the surroundings. This place is much larger than the Red Mill. To serve the hundreds of customers already present, there are several counters equipped with neon lights of different colors—blue, red, and green. In the middle, there's a huge dance floor where sweaty bodies, drenched in alcohol, sway against each other in a white haze that reaches their waists. This sight is surreal. I've never seen such an atmosphere.

"Let's check this place and then head to the bar," Niklas whispers in my ear.

The music is so loud that I struggle to hear what he's saying. I cling to him and move forward, looking around me. What am I supposed to be looking for?

Oh, right! Rodrigo and his men. Or just Rodrigo, because I wouldn't be able to recognize the others.

There are so many faces to analyze that at times my vision blurs. Men, Women, white, tanned, black skin, long hair, short hair, shaved, bearded, so many details to take in, and the lights that blind me on several occasions don't help.

I glance at Niklas, who, despite me wearing heels, is still taller than me. With his serious expression, he continues to search for his enemy. There's a certain ferocity emanating from him, which was confirmed a few hours earlier, when I discovered him torturing a man. I should have run away and said goodbye once and for all, but deep down, I always knew that his dark side held horrible secrets. So why run away? No, I couldn't. I love him too much for that.

We spot Gunkil and Fredrik, gathered around a drink at one end of the blue neon-lit counter. They wave to us when they see us.

"Anything?" asks Niklas.

"No nothing at all, and we can't question anyone without risking getting noticed," Fredrik replies, taking a sip of his beer.

"Let's just hope Torston told us the truth," Gunkil says.

I meet his gaze, noting his dilated pupils caused by the low lighting and the cocaine in his system. He's always been the craziest one in the gang. Niklas told me about his drug addiction when we talked about his club in Kiruna. Gunkil managed it for a while, but he was constantly getting high at work. He fired him and forced him into rehab, but sometimes he relapses or uses occasionally drugs, like today.

"What do we do if he sees us first? He might attack us," I interject, looking at them one by one.

"Rodrigo isn't stupid; he wouldn't do that in front of so many people. It would cause chaos, and we wouldn't see anything. However, he might try to run away, but my men outside would inform us," Niklas responds.

The wait could be long; Rodrigo isn't expected to arrive before 11 p.m., from what I understand. We sit at the bar with our drinks. Niklas chose a pure vodka; as for me, I prefer to soften the drink with orange soda.

"If you want to leave at any time, just let me know," he says in my ear.

I shake my head and lean toward him. "I'm staying with you until the end; I'm not changing my mind."

Even if my heels are starting to hurt a little. I shift from one foot to the other and finally sit on one of the stools available to us.

Around us, everyone is dancing, talking, laughing. The carefree expressions I see make me wonder what image my group and I must be projecting. We talk amongst ourselves, looking serious. Niklas and Fredrik are speculating about what might happen tonight. Gunkil seems to have regressed to his teenage years, engrossed in his phone and giggling occasionally. His state baffles me, I wonder what he feels, sees, and hears. He's clearly not lucid and drinking beer after beer is definitely not the best idea he's had. Oddly, Nik doesn't say anything to him, just gives him a few disapproving looks between words with Fredrik.

As for me, mostly an observer, I just nod at their theories while casting a caring glance toward Gunkil, who strangely reminds me of my mother. I usually avoid thinking about her because it hurts, and the brutality of her death has never allowed me to fully grieve. What if Gun overdoses too? As eleven o'clock approaches, Niklas and Fredrik decide to make another round of the club to see if Rodrigo has arrived. I take this opportunity to change stools and get closer to Gunkil.

"Are you okay?"

"Doing great, yeah. And you? No disrespect, but you look damn sexy tonight. Don't tell Nik, he'd be furious," the young man chuckles, putting his phone away.

I nod and moisten my lips. It's quite warm, and my throat is dry, so I finish my drink. Shifting uncomfortably on my stool, I struggle to bring up the topic.

"Gun, I was wondering, are you careful when you… when you, well you know," I try to make him understand by passing my finger over my nose.

He immediately bursts into laughter, understanding what I mean. He throws an arm around my shoulders and sways me side to side with him before letting go.

"You're so cute, you can't even say it. I know what I'm doing, but thanks for worrying about me."

He digs into his pocket and pulls out a small white bag and his credit card. My jaw drops in surprise. I glance around to see if anyone noticed. I lean close, and whisper, "Are you crazy doing that here?"

"Don't worry, no one will say anything. Everyone does it."

He's completely nuts. How much has he already taken? What if this dose is too much? Gunkil places his card on his thigh and pours some powder on it. Using a second credit card, he makes a perfectly straight line. He rolls up a five hundred kroner bill and places it on the line. I grab his wrist to stop him from going any further.

"That's enough, don't do it."

He chuckles and shakes off my grip. "Still so uptight, huh, Lovisa? Even back then, you never dared to have fun."

"I know how to have fun without that crap."

He looks at me, but his gaze is vacant; a part of him is absent, probably dulled by the cocaine. He leans forward and, with the rolled-up bill, snorts the line. He then throws his head back and rubs his nose.

"Wow! That's good stuff."

He slaps the table with his palm and laughs at something only he can understand. I scan the crowd for Niklas, but the light show and the hundreds of people in the room make it impossible to find him. I have to handle this on my own.

"Do you want to step outside? The fresh air will do you good."

"Wait, I'm not finished."

What? I watch him empty the rest of the bag onto his credit card. He can't be serious.

"Stop! You're going to kill yourself."

He shakes his head and makes a somewhat straight line. I try to knock his card to the floor, but he pulls it away. How can he still have speed reflexes? His blue eyes, with pupils so tiny they're almost scary, gaze at me mischievously.

"The only way to stop me is to take it yourself. Sniff it."

Did I hear that right? I laugh nervously.

"You're not serious, right? And what's stopping me from just throwing it away?"

"Up to you. If you throw it away, I'll get more. I'm sure there are dealers in this club."

He pretends to look around and offers me the card and the rolled-up bill.

"Just once. Come on, Granberg, relax."

Gunkil would easily find someone to supply him with what he wants, I have no doubt. I take the card and look at the white powder, glowing under the blue neon lights. Nothing stops me from throwing it on the floor, except maybe the overdose Gunkil might have if he gets more elsewhere.

"What does it feel like?" I can't help but ask.

"It's like being a free electron. There's all this power inside you that's hard to control. You feel like you can do anything, and in a way, you can. Your mind is sharper, it's like accessing parts of your brain that have been asleep for years, like doors opening up," he explains, his eyes gleaming.

Is this what my mom felt every morning when she took her dose? I've always judged her without ever trying to understand her, and now, I'm about to do what I once hated so much.

What Gunkil described is tempting, but I know that every experience is different; it doesn't mean I'll feel the same as he does.

I bite my lips, looking over my shoulder.

"Nik would be against it."

Gun snorts, then smiles.

"He's a killjoy since he can't take anymore because of his heart. A few years ago, he was taking this stuff every night. Come on, just once."

Just once.

How many people have said that and ended up overdosing five years later? Even knowing this, the temptation to try something new grips me. I don't want to be the good Lovisa who listens to everyone. I want to make my own choices, even if it means hitting a wall sometimes.

"Just once, and then you stop for the night, okay?"

He shakes my hand to seal our agreement. I grab the rolled-up bill and place it at the beginning of the line. My mouth is suddenly goes dry, and a shiver of excitement runs through me. I bend over, place my nostril at the edge of it, and snort the entire line. I grimace and rub my nose, throwing my head back.

"Bottoms up, baby!" Gun teases, taking back his card and handing it to the bartender, which he gives to the bartender, ordering another round for us both.

"How long does it take to kick in?"

"It's very fast, two minutes tops, maybe less since it's your first time."

My heart races with excitement but also with apprehension; I don't know how my body will react to this foreign substance. What if I have a bad reaction? Or an allergy, who knows? Considering all the components in this powder. So white, so pure. Like snow. I love that, ordering another round for us both. It smells too, that freshness, carrying the scent of the sky and clouds that are out of our reach. If I think hard enough, I can almost feel its coolness on my body, wrapping around me like a coat of ice.

I feel good, light, as if I'm floating on a cloud. What a nice sensation.

"I still don't feel anything."

"Oh no? Are you sure about that?"

Gunkil waves his hand in front of my face. His fingers multiply into a dozen before returning to five. I start to laugh and look at my own hands.

"I think it's working," I giggle.

I pick up my drink and take a long sip. My common sense tells me not to drink too much after what I just took, but I don't want to listen. I want to let go without restriction. A part of me whispers that tonight isn't the right night to experiment with new things, that Rodrigo could arrive any minute and the situation could turn dangerous at any moment, but it's too late.

I take off my leather jacket. My lace bodysuit has long, fitted sleeves. I'm aware that this daring and incredibly sexy outfit will attract attention, but I'm hit with a wave of heat. Gunkil lingers on my cleavage for a moment before looking away.

"Let me show you something."

He grabs a handful of peanuts from a nearby guy's bowl while the guy's back is turned and moves his barely touched beer bottle away.

"I bet you I can throw them in the bottle."

If he can do that under the influence of cocaine, I can't imagine how skills he must be when he's sober. The bounty hunter focuses on his target and start tossing the nuts one by one, missing each time. Far from being discouraged, he continues with my encouragement. On the last one, he barely makes it. He high-fives me and raises his arms in victory. We laugh until our stomachs hurt.

"What's so funny?" Niklas says, coming with Fredrik.

Judging by their disappointed expressions, I guess they still haven't found Rodrigo.

"I was showing Lovisa my shooting skills. So, any new?"

Unlike me, who is completely high, Gunkil seems to have a startling lucidity and wears a serious expression.

"He won't come, but I talked to a bouncer who complained about getting paid peanuts. He's been working here for a while and he recognized Rodrigo from having seen him here before. He said he'll be here tomorrow late morning," Niklas explains, wrapping an arm around my shoulders.

With his fingertips, he caresses my skin through the thin fabric of my blouse. A long shiver runs up my arm and to my neck. The spot he touches feels like it's on fire. My skin is more sensitive and on the lookout for any sensation. Nik's gaze lingers on my chest, which I push forward, driven by audacity his desire.

"Our hotel isn't far, we're leaving," Fredrik informs us, standing next to Gunkil.

I hope there's a bath; it's been a while since I had one.

"You're quiet. Are you okay, babe?" Niklas asks.

I nod and smile. I blush at the thought of what I just did. How can I tell him that I did cocaine? He has no right to tell me what to do, but I don't want to incur his wrath if he disapproves. I decide not to tell him and snuggle against him. I feel a surge of love so strong that I want to kiss him all over. I devour his full lips with my eyes and get up to wrap my arms around his neck.

"I want to kiss you, and dance too, but first, I want to kiss you!"

Full of enthusiasm, I don't wait for his permission and rush on his beautiful dark pink lips. My eagerness surprises him, but he quickly responds to my kiss and holds me tightly. I feel protected and safe in his arms, and I love it. The sensation that nothing can happen to me when I'm with him is very comforting.

He slides his lips to my ear and kisses it.

"I don't know what's up to you, but I love it."

If only you knew.

I smile and grab his hand. "Come dance with me, no violence tonight, you can take a break."

Niklas resists when I try to pull him along.

"Nah, I'm not in the mood for that. Let's just leave."

"Just one dance. Just one. Come on, please."

I bounce impatiently, tugging on his hand. He eventually groans and pulls away. He rubs his hand and glances at his injuries.

"You're no fun," I pout, making a face. "Oh well, you'll just have to watch."

I give him a playful smile and walk backward. His darkened gaze doesn't leave me for a second as he sits down in my spot.

I'm going to show him what he's missing.

I make my way to the dance floor and manage to get to the center, still under Niklas' watchful eye.

Just like Gunkil described, a powerful energy makes every cell in my body vibrate. I want to run, dance, and party all night long. I feel like the world belons to me, and I can do anything I want.

Following the rhythm of the music, I sway my hips, using my hands on my body to accentuate the sensuality. I let the notes cradle me, just like I've done thousands of times playing melodies myself. Music has flowed through my veins for so long that I can't imagine living without it. It will always be part of my life.

I glance at Niklas, who is now standing to watch me better. Next to him, his best friends are chatting. For a brief moment, I wonder what they're talking about.

Come on, Nik, join me.

I close my eyes and focus on the music, letting the warm, rhythmic notes wash over me. They penetrate every part of my body and makes me feel transported. From behind, two firm hands grab my hips. I can't help but smile, feeling victorious.

"I knew you'd come."

I slide my hands behind me to grab his neck. His neck feels lower than usual. Did he shrink like clothes in a high-heat dryer? I turn around and find myself face to face with a stranger. Shorter and thinner than Niklas, he's the complete opposite with dark eyes, hollow cheeks, beardless, and spiky blond hair set in gel.

"Let go of me!" I shout immediately.

"Relax, honey, we're just having fun."

Fueled by a surge of courage, I clench my fist and punch him in the nose. It shatters under my knuckles, and blood pours out. He releases me and clutches his face.

At first, I don't feel the pain in my hand, but a little voice in my head tells me I'll pay for it tomorrow.

"You broke my nose!" scream the blond, spitting a few drops of blood at my face.

He is quickly joined by three other guys, probably his friends.

"That bitch broke my nose," he repeats, looking at the blood in his hands. "You'll pay for this!"

He rushes toward me, but Niklas, who witnessed the scene from afar, comes to my rescue with Gunkil and Fredrik. He places his big hand on the blond's chest and shoves him back with a swift push.

"Stay away from her, or your nose won't be the only thing that gets broken."

His threat sets off the fight. *Blondie* and his three friends attack Niklas. Gunkil and Fredrik step in, each taking on one guy. That still leaves two for Niklas, and while he can handle them alone, it's not a fair fight.

He needs me.

While Nik deals with my attacker, I tackle the second man, a brown-haired man with a plain face. I dig my heel into his foot, making him double over, and knee him in the head, pressing down on his shoulders. My Viking's lessons are paying off.

I feel powerful and invincible. I can do anything. The possibilities are endless. I shake my head, realizing I'm losing focus. When I come back to myself, I see the dark-haired man's closed fist coming down on my face. A metallic taste floods my mouth. I wait for the pain.

I wait.

I wait.

Nothing? Nothing at all. Not an ounce of pain. Is that normal? I laugh and jump on him, knocking him to the floor. We roll, pushing other customers, who start fighting too, caught up in our frenzy. I get, straddling him, and punch him in the stomach. He hits me back. I collapse to the floor and see him vanish into the crowd. Where did he go? I'm not done yet! My head spins, and my vision blurs. I stand up and turn around. I spot Niklas a little further away; he's still fighting with the blond, who's in a bad shape.

"Nick!" I shout, trying to weave my way toward him.

Around me, a general fight has broken out. Everyone is hitting each other. The bouncers are probably intervening at the edges.

"Nick!" I scream again.

He doesn't hear me; there's too much noise, too many people, and too much commotion. The more I try to get closer to him, the more I'm pushed back. A woman bumps into me. That's the last straw. She turns toward me, and before she can react, I slap her. I'm not usually one to fight, but at this moment, my primal instincts take over, wanting to avenge everything I've endured. Rikard's face appears all around me, urging me to punch anyone who gets too close. I won't let anyone push me around anymore. Suddenly, he's there. Dressed in a nice black suit, my ex-boyfriend looks at me with that smug expression he always wears when he has something to criticize me for. Anxiety grips me; I want to curl up on myself to protect myself before I remember that I can, no, that I know how to defend myself.

"Lovisa, there you are."

He moves quickly, reaching his arms out toward me. I let out a scream worthy of a hysteric.

"You'll never touch me again!"

I punch him square in the face. He groans and grabs my shoulders, making me close my eyes. When I reopen them a second later, Rikard is gone, and Niklas is holding me. Where did he go? My heart beats fast, too fast, and too hard. Panicked, I look around for that monster.

"Where is he?"

"Who are you talking about?" asks Niklas.

"Rikard! He… he was there, then he wasn't. And now you're here. Oh, Niklas, you found me!"

His concerned face studies me, then his eyes widen.

"Holy shit, Lovisa, are you high?"

Oh, yes, I am! I took cocaine. With Gunkil. By the way, where is he? I try to look behind Niklas, but he holds me tight and lift me onto his shoulder. I scream in surprise and start laughing as my head is upside down. I feel like a kid.

He makes his way through the crowd, pushing aside anyone in his path. We head toward the exit.

"My jacket!" I shout, straightening up and pointing toward the blue neon bar. "My gun is in my jacket! What if someone steals it?"

Niklas's body vibrates under his growl. He turns back and quickly grabs my jacket. At the entrance, blue and red lights flash. The police. We rush out.

Outside, it's chaos. Customers scatter at the sight of the authorities. Niklas sets me down only when we reach the car. Gunkil joins us, his eyebrow bleeding, and Fredrik has a bruise forming on his cheek. I turn my attention to Niklas to check for injuries. He seems okay, except for the blood on his knuckles. Did his wounds get worst?

"We need to get out of here, fast," Niklas shouts to be heard over the noise.

In the distance, Oscar gets the signal from his boss to leave. He releases his driver who drove me here and orders him to take Gunkil and Fredrik away.

"Get in," Niklas orders me, his voice devoid of any warmth.

Uh-oh, this is going to hurt.

I climb into the front seat and let him buckle my seatbelt. Does he think I'm helpless? He circles the car and gets into the driver's seat. With controlled speed, he backs up quickly and makes a sharp turn with a squeal of tires.

"What were you thinking, doing coke? It's dangerous."

I giggle and put my hand over my mouth to try to calm myself down. Is he serious? He's lecturing me when he used to do it himself.

"Stop fucking laughing. Did Gun give it to you? He'll regret this."

His anger radiates from him like scorching heat. The atmosphere in the car becomes suffocating forcing me to open the window. The icy air freezes the sweat on my forehead, making me uncomfortable. I close my eyes.

"Don't do anything to him. I'm an adult, and it was my choice."

Even though I did it to stop him from taking more, the desire to try something new pushed me to give in. A new thought for my mother crosses my mind. Is this what she felt? This euphoria and this feeling of being able to do anything? It's so good and terrifying; I feel like I'm aware of everything. The cold on my skin, the icy sweat trickling down my back, the leather of my pants rubbing against my legs, and the lace caressing my body with every movement. Niklas's harsh words go in one ear and out the other. I hear his voice, but his words are muffled as if behind a thick window, incomprehensible.

He snaps his fingers in front of my eyes to get my attention.

"Are you listening to me? Damn, you're really out of it. It's going to be a cold shower for you when you get at the hotel."

A shiver of fear runs through me. I look at him in terror and cling to my seatbelt, pressing myself against my seat.

"No! Not the cold shower, why are you doing this to me?"

Why does he want to punish me? I didn't do anything wrong. I shake my head and swallow the tears threatening to fall. Niklas's hand on my thigh makes me jump.

"Shit, babe, it's not what you think," he reassures me.

His voice softens, and he sighs. "You're going straight to bed, okay?"

I nod and focus on the road, forcing my mind to settle, but it keeps jumping to various thoughts, both happy and upsetting, especially when I think about my mother. The engine's purr and the warmth of the car, after I close the window, gradually calm me down. My heart slows down to a normal rhythm, and my body relaxes more and more. With half-closed eyes, I end up falling asleep.

Ow. My cheek.

What's wrong with it? I run my tongue over the inside of my cheek and find a wound that starts throbbing again. I touch it with my numb hand and slowly wake up. Wrapped in a thick blanket and in Nik's arms, I recall the events of the last night under the cold morning light that comes in from a large bay window.

The club, Rodrigo not showing up, me taking cocaine, then the massive fight. It all comes back to me in painful fragments. I fought? That realization surprises me. Normally, I would have done anything to avoid a physical confrontation. I look at my stiff hands, and slightly red around the knuckles.

Wow! I fought! And I was good. I received blows, but I gave them back too.

I lift my head and look at my handsome Viking, sound asleep. He rescued me in that chaotic crowd, like always. I have no doubt about his presence by my side when things get tough.

Slowly, I pull away from his arms and realize we're in our underwear. I don't remember undressing, or even getting here. It's a spacious hotel room with all the necessary comforts.

A luxurious suite, even.

I fumble my way to the bathroom, where I find a light gray, cotton robe and put it on. I inspect the pristine white bathroom. A large, deep bathtub takes center stage. Further on, two sparkling sinks with silver faucets look as if they've never been used, they're so clean. I feel dirty from head to toe, so I take a quick shower and then run a bath to relax in. I stay in the steaming water for a long time as it gradually cools. My mind is still a little foggy, but slowly that hazy state lifts, and I can finally think clearly.

"Can I join you?"

Niklas stands in the doorway. I smile at him and nod, pulling my legs against me to make room. After taking off his boxers, he comes in front of me.

"How are you feeling?" he asks.

I bite my lip, embarrassed as I recall my behavior from the night before.

"Not too bad. And you?"

We're both pretty banged up. Niklas' knuckles are purple, and his left cheekbone is a bit swollen. Our wounds are similar, though my hands are much less damaged.

"A fight from time to time keeps you in shape," Niklas jokes, resting his arms on the edge of the bathtub. "You were very restless last night, probably having nightmares."

I don't remember anything, and maybe that's for the better. We sit in silent for a few minutes before I finally can't hold it in any longer. "Are you mad at me? For the cocaine and the fight."

He presses his lips together and grips the tub with his large hands before letting go.

"I was very worried. I didn't know how much you had taken or how you'd react. What got into you to follow Gunkil in his crazy antics?"

"It was either that or let him take it himself, and he had already consumed so much that I was afraid he'd overdose."

"And the thought of you overdosing didn't cross your mind? Damn it, Love, you should have come to me."

I press myself against the tub, pouting. I hate feeling like I have to justify myself to him.

"What if, deep down, I wanted to try it? To let go at a party like anyone my age? I wanted to an experience something that wasn't like me. And you know what? I don't regret it. Yes, it was scary at times, but it was also exhilarating. I know I won't do it again. I don't want to become addicted like… my mom."

I once accused her of being weak, and he thought of becoming like her scared me then. I didn't want to be dependent on a drug. Now that I understand its effects, I can see how she might have succumbed to such sensations while juggling multiple jobs to support us.

Niklas pulls me between his legs and holds me against his chest, my side pressed to him. I look into his eyes. They're lighter than usual, probably an effect of the bright bathroom lighting.

"Your situations aren't the same; it won't be the same for you. And I'm here. Your mother had Hendrik; he never stopped her, and for that, I'm sorry. He was part of her problem, and as his son I feel responsible too."

I place my wet fingers on his beard rest my forehead against his.

"Don't carry that burden. Your father is guilty of many things that don't concern you. You're not him, and I'm not her."

No, I'm not my mother and never will be. I prefer to hold onto the good memories I have of her and erase the bad ones that tarnish her legacy. I must accept my painful past and move on.

"Today, I want you to stay here, you'll be safe."

"You're going to find Rodrigo, aren't you?"

He nods.

"I told you I wanted to come with you."

"With what happened yesterday, I'd rather you rest. I'd feel better knowing you're here than having a dozen loaded guns aimed at us."

I turn pale.

"No…"

"Love, you're not trained to handle with all this violence. I am."

In a way, I am too, since life with Rikard wasn't always easy.

We get out of the now almost cold water and slip into our robes after drying off.

After a hearty breakfast of pastries, coffee, orange juice, and a hot tea for me, I excuse myself to get dressed. I put on a gray turtleneck sweater with skinny jeans and cozy, fur-lined boots that feel great to wear.

I tie my hair into a high ponytail and settle into the beige fabric corner couch. Niklas, on the other hand, is dressed in jeans and a fitted black sweater with a bulletproof vest underneath. He has his holster strapped to his shoulders, loaded with his weapons. Everything looks good on him, and I can't help but admire him for a moment. He's standing by the large window, discussing strategy with Oscar.

Boring. I can't participate, so I browse social media looking for interesting music topic.

Message.

I open it immediately without even checking who it's from.

[You've blown your chance to get your damn violin back,

I'll throw it away tonight.]

Rikard.

[Don't do that!]

[And who's going to stop me?

Your thug boyfriend? You?]

I put down my phone and stand up.

I had completely forgotten the second reason for my coming to Stockholm.

I grab my leather jacket and put it on. Niklas took the weapon that I hid in my pocket to put it safely in a bag containing his guns. Luckily, he forbade the staff from to come here, otherwise they would immediately call the police.

"I have to go," I inform my boyfriend as I search around for his car keys.

"Where to?"

"To my old apartment to get my violin. Rikard wants to throw it away."

We had agreed he would come with me, but given the circumstances, that won't be possible now.

I finally find the key on the entryway table and turn to see that Niklas has joined me in a few quick strides. I grab my purse and rummage through it, looking for Rikard's spare keys, praying that he hasn't changed the locks.

"Now? I have something else to do!"

"I *need* to get it back."

"We're at war, and you're talking to me about a stupid violin?"

Niklas is on edge, so I don't hold it against him.

"I know you don't understand, but it's important to me."

He sighs loudly. "Can't you wait until I've dealt with Rodrigo so we can go together?"

I'm not going to get out that easily. "I can manage on my own. He won't be here until tonight, so it's now or never."

He growls in frustration.

"I can't manage everything at once. Wait for me, and we'll go together."

Is he listening to me at all?

"Nik, I'm not asking for your help, I'm just letting you know that I'm going. You don't have a say in this."

Well, that's a bit harsh, but I don't see another way to make him understand that I need to go. He glares at me for a long moment.

"Take one of my men with you then. I refuse to let you go alone."

"If it makes you feel better."

Niklas steps out into the hallway and returns a minute later with a tall, dark-haired man, almost as tall as he is. He takes his keys from me.

"He'll take you in his car. If there's any trouble, let me know immediately."

I kiss him and leave the room, feeling a sense of apprehension. I haven't been back to my old place for a few weeks, and I wonder if my things are still there. If I can get some of my belongings back, that would be great. I haven't had confirmation that Rikard isn't there, but usually, during the day he's at one of his father's dealerships, barking orders at anyone who passes in front of him. If his car isn't there, I'll be able to get in and get out quickly.

24

Niklas, 19 years old

I can finally breathe. Hendrik is off on a trip with his pit bull, Sören. The day that guy takes a bullet will be a day to celebrate. He's the worst of my dad's employees. While they're gone, I'm slacking off on all the work he dumped on me. I don't give a damn about the finances of this dump he calls a hotel! If it were up to me, I'd tear it down and put up a strip club, but those puritans in Kiruna are too backward to accept that kind of place. My family's influence has its limits; it can't completely corrupt the town council where several people are against Hendrik. He wants to give me more responsibility and wants me to use my fists as much as my brain, but if I have to choose, I'd rather smash someone's face than deal with complaints.

***

What was I thinking, letting her go without me? Especially to that idiot's place? My instincts tell me to follow her, but my reason says to stay and handle the more urgent problem. That girl never listens to me; she always does what she wants. Once all this is over, I'll go find her.

In the hotel lobby, I wait with Oscar and the rest of my men for Gunkil and Fredrik to join us. I haven't seen Gun since yesterday, and I've got a few words for him. Him doing cocaine is his problem, but dragging Lovisa into his crap makes it my problem. He can be a real idiot when he wants to be.

Around us, guests come and go, casting curious glances our way. A group of ten men dressed in black tends to attract attention.

The doors finally open, revealing my two best friends. Fredrik, looking fresh and rested, and Gunkil, with dark circles under his eyes but a smile on his face, dimples that women love. Before he can say a word as they approach, I send my fist into Gun's face.

"Nick! Stops!" Fredrik intervenes, pushing Gun back.

Gun groans, holding his cheek. A few shocked looks turn our way, and the receptionist hesitates, unsure whether to intervene or not. Ultimately, he stays behind his counter. Good choice, kid.

"It's fine, I deserved it," Gun says, moving his lower jaw to make sure nothing's broken.

I didn't hit that hard.

He glances at me sideways.

"Are we even now?"

"Yeah," I grunt, rubbing my knuckles. "You're lucky she's okay."

Gun doesn't reply, just rubs his sore jaw.

With everyone present, we head out. All armed under our coats, we leave the hotel and split into four cars. I'm with my friends, Fredrik in the front and Gun behind me.

"If he's here, leave Rodrigo to me, I'll take care of him."

"Do you think he'll have a lot of men waiting for us?" Gun asks.

Sometimes I wonder what his parents did to him when he was a kid to make him love the taste of blood so much. He takes insane risks and always acts impulsively.

"We're not taking no chances. Do you think you can control yourself for once?"

I adjust my rearview mirror to catch his eye. His mischievous grin annoys me; he seems to take nothing seriously.

"I'm not a killer," Fredrik says quietly, eyes fixed on the road.

He's the most pacifist of our group. I've always wondered why he sticks with us. Our friendship has lasted so long that I've forgotten when we first met.

"Rodrigo threatens my business, my safety, and everyone around me. He leaves me no choice."

"Really?"

He finally looks at me.

"What do you want? That I give up everything my father built out of fear of retaliation? If I give in to him, I will have to do it for everyone else who wants something from me."

"Forget it, man. His parents aren't going to leave him anything, he can't understand," Gunkil cuts in, scrolling on his phone.

"Shut up!" Fredrik snaps, glaring at him. "You know nothing about my family, so shut your big mouth before I shut it for you."

It's rare to see Fredrik lose his cool, which is why his threat ends this conversation. Fredrik comes from modest means. His mother doesn't work, and his father owns a grocery store in the center, which works well. He got into our school on a scholarship. He's the one with empty pockets but a mind filled with knowledge from books.

In front of the Charm, not a soul is in sight. The club is on a deserted street, rarely busy when the place is closed. To avoid detection, we parked farther away.

The instructions are simple. We slip inside, only shoot if absolutely necessary, and the first one to find Rodrigo alerts the others.

"Be careful," Oscar advises as he and his men go in first.

It's the first time I've had my men's lives in my hands. If the mission goes south, their deaths will be on my conscience. Before, they answered to my father, and I was one of them, following his orders. Now, they carry out mine. Hendrik never cared about those who worked for him; he thought everyone was replaceable. He barely regretted Sören's death, his loyal dog.

I see things differently.

As planned, I go through the back with Gun and Fred. With my two Goldens in hand, I push open the door and enter. I walk along a hallway lined with crates of empty liquor bottles. At the end of the hallway, there are three doors. I signal to Gunkil to take the right door and Fredrik the left one, while I take the one in the middle. Behind mine is the main room, where my men and Oscar are. They have three guys in their grasp, probably employees judging by the badges on their chests. On their knees with guns to their temples, they stay silent, fearing for their lives.

A quick glance around tells me there's no one else in the room, which looks nothing like it did the night before without its lights and smoke machines.

I look at Oscar, who nods toward a door behind which voices can be heard. My comrades return to my side, silently indicating they've found nothing.

Guns raised, I approach the door Oscar pointed out. My heart starts pounding faster with every step.

I'm almost there.

I position myself to the side of the door; Gunkil, Fredrik, along with two other men, Gregor and Istvan, press against the wall. With a nod indicating everyone is ready, I knock on the door three times. The voices inside are immediately fall silent. Oscar presses his gun a little harder against the temple of a man named Josh, urging him to get Rodrigo to come out.

No trouble, buddy, and you can leave here alive.

"Sir, I'm bringing your drinks," he announces in a clear, loud voice. From his position, he will be heard on the other side of the door.

A chair scrapes the floor, then heavy footstep heads toward the entrance. As soon as the door cracks open, I kick it in, sending the man behind it sprawling. I enter the room with my men close behind. My guns quickly find Rodrigo, who stands up suddenly. Initially taken aback by this unexpected interruption, he then starts laughing.

"Niklas, my friend, it's been a while."

"Cut the crap with me, asshole. Don't move."

With everyone armed, my men and Rodrigo's, numbering six each, as well as his prospective partners, face off. Even though they're outnumbered, I don't underestimate their strength and watch their every move closely.

The room is rather narrow, leaving us little space for us. In case of a gunfight, there will be very few ways for us or them to dodge a bullet.

"You're going to come with us quietly, and I promise you a quick death."

Rodrigo looks smug and doesn't seem impressed by my threat.

"How did you find me? I've been very careful about my appearances."

My lips stretch into a dark smile.

"Unlike Torston, who spent his last hours wallowing in his own filth and half drained of his blood."

A shadow passes over his face. This is what I was waiting for. That little spark of fear that should be present considering what I have in store for him if he doesn't comply. With a slight nod of his head, he slowly walks around the table; his men follow him.

"That little shit is lucky to be dead. I don't accept betrayal. Right, Niklas?"

His removal from his position is a betrayal to him, and I'm

probably no better than Torston in his eyes.

"You have to know how to lose, Rodrigo."

"Never."

Tense, I step back with my team, guns aimed at their chests. Each step is calculated, every reaction monitored, and every breath held to sharpen our focus in case of a sudden attack.

Everyone is on edge, except for Rodrigo, who seems to have some information that escapes me. Either he has a plan, or he's arrogant enough to think I'll let him go.

"Move back," I command, freezing in the middle of the room and pointing to a row of tables stacked on top of each other a little further away. "There!"

They complied in silence, under their leader's approval. Without him, bullets would probably have flown already.

He's the only one unarmed.

He's too confident for my liking.

"What are you going to do, kid? We're here, you found me. What's your plan?"

He tries to belittle me in front of my men, to make me look like a child and discredit me, but it won't work. He forgets that my father was Hendrik Ekman, who taught me everything, often in the most unpleasant way.

"Your men are going to gently put their weapons on the ground, and you're coming with me."

"Is that all. Anything else?"

Rodrigo starts laughing and claps.

"Congratulation you on your rise to power, kid, but you don't take down the big boys with a snap of your fingers."

His laugh turns cold, menacing. He stops abruptly and gives me a murderous look.

"Killing me won't be easy, I've more than one trick up my sleeve, and I never go anywhere without a backup plan."

Focused on his vile mouth, I don't immediately see the furtive movement he makes against his thigh. A click is heard. What is that? The screech of tires sounds outside. More of his men are here to rescue him. Clever. Very clever.

"You thought you had me trapped, Niklas? Not today."

The bastard. That's why he wasn't shitting on himself at the thought of living his last moments.

"Your men won't stop me from shooting you," I retort.

Rodrigo scratches his scruffy beard and gives me an arrogant smile. "And then what? Huh? Do you think everything will stop after I'm dead?"

He dares to take a few steps in my direction. To discourage him from going any further, I raise my gun to his face. He stops.

"Be sure that everyone you know, your friends, your employees, and even your whore mother will be killed on the spot," he says, looking me in the eye. "But don't worry, I won't kill Lovisa. No, I've a better fate in mind for her. She'll be my personal little slut and will do my every desire."

He slides a hand between his legs to grab his cock, making bile rise in my throat.

"She must be damn good in bed, that woman's body…"

Images of my girl probably flash through his perverted mind, and the idea makes my blood boil with rage. He dares to provoke me with several guns aimed at him. My body trembles slightly with fury, and I tighten my grips on my Goldens guns so as not to lose my control.

"I'd love to stay and chat, but I've business to attend and an empire to destroy. Yours."

The motherfucker. Despite the delicate situation and a gun pointed at his head, he still managed to taunt me. Far from being intimidated, he turns his back on me and walks toward the door I came through. I can't let him escape, not when we're in the same room. The building must be surrounded by his men. They'll kill us as soon as we step outside.

"Rodrigo!"

If I'm going to die today, it will be taking him with me.

"Don't let him get away!" I shout, firing the first shot in his direction.

Immediately, shots ring out around us from both sides. Quickly, my ears start to buzz, and every sound becomes torture, but I don't have time to worry about my hearing. My eardrums could burst and bleed, I'd continue the fight.

I rush into the fray, certainty that my men will cover me. I shove everyone in my way and shoot at anyone who points their weapon at me. Some collapse, likely wounded or even dead. Their loyalty will cost them their lives.

Rodrigo is gone. He didn't try to fight to save himself, abandoning his men behind him.

I burst through the door he went through and run down the hallway to the exit. There, I see Rodrigo near a car, about to climb in. He turns toward me with a mocking smile. Seeing red, I empty my gun in his direction. I managed to hit him in the thigh. His scream of pain alerts the men with him, who open fire on me.

How many of them are there?

I take cover behind the iron door and hear the car speed away.

"No!" I scream, pushing away my makeshift shield to chase after the vehicle.

Too late. He got away. Again!

Furious, I head back inside, where the gunfire has stopped. My stomach in knots, I cautiously approach the main room, unsure of what I'll find. Armed with my audacity and my empty guns, I point them in front of me as I push open the door.

"Did you get him?" Fredrik asks me immediately, his cheek grazed by a bullet.

Beside him, Oscar is lifting a bloodied man.

"He got away, but I managed to wound him."

Rodrigo's man laughs, his teeth stained with blood.

"He's going to kill you and your entire family. All of you are going to d—"

I don't let him finish and put a bullet in his head after taking Oscar's gun. The echo reverberates through the room. In the distance, police sirens wail. That will scare off Rodrigo's last men and give us time to get out of here.

"What are our losses?"

"Three dead and two injured. As for Rodrigo's men, aside from those who escaped with him, we got them all."

My eyes search for our wounded. Gunkil is holding his bleeding arm but shows no sign of pain.

A little further, Gregor lies in a pool of blood with a significant wound in his stomach.

"We need to get them back to Kiruna as quickly as possible. Dr. Söderholm will take care of them."

My men obey, carrying Gregor after checking the street, and pile into their cars. I approach Gunkil and tear the hole in his jacket wider to assess the extent of his injury. He grimaces as I handle his arm but doesn't make any comments.

"You'll be fine. Söderholm will get you patched up in no time. How are you feeling?"

"I'll feel better when we're out of here and I have a glass of vodka in my hand."

I smile and nod. He hasn't lost his sense of humor.

"Let's go."

I rush to my car and see the flashing police lights in the distance. *Just in time*. They were quick.

I start the car and make the engine roar as I speed away. In the back, Gunkil improvises a bandage around his arm with whatever he finds in the rental car's first aid kit.

"That was wow, spectacular!" Gunkil exclaims, once we're far from the club. "I've never killed anyone before, it was—"

"Bloody," Fredrik finished grimly, looking at his hands.

I focus on the road.

For me, this isn't the first time. That's why I can take the shock more easily, even if it's not easy to take someone else's life. The deeper I sink into darkness with my wrongdoings, the further I drift from the person I once was.

"You did it to protect your own," I try, glancing at him.

"Tell that to their mother, their brother, or worse, their child."

Even Gunkil, who would usually mock Fredrik for his drama, stays silent. He's not a man of action, I've always known that. He doesn't belong in this conflict. I was wrong to bring him into it.

"You're going home," I say. "You'll be more useful to us behind a screen."

"Are you kicking me out because I don't think like you?" Fredrik snaps.

"I'm keeping you away so you don't *become* like me," I tell him.

A monster? A heartless killer? How should I describe myself to make him understand that he isn't the problem?

Oscar breaks the silence by calling me. I tap the car's touchscreen to pick up.

"We managed to stabilize Gregor. He should make it through the flight, and Dr. Söderholm is aware of our arrival."

"OK, I'll pick up Lovisa at the hotel. She should be there by now, and we'll meet you."

I hang up and call her immediately. Her phone rings, then goes to voicemail. I end the call, containing my nervousness as much as possible. She can't manage to answer on the first ring, unbelievable!

"Stay in the car, I won't be long," I order once we're at the hotel.

Parked a little before the building's entrance, I leave the engine running. During the drive, Gunkil started getting cold; I suspect he's hiding the seriousness of his condition. We're similar in that way.

I take the elevator and press the top button. Our suite is so high up it would give even the greatest stuntman dizzy. I unlock the door with a key card.

"Babe, you here?" I call out, venturing into the main room.

Nobody. I search the rest of the room. Everything is untouched since I left. Is the apprehension I've been trying to suppress since she left justified? I call once. Twice. THREE TIMES. Nothing. Just that damn voicemail.

Something happened.

No. Impossible. I would have sensed it… Suddenly, a detail comes back to me, Jan is with her. I dial his number. He answers me on the three rings.

"Boss?"

I sigh. Finally, someone answers.

I pinch the bridge of my nose and step out of the room to call the elevator that has gone down in the meantime.

"Jan, finally! Where are you?"

"Still at Miss Lovisa's old place. I'm waiting for her."

What? What the fuck is this?

"You didn't go upstairs with her?"

"She refused. She wanted to pick up some things."

Who's his boss? Her or me? I had demanded him not leave her side. I growl and get back into the elevator. furiously, I press the bottom button several times.

"How long has she been inside?"

Jan pauses, probably calculating, before answering. "Less than an hour, boss."

What! You have to be kidding me! My blood runs cold, and I feel like I'm going to pass out. I lean against the elevator wall behind me, my heart pounding.

"An hour for a *fucking* violin? Didn't you think it was a bit long?"

"I… She had other stuff to pick up, too," he tries to justify.

"I don't give a fuck. You weren't supposed to your eyes off her!"

Is he being so stupid on purpose? Oscar told me that he is an outstanding shooter, but he is not known for his thinking skills.

"Send me the address, I'll be right there."

"Shall I wait for you?"

Good question. Lovisa isn't answering, and she's been up there for over an hour. If he goes up before me and finds her tied up, hurt, or worse, dead? I can't bear the thought of seeing her lifeless body, but even more, I can't stand the idea of Jan seeing her like that.

"Yeah," I growl as I exit the elevator.

I hang up and quickly receive the address. I inform Gunkil and Fredrik of the change of plan and hit the road. My best friend, in bad shape, will have to hold on because the woman I love may be in danger.

Damn it, Lovisa, what kind of mess have you gotten yourself into?

25

Lovisa, 18 years old

I'm ... free. No more school, no more boarding school, no more rules. Why does this idea make me feel both euphoric and terrified? No one came to my graduation. I got a lovely letter from Alfrida, who I've been corresponding with since I left Iron House. Hendrik also called, telling me he would continue to support me within reason and reminding me that even though I'm of age, I'm still at his mercy if I come back. I quickly found work in a café; this salary helps me to continue my violin lessons until I find a job in music. Now alone, I will be able to live my life as I see fit. I can live my life the way I want. For the first time in a long while, my heart feels lighter, and breathing seems less painful.

***

An hour earlier

The familiar streets of Stockholm take me back a few weeks, and for a brief moment, everything I experienced with Niklas disappears, and I fall back into my old life with Rikard.

Jan parks in the building's lot. I take a look at the other vehicles—Rikard's car isn't here. The coast is clear.

"I only have for few minutes," I tell Jan as I get out.

He follows me.

"Niklas asked me to come with you."

"It's not necessary. I won't be long."

The worried look on his face reminds me that this is a non-negotiable order from his boss.

"Look, I won't say anything. Wait for me here."

Jan finally nods and leans against his car. If Rikard were here, I might need his protection, but that's not the case.

I adjust my jacket and cross the small parking lot reserved for the building's tenants. The building is about a hundred years old. It has five floors, each with a huge loft. The walls are high, with original moldings on the ceiling. The Victorian-style lobby is impressive. The black marble floor shines from being polished several times a week. The high walls of a sober gray are devoid of any decoration. To my left are the black mailboxes for each tenant. Without much surprise, I see that my name is no longer listed next to Rikard's. Why do I feel a twinge in my heart?

It's as if you never lived here.

I call the elevator and watch the cage descend slowly, with its mesh and two glass doors. I really like this vintage charm of the building, and this authentic elevator has remained the same since its creation. I press the button for the top floor.

My heart is beating so fast and hard that it's painful. I know that Rikard isn't here and I have the right to come and retrieve what is mine, but this is no longer my home. Was it ever my home? I was never able to make this place truly mine.

Once on the right floor, I head toward the towering brown doors. I take out my keychain and find for the key that fits the lock. It slides in perfectly, so I slowly push the unlocked door. The hall hasn't changed. The coat rack is in its place near a small table where I usually put my keys, and the shoe closet opposite is still closed. The beige short-pile carpet covering part of the dark floor hasn't moved either. What was I expecting? I haven't been gone for years. It's too soon to spring cleaning and completely change the decor after a breakup.

In front of me, a long, fairly wide hallway with several doors leads to various rooms like the bathroom, two bedrooms, an office, and a laundry room as large as the kitchen. At the end of the hallway are the dining room and the living room. From there, we have access to a balcony that almost entirely wraps around the apartment and is wide enough to hold a small table and four chairs. I remember all the meals we had there with our friends.

I shake my head and head toward my former room, behind the first door on my right. I can't let my memories distract me from the purpose of my visit. Rikard sent me a picture of the violin on the bed, so hopefully it's still there.

I feel as if I'm entering a sacred sanctuary, where my presence is unwelcome. Just like in the entrance hall, nothing has changed. The enormous bed has new bedding in various shades of blue with a dozen pillows I used to painstakingly fluff and arrange every morning. I hated that.

My violin isn't here.

I look under the bed. Nothing. The closet has no instruments, only my clothes and Rikard's. I run my hand over my tops. Did I really have this many things? I always felt like I was wearing the same outfits. I'm tempted to take my favorites, but what's the point? Most of them were gifts from Rikard.

I leave and head toward the living room but stop in my tracks when I hear a noise from the bathroom. I freeze in front of the door, staring at it in horror. Could it be Rikard? I didn't see his car. My heart in my throat, I want to turn back and flee, but then I see my violin on the leather sofa. I curse myself and run to it. It's intact.

What a relief!

I can leave. I clutch my instrument and focus on the exit, walking quickly. Then the horror strikes. The person I dread most step out of the bathroom and blocks my path.

As shocked as I am, he stops dead. Thick, humid heat escapes from the room.

"What are you doing here?" we ask at the same time.

Under different circumstances, it would've made me laugh, but right now, all I want is to escape.

"This is my place," he answers.

"I thought you wouldn't be here. I didn't see your car."

He gives a nasty smile. "It's in the shop until tomorrow. How did you get in? Oh, I see, you still have the key."

I don't know what to say, as if I I've lost the ability to speak. Instead, I hand him my key, which he pockets.

"I'll change the locks; rats come and go as they please."

This kind of remark doesn't surprise me coming from him. He always loved to belittle those he deemed inferior. And now, I'm one of those people.

"You came to steal from me, is that it?" he asks, eyeing the violin.

It's not a stealing if the belongs to us.

"So, what, you lost your tongue? Speak!"

His harsh tone startles me. I lose all my means. I try to summon the courage I've built up these past few weeks, but it's gone, even Niklas's self-defense lessons seem to slip away.

"I don't want any trouble," I murmur, clutching my instrument. "You can keep everything else; just let me take this."

I try to move around him, but he blocks my way. Rikard laughs. "Look at you, still so pathetic. So, what's your life now? Living off another guy like a leech?"

So much cruelty come out of his mouth. Does he not realize how mean he's being? The guilt I once felt toward him after our brutal breakup and Niklas's beating fades away. My lungs fill with air, giving me the courage I need to respond. "You'll never grow up. When we were together, I hoped that you'd change, that I could make you change, but no. You'll always be an arrogant jerk who thinks no one is good enough for you."

He laughs again. "But look at you, she has a voice now. I may be a jerk, but at least I'm not a leech who clings to others to survive."

His accusation infuriates me. He always underestimated me and dismissed my financial contributions to our lives. Sure, I never earned as much as he did, but unlike Rikard, the job I have and the money I earned, I owe only to myself, which isn't the case for him. His parents gave him everything, and he calls me the leech? I snort in disgust. He doesn't deserve another minute of my time; he'd only use it to tear me down further.

"I have to go; someone's waiting for me."

I manage to slip between him and the wall quickly heading for the exit. His heavy footsteps follow me.

"Going back to your thug of a boyfriend? Is he here?"

"No."

Rikard swiftly spins me around and pins me against the wall, his face darkened with a cruelty I've seen too often in him.

And that never bodes well.

"So, you came alone."

Why do I feel like I should have lied about that?

"Let me go, and you'll never hear from me again."

His dark gaze slides over my body.

"We ended things on such bad terms. How about we start over, huh? One last kiss."

Did I hear that right? He's out of his mind. After everything that happened between us, I should give in to his twisted request? I place a hand on his chest as he tries to move closer.

"I'm leaving."

Rikard grabs my arm and grips it tightly to hold me back.

"Let go of me!" I shout.

"Just a kiss, that's all I'm asking," he demands, pulling me closer.

"You're completely insane, let me go!"

I try to back away, but he has no intention of letting go. His strength is superior to mine, but I'm not going to give in. I stomp on his foot as hard as I can. For a brief moment, his grip loosens, and I take advantage of it to break free.

"Come back here!"

His threatening tone sends chills down my spine and propels me to run away as fast as I can. He chases after me, his hand grabbing my shoulder. Instinctively, having lived this scene many times before, I turn around and use the violin to hit him over the head. His body slams against the wall, and a few drops of blood fall on his right cheek.

We both freeze at my action before he recovers and stands up, slightly staggering, probably dazed from the blow. The expression in his eyes reveals a murderous madness I never knew existed.

"It's much more than a kiss that I'm going to take from you."

I swallow hard and drop the violin, raising my hands to try to calm him.

"That's not what I wanted to do. Let's stop here, I'll leave, okay?"

I slowly back away, never taking my eyes off him. The fear of blinking and finding him on top of me, tearing my clothes off, grips me.

A mad, cruel laugh escapes his lips, which I once found perfect, but now only evoke disgust at the thought that they ever touched me. I turn and dash for the exit. Quicker than me, he grabs me by the hips and lifts me off the ground, dragging me into the bedroom. I scream at the top of my lungs.

"Help! Help!"

"Scream all you want! Remember, we soundproofed everything last year."

He throws me onto the bed and climbs on top of me. I struggle to bend my legs between us and push him away. Rikard puts his full weight on me, nearly suffocating me.

"Get off! Get off!" I shout, scratching his face.

He slaps me, unfazed by my cries, which only seem to fuel his sick cruelty. He forces my legs to straighten so he can wedge himself between them. Helpless, I let out one final scream before he muffles it with his large hand, covering my mouth and part of my face. He presses down on my nose, cutting off my air. Panicking, I try to break free and thrash wildly under his massive body. The air quickly runs out.

"You'll regret all your choices," he threatens, trying to slip his hand between us to reach the zipper of his pants. "Stupid bitch. You thought you were clever, huh? Let me tell you a secret, you're just an empty doll on someone's arm, and if you open your mouth, it's clear there's nothing inside."

Hot tears blur my vision, streaming down my face. His harsh words pull me back to a conversation I had with Niklas shortly after my breakup with Rikard.

***

Curled up in front of the fireplace with a cup of tea in my hands, I explain to Niklas my conversation with his father with his father while he was unconscious on the floor.

"I was scared at first that he would let Sören do horrible things to me, but in the end, he wanted to negotiate my departure. If I left quietly so he could raise you to be his successor, he promised I'd have a good life. He saw me as your weak point that needed to be eliminated."

I stare at my steaming cup, the warmth pleasantly heating my fingers.

"He said a pretty girl like me deserved the best and that my looks would open all doors. According to him, I didn't need intelligence to succeed."

At the time, I hadn't understood the full weight of his words. I was a sixteen-year-old girl dreaming of a life filled with music, and the fact that Hendrik supported my project by saying I needed nothing else never made me suspect that he was implying I should stay stupid to be appreciated. As I grew older, I realized the true meaning of his words, and even though he didn't see it, I made sure to learn every day to prove I wasn't the airhead he wanted me to be.

Niklas wraps me in his arms and plants a comforting kiss on my temple.

"Never let anyone belittle you or say you're worthless again. I know you're full of qualities, and people like my father or Rikard aren't even close to your level."

His words are a balm for my heart. He manages to boost my self-confidence, and it feels so good.

***

I won't let anyone manipulate or hurt me again. On the verge of passing out, I draw on my last reserves of strength and recall an infallible technique I learned during my self-defense classes. I grab Rikard's face and press my thumbs into his eye sockets as hard as I can. H He groans and instantly releases my mouth, backing away. I gulp in air and roll to the side to escape him. Falling to the floor, I crawl toward the door, coughing. Behind me, Rikard whimpers like a wounded animal. I just need to reach the door, and it will all be over, but my ex-boyfriend's determination to hurt me knows no bounds. He quickly gets back on his feet and charges at me, growling.

"You're not getting away that easily."

He grabs my ankles and drags me toward the bathroom. Mist surrounds us, and the humid heat draws my gaze to the bathtub. U Realizing his intention, I cling to the doorframe, screaming for help. With a sharp tug, he pulls me loose. Not giving me a moment to recover, he grabs my hair and brings his face close to mine. I moan, holding his wrist, trying to make him let go. Out of breath, we engage in a visual battle until I close my eyes as he tightens his grip on my hair.

"You're going to taste real pain," he assures me.

Hasn't that been the case since we met?

My eyes widen as he leans me over the bathtub.

"No, don't do th—"

A rush of hot water floods my mouth as he dunks my head into the tub filled to the brim. scream, swallow water, and choke. My arms push against the edges to try to pull back while my feet slip on the wet floor. He lifts my head. I spew a torrent of water and cough violently. My body, in shock, trembles all over.

"Please, stop!"

He chuckles and dunks my head back into the water. This pain crushes my lungs. My throat contracts in vain. It's unbearable. Rikard lifts my head again. I vomit up everything in my stomach along with the water.

"Look what you've done!" he growls, yanking my hair.

He'll end up pulling it out of my head, but for now, that's the least of my worries; I think of surviving.

"Stop, please, I understand! I'm a bitch, a parasite, all you want, but stop." I beg, hoping he'll end the torture.

"I'll stop when you're dead," he spits.

Has he always been like this? Rikard is a bad person, but a murderer? I couldn't have live with such a man without realizing it, it's impossible. But the evidence is overwhelmingly clear. He's going to kill me. And why? Because of a bruised ego? I swallow my tears and let my anger explode.

"You'll pay for it. One day, someone will come and kill you, and you'll end up in hell. You're just an asshole with whom I wasted four years of my life! I will always regret meeting you. You deserve the worst sufferings!"

Rikard crouches behind me and speaks into my ear. His mouth razing my skin, which disgusts me.

"Thanks for making this so easy for me."

Knowing what's about to happen, I hold my breath as he plunges my head into the bathtub again. I can't accept dying; I'm too young and have barely lived! And Niklas? He would be furious, and who knows what he would do.

I try to escape, flailing my arms backward to grab him. I dig my nails into the hand holding me and scratch it until it bleeds, while the other hand hits the small cabinet where I used to place my phone during my baths. Frantically, I find something hard. A candle? Rikard punches me in the ribs. I expel the air from my lungs and choke on the water.

Without hesitation, I grab the cylindrical object and manage to kick his knee. He loses his balance and falls.

This is my chance.

I lift my head out of the water, inhaling deeply, and turn to Rikard, who is on his knees. I raise the candle and strike him in the face with it. Half-lying down, I push myself up against the bathtub. The floor is so slippery that I can't stand. Fighting for my life has drained my energy, but as Rikard rises to attack me, I muster all my strength and kick him in the stomach. He slips and falls backwards. He slips and falls backward. His skull hits the tile so hard that I hear it crack.

Then… nothing.

Silence, except or the agitation of the water behind me.

I don't dare move, fearing he will get up and resume his attempt to kill me. The water in the bathtub calms, and the splashing stops. Soon, the white tile turns a light reddish color. This blood is coming from Rikard's head. He's bleeding profusely. I should help him, but I can't move. He might already be dead.

My eyes remain fixed on his face, which turns pale as all the blood drains from his head through his skull. What have I done?

If it wasn't him, it would have been me.

I let myself slide down against the tiles, sobbing. Stunned with cold, I can't stop the trembling that shake my body. I curl up on myself, letting the darkness envelop me and plunge me into a semi-conscious state, drifting between my confused thoughts and the present moment with the corpse of my ex-boyfriend.

✱✱✱

How much time has passed? Ten minutes? Twenty minutes? An hour? More? I slowly open my eyes. It's still light out, so it must still be daytime, but is it the same day? What woke me up? Groggy, I listen without being able to move. There are loud banging noises around me. What's happening? My gaze falls on Rikard, who hasn't moved. So he really is dead, and it's my fault.

"Lovisa!"

Who's calling me? Rikard? I stare at his pale lips, but they don't move. No, it's not him. The smell of death hangs all around me, confronting me with the harsh reality of the situation, yet I can't move. I remain frozen, staring at him, my cheek pressed against the wet tiles and my arms wrapped around my legs. I squeeze them so tightly that my stiffened limbs scream for me to finally relax, but I can't.

"Lovisa!"

Who the hell is that? The sound of wood splintering makes me flinch slightly. Someone shouts my name again, and hurried footsteps approach. Then a large figure bursts into the bathroom.

"She's here!" a familiar voice yells.

Two other figures appear; I glimpse them out of the corner of my eye but can't turn to face them.

"Get out of the way!" growls a voice that makes my heart jump.

Someone is pushed aside, and another takes over. I feel his scrutinizing gaze on me. His voice laden with emotion, he pleads, "Please let it not be her blood."

Niklas.

He's here, he came for me.

Finally, I blink extremely slowly, or is it just an illusion, and struggle to speak with a hoarse, exhausted voice, "It's his."

A collective sigh of relief washes over us. Gently, Niklas wraps his arms around me to help me sit up. He hesitates to touch me further, examining me closely.

"She's cold. Jan, bring me something to cover her," he instructs.

Sliding a hand under my chin, he lifts my face. I can't bring myself to look at him. If he can read me like I think he can, he'll see a soul torn in two and the eyes of a murderer. I close them and let a tear fall.

"It was… it was…" I murmur, but I can't say more.

"Love," murmurs in turn, gently stroking my cheek swollen from Rikard's slap.

I recoil.

No! That's not what I wanted, but after all that madness, my body rebels against human contact. Jan returns with a blanket, which Niklas wraps around me.

"Call Oscar to clean up. Fredrik, go check if anyone's around; we can't have anyone seeing her like this."

"We have to hurry, Gunkil is in bad shape."

Gunkil is hurt? I remember they were supposed to catch Rodrigo. Did they? I cast a tense glance at Niklas to see if he's injured, but he seems unharmed. It's been a hectic day for everyone.

"I killed him," I manage to say, lowering my head to the body at our feet.

"If he hurt you, he deserved it. I would've done it myself if I'd gotten here sooner," Niklas says, his voice full of anger, but not directed at me. His face looks like it's aged ten years. I've put him through a lot since I came back into his life. I'm adding another layer to everything he's had to endure since his father's death.

Fredrik quickly returns, reporting that everything's clear. The advantage of living on the top floor is that no neighbors are likely to come up here. As we descend the stairs, we don't encounter any other tenants in the building. Did any of them hear what happened? If they did, did they just turn a blind eye, figuring it wasn't their business? I prefer not to think about it.

Nestled in my boyfriend's arms, I refuse to leave them when he settles me in the backseat, next to Gunkil, who's as pale as snow.

"Gun…"

He offers me a weak smile and accepts the comforting hand I extend him.

I catch my reflection in the rearview mirror and recoil in horror at the state of my face. One side is covered in Rikard's blood, as are my hair. I look frightening!

Niklas slips in beside me and pulls me close. Fredrik takes the wheel and drives away swiftly from this place of misery, with Jan following behind.

No one speaks, there's no background music to mask the silence. Lost in my thoughts, I replay the past hour over and over again. he more I dwell on it, the more my feelings of sadness and guilt grow. I wish I could just sleep and forget about it all, but I'm sure my dreams would torment me too.

When we finally arrive at the private jet, I immediately notice the injured man lying on the floor under a blanket stained with dark blood. There's only one man accompanying him. I question Niklas with my eyes as we settle into our seats across from his best friends. Fredrik is putting Gunkil's arm in a sling to support his injured arm.

"Three of our men are dead, and Gregor was wounded in the abdomen," Niklas explains.

My eyes widen as I clutch the blanket to me. My soaked clothes chill me to the bone, adding to the shock that makes me tremble.

The pilot takes off without delay after receiving his orders.

During the flight, Niklas is in constant communication with Oscar, who stayed behind to clean up the apartment and dispose of Rikard's body with four of their men.

Dispose of him…

The thought makes me nauseous. As if he never existed, Rikard will simply be erased from the Earth. Body and soul. If I hadn't insisted on retrieving that stupid violin, none of this would have happened. My internal agony must be palpable. Niklas takes my hand and rubs it between his.

"It's not your fault," he says.

"I should have listened to you and not gone there," I lament.

If he throws an *I told you so* at me, I wouldn't blame him. After all, he had asked me not to go without him.

I take a deep breath, building up my courage, and explain to him what happened before my memory starts to blur the events to protect me. I'm aware that everyone is listening attentively, but I owe them the truth. I shed a few tears when I recount the bathtub ordeal. I still feel the horrible sensation of water in my lungs and nearly stop talking several times, but I force myself to spill everything in one go. When I finish, Niklas remains silent, his face closed off. What is he thinking? Oh no! What if he doesn't see me the same way now? Fredrik breaks the unbearable silence.

"It was self-defense. You couldn't have done anything else."

Niklas and him exchange a knowing glance.

He's right, but why do I feel so guilty? Gunkil, beside Fredrik, sits up straighter in his seat. He looks bad and urgently needs care.

"From the moment I saw him, I couldn't stand him. Only jerks go after women. He got what he deserved," Gunkil says in a hoarse voice, with a smile on his lips. "You're a real tough cookie, actually. I'll watch my back around you."

I can't return his smile and turn to Niklas, waiting for some kind of reaction from him.

"Fred, take me to pee, you'll hold it for me," Gun says.

Fredrik snorts in disgust but gets up to help Gun walk to the bathroom.

"Is he going to be okay?" I ask, worried.

Niklas glances in Gunkil's direction and finally nods.

"It'll take a lot more than that to bring him down."

Our eyes meet, and I don't see any judgment from him, just compassion for what I've been through. He keeps my hand in his and eventually intertwining our fingers.

"Say something. I won't blame you if you chew me out," I say.

His expression changes from compassion to surprise in a split second.

"Chew you out? Love," he sighs, unfastening my seatbelt to pull me onto his lap. "You were practically killed; the least I can do is congratulate you for fighting back and still being by my side."

"No blame, then?" I ask, on the verge of tears, relieved t that at least I haven't destroyed that.

"If you were dead, I'd have cursed you for the rest of my life and stopped you from resting in peace."

He runs his hand over my cheek in a gentle caress. He's so tender in this moment that my heart melts with happiness. I bite my lip, placing my hands on his chest, the blanket falls to the floor.

"Heading over there, I didn't imagine what was really going to happen. Oh, Nik, I truly had no idea, and I regret letting him manipulate me once again."

Now he won't be able to do anything to me or to anyone else. The thought of his worried parents searching for their son weighs heavily on me. Oh, no, Martha and Glen. What will they do without him? He was a monster in my eyes, but to them, he was their only child.

"His parents will wonder where he is. Oh my god…"

I run my hand through my tangled hair to pull it back; my elastic band snapped during my struggle with Rikard. A handful of hair remain in my hand.

"Oh no…"

Panicked, I run my hands through it again and pull out more handfuls of hair. I stand up abruptly.

"Wait," Niklas calls out to me.

He takes the hair from my hand and runs his fingers over my scalp as I sob. Without me seeing it, he gets rid of it returns with a bottle of water and two pills.

"Take them, they'll help you sleep."

I do so and sit back down, letting him cover me with the blanket. I'm afraid to fall asleep and be tormented by Rikard's ghastly face. What if he haunts my thoughts for the rest of my life?

26

Niklas, 20 years old

We gathered with the gang one last time before our paths diverge for good. Sven is going abroad to work, and Lucia has decided to become a vet and is going elsewhere for her studies. Only Gunkil, Fredrik and Jonna will stay. Everyone leaves someday, and for me, the breakup of our group began with Lovisa's departure. After one last beer in a local bar, only Jonna stayed. Talking to her strangely felt good. She reminded me of the good old days when Lovisa was around. Except for her blonde hair, I find her similar to Lovisa. Perhaps it's this physical trait that led me to sleep with Jonna. What I do, what I am, doesn't bother Jonna, and I'm certain she won't abandon me.

***

I've never appreciated watching a woman breathe as much as I do right now. Lovisa's chest rises and falls slowly, filling with that vital air. When I think that just the day before yesterday her lungs almost didn't fill with oxygen anymore, that her heart almost stopped beating. This thought revolts me. How could I have been so negligent toward her? I should have insisted that she stay in the room. I broke my promise about her safety. I assured her that no one would hurt her anymore. The shock passed, now a part of me resents her for making me so weak and powerless against all external threats. I can't protect her from everything.

She is my weakness. My flaw. The one that will cause my death.

If I had known what was happening to her earlier, I would have rushed to her aid and abandoned my mission with Rodrigo, and that's unacceptable on my part. What kind of leader am I to abandon my men at the last moment? In her presence, I forget my duty to them, and I can't accept that.

But I fucking love her so much. My heart could stop beating for her.

"Is everything okay?"

Alfrida interrupts my thoughts by bursting into the room, arms laden with a tray containing two delicious meals. Since our return, she has stayed overnight in one of the guest rooms to watch over us.

"She's just sleeping; the pills are working well."

"Do you think it wise to keep her asleep? She hasn't moved from this bed since you got back."

Lovisa was so agitated on the plane and when she woke up. Her incoherent and almost insane ramblings posed a danger to her.

"It's for her own good. I'll let her wake up in her own time; she needs to eat."

No food crossed her lips, and the impression that she has already lost weight preoccupies me. She's so thin that her fragility is evident. Has she always been like this? I remember a well-fed teenager.

Dr. Söderholm visited us this morning; he took care of my injured man, but also Gunkil; they're both resting at his clinic. According to him, Lovisa will eventually recover, but she will need a lot of support. As for her weight, he's not worried, so I deduce that I'm the one worrying too much.

After placing the tray on the desk, Alfrida affectionately strokes Lovisa's cheek and kisses her forehead. "My dear child, when will fate stop being so cruel to you?"

With pursed lips, I echo the governess's thoughts as I watch Lovisa, her face peaceful, sleeping. We've experienced so many painful trials that it becomes a nameless banality that no longer surprises us. I'm no longer amazed by the difficulties we face, and I would even find it strange if good things happened to us.

Alfrida leaves us in our bubble of serenity. I only left the room to speak with Oscar. He took care of Rikard's body and cleaned his home to erase any traces of our presence. O Oscar does a lot for my family for so many years that sometimes I forget to thank him. No obstacle scares him; he rises to every challenge we impose on him. In parallel with my conversations with him, I exchange emails with John Gray, who is finalizing the purchase of the Rosell companies. Soon, they will be mine. I love taking on challenges, and managing shopping centers at my age will be an achievement that I will enjoy achieving.

An hour later, Lovisa emerges from her long sleep, her face exhausted and so deeply sad that it breaks my heart. I wish I could take away all her guilt so she could feel better.

"Good evening, my love."

I kiss her and place a pillow behind her back as she sits up. I bring her the tray with her meal—having finished mine a long ago—and place it on her lap.

"Hi," she murmurs, pushing her hair behind her ears. "Have you been here all day?"

Her emerald eyes look at my casual attire and bare feet.

"I wanted to keep an eye on you even though Dr. Söderholm said you were okay."

She slightly furrows her brow, wrinkling her forehead.

"I vaguely remember his visit. Everything is so confusing."

Her thoughts clouded by medication don't allow her to say more. She takes her glass of water and drinks it all.

"Alfrida made you food; I'm going to warm it up for you."

She shakes her head, picks up her cutlery, and eats by cutting her food into small pieces. Given the circumstances, I can't blame her for this lack of appetite.

"I feel stupid asking you this, but how do you feel?" I ask.

Lovisa gives me a weak smile and shrugs. "Like I've been run over by a truck."

It doesn't surprise me. She immediately moves on to a contentious topic, "He's disappeared, isn't he? I mean Rikard. We'll never hear about him again?"

The worried look on her face unsettles me. Does she doubt my abilities? I place my hand on her leg, through the blanket, and look into her eyes. "You have nothing to fear, no one will trace it back to you."

Her utensils clatters on her plate as she sets them down. She pushes the tray aside and rests her chin in her hands, taking a deep breath. Her face takes on a determined expression.

"They'll eventually trace it back to me. The culprits always get caught."

I smirk. Really? My family is proof they don't, you just have to do it right.

I move next to her and wrap her in my arms, kissing her hair.

"If they try to get you, I'll move heaven and earth to save you."

The apparent silence that follows my words is deceptive. Our minds are racing, probably is a confusing way for Lovisa. I encourage her to eat a little more before her stomach refuses another bite. After that, she falls asleep again. I take the opportunity to slip away, putting on my shoes to go smoke a cigarette in the garden. Oscar joins me shortly after.

"How is she?"

"Better, I think, we'll see in the coming days."

He nods and immediately continues, "As we suspected, Rodrigo didn't show up at any hospital in the area, or if he did, he used another name. We haven't found him yet."

At least I have the satisfaction of seriously injuring him, his pants were soaked in blood. Maybe he succumbed to his wound? I dare to hope.

"We should expect retaliation. If he's still alive, he'll want revenge quickly," Oscar says, shoving his hands in his pockets.

"You're right. I think it's best not to bring the cleaning staff anymore, for their safety. As for Alfrida, I know she lives on the property, but she would be safer elsewhere."

The housekeeper may not agree, but she'll comply with my will. For her own good.

I exhale the white smoke in front of me. It rises into the air and disappears into the darkening sky.

"I know you want to be with her, but what are you going to do about Lovisa?"

If she stays here, I don't know what will happen to her mental health. For now, she needs to leave, even if it's just until Rodrigo is taken care of.

"She'll leave with Alfrida, make sure that the house in Greece is ready for them."

My family has several residences outside of Sweden, including one in Greece, where I spent many vacations when my mother was still with us. It's a beautiful little house on the beach in Crete. An idyllic landscape that will help Love to take her mind off things.

"Have you taken care of Gun and Fred?"

Oscar pulls out some documents and hands them to me along with a pen. I sign several pages. Ash falls on the papers, I blow it away and hand them back to him.

"What did they say?"

"As you predicted, they refused, but they know you'll do as you please."

I smile faintly, they know me well.

Putting my men's lives in danger doesn't bother me, they're paid to protect me and they know the risks. But when it comes to my best friends, my brothers, it's different. Gunkil downplayed his condition; his injury was much more serious than he let us to believe, and if he hadn't gone to the hospital in time, he would probably be dead. I can't work with them anymore. That's why I ended our partnership. As compensation for their services, I decided to give them a substantial amount, transferred to an account they'll have access to when they decide to accept it. For now, this offer infuriates them, as they want to be by my side and fight Rodrigo, but I don't want their deaths on my conscience.

I stub out my cigarette and put a hand on Oscar's shoulder, squeezing it as I look him in the eyes. He smiles back and nods. I head back up the stairs and go straight to find my pretty redhead. But when I enter the room, she's not there anymore. Noise from the bathroom catches my attention. As I approach, I see Lovisa kneeling in front of the toilet.

"Are you sick?"

With one hand, I lift her hair, and I place the other on her sweaty forehead.

"'m feeling better now," she admits, flushing the toilet.

She stands up with my help and rinses her mouth with water several times before brushing her teeth. Lovisa is wearing one of my T-shirts, much too big for her.

"I'll ask Alfrida to bring you something else to eat."

She swallows and shakes her head as she rinses her mouth again.

"Just the thought of swallowing anything makes me feel nauseous."

I don't like the idea of her getting sick. I pull her into my arms and carry her to the bedroom. So light... I scrutinize her exhausted face, pressing my lips together.

"Would you like to go to Greece?"

"Do you want to travel with everything that's going on right now?"

I sit on the bed, keeping her on my lap. I'd like to relax and go with her, but the timing isn't right.

"Not me. You and Alfrida. You'll settle in my house in Greece for a while."

Her face contorts into a grimace, giving her an even more exhausted expression. Her pale skin turns almost translucent under her strained features. Her chin trembles slightly, she stands up and hugs herself.

"I knew it. You don't want me anymore."

I must have misheard. I follow her as she starts pacing around the room. Her body is restless, her movements are sharp and tense. Where does she get this new energy from?

"What are you talking about? If I'm sending you away, it's for your safety."

"Liar! Liar…" she accuses me, ending with a nervous laugh. "I'm no longer the innocent, unblemished young woman. Now, my hands are stained."

What's all this nonsense? Damn, she's completely delusional. I try to approach her, but she avoids me.

"Listen, you must have your reasons for thinking that way, but you're wrong. I love you, Love, and I just want to keep you safe."

Her mind must be really confused to think like this. How could she believe that I wouldn't want her anymore after what she's done? Nothing she could do would ever push me away from her.

"I'll never blame you for your actions," I try to reassure her, taking hold of her hands and squeezing them when she tries to pull them away. "Hey! Hey, calm down. Calm down. I've killed more men than you can imagine. My hands, my whole body and my soul are stained with the blood of all my victims, and yet, you're still with me. So, tell me why would I reject you for defending yourself against that rapist?"

My reasoning seems to find its way to her mind, because her body stops its frantic movements and calms down. Again, her lower lip trembles, she struggles to hold back her tears. My little warrior. My heart swells with love and pride. She's still standing after all she's been through, and that's what matters most.

I guide her to the bed, where we lie down, our legs intertwined. I manage to get her to eat some fruit and drink water. Watching her nibble on her slices of nectarine, I wonder how I would go on living without her by my side. When she leaves, she will take my heart with her, and maybe I'll be able to work properly without worrying about her safety.

27

Lovisa, 19 years old

After three years, I gave in. I resisted the urge to search for him on the internet for so long. Nowadays, all young people are on social media. There's no reason why Nik wouldn't have an account on one of the most popular platforms. Looking at his photos feels surreal, like I'm observing a stranger. I'm fascinated by his transformation. He's no longer the teenager I knew. He has a beard and wears such a cold pout in some photos that he reminds me of Hendrik.
One hashtag keeps coming back: Love. My heart tightens at the sight of that word. Niklas still thinks of me.

***

Time heals all wounds.

I've always attached great importance to this phrase. Throughout my short life, where misfortune has struck me often, I've always bounced back. And what happened with Rikard is no exception. He still haunts my dreams, even though three weeks have passed since that fateful day, but I manage to get up in the morning without collapsing into tears. Maybe being away from Sweden plays a part. Greece is such a beautiful country, the weather is much milder than in my homeland. I feel good.

Even though I miss *him*. Terribly. His absence weighs on me, my heart bleeds again, and I feel incomplete. We talk on the phone every day, but it's not the same as feeling the warmth of his body against mine, smelling his skin, or the sensation of his lips on mine. I miss everything about him.

"You're daydreaming again, my dear."

Sitting on the balcony of my room, gazing out at the horizon, where the peaceful and cold sea could chill me to the bones if I ventured into it, I didn't hear Alfrida approach.

"As usual, Frida. Are you going to the market today?"

She nods, coat over her shoulders, wicker bag in hand, and scarf around her neck.

"You don't mind if I stay? He'll be calling soon."

With Niklas, we have agreed on a specific time to avoid missing this call that we are waiting for.

"Of course not. I'll bring you some baklava."

These pastries are a delight for my taste buds. Every morning, Alfrida makes sure I have them with my tea. She knows how to please me. This little stay among women is pleasant, although strange at first. We're not used to living together anymore. Quickly, the housekeeper took ownership of the place and managed the house like she does for Iron House. I'd like to feel at home too, but my home is wherever Niklas is.

Alone again, I admire the landscape one last time before closing the terrace doors. The house is impersonal, and nothing indicates that a little boy and his parents used to spend their vacations here. No photos, toys, or even clothes. This place seems like it never hosted the laughter of a family. In comparison, even Iron House seems warmer.

In my pocket, my phone vibrates repeatedly. A ball of anxiety overwhelms me and twisted my gut when I see the name *Ulrik*, a friend of Rikard, appear on my screen. He keeps contacting me despite my efforts to remove him from my life. Every time I block him, he finds a way to talk to me. I suspect he's put the police on my trail. A witness must have seen me going to my ex-boyfriend's place. He probably provided my new address, and the local authorities came to see Niklas. But what the Stockholm police don't know is that Nik is untouchable in Kiruna. For form's sake, they came to question him about me, but they didn't try to find me and gave an inconclusive report to the inspectors handling Rikard's disappearance.

I'll probably regret it for the rest of my life to have committed such an act, but every day I try to convince myself that he was just a monster about to kill me. It was him or me. I have to move on now. *I must.*

As expected, at exactly one o'clock, my phone rings, and my heart leaps with joy. A great distance separates us even though the time zone is almost the same, except for one hour.

I hurry to answer so as not to keep him waiting and bring the phone to my ear. The sound of his distant voice makes me both sad and happy.

"Hi, babe."

Simple, banal, and yet, I love hearing him say that! I can't help but smile and sit on the edge of the bed.

"Hi. As always, you're right on time."

His laugher warms my chest and releases endorphins of happiness throughout my body.

"I wouldn't miss this for the world. I have to accompany my men on a stakeout where Rodrigo was spotted in Kiruna. We're almost there, Love."

My smile fades. It's good news, but the fear of losing him is even greater now that I'm no longer by his side. So many miles separate us, and I have no way of coming to his rescue if anything happens to him.

"Can't they go without you?"

I know, it's selfish of me to want to protect his life at all costs when his men face the same danger. But I love him so much that his life will always come before anyone else's.

"It's is my fight. I need to be with them."

"I know," I mumble, pulling at a loose thread on the blanket embroidered with lovely hyacinths. "It would be easier if I were with you. This distance is unbearable, I can't stand it anymore."

This isolation is intolerable, and when I'm outside, Alfrida and two bodyguards follow me everywhere. I'm never free to move; there's always a pair of eyes watching my every move to ensure I'm safe.

"This situation is temporary; everything will be back to normal soon."

He's been telling me that for so long that I feel like I'm dealing with an automaton listing options when you call a company.

"If only you could come for a day, just one. We could catch up, relieve all this pressure," I say trying to persuade him.

"And I have a lot pressure to release."

I can sense his smile through his words. I imagine him sitting in his office chair, spinning a coin on the aged polished wood. He often does that when he's on the phone, or he plays with his wolf-head signet ring.

"Can I call you tonight when we're lying in our beds and alone?"

"Sounds good, I didn't know you were so naughty."

"There are a lot of things you don't know about me, Viking," I giggle, biting my lip.

The warmth of his smile is a soothing balm for my soul, tortured by his absence. I can see his eyes squinting, forming little wrinkles at the corners, and his beautiful white teeth contrasting with his brownish-blond beard.

"That nickname is going to follow me for the rest of my life, isn't it?"

"You can be sure of it!"

This nickname comes from one Halloween night, a year after I arrived in Kiruna. For the occasion, he had dressed up in a Viking costume and was shouting lines from Conan the Barbarian, entertaining everyone. That party at our place was unforgettable. n high school, the students would shout a line from the movie every time they saw him, making everyone laugh. Back then, he was much thinner and way less muscular than he is now, which made him look ridiculous in his costume, but he wore it with such confidence that no one dared to criticize him. As for me, I wore a bumblebee costume that wasn't scary at all. Nevertheless, it was comfortable to wear and everyone let me pass because it took up so much space.

"What's the best in life?" I quote, biting my lip and smiling.

He laughs through the phone. *"To crush your enemies. See them driven before you. And to hear the lamentations of their women.*[1]*"*

I join in his laughter, which makes me feel good.

"Do you remember Lucia and Sally's costumes?" I ask, trying not to laugh again.

"Um… No. Oh yes! In—"

"In a hot-dog costumes!" we say together.

We burst into laughter. Lucia was the sausage and Sally the bun. Unfortunately for Lucia, all the padding had fallen off her legs, making her look like male anatomy in erection. She won the contest that night.

I lie on the bed, looking at the white ceiling adorned with moldings of angels surrounding a crystal chandelier. I'm staying in the master

---

1   Line from the movie *Conan the Barbarian*.

suite, the biggest room in the house. The canopy bed would make any little girl dream. I calm down before he does and turn over onto my stomach.

"If only for one day, I wish we could go back to being those teenagers."

"Me too."

He pauses. I hear murmurs from his end and wonder who's distracting him.

"Love, I have to go, but I'll talk to you tonight, okay?"

"For our naughty date?"

He's laughing. "Yes. See you tonight."

Every time I hang up, my heart feels lighter and my loneliness seems less painful. But the emptiness of my room quickly brings me to reality, showing me that this illusion is fleeting. This large, cold room feels even more daunting at night. Everything is oversized. The house seems to have been designed to accommodate a multi-generational family.

Later in the day, Alfrida returns with food and a smile on her face.

"I have good news! There's a puppet show tonight in the square; I know it's for kids, but it could be fun for us. What do you think?"

I admire her effort to make me feel better. I slip behind her and wrap my arms around her shoulders, resting my chin on one of them.

"Thank you for everything you do. Let's do it, it might be nice."

I'll send a message to Nik to let him know of my plans and that I might not be on time for our naughty date.

Frank, a man assigned to us, clears his throat to get our attention and signal his presence.

"M. Ekman wouldn't like you being out at night."

I smile and take an apple from one of Alfrida's bags. "Let him come to Greece to stop me."

"It's for your own good."

I snort and shake my head, my red locks twirling around me.

"Are you going to lock me in my room like a child? No! So, we're all going to that show. Got it?"

His eyes widen slightly before returning to a neutral expression. Getting ordered by a woman can't be easy on his pride, but I don't care. Since I've been here, I've obeyed wisely without complaining. When

I arrived, I was a wreck consumed by grief. Now that I'm on my feet, there's no way anyone's deciding what I do with my days.

"Lovisa dear, come sit and have a little drink with me, it'll relax you."

"I'm perfectly calm," I reply, glancing at the bottle of beautiful pastel pink liqueur.

Strawberry liqueur. I wrinkle my nose and wave away the glass she filled, sitting down and biting into my apple. Frank slipped away at the housekeeper's request, who then takes a seat next to me. She places her wrinkled, soft hand on mine and pats it affectionately.

"Poor Frank, you don't make his job easy. Why are you so hard on him?"

Am I? I didn't think I had been awful to him. I chew my piece of apple slowly, staring at the fruit with more interest than necessary.

"Tell me what's bothering you."

Isn't that obvious? This beautiful gilded cage holds me against my will and keeps me from the man I love. I want to go back to my country, but I'm not allowed yet. I sigh loudly and look into her age blue eyes.

"How do you stay so calm with everything going on back home?"

Alfrida's smile, full of wisdom and knowledge that I lack, stretches her thin lips chapped by the cold. She grabs her glass of strawberry liqueur and drinks it in one gulp, much to my surprise.

"I've lived long enough to know that everything works out eventually. But do you know my secret? After a day of work, I sit in my chair with a glass of fruit liqueur and thank heaven for the good things that happened that day."

I burst out laughing. The comical image of Frida in a bathrobe and curlers, sipping a glass of alcohol, flashed through my mind. She affectionately pats my cheek before getting up.

"In a few years, you'll see that all these complications were worth it because you'll have a wonderful life. Now, finish your drink and help me put away these groceries if you don't mind. My old back is killing me."

I nod and stand up, looking at my glass. I sniff its contents and grimace, placing it by the sink.

"You can have it if you want."

I grab a bag of potatoes and hefted it.

"Are you planning to feed an army?"

"They keep for a long time, and who can resist a good deal."

Right now, we could easily afford groceries without needing promotions, but some habits are deeply ingrained. Alfrida, like me, comes from a modest family where coupons are important.

Groceries put away, I leave the housekeeper to prepare dinner. I put on a warm coat and head outside, climbing the path that leads to the beach. Glancing behind me, I see Jan, the second bodyguard, watching me at the top of the path. He doesn't follow me by my order. From where he is, he'll see anyone approaching before I do. At this late winter period, the beach is mostly deserted.

The gray sky and mist hanging over the sea don't diminish its charm; on the contrary, they enhance it. The waves lap in front of me, some crashing against the rocks a bit further out, creating more movement in the ever-restless water. At first, I didn't dare venture onto the beach. The thought of falling into the ocean, even if I could stand, made my stomach turn and filled me with panic. But each day, I forced myself to walk on the damp sand to overcome this fear. And it's working; I'm now less than a meter from the water.

I take out my phone and take a picture with the sea behind me, sending it to Niklas with the caption: "No snow here, just a beach waiting for you."

The weather is much milder than in Kiruna, which is nice. There's no snow or icy wind in the evening. It rains a lot, several times a week, keeping us indoors and contributing to my often gloomy mood. Plus, there are no northern lights dancing in the sky at night, and I must admit, I miss that splendid spectacle.

Barely a moment after sending the photo, I get a reply. A photo, actually, of him in his car with a heart-melting smile, saying, *I'm with you every moment. You have my heart.* These words make me want to catch the next flight to Sweden to be with him. How does he expect me to be patient with messages like this? It makes him even more irresistible and essential to my life. If we were in a romance novel, I'd be plucking flower petals, reciting, "He loves me, he loves me not." This man is going to be the death of me with declarations like this.

I would gladly damn myself for him.

✳✳✳

In the evening, after dinner with the two bodyguards—a scene that would scandalize Niklas, who would probably insist they eat after us—we head to the puppet show taking place in a cozy little square a few minutes from the house.

"Look, Frida, isn't it beautiful," I exclaim, spotting all the lights decorating the theater that had been set up just a few hours earlier.

In front of the small stage, wooden chairs are arranged in several rows, surrounded by flaming torches warming the air. The smell of hot sugar wafts from several stalls, whetting our appetites. To my right, one of the vendors is selling candied apples, sugar-coated peanuts, and giant cotton candies. This magical sight delights me more than I could have imagined. Even the bodyguards forget their role for a moment to take in the decor of this place.

"It's very pretty, dear, we're going to have a great time. Let's pick our seats, there's such a crowd."

People are streaming in from all the streets that lead to the square. Children, parents, couples, and friends gather near the stalls or head toward the seats. A collective excitement surrounds us; I feel everyone's enthusiasm and find myself momentarily forgetting my worries.

"I had no idea puppets were so popular," I say.

The show will probably be in Greek, so we won't understand much, but that doesn't matter. The evening is just beginning and I already feel good. We settle into the third row, with Frida and me flanked by Frank and Jan. Once again, they put on a professional mask, making me smile with amusement.

"Relax, guys. A serial killer isn't going to jump on stage and start slashing at the puppets."

Jan, sitting to my right, gives a slight smile but doesn't respond. Worse than damn robots, those two. I don't insist any longer and snuggled up against Frida's shoulder, who shares my good mood.

"Thank goodness I have you," I whisper in her ear, smiling.

She pats my hand, nodding.

A man climbs on stage and introduces himself. Though I can't understand his language, I assume he's the director of the play we're about to see. Curled up in the arms of Alfrida, I watch the human-sized puppets move in front of us. Several feet above them, the director and his assistants control their puppets, lending their voices for the evening. I don't understand a word of what they're saying, but the laughter of the crowd triggers my own. The giant puppets move so eerily at times that it seems real. I'm captivated by their craftsmanship. Not everyone has this talent; I would be incapable of animating toys as well as they do. It must require a lot of coordination.

During intermission, I get up to buy us some snacks for the rest of the show. I look for the shortest line and stand behind two people waiting. As I wait, I take out my phone and snap a selfie in front of the food stand, smiling. I send the picture to Niklas with the caption: "A sweet kiss just for you."

When it's my turn, I point to four bags of popcorn with four lemon sorbets. My English is rudimentary, and the vendor only half-understands me. I complain in Swedish, "Why didn't I pay more attention in class? I just want popcorn and lemon sorbet."

A man chuckles behind me. When I turn to glare at him, the large scar running vertically down his left cheek catches my attention. Unfazed, he steps up next to me. In perfect English, he places my order, then looks at me and asks in my native language, "Just for you?"

I'm taken aback and don't respond immediately.

"No, for four."

He speaks Swedish! Since I've been here, I haven't met anyone else from my homeland. Suspicion makes me wary. What if he's here to kill me? He could be one of Rodrigo's men. I swallow and scrutinize him, trying to detect anything suspicious. I eye his closed jacket, easily imagining a weapon hidden beneath. While I analyze him, he places his own order and pays for two bottles of water and a large assortment of biscuits.

"It's not easy to make yourself understood in another language, is it?" he asks me, before quickly adding, "I have to go. My wife is waiting. Glad I could help."

He doesn't wait for my answer and disappears into the crowd. I watch him sit next to a woman. Shaking my head, I realize I'm becoming paranoid, imagining danger everywhere. Prompted by the vendor and the impatient customers behind me, I pay and return with my loot, nearly dropping the sorbets due to the rush of people toward the stands. Everyone is in a hurry because the show is about to resume.

To my surprise, there are far more adults than children. Maybe it's due to the hour? Or to the cold, which is harsher than the previous evenings. My frozen fingers long for warm gloves and a blanket on my lap. Despite the cold, I'm having a pleasant evening. I'm crazy for not getting hot drinks, but the sorbets were too tempting. I love the tangy flavor that makes my mouth water before I even taste it. Besides, when Niklas and I were teenagers, we used to have them after school. I kept up this little tradition after I left Kiruna for boarding school, whenever we could go out on weekends.

The evening ends with a nursery rhyme that everyone starts singing. I hum along while swaying with Alfrida, arm in arm, and clap as the puppeteers take their bows. Free hot chocolate and coffee are distributed. We drink them quickly to head home. The evening was enjoyable, but we're exhausted, and Alfrida is nearly asleep in her chair. Before going to bed, I check my phone one last time. A message from Niklas says he's postponing our flirty call. A little disappointed, even though I had asked him to reschedule, I slip under the cool sheets and place my phone by my pillow, just in case he tries to contact me again.

✳✳✳

The following days blend into one another. Wake up, eat, go to the market, eat, take a walk, watch TV, call Niklas, eat, sleep, and sleep some more. This routine becomes a habit that I stick to every day.

The market we go to is vast and varied. It offers so many foods and items of all kinds that it's hard not to find what you're looking for. Alfrida carefully selects beautiful red apples for the pie she plans to make for tonight's dinner. My mouth waters just thinking about it. With her is Frank, helping carry the heavy bags. On my end, Jan advises me on my choices for home decorations. I want to brighten up the place with some green plants. I'm not sure if I can keep them alive, but I figure it will keep me busy for a while before I get bored with this activity.

"Can you ask the vendor to wrap these two ferns for me?" I say to Jan.

Jan is much better in English than I am, and if it means I can have a few minutes without him hovering around, I'll give him all the most trivial tasks.

I move over to some purple flowers, wondering about their name. A pleasant, light sweet scent comes from them. Their delicate appearance makes me hesitant to buy them; they'd surely die.

A tattooed hand enters my field of vision. The numbers between the thumb and index finger catch my attention, so I look up at the man beside me, intrigued. Short, tousled brown hair. Hazel eyes too small for his face and a mouth twisted in a nasty sneer. But what stands out most is his scar. The Swede from the theater.

"You?"

"We meet again."

A malevolent aura emanates from him, and the wariness I felt toward him returns. I put down the purple flowered plant and move away, glancing sideways at Jan, who is talking to the vendor. To my surprise, the stranger follows me, pretending to be interested in the various potting soils.

He's following me.

I step back again, and he quickly grabs my wrist to stop me.

"Let go of me or I'll scream," I order, pulling on my arm.

He complies but keeps his wicked smile.

"Go ahead and scream, bitch, and the old lady will die along with your two buddies."

His tone freezes my blood and roots my feet to the ground; I don't dare move. He takes a deep breath, satisfied with his effect, and steps closer to me.

"Wise decision. Pretend to be interested in what's in front of you."

I swallow hard and cast an uncertain glance at the seed packets on the table. I hold my breath waiting for what comes next.

"Do you know who sent me?"

He plays with some onion bulbs, crushing them in his fist without caring if the vendor sees.

"Rodrigo," I whisper.

Who else could it be? A tough-looking, tattooed man who speaks Swedish—it has to be one of Rodrigo's men. I thought I was safe so far from home. And yet…

"How did you find me?"

"We have our sources. It took some time. You were well hidden, almost slipped through our fingers."

I risk a glance at Jan and pray he comes over.

I bite my lip and slowly slide my hand into my pocket to grab my phone. But I'm as subtle as an elephant in a china shop; Rodrigo's man grabs my wrist and takes my phone.

"Trying to fool me?"

He puts my phone in his jacket, which he then lifts slightly to show me his weapon.

"Here's what's going to happen. You're going to lose them and meet me in two minutes at the tobacco shop. You know where that is?"

I nod, my mouth suddenly dry and my throat tight.

"If you try to warn them, the men with me won't hesitate to kill the old lady and the other two."

He spits out his words with such disrespect for Alfrida that I want to slap him, but playing hero at such a critical moment would be risky.

As soon as he gives his instructions, he disappears into the crowd.

I suddenly look around, searching for any suspicious-looking men. But there's nothing.

It would be so easy for me to rush to Alfrida and beg her to hide, but not knowing if he's telling the truth about his accomplices ready to shoot if I disobey, I can't take that risk.

With fear in my stomach, I slowly move away from the stall and weave through the numerous passersby in the main aisle. My legs can barely hold me up; they are numb and threaten to give way if I'm not careful.

The tobacco shop is on the other side of the market. Without losing a second, I gather all my courage and start running, apologizing to the people I bump into. My heart pounding, I spot the wooden sign with a pipe drawing on it.

Just in time.

I rush to the store. As I'm about to push the door open, arms grab me and shove me into the alley beside it. Rodrigo's man, now away from prying eyes, openly threatens me with his gun.

"Good girl. Now, let's go."

"Where?"

"To see your man," he sneers, pushing me ahead of him. "Wouldn't want to miss seeing him one last time, now would you?"

28

Niklas, 21 years old

Years go by, and I keep sinking into such deep and dark waters that sometimes it feels like I'll never be able to surface again. And for what? There's nothing good for me outside of my father's business. At least there, I leave my heart out of it, and only my head acts. Damn, I disgust myself. Why do I still miss her? I should have forgotten her by now, yet I see her everywhere and in every woman I sleep with. I wish I could tear my heart out so I wouldn't feel anything anymore, because even in the depths of the abyss, it still beats for her.

***

I knew it would be difficult for me to find Rodrigo again. Our confrontation has made him much more vigilant, and so far, I haven't been able to track him down. Once again, a false hope enrages me—one of my men, Gunnar, thought he had spotted him. Unfortunately, that idiot was mistaken.

So here we are, back to square one.

I hate this waiting. Under different circumstances, I might have enjoyed this cat-and-mouse game more, but I need to keep Lovisa away to protect her. I managed to stay out of her life for years. Now, she's back by my side; we're together, and every minute spent away from her puts me on edge. During our calls, I'm always vague about my feelings, but deep down, my heart bleeds every time I hear her voice from thousands of miles away. This distance is also why I've decided never to leave her again.

A week ago, I went to a jeweler to pick out a ring. Once this mess is finally over, I plan to make Lovisa my wife. This thought makes me smile—I had promised myself I would never get married. My best friends would laugh at me if they knew what I was about to do, but I know they'd be happy for us.

In the meantime, I received an annoying phone call: Antonin Bourgois, the son of jeweler Jean Bourgois, contacted me to report a problem with the ring. He asked me to come and check it out. I don't know what it's about, but his worried tone left me no room for hesitation. Besides, everything has been quiet these past few days.

Iron House will still be standing when I get back.

But with the looming threat, I don't go out without my two Goldens strapped to my holster, fixed by Ogs.

The jewelry store, famous in the region, is located in the affluent part of the city. Everyone knows to come here for quality, often unique, pieces. It has security cameras all around the shop and a private parking lot where only my car is parked.

After I parked, I enter the shop as the door unlocks, a necessary security measure for this type of business. Inside, the artificial spotlights directed at the showcases displaying all the jewelry hurt my eyes. It takes a moment for me to adjust.

At the counter, Jean greets me with one of those dazzling smiles that shopkeepers often have. He's dressed in an elegant cream-colored suit that fits perfectly on his slender frame. His brown hair, streaked with silver, is neatly slicked back, and his thin rectangular glasses rest on a long nose. His unique appearance has always amused me.

"Mr. Ekman! How are you?"

"Fine, thank you," I reply, approaching the counter. "Antonin told me there was an issue with the ring. What's going on?"

Jean furrows his thick brown eyebrows speckled with gray and adjusts his glasses.

"He told you that?"

I nod, tapping the glass display case that showcases luxury watches. Mr. Bourgois seems annoyed, although he doesn't let it show. He quickly regains his composure and smiles again.

"One moment, please."

The jeweler disappears into the back room. My family has been one of his oldest clients, so he has no problem leaving me alone with his livelihood. Besides, everyone knows money isn't an issue for me, even if, when I was young, it didn't stop me from stealing alcohol or cigarettes for fun with my gang. And anyway, all the jewelry is protected and locked up.

Jean returns a few minutes later, holding a small black velvet box in his hand.

"It must have been a mistake. Here's the ring, and I have good news, it's ready."

He opens the small box. In the center, there's a silver ring set with a large ruby. Its warm, deep color symbolizes the love and passion that bind us. All around, small transparent diamonds sparkle. The jewel is unique.

"You're going to make her very happy. This ruby will enhance her beauty, and everyone will have eyes only for her."

I smile and take the ring, moving it from side to side. The light reflects in the precious stone, revealing all its perfectly cut facets. Each diamond surrounding the ruby is unique; no two stones are alike, but when assembled, this isn't noticeable.

"She doesn't need a jewel for that."

I remember four years ago, in that immense concert hall where I admired her playing her solo. She was stunning in her emerald-green, mid-thigh-length dress. She was so beautiful. Every sound from her violin drew me closer to her; invisible threads encircled me with each note, and even though I had promised myself that day never to see her again, deep down, I knew our paths would cross again.

"You've done an excellent work."

I refuse the bag and put the box directly in the inner pocket of my leather jacket, which scandalizes the jeweler, who prides himself on presenting his creations well.

"I hope she says yes."

"Thank you. Goodbye."

Lovisa won't say no, the bond between us is too strong, but out of tradition, I will propose to her properly. All I have to do now is wait for her return.

Once in the deserted parking lot, I walk to my car. I pull out my keys, twirl the keychain on my finger, and unlock my door. The screech of tires makes me jump. I turn around just in time to see a black van screeching to a halt in front of me. The side door slides open, and two men with guns jump out. I drop my keys and reach into my jacket, pulling out my guns. Without hesitation, I start shooting as I duck behind my car for cover.

"Shoot, damn it!" the driver yells, rolling down his window.

"The boss wants him alive!"

Who? Rodrigo? e's the only one with the guts, or the cowardice, to send his men to attack me. So far, none of my father's enemies have dared to mess with me.

I take advantage of their hesitation and pop up, shooting the nearest man in the neck. Blood spurts everywhere, and a horrible gurgling sound escapes his mouth as he chokes on his own blood and collapses. The adrenaline pumping through my veins gives me the courage to charge at the second assailant outside the van. I smash his nose with the butt of my empty guns. Blood soaks the man's face as he pushes me away, hitting me in the stomach and abdomen.

"People are coming!" the driver yells.

The guy I wounded tries to drag me into the van, but a punch to his jaw makes him let go. He curses at me and lands one last punch in the middle of my chest. I gasp in surprise and stagger backward. It feels like my heart is being torn apart from the inside. The pain is intense and unbearable, and I fall to the ground.

"Let's get out of here!"

They quickly grab the body of the man I killed and flee as passersby rush into the parking lot, alerted by the commotion. Unable to move, I watch the van speed away with another screech of tires. A panicked woman in her fifties approaches and screams in horror at the sight of the guns at my feet. She leans over me, her face filled with concern.

"Are you okay? Sir?"

She looks me over and pulls out her phone when she sees me struggling. My face twisted in pain, I can only clutch my chest, trying to ease the agony in my heart. It doesn't work.

"Call Dr. Söderholm's clinic, I need… to go there," I manage to articulate through gritted teeth.

The doctor is famous throughout Kiruna. His posters are plastered at every bus stop.

"Tell them… I'm Niklas Ekman."

My voice fades, becoming a distant echo. My vision darkens until the void swallows me. I'm plunged into an endless fall, deeper into myself, with no escape.

***

My body is… cold. I can barely feel my fingertips and toes. I'm lying against a smooth, cold surface—I'm no longer on the asphalt of the parking lot, but where am I?

"Is he ready?" a familiar voice asks to my right.

"The catheter is in place, and the anesthesiologist is ready," a woman replies to my left.

A blinding light assaults me when I try to open my eyes. I groan and raise a hand to my face, but it's stopped by a needle in the back of my hand, connected to a long, clear tube.

"Mr. Ekman, don't move."

Dr. Söderholm leans over me. His graying hair is covered with a scrub cap, and his usual white coat over his suit has been replaced by green scrubs. A surgical mask covers his mouth and nose, and he's wearing gloves. The setting of the operating room quickly becomes apparent.

"What the hell am I doing here?" I exclaim, a touch of panic in my voice.

"You were brought unconscious to my clinic. It's your heart."

That damn heart acting up at the worst possible time.

I hold back a swear and glance around at the people surrounding me. Including the doctor, there are four—two men and two women. They're staring at me, frozen as if facing a predator.

"That doesn't explain why I'm on this table freezing my ass off," That doesn't explain why I'm on this table freezing my ass off.

Even through his mask, I can sense his tight-lipped expression. He clears his throat.

"We can't wait any longer, Mr. Ekman. Your heart can't take much more of this without external help. Let me operate you."

I stare at him, dumbfounded, resisting the urge to strangle him when I realize he was about to operate on me without my consent.

"I didn't give you permission."

The old doctor sighs and signals to his team to continue with the preparations. He locks his blue eyes with mine.

"You gave it to me the day you invested in my clinic, asking me to do everything to keep you alive, and that's what I'm trying to do today. You invested all that money to benefit from my skills."

He silences me with his argument. I know he's right, but it's not the right time. They tried to take me, and something tells me it's just the beginning. But will my body still follow me in this battle?

Today, as I lay on the asphalt of the jewelry store parking lot, I briefly thought I was living my last seconds. It will probably never be the right time for this operation; sooner or later, I'll have to let it happen.

"I need to make a call first."

If I'm going to be out of commission for a few hours, I need to inform my team.

"Mr. Bäck has been informed of your condition."

Oscar probably knew what Dr. Söderholm had in mind and didn't stop him.

"Fine. Get me back on my feet," I capitulate, reluctantly.

I need to recover quickly, for my own safety and for the safety of those under my protection.

Through the catheter, the man I assume to be the anesthesiologist injects a substance that forcefully enters my veins.

"I won't feel anything, but I'll be conscious, right?"

The nurse exchanges a heavy look with Dr. Söderholm, who takes the mask from her. He places a reassuring hand on my shoulder and places the mask over my nose and mouth.

"It's a procedure with local anesthesia, but in your case, I prefer you to be completely asleep."

A sense of betrayal boils deep within me and spreads throughout my body.

"Bastard. You're… you're… going to…pay…"

My mouth goes numb, as does the rest of my body, which feels like it weighs a ton.

My mind drifts away from reality before fading into nothingness.

29

Lovisa, 20 years old

I can't believe it. My dream has come true! After several intense auditions where I gave my all, I've managed to join an orchestra that performs regularly throughout Sweden. For now, I'll be just another violinist among many, but I promise myself to give everything I have to stand out and become the solo violinist. I'll surpass Aria Korkova, a young Russian with undeniable talent, but who doesn't know about my determination to be the best. Niklas would be so proud of me; he always told me I would be a great artist, that my talent would be recognized. According to him, I was a fighter, and I will make my name known in the world of music. He always believed in me.

***

When I woke up this morning, I didn't expect to end up being taken hostage and forced to return to Sweden. On the plane, my captor no longer has his gun, but the threat is still very real.

"If you make one wrong move, they're dead," he told me, tapping his phone. "Just one call from me and it's over for them."

The idea of snatching his phone crossed my mind, but something tells me he would foil my plan in less than two seconds and make me pay for it immediately. After all, I'm not his main target, just a means of pressure against Niklas, and even though I'm important in Rodrigo's eyes, there's no guarantee that my captor wouldn't make me pay for my disobedience in some other way than death.

After stealing my papers and passport, he assured me that a team would remain in Greece to hold the others hostage. Very talkative, he added that he had left a message for Alfrida and the men with my phone to lure them to the beach house.

The flight lasts for several hours, during which my nerves are so on edge that any noise makes me jump. I don't know what's going to happen, but the closer we get to Sweden, the greater the danger becomes. I'm in a real mess, and I know the aftermath will inevitably be worse.

***

Sitting in an old car of an unknown make, I tighten my seatbelt and stare at the road ahead. Beside me, my captor drives in silence, occasionally breaking it to throw lewd jokes my way. A gun is hidden in the glove compartment; he quickly grabs it, wedging it between his abdomen and his pants. My attention drifts to it from time to time. It would be so easy to take it, but would I be capable of pulling the trigger? After the umpteenth time, he catches my gaze and snickers.

"It's big one, don't you think?"

I grimace in disgust and cross my arms over my chest to shield myself from his prying eyes.

"You know, I could ask the boss not to kill you. You could stay alive if you behave," he suggests.

His tattooed hand slides over my thigh. I recoil and swiftly push it away, glaring at him.

"Don't touch me, you filthy pig! I'd rather die than buy my freedom by sleeping with you," I retort.

He chuckles and places his hand back on the wheel, abruptly speeding up.

"You're just a lackey who only obeys. I doubt Rodrigo even knows your name," I spit out, hoping to wipe the smirk off his face.

Touché.

His nostrils flare, and his eyes widen for a brief moment. His fingers grip the wheel tightly, his knuckles whitening. A wicked smile stretches his lips.

"I'm going to kill you, baby, but before that, we'll all take turns with you. You'll be in so much pain that you'll beg me to put you out of your misery," he threatens, his tone chilling.

A shiver of terror runs down my spine, and the little courage I have left fades away. I swallow back the bile rising in my throat and sink as far back into my seat as possible. His words, spat out with such coldness, make me pray for Niklas to wipe them all out.

The car slows down when we reach Iron House. The gates are already open, and bright red blood stains the snow. I part my lips and sit up, craning my neck forward. Two men emerge and greet my captor as he enters the estate. Off to the side, two corpses lie side by side. Niklas's guards.

The war has begun.

What will I find in the villa? And what if… What if everyone is dead? The jolts slightly, making me jump as it hits a pothole that Nik usually avoids. All around me, the forest reverberates with shouts and gunfire. I half expect to see more of Rodrigo's men emerge at any moment. The downside of Iron House is that the estate is more than forty minutes away from the town or any form of habitation. We're isolated from everything. While I used to appreciate this detail because it ensured a certain calm, right now, all I want is for the authorities to hear the chaos reigning here and intervene.

In front of us, a body lying in the middle of the road blocks the way, but this detail doesn't stop the driver, who accelerates to drive over it. I swear I heard his bones crack; a shiver of horror runs down my spine. I look at my captor with fear.

"If he wasn't dead before, he is now," he says nonchalantly.

I turn to see the crushed body sunk deeper into the snow. I can't tell if it's an ally or an enemy. Regardless, the man beside me doesn't seem to care; it didn't stop him from running over him. He reeks of sadism, and in the heat of the moment, he must be the type to enjoy inflicting pain on his opponent.

He parks carelessly in front of the house, where three scary-looking men are waiting for us. My captor grabs his weapon and steps out of the car. He circles it, sliding over the hood, drawing admiring whistles from his colleagues, and roughly pulls me out of the vehicle.

"Siv! Finally, you're here," greets a burly man with an impressively long black beard. "Everything went well?"

"Yeah. Where's the boss?" Siv replies.

Siv drags me up the steps to the porch, and we ascend the few steps— where large drops of dried blood have been crushed by previous shoes—which lead into the villa. Whose blood is this? Fear grips me as

I look around, suppressing a tremble. Among all these unfamiliar faces, I search for an ally to turn to.

"He won't be long. Get inside before you catch a stray bullet," the burly man warns.

This warning doesn't seem directed at them; they're willing to risk getting shot.

"There are always sacrificial lambs, those who know they're here to die and not survive." Niklas had whispered this to me after we left Stockholm, just after losing three of his men. The sacrificial ones take more risks because they have nothing to lose. Do Rodrigo's men think the same way?

"If you behave, I'll let you pee. You must have needed to go since this morning, right?" Siv murmurs in my ear, pressing his gun against my ribs.

I hold back a sharp remark and move forward, s scanning the living room we pass, then the library. Empty. There's absolutely no one, and the gunfire outside is diminishing, surely as bodies fall to the ground or hide. To my left, two men descend, greeting Siv behind me.

"Nothing up there, except this." A blond with tousled hair waves several wads of cash. "Jackpot," he adds, kissing the money.

"Maybe there are more hiding spots to discover. So, sweetie, do you know where your boyfriend hides his cash?"

As I pass by them, the blond generously pats my buttocks. My hand immediately lands on his face. The gesture surprises us both. I quickly step back as he approaches, his lip slightly cut.

"You're a tough one," he spits, licking the drop of blood from his cut.

"I'm telling you. She doesn't like to be touched," Siv intervenes, running his fingers lightly over my upper arm.

"I feel sorry for her man."

The three men chuckle. I'd like to wipe the smiles off their faces, but I'm clearly outnumbered, and that won't work in my favor if they decide to take advantage of me in the worst possible way. I glance sideways toward the kitchen, which also seems deserted. Where is Oscar and all his men? Are they fighting in the forest? Siv calms down as his accomplices and head toward the house's entrance.

"Looking for someone, doll? No one's coming to help you; we've taken care of everything."

I go pale. *Taken care* in his mouth bodes the worst.

I moisten my lips, unsure if I want the answer, yet I have to know. "What did you do?"

His smile widens, revealing large, perfectly aligned teeth.

"We led them on the wrong track, and by now they're probably all dead," Siv giggles, scratching his head with the tips of his gun. "And you want to know how we did it?"

I don't know why, but the urge to make him talk to gain a few extra minutes of survival overwhelms me. I slowly nod my head.

"The old guy with the big scar on his neck hired some men a few weeks ago. One of them works for us," he begins, referring to Oscar. "After snooping around, he found where you were hiding, and today, he made Rodrigo believe he was outside of town, and that idiot bought it. So, they left a few men here, and the rest went off to get slaughtered like sheep in a slaughterhouse."

Oscar's dead? If they defeated a man like him, it means Niklas will be left alone. If he's still alive.

A ball of anxiety gnaws at my insides at the thought stumbling upon Nik's lifeless body. I struggle to ask the question.

"Where…where's Nik?"

Siv was waiting for this question; his eyes gleam with malice.

"He's at the hospital, in the hands of a doctor, he had a problem or something."

I almost fall backwards. It must be his heart. It has to be. Damn it, I told him to be careful! overwhelms me, stronger than before. I swallow hard and close my eyes. My ears buzz and my head spins. This is not the time to faint. I quickly do a breathing exercise to calm myself. If he's at the hospital, I need to go there to warn him about what's happening. I don't know how to get there, but first, I need to shake off Siv, who's enjoying my distress. He thinks I'm harmless; he's no longer aiming his gun at me. This excess of zeal works to my advantage.

Now.

I close my fist and apply an infallible technique that Niklas taught me to destabilize his opponent. With all my strength, I hit him at his Adam's apple. He emits a surprised groan and staggers back, gasping for air. I take advantage of his dizziness to escape through the kitchen. From there, I quickly look around. In the late afternoon, the sky begins to darken gradually. I need to hurry to make use of the natural light before being plunged into darkness. The only emergency exit I know has been barricaded for a long time. I have no choice; I'll have to go back through the main entrance of the estate. I skirt the house, keeping as low as possible to avoid the windows. When I reach the end, I hear the men on the porch. They're still there.

Shit!

If they see me, they'll make me regret my escape attempt. I step back, holding my breath and praying they don't see me. Eventually, Siv shouts, alerting his comrades, who rush inside. I wait a moment then start running as fast as I can.

A man who stayed behind sees me and raises the alarm. There are so many of them! What was I thinking, that I could shake them off so easily? I curse myself and pivot to retreat, but I bump into something hard. Another man. I quickly raise my head, terrified of what's about to happen.

"What… You!" I exclaim, stepping back.

A tall, curly-haired redhead stands before me, displaying a wicked smile. I don't remember his name, but he had come to the store as a potential buyer. I quickly realize that I've been the victim of a charade. He's one of Rodrigo's men.

"Surprised? By the way, I didn't tell you, I'm not interested in your business," he says, finally chuckling.

In one of his hands, a slim knife glimmers slightly. He twirls it from one hand to the other as he advances. Like a predator, he stares at me with a certain interest. I hold my breath as he raises the blade in front of his face to examine it with a sickening joy.

"You know what I like about knives? No flesh can resist them. You want to try?"

30
Niklas, 22 years old

I came across a letter from Lovisa this morning; Alfrida must have dropped it from her apron. I shouldn't have read it, but it was stronger than me. talks about her beginnings in the orchestra she joined. A tiny part of my heart rejoices at this news, but the other hates her for having the right to happiness. Yet, I love my life as it is, this violence that surrounds me, it's me now, and I've accepted it. My father is finally satisfied, it's been months since he blamed me for anything. I am one of his best soldiers.

Without really knowing why, I contacted the staff who take care of the orchestra and asked for a bouquet of orange roses to be delivered to her after each performance, specifying that it had to remain a secret. Money buys everything, like silence.

***

Still groggy from the anesthesia, I didn't wait a moment to demand my phone when the nurse brought me back to my room. I quickly check my messages. None are from Lovisa. She must not know about my condition, otherwise she would already be here. That's not a bad thing; I don't want to worry her for no reason.

I call my voicemail to listen to Oscar's message, glancing at my left arm slung in a sling against my chest. I have to keep my arm still to avoid dislodging my stitches.

"One of our men spotted Rodrigo. It might be a false lead, but I have to check it out. I left some of our guys at Iron House, and Dick and Jonas will stay at the hospital to watch over you in case of a new attack."

soon as possible. Take

This call is from two hours ago. He should be done by now, so why haven't I heard from him? And where are my men? I didn't see anyone when I entered my room.

Something is off.

I call Oscar while placing a hand on my chest. The surface area is numb; I can hardly feel anything, but inside, every movement, every heartbeat stirs up what they've implanted in me. I feel like a fucking robot. This thing better do its job, or I'll rip it out, even if it means opening up my chest. Electrodes are stuck to my chest and connected to a machine where I can check my regular heart rate. My left hand still has the catheter connected to a drip, restricting my movement. Plus, a drain from which blood is slowly trickling is attached to the still fresh scar. It's all handicapping me.

After several unanswered rings, I reach Oscar's voicemail.

"Answer, damn it. Oscar!" I call out through his voicemail. "Tell me you got that motherfucker."

I hang up and bring my right arm on my forehead, but this gesture causes an unexpected pain in my chest. I growl, "Nurse!"

In the distance, a pair of heels clack on the floor. The sound is regular, fast. It must be coming from a woman who knows how to walk in heels easily. I love women in high heels, and by observing them, I've learned the different strides and the kind of women who wear them. I close my eyes and call for help again, to get a damn painkiller. In the recovery room, I had nothing, as I had just emerged, but it's been a while.

"Nurse!"

The heel clacking stops, and a woman giggles outside my door. The bed's backrest is halfway up, so I tilt my head toward the door. It opens slowly, and the woman in heels enters my room.

"You've always been impatient."

That voice… Tell me I'm dreaming!

Jonna appears. I don't know what silly movie remake she thinks she's in, but she's going all out. She's wearing Lovisa's lost fur coat from the Red Mill.

Underneath, she's in tight leather pants and dark boots with thin heels. Her blonde hair is pulled back into a tight high ponytail. Her crimson lipstick highlights her lips.

"What are you doing here?" I bark.

The condescending look she gives me doesn't faze me. Her hostile attitude has never affected me in the past, and it's not about to change, no matter how weak I am now.

"I heard you were unwell. I came to see how you were doing," she says.

I squint at her pinched face and scoff, tilting my chin up. "Bullshit. Tell me why you're here."

She smiled, showing her white teeth. Jonna slowly approaches me, casting an amused glance over my entire body.

"I wanted to see your face when I tell you Rodrigo was here."

So, it was true; he's in Kiruna. I snort disdainfully. "You're too late; Oscar already told me."

Her chuckle annoys me; I want to wipe that smug smile off her face.

"Oh, poor thing, haven't you heard? He's dead. They're all dead. All of them."

This time, I can't tell real from fake.

"You're lying," I try.

No one can kill Oscar; it's impossible. I refuse to believe her. He's been working for my family for decades. He can't die under my command.

The device next to me goes haywire, showing my heart rate skyrocketing. A pang tugs at my heart. It beats fast, too fast and irregularly. The defibrillator in my body sends a small shock to help it calm down. It's a strange sensation, an internal spasm that I can't see but can feel. It's a bit painful but bearable.

"I'm not lying. He's dead, and you're next. You and… Lovisa."

"You'll never find her."

I've made sure she's safe. Other than Oscar, no one knows where she is. Yet, Jonna exudes confidence and spite. Her blue eyes darken, and her smile turns malicious.

"She's here in Kiruna, with our dear Rodrigo."

To prove her words, she takes out her phone and shows me a picture of Lovisa, tied to a chair. Her terrified expression and tear-stained eyes pierce my gut. My lower lip trembles slightly with the rage consuming me. Jonna scrutinizes me with interest, reveling in my distress.

"That's what I wanted to see," she says.

I slowly raise my head and struggle to look at her without throwing myself at her.

"You motherfuckers," I mutter through difficulty. "I'm going to kill them all, and you too, you dirty bitch."

She's close to me, too close for her own safety. I grab her by the throat and pull her toward me to get a better grip. She struggles, whimpering, and digs her fingers into my chest, near my bandage. I growl in pain and eventually let go when the dressing turns red. Jonna backs away, coughing, and glares at me.

"You can't do anything! Accept your fate. You've lost."

I put a hand to my bandage and lift it slightly. Several stiches have come loose.

"Are you doing all this because I dumped you? There's something wrong with you. Do you realize you're involved in murders?"

"I could have made you happy, but you chose Lovisa. She's too fragile and broken for you; you need a strong woman!"

I scoff and shake my head, giving her a disgusted look.

"You're just a viper, and believe me, you're going to pay for your betrayal! Pray for my death."

For the first time since she's been here, Jonna is finally looks scared. Her blue eyes widen. I don't have time to relish in this sight; sweat beads along my forehead, and the room around me starts to sway.

"You're finished, he'll kill you."

She slides a hand into my hair to pull it back, but I barely react. Truth be told, her gesture doesn't hurt me; it's nothing compared to my chest.

"One last thing, I wanted you to know before you die. Your damn foxes, I took care of them. I hired a man who took pleasure in slaughtering those beasts."

I wasn't expecting this announcement, and my blood drains from my face. She dared to go that far!

"The cameras and the backup generator, that was you?"

"Kinda. Azerty took care of the computer side, and a mole in your men took care of the generator."

She chuckles as she releases me.

"You don't even know who you're hiring. Poor thing, you've dug your own grave."

You bitch. I'm going to kill her, Azerty and that traitor. But who? Oscar has always been careful about the people he hired.

"You'll pay for this. I promise you won't get away with this."

"Your words may have had an impact before, but now they're just hot air. You're going to… die…"

My heavy eyelids close for a moment. I'm so tired, but I have to resist. When I come back to myself, Jonna is gone, and the room is dark. Damn, I fell asleep! I grab my phone and widen my eyes. I slept for almost two hours! I rip off the sheets and sit up, groaning. Nausea washes over me and immobilizes me. I have to pull myself together quickly. I don't know if Lovisa is still alive or if Rodrigo is still in Kiruna. I remove my IV; a spurt of blood flows from my skin to the floor. I also get rid of my splint.

The sensors on my chest, once torn off, show cardiac arrest on the screen beside me. A few moments later, as I stand in front of my wardrobe where my clothes are, a nurse bursts in, alarmed. When she sees me standing and still alive, she turns off the screen and turns to me.

"Mr. Ekman, what are you doing? Go back to bed. But… you're bleeding?"

She opens the drawer of the bedside table and takes out a bunch of sterile compresses which she presses on my hand, awkwardly as I dress.

"I have to leave, let Dr. Söderholm know not to worry."

I may not survive tonight, but I prefer to keep this information to myself. I grab the roll of tape I see in the drawer and wrap it around my chest to secure the drain against me. I'm not crazy enough to pull it out.

I put on my leather jacket and grumble; the wide movements awaken the pain in my chest.

On the shelf in front of me is the small black box containing the ring for Lovisa. This is not how I imagined spending this day when I woke up this morning. I stuff the box into the inner pocket of my jacket. I grab my keys and tuck them into the pocket of my jeans.

I'm ready.

As I'm about to leave, the nurse blocks my path, determined to keep me within these four walls.

"You're not allowed to leave, return to your bed and let me call the doctor."

I take a deep breath to avoid getting angry. I'm already tense enough, and her refusal to let me pass puts my nerves to the test.

"I don't have time for this bullshit. Get out of my way. Right now!"

I push her away roughly and leave the room. I toss the blood-soaked compresses to the floor and call the people I didn't want to disturb.

"I need you. Iron House is surrounded, they have Lovisa, and my team is dead."

I growl and stop, leaning against the wall. My body is freezing, then boiling with rage, and the sweat on my forehead chills my skin under the air conditioning above my head.

"Is it war?" Gunkil asks on the phone.

"Bring everyone."

I hang up and wipe my forehead. I'll arrive at the estate before him; I have to prepare the ground to make their task easier. Behind me, the nurse calls out to me. Damn it, can't she leave me alone? I straighten up and drag myself outside. My chest burns, and the urge to scratch myself until I bleed itches. I have to muster a lot of willpower not to tear everything off.

Outside, the wind lashes my face and gives me the energy to head toward a car in which its owner is dropping off a woman. As he exits the vehicle with his partner, I take advantage of his moment of inattention and slip into his Volvo. The man's cry is muffled by the roar of the vehicle.

I gather my thoughts and evaluate the possibilities and various scenarios that could happen tonight. Each plan ends with Lovisa's death and mine. I can't think clearly. I hit the steering wheel and crack the joints in my neck.

"Okay, let's start over."

If I have to die tonight, it will be by saving Lovisa; I won't accept any other possibility.

31

Lovisa, 21 years old

For a while now, life has been good to me. I created strong bonds with the people in the orchestra, I found a great little apartment, and I'm receiving flowers from a secret admirer. It's so exciting! But what's even more exciting is that I met him tonight. He's so handsome! His name is Rikard and he's so good-looking. I've never met such a charming man. We had dinner together tonight, and I have a good feeling about him. For once, for a few hours, I didn't think about Niklas, and my existence didn't seem so hopeless as before. Maybe he's the one I've been waiting for? We plan to see each other again tomorrow. I can't wait to see how it goes.

***

As I'm tied up in this chair, the thought that my life hangs by a thread crosses my mind. There are so many things I would have liked to do that I probably won't be able to do. I found Niklas only to lose him a few weeks later. We're going to be separated again, and being a non-believer, I know that once we're dead, we'll be lost forever. If only one of us survives tonight… But Niklas, knowing I'm here, will never run away to save his own skin, and for that, I love and hate him even more because he risks his life for me.

Our love will destroy us.

Rodrigo and his men are counting on it to do what they want with . Moreover, the Spaniard hasn't arrived yet. My new captor with sharp knives taunts me by touching his weapons spread out on the kitchen counter. He enjoys the horror that appears on my face as he explains

of his blades and what his

victims. T The idea of being slashed by one of them sends shivers down my spine. Given the choice, I'd rather take a bullet to the head than endure a thousand sufferings at his hands.

"I know how to cut flesh for as long as possible before the body gives out. I could show you," the tall redhead offers me with a coldness that would make you piss yourself.

I swallow, a drop of sweat running down my cheek. My body is under such tension that I'm surprised my nerves haven't given out already. My arms ache, tied behind my back; the bindings around my wrists are way too tight, and I suspect they did it on purpose out of pure sadism.

In the house, as well as outside, calm has returned. I don't know if there are still men with Nik in the forest. Perhaps they're hiding? I haven't heard Krigare since I arrived, and the thought of his bloodied body lying in the snow pains me greatly. I still hope to hear him bark, but every time I listen, only the muffled conversations of Rodrigo's men reach me. When the doors are closed, it's hard to hear anything outside.

The sound of the clock annoys me, the ticking of the second hand increases my anxiety. Time passes at such a slow pace that the feeling of being in another dimension makes me believe that all of this isn't real.

From time to time, the redhead's radio crackles, and snippets of conversation reach us. They communicate through their walkie-talkies, but my captor never responds; all his attention is fixed on me. A suffocating darkness emanates from him. In his gaze, I can read all the imaginable tortures he dreams of inflicting on me, and begging would probably be useless. But perhaps he would be more responsive to other words from me?

"How much does Rodrigo pay you?"

He chuckles as he puts down his knife and walks around the counter. I've hardly spoken since he's been here.

"Too much for you to afford for my services."

"Niklas has a lot of money, much more than your boss. We could pay you double… triple!" I correct myself as I see him lose interest in my proposition. "We can make a deal. You'd be a winner."

He sucks in his lower lip before releasing it, thinking.

He grabs one of his knives, small and thin, the size of a hand, and steps forward. The blade pointing in my direction, I already see the tip piercing my eye but instead, it slips behind me and cuts my ties. An immense relief radiates from the tips of my fingers and travels up my arms. I massage my sore wrists and stand up immediately.

"Thank you, you won't regret it. As soon as I find Niklas, we'll pay you."

Still behind me, the redhead starts to laugh, first discreetly before bursting into a chilling laughter. I turn sharply toward him.

"Did you really think I was going to let you go?"

"But—"

"What? You're going to pay me, is that it?"

Dangerously, he steps in my direction and punches me in the stomach. I stifle a cry of pain and double over, contracting to manage this agony.

He leans in close to my ear and whispers, "Silly girl. W When you and your guy kick the bucket, everything you see here will belong to us. I don't need your breadcrumbs."

He grabs me by the hair and throws me back into my chair, chuckling.

"I'll take pleasure in cutting you into pieces."

The intense, throbbing pain prevents me from replying. I clutch my stomach with my arms and remain slumped on my chair. If I don't move, he probably won't hit me again.

"Come on, Vidar, is this how we treat our guests?"

In the shadow of the corridor, Rodrigo appears. With a limping step, he enters the kitchen, adding more darkness to the already oppressive atmosphere. Niklas had told me he had injured him in the leg; evidently, he's still suffering. Vidar returns to his place behind the counter and neatly puts his knife back in line with the others.

"Good evening, Lovisa."

His presence here is like an affront to Niklas. He's desecrating our home by coming without permission. I glare at him as I slowly straighten up. The pain makes me more lucid and aware of events around me. It warns me to be vigilant for what's to come.

"You should be dead."

It's more of a wish than a statement.

"Almost was."

Rodrigo positions a chair in front of me and sits down. In his left hand, he holds a gun that seems to be coated in gold. It's a bit too flashy for my taste. Much like my pink Walther PPK.

My gun!

At that moment, I think of the hiding spot under the floorboards, which is behind me at the back of the kitchen. Niklas had hidden it there along with a bundle of cash and a box of ammunition. I'll never reach it without getting myself killed. I curse myself for not thinking of it when I tried to escape.

Rodrigo's hand on my thigh snaps me out of my thoughts.

"I wonder if… knowing that you'll be my whore while our dear Niklas gets eaten by worms might be the final blow I deliver before I kill him. What do you think? Can you imagine his agony knowing he can't do anything about it?"

I swallow needlessly, my mouth dry. He watches my reaction and smiles.

"Or should I kill you in front of him? What do you think, Vidar?"

He half-turns to his henchman.

"If it were me, boss, I'd kill them both, very slowly," Vidar answers.

"No survivors, I like that," says Rodrigo.

I shudder and finally push his hand away, which seems to itch on my thigh.

"We'll soon find out, our dear friend paid him a visit at the hospital, he's been informed of the situation."

We lock eyes. I am the bait that will destroy Nick, and Rodrigo knows it.

"Nik will come, and he'll kill you all and wipe that smug smile off your face."

Rodrigo straightens up in his chair and looks at me with amusement.

"I wiped out Niklas's little army in a snap, and you think he alone can stop us? Here's what's left of his men."

He whistles. The sound of commotion from the front hall grows louder. Two burly men drag behind them a man I quickly recognize as Oscar. He has a wound on his chest, his white shirt stained with blood.

"Oscar!" I cry, trying to stand up, but Rodrigo forces me back down.

He's alive! There might be hope for the situation to turn in our favor. But seeing the severity of his condition, my hope quickly fades.

"You're nothing but a monster!"

Oscar weakly lifts his head and gives me a glassy-eyed look. He's barely conscious. How much blood has he lost? Too much. The two men let him go, and he collapses onto the wooden floorboards with a painful groan. He's proof that any man can fall.

"I've seen him in better shape," Rodrigo laughs. "He's found his place, at my feet, and soon he'll be joined by his master."

His arrogance will be his downfall. He's so sure of himself that it sickens me. I've never wished death on someone as strongly as I do for him.

"You disgust me! You're not worth half the man he is!" I shout, spitting in his face.

His reaction is immediate. He slaps me so hard I fall to the side. My ear rings and my cheek throbs.

"I hate vulgarity," Rodrigo growls, standing up.

He pulls a handkerchief from his pocket and wipes his face before tossing it to the floor.

"I'll teach you some manners."

Immediately, he brings his foot down into my ribs. A pathetic whimper escapes my mouth, quickly followed by another.

Lying on the floor, I wonder how many blows my body can take before it breaks in two. Rodrigo, indifferent to my pain, kicks me over and over. I protect myself as best I can, but I soon crack, panicked.

"Stop! I beg you, please stop!"

I sob, curling on myself. Rodrigo, panting, finally stops and forces me onto my back with his foot.

"Give me a good reason to stop. Talk!"

Suddenly, the kitchen and the rest of the house plunge into darkness. Everyone freezes.

"Shit! Spread out and find me the problem, and fast!"

Rodrigo leans down toward me, a wicked smile on his face. The moonlight filtering through the windows and the glass door illuminates us.

"Looks like Niklas is back. How about we give him a proper welcome?"

32

Niklas, 23 years old

Sören, my father's loyal dog, is dead. No one will miss him, especially not me. So, Hendrik took me with him to visit each district where he had meetings with his lieutenants. When I saw Rodrigo again, that bastard hadn't changed a bit. He still treats me like a kid, which pisses me off. I asked my father if I could teach him a lesson, but he said that as long as he's in charge, I will never lay a hand on any of his men. Those words didn't fall on deaf ears. When I was younger, I promised to get rid of him; today he's given me another reason to put a bullet in his ass. Things will be different under my command. I'll raise the Ekman name to an international level. Everyone will know us, not because of the cartel. This business, while profitable, isn't my life's goal, but I keep that thought to myself. My father would kill me just for considering the idea of quitting and leaving.

***

With only my two hands as weapons, I move through the forest of Iron House. Not knowing the extent of the damage, I chose to park outside the estate but, to my surprise, there was no one at the gates. All around me the woods are silent; only the wind rustling and cracking the tree branches makes any noise. It's as if everything is normal. The blood at the entrance gives me a glimpse of what must be happening further in I don't know how many of my men have died or even if Lovisa is still alive

If there is a god up there, let him protect her.

I'm not a believer, but in this situation, I'm ready to believe in anything as long as it turns events in my favor.

It would be madness to show up unarmed at the doors of my house; that's why the entrance to the underground bunker, connected to the villa by a tunnel, is the best option. Plus, it has all the equipment needed to fight Rodrigo and his men.

Damn, I hope Gunkil will arrive with reinforcements. I had promised myself not to involve him in my affairs anymore, but he's the one I trust the most, after Oscar, to help me.

I know this forest like the back of my hand, having roamed it for years. I approach a very old tree, a birch with a white wolf emblem carved and painted black in the center.

The sign.

A quick glance around assures me there's no one around. I circle the tree and bend toward a platform made of woven vines covered in snow. Only a big piece of wood sticks out. I pull on it, lifting the plank. Beneath it, two large iron doors. Using a key I always carry, I unlock the padlock and yank it open. This seemingly simple act takes more strength than I expected. The pain in my chest flares up, and I curse myself for not taking any painkillers before setting out. No time to wallow in self-pity; I have to move and put an end to this mess.

I go down the stairs and switch on the light. A large room is illuminated in bright white. My eyes burn for a moment before adjusting. To my right, several lockers and a bench are set up for changing. Further in, there's a rudimentary shower with a sink and toilet. Directly ahead, several cabinets locked with padlocks contain all the firearms needed for a war. Nearby, a box holds the keys to open them. Right next to it is the backup generator.

On my right, a safe was built into the wall. I open it with a code I change every month. Inside are several gold bars, bundles of cash, two Golden Eagles, brass knuckles with a wolf's head on the index finger, and a tablet. I tuck the guns behind my back, slip on the brass knuckles, and grab the tablet, which I turn on. I immediately access the exterior cameras. I spot the men around the villa. There are too many of them for me to handle alone. Next, I select the interior cameras. These are hidden and only Oscar knows their locations. I scan the images from the living room, the library, the entrance hall, and finally the kitchen. The camera is hidden in a porcelain chicken figurine perched above the fridge. Rodrigo, accompanied by another man whose face is familiar, is holding Lovisa hostage. She's sitting on a chair, curled up. Her face, twisted in pain, and the thought that they might have touched her, fills me with rage.

"Hang in there, babe, I'm coming."

She won't spend another minute in their company.

I put the tablet back in the safe and close it. Taking the keys, I unlock the armory, grabbing a bulletproof vest which I put on after taking off my leather jacket. The difficulty of this simple action feels ridiculous; every movement tugs at my scar, but I can't risk getting hit by a stray bullet.

Next, I cut the power to the villa and disable the backup generator. I'll have a better chance of surprising them in total darkness. Ready for the attack, I open the door leading to the tunnel connected to the basement. Gun in hand, I venture into the cool, damp air of the gallery. I don't need my eyes to see; it's a straight line, and at the end, I know where to find flashlights.

I walk about a hundred meters before reaching the end of the tunnel, where I place my hand on the sliding cabinet. I hold my breath for a moment, hearing voices on the other side. Slowly, I slide the cabinet to the left, leave an opening. Using their phones, two men are illuminating the area around them.

"Look harder, check the walls for any boxes."

"Isn't that stuff usually upstairs?"

"Not necessarily," one of them snaps. "We need to get the power back on before Rodrigo takes it out on us. He's totally lost it."

Their phones pointed in front of them, they move away from the cabinet, which I quickly slide open to sneak into the basement. Stealthily, I creep toward them. One of the men, the closest to me, is about my height. I raise my weapon, squinting to see his head, and strike him hard with the butt of my gun. He collapses heavily to the floor. The other reacts instantly, trying to turn around, but I'm faster. He's shorter than me, so I easily wrap my arm around his neck and squeeze. He struggles, elbowing me in the ribs. I grunt but don't loosen my grip.

"He—"

I put my hand over his mouth and squeeze his neck so tightly a sickening crack is heard. His body goes limp, and he collapses.

"Have you found it?"

A radio clipped to his belt crackles with a voice from his interlocutor. I pick it up and listen to the exchanges between Rodrigo's men.

"Nothing at the front."

"We're heading back to the entrance, there's movement."

Movement? I regret cutting the power. I could have seen what's happening.

I keep the radio, grab a flashlight near the entrance, and climb the basement stairs without encountering more of Rodrigo's men. Halfway up, I hear Lovisa's plaintive voice, breaking my heart.

"Stop! You're going to kill him!" she screams.

Who is she talking about? Did someone join them while I was in the tunnel? I set the radio and the unlit flashlight on the last step. At the door, I slowly turn the handle and crack it open. A shadow darts by quickly but doesn't stop, heading toward the entrance. I slip out of the basement and press against the wall, my gun leveled by my cheek and the second one I draw against my shoulder. A glance down the hallway shows the door is open. In the distance, I hear the roar of several cars speeding into the estate, as well as motorcycles, but I can't tell if they're friends or enemies.

"Do you want to take his place? Just say the word, sweetheart, and I'll have Vidar carve a nice smile on your face with his blades."

"You're a psychopath, and I hope Nik comes and kills you!"

Yes, babe, I will.

My little warrior, even among hyenas, stands strong. A surge of pride fills me, but it's quickly replaced by anxiety as two men walk past me, heading to the kitchen.

"Cars have entered the property and motorcycles slipped through the woods. Our men are awaiting your orders."

"Kill them all, I don't want that bastard getting any reinforcements."

The two men leave quickly, exiting the villa. I approach the kitchen slowly. On the floor, Oscar's body lies half in the hall and half in the kitchen, bleeding profusely. His face is battered. I don't know if he's still alive, but seeing such a large man in this condition makes me question my own physical capabilities.

"Where was I? Ah yes…"

"Wait!"

What's happening? I move silently, breathing slowly and almost inaudible.

"Give me one good reason."

"Because… because I'm pregnant."

I stop, unable to take another step. Lovisa, pregnant? Since when? Why didn't she tell me?

Holy shit… Holy shit!

From where I stand, despite the darkness, I can see Lovisa sitting with Rodrigo standing in front of her, ready to hit her. This sight snaps me out of my confusion. I don't know what to think about this new revelation, but I know that Love needs me. I burst into the kitchen, aiming one gun at Rodrigo and the other at the redhead behind the counter.

"If either of you moves, I'll put a bullet between your eyes," I growl, ready to shoot.

33

Lovisa, 22 years old

When Rikard slapped me for the first time, I thought it was a dream. We were just talking, him fiddling with my phone, and me heating a dish from a renowned chef that we had ordered. He didn't like the messages exchanged with a colleague from the orchestra, despite their innocence. No matter how much I pleaded my case, he didn't listen to me and accused me of cheating. He then regretted his action and apologized. I believed him, but deep down, I knew he was lying. Call it a sixth sense or some similar nonsense, but I knew. He did it again, harder, more often, and always without reason. And I stayed with him despite everything. Why? Why do I subject myself to this? Is it because I must like it deep down, right? Yet he makes me feel dirty and unworthy of his love. Love is supposed to be beautiful, supposed to be good, so why do I stay?

***

He's there.

He's really here!

It's not a hallucination; everyone sees him, don't they? Niklas is illuminated by a beam of moonlight, allowing me to see him fairly clearly. I can't take my eyes off him, examining his face. His tense features and the sweat on his forehead reveal the physical ordeal he's enduring. I still don't know what happened to him, but his condition worries me. None of my captors dares to move under the guns pointed in their direction.

How long has he been in the house? Near the kitchen?

"*Because … because I'm pregnant.*"

I turn pale. Did he hear me say those words? This isn't how I wanted to tell him the news. After taking the test in Greece, which turned out positive despite being on the pill, I kept it hidden and told no one, especially not Niklas. I couldn't do it over the phone. Besides, I have no idea what he thinks about having kids. I don't even know what I think. Am I going to keep it? Will Niklas want it? We need to discuss this… baby. Anyway, my protective instinct for my life and his kicked in, and I don't want anyone to hurt him. If Niklas and I made mistakes in our life choices, living in danger and death, he didn't ask for any of this.

I nervously bite my lip and try to read his eyes, hoping to see a response, but all I find is darkness and anger. He has slipped into the role of the cartel leader to handle the situation better. No room for emotions, he needs to stay focused.

"Niklas! You almost made me wait," Rodrigo says, turning his back to me.

His gun is aimed at my boyfriend; as for Vidar, he's holding two small knives capable of cutting through any human tissue. The kitchen's dim light doesn't prevent anyone from seeing each other, although visibility is lower than with the lights on.

"Step away from her," Niklas demands, approaching slowly.

His gaze moves from Rodrigo to Vidar. With a flick of his gun, he orders Rodrigo to switch places with him to protect me behind his back. Without taking his eyes off them, he addresses me. "Can you stand up?"

I nod before realizing he can't see me.

"Yes," I say out loud.

"Okay. Do you remember where your gun is? Go get it."

I stand slowly, as if any sudden movement might trigger the shootout that's about to erupt. I walk around the table, bumping into a chair that creaks, and head to the cabinet at the other end of the room. From there, I bend down with a groan, my stomach aching, and the thought of losing the child because of all the blows I've received fills me with horror.

"How are you, Niklas? I heard you had a stroke," Rodrigo says.

A stroke! Was that's why he was in the hospital? Lord… And he's already up!

My boyfriend snorts before answering, "Shut up, I don't want to hear you. Hurry up, Lovisa."

I remove two boards at the base of the sideboard with the

engraving of a wolf's head surrounded by a forest at the top and access the hidden compartment. I grab my Walther and Nik's gun and bring it to him. Following his direction, I wedge it behind his back and stand beside him, pointing my gun at Vidar.

"Look at you," Rodrigo sneers. "Two lovers about to die, still clinging to the idea that you stand a chance against me."

I don't know how many men he has, but he won't get away with it against Nik. And I won't let him without a fight. If I'm going to die tonight, I might as well die by his side.

"You should have left without making a fuss," says Niklas.

"Oh, but I wasn't planning to leave without taking your life," Rodrigo answers.

Niklas snorts disdainfully, keeping both guns aimed at Rodrigo. "Is your pride that wounded? I didn't know you could be so easily hurt."

Rodrigo's nostrils flare and his eyes widen. He slowly raises his gun in our direction.

"If you hadn't screwed everything up the moment you took over, I would have been a valuable ally. But you let a little pussy get inside your head," he spits venomously, looking at me before smiling. "Yes, I know why you pushed me out."

Am I the cause of this conflict? A ball of guilt tightens in my gut. I look to Niklas for denial, but he says nothing.

"I keep my word."

The tension between the two men is palpable and oppressive. We're all ready to pull the trigger and start a real bloodbath.

"We're under attack!" someone yells through the radio on the counter.

A shiver of fear runs up my spine. Dozens of gunshots ring out. In the hall, flashes of light burst from the open door, coming from car headlights and guns. This commotion confuses us all. Niklas turns his head toward the noise. That brief moment of inattention is all Rodrigo needs to go after him. With a powerful kick to his chest, he knocks him to the floor. His bulletproof vest protects him from gunfire, but not from blows. He groans, his face contorted in pain, and fires at Rodrigo without hitting him.

"Nik!"

I grab his arm and to help him up, but he pushes me away.

"Get out!"

"I won't leave you!"

Niklas fires again in the direction of the two men hiding behind the counter. He grabs my arm and squeezes hard. Too hard. His gaze pierces through me.

"You have to go, don't argue!"

"You need me!"

"No, I don't," he growls, placing his hand on my belly, "but he does. Save him, save yourself."

He pushes me again, forcing me to get up. Near the door, hesitation roots me to the spot.

"Get out!"

An electric jolt runs through me, my legs lift off the ground, and I sprint into the forest.

Run. Don't think about anything. Run faster. Think about him, the little one growing inside you. But Nik needs me, how can I leave him so easily? I bite my lip until it almost bleeds. For once, I have to listen to him. Enough of doing things my own way.

Even without a jacket, I'm not cold; this frantic run keeps me warm and on edge. The further I get from the house, the less the gunshots reach my ears. My heart pounds so loudly it drowns out all other sounds. My fingers, gripping my gun too tightly, ache and want to let go, but since it might still save me, I cling to it like a lifeline and don't loosen my grip.

Instinctively, I listen for hurried footsteps behind me. I half-turn and, despite the darkness, recognize Vidar chasing me.

Oh no!

I try to pick up the pace, but my physical condition doesn't allow it. I've never been a fan of running or sports. The closer Vidar gets, the tighter the vise of fear and dread of falling into his clutches squeezes around me.

He curses at me, covers the last few meters between us, grabs me, and we tumble into the snow in a painful fall, adding more bruises to my already battered body. Amid grunts and plaintive groans, we struggle—me to escape, him to end my life. I see his blade glinting in the moonlight before it slices into my upper arm. Despite the cold seeping into my flesh minute by minute, the sharp pain makes me scream. Blood spurts from the wound, staining my sweater. I kick him to push him back and point my gun at him, miraculously still in my hand. This desperate move makes him laugh.

"Oh, you're going to kill me, huh?"

He remains seated in the snow, lifting his head to challenge me. His blade, still in his hand like an extension of his arm, never leave his grasp.

"You don't have it in you, girlie. It takes guts to kill someone."

I narrow my eyes, furrowing my brow. Sometimes it's not about guts, but about a survival instinct that takes over. I place my other hand on my gun, pushing aside the pain shooting through my arm.

"You won't be the first person I've killed."

His eyes widen before I fire, determined, in his direction. I should have taken Niklas's shooting lessons more seriously because I miss my target by a hair. The redhead stands frozen, staring at me, before rushing at me. I fire again, but he dodges.

Shit!

Without thinking, I throw my gun at him and get up. I run, ignoring the pain in my arm as blood soaks my sleeve more and more. I've barely recovered from the previous chase, my legs trembling, struggling to keep me upright. But if I don't outdistance him, he'll slash me again before giving me the final blow, probably by slitting my throat.

"Come back here, bitch! You tried to kill me!"

Me? He started it. He's like the hunter who becomes the hunted and doesn't like the fate he wanted to impose on his prey.

The air suddenly cools, and I realize we're approaching the frozen lake. Well, not so frozen anymore—the ice has started to crack, creating even bigger holes on its surface since the last time I was here.

This is it.

If I can lure him onto the lake, I can make him fall into the icy waters. I risk falling in with him if I'm not careful, but what other choice do I have? I'm clearly outmatched, and he still has his knife. Physically, he could snap me in half. Water has always been my enemy; tonight, it needs to become a formidable ally.

I dodge several low-hanging branches and don't stop, even when my hair gets caught in those I can't see. I have the advantage of being on familiar terrain, and I need to use it to stop him. With my guts in a knot, I change my course toward the lake.

The vast expanse of frozen water looms on the horizon. I'm almost there. I push aside a large branch blocking my path and step onto the ice, slowing down to avoid slipping.

"Stop!" Vidar yells behind me.

I don't listen and keep moving, looking around. The whiteness of the ice reflects under the moon, giving us natural light in the surrounding night. It allows me to scan the ground for what I need.

"I told you to stop!"

A gunshot rings out beside me, in the air. I freeze immediately, just a few steps away from a hole in the ice.

"I really hate using firearms, but you forced my hand. Turn around."

I swallow and turn around, shivering from the cold. The ends of my body are red and frozen. Every breath is visible as white smoke, each one burning my lungs with the cold air.

Vidar holsters his gun and starts tossing his knife from one hand to the other as he approaches.

"Finally, the moment I've been waiting for. You've been more trouble than I anticipated."

"You didn't think I'd let you kill me that easily, did you?" I retort, trying to keep my teeth from chattering.

I let him come closer. The ice beneath his feet cracks and shifts noticeably, but he doesn't seem to notice.

"I can give you a clean, quick death or a slow, painful one. Personally, I prefer the second one."

He stops, waiting for my response. Either way, I'm going to die. But things could be different if I play it smart.

"A quick death would be preferable, but it doesn't matter what I choose, does it?"

From the beginning, he's boasted about his torture skills, so I don't see why he'd spare me. He's toying with me, it's obvious.

He starts walking toward me again, gripping his knife in his right hand.

"You're right, I'll get more pleasure from hurting you. It's hard to break old habits."

The closer he gets, the more the ice groans under our feet. I stay still, feeling the edges of the hole just centimeters from my heels, and let him come to me.

A little closer.

He steps forward.

A little closer.

He gets nearer.

A little closer.

The blade, now coated with my coagulated blood, is so close it could slice me at any moment.

"You're mine."

Dramatically, he raises his knife above his head. The madness in his eyes spurs me to continue with my plan. The guilt I felt about trapping him to drown vanishes. I dive to the side, hitting the ice hard as it cracks under my weight. My elbow plunges into the water, and I grit my teeth to keep from panicking and kick the back of his knee. He drops to the ice, his body leaning forward. I get up and groan as his knife cuts my chest again. I manage to slip behind him, sliding on my side, and push him into the water. He splashes me, making me even colder. I stay half-lying down and watch in horror as he emerges, his face contorted with rage, shouting at me.

"You refuse to die!"

I freeze for a moment, watching him cling to the edge, trying to climb out.

"I've never had more reasons to live than right now."

With a heavy kick, I strike his face. His nose shatters under my shoe and bleeds profusely. Vidar immediately sinks. Bubbles break the surface and eventually disappear. Fearing he might resurface, I stare at the hole for a moment.

"Lovisa!"

Startled, I turn quickly and look toward the forest. A shiver of excitement and cold runs through me. Could it be—? I stand up and scan the surroundings. The distant voice echoes through the trees again.

"Nik!"

My voice cracks in the night air.

In the distance, are moving in all directions.

My heart pounds so hard in my chest it feels like it might burst.

Is it all over? I'm alive, and so is Niklas. I sigh with relief and allow myself a smile.

It's over.

It's—

A hand grabs my leg and pulls me down, and I fall flat on my stomach. A metallic taste fills my mouth, and a trickle of blood stains the ice. I look behind me and, horrified, realize Vidar is still alive. Pale as death, he pulls me, dragging me into the water.

"If I die, you die with me!"

I scream as loudly as I can, clawing at the ice with my nails. I have nothing to hold on to except my fingers, which I try to dig into the cracks.

"Help!"

With my body half-submerged in the water, I already feel the currents trying to drag me down with him. The water is so freezing that it makes my breath short and choppy. How is Vidar still alive? In a final effort, I shout again with all my might, "Niklas!"

34

Niklas, 24 years old

All the hard-earned respect from my father vanished when my heart problems arose. In his eyes, I became weak, no longer fit to do my job properly. This motherfucker is trying to push me out of the family business. And why? Because, according to him, I'm not capable of taking over. Yet, he suffers from the same condition! It's the pot calling the kettle black. Despite this anger eating me up, part of me is relieved at the idea of leaving all this behind to start a new life. Maybe even leave Kiruna?

***

Just as Lovisa escapes, Rodrigo empties his gun in my direction. Like me, he's now out of ammo. The kitchen is riddled with bullets.

"Find her and kill her!" Rodrigo orders to his guard dog.

The redhead vaults over the counter, grabs a knife, and rushes out the door as fast as lightning.

"No!"

I get up, grabbing the weapon from my back, and try to follow, but Rodrigo grabs my shoulders and pulls me back. He spins me around and punches me square in the jaw, my teeth clashing together. I drop my gun while dodging his next blow.

"We have a score to settle, the two of us," Rodrigo says.

Rodrigo doesn't give me a chance to react and punches me in the face again before attacking my chest. Electric shocks painfully pierce my heart, the last thing it needs. He's wrecking the device freshly implanted under my skin. Bastard. Such a low blow doesn't surprise me from him.

e, I barely manage to

"Is that all you've got?"

He laughs at my weakness and throws me to the ground. Straddling me, he slams his fists into my face, nearly knocking me out. His hands wrap around my neck, squeezing tighter and tighter.

"A pitiful death for a pitiful man. That's all you deserve, dear Niklas."

I jab my elbows into the crook of his arms, but he tightens his grip. I'm gasping for air, my face reddening as blood rushes to my cheeks.

"Coward!" I manage to choke out, hitting him in the ribs to try to push him off.

"In war, all blows are allowed to defeat your enemy. You should known that by now."

A well-placed punch to his abdomen with my brass knuckles makes him double over, his fingers loosening slightly. I manage to push him away, coughing violently. Gasping for air, I search for my weapon, but Rodrigo grabs it faster. I groan and stay down as he stands, pointing the gun at me.

"The game is over. You lost. Any last word?"

"Fuck you," I spit, wiping the blood from my lower lip.

He laughs.

"I expected nothing less from you. Maybe I'll change my mind and let Lovisa live. You'll die knowing that everything you had is mine, including your little whore. And your brat, I could take it and raise it, or force her to abort and live with that for the rest of her days…"

A deep rage echoes inside me. This isn't the first time he's claimed Lovisa, and he's not the only one. Azerty tried to intimidate me with this threat, and I dealt with him. I get up, trying to ignore the pain, and press my forehead against the cold barrel of the gun. Its coolness soothes the fever that's slowly consuming me.

"Go ahead, shoot, but don't miss, because I won't miss you," I growl, pressing my forehead harder against the gun.

"You're completely insane, poor thing. Power has gone to your head."

He scrutinizes my face, searching for any trace of madness in my eyes, but finds nothing. Before him stands a man determined to see things through to the end. I smirk.

"Maybe, but I'll always have a bigger pair of balls than you."

I quickly duck and strike his injured leg with all my might. He fires into the air, groaning in pain, and falls to his knees. The wound might be closed, but inside, it's still raw and sensitive. I snatch the gun from him and turn it on him. Knowing his final moments are near, he rises proudly to his knees and examines me with an enigmatic smile.

"We could have made a great team, you and I. I hope she was worth it, because things won't calm down after my death."

Maybe he's telling the truth, but there's no going back now; it's too late.

"Lovisa is the main reason for all this, but you have to admit, your district has been declining for some time. You weren't doing your job well enough," I spit out.

He remains silent for a moment before lifting his head proudly.

"Maybe. You'll succeed Hendrik wonderfully. Just as cold and ruthless as him."

I grimace. Look like my father? Never. I'll never belittle my family members or friends, never hit them or force them to become something they're not. I'm far from my father, and his example will always be a cautionary tale to avoid repeating his mistakes.

"I know what you're thinking, but you look a lot more like him than you think. Time will tell."

I slide my finger over the trigger and nod.

"And you won't be there to see it."

I pull the trigger. The bullet, fired at such close range, pierces Rodrigo's skull through his eye and lodges in the counter. The detonation echoes throughout the house and makes my ears buzz, already badly damaged by the previous shots.

Beams of flashlights from the hall move toward me. I raise my gun, ready to fire.

"We're armed and there are more of us. Surrender!" Gunkil's voice shouts.

"It's me, Nick."

Gunkil, Fredrik, and several men rush in. The relief of my best friends seeing me still alive touches me. I place my hand on Gun's shoulder and nearly collapse from exhaustion.

"Are you okay, man? You look terrible," says Gunkil.

"It'll be better when all of Rodrigo's men are dead."

Gunkil laughs and pats my back. His gaze shifts behind me, widening. Before I can react, he shoves me aside. A gunshot reverberates through the kitchen. My best friend collapses to the floor.

"Gun!" Fredrik and I shout in unison.

The men who came with them rush out, firing at Rodrigo's men.

I drop to the ground and press my hands against the bloody wound in Gunkil's abdomen. He's losing a lot of blood.

"Why the fuck did you protect me?" I snap, more panicked than angry.

"Hey… I always have your back, don't I?"

His voice begins to fade, losing its naturally cheerful tone. Breathing becomes difficult as blood trickles from his lips, dampening his pale skin. A lump of fear turns into grief, blocking my throat as I realize what's happening.

"Don't leave me, brother."

I loosen the pressure on his wound, causing blood to flow faster. I grab his hand and squeeze it. Across from me, Fredrik holds Gunkil's other hand, watching his best friend and colleague slowly die, unable to say anything. Normally, Fredrik is the one who finds the right words in any situation. His eyes shine with tears he struggles to hold back.

This isn't the ending our trio envisioned. Things weren't supposed to go this way.

"No hard feelings, okay?" Gunkil whispers.

His labored breathing calms. His chest stops moving, and the fingers once tightly gripping our hands go limp. His eyes, fixed on the ceiling, no longer sparkle with mischief.

It's over.

I let my tears fall. I've just lost my best friend, my brother, the one who's always been there for me since I was a kid. Twenty years of friendship destroyed in an instant. Not far away, Oscar, who I couldn't save, is also dead; his body hasn't moved for some time.

Fredrik faces his own grief. I want to comfort him, tell him everything will be okay, but I can't. I've never experienced anything like this, and not even my father's death affected me this deeply.

Lovisa's scream pulls me out of my grief. I snap my head up and look toward the garden door.

"She needs you," Fredrik manages to say, his voice heavy and deep.

I give one last glance to Gunkil, grab my gun and a flashlight, and run into the forest. The vest feels more like a hindrance, so I discard it and immediately notice my shirt soaked in blood. I don't have time to dwell on my wounds; Lovisa is in danger. Her piercing cry urges me to run faster, even though I don't know exactly where she is. I call out to her, listening carefully to the sounds around me, trying to pick out her voice among the trees, but nothing. I keep calling her name as I look around.

Hold on, Love, I silently plead.

My heart pounds painfully against my chest, and my lungs burn in the icy air I breathe. Every breath, every jolt of pain, hurts me more. If I survive this night, I'll honor my promise to Lovisa by taking her on vacation far from here and staying in bed for at least a week.

I'm torn between wanting to collapse into the snow and flying to Lovisa to save her from this lunatic. Both desires, equally strong, do nothing to alleviate my torment. My head spins, and my body struggles to keep running. At any moment, I might collapse.

Behind me, I hear men shouting, and I spot lights illuminating the woods. Their help is welcome. This moment of distraction causes me to stumble; I fall to my knees, hands sinking into the snow. Desperately, I scream at the top of my lungs, "Lovisa!"

Against all odds, her voice resurfaces, and I hear her scream and call out to me again. With difficulty, I pinpoint the location of the sound and head toward the lake. A sense of dread pushes me to quickly get up and start running again to reach her as soon as possible. At this time of year, the ice begins to melt, and the waters take over. It is dangerous to venture out there. The lake extends beyond the property, so there's a natural current that can be fast in some places. I push aside the branches blocking my path and find myself facing the lake.

A horrifying sight greets me. In the distance, Lovisa's body is halfway submerged in the lake. Without thinking about my own safety, I sprint onto the cracking ice beneath my feet in some places.

"Lovisa! Hold on!"

I slip but don't stop. I'm only a few feet away from her now. I toss my gun aside. Her hand reaches out to me, her frightened face begging me to save her. I dive on the ice, trying to grab her, but the water suddenly sucks her down and swallows her into its depths.

"Lovisa!"

I plunge my arms into the water and blindly search for her, but they come up empty, finding no body. It can't be. I can't have lost her the moment I found her again! My nerves saturate and crack, I feel like I'm losing my mind.

"Lovisa!"

35

Lovisa, 23 years old

Life isn't just about suffering and enduring the cruelty of others. I'm so young, I haven't lived yet. This toxic relationship suffocates me and changes me every day. I won't let him destroy me. I don't know when or how yet, but I'll get out of this situation if Rikard doesn't change.

***

I barely had time to catch my breath when the icy waters sweep me under ice sheet. I'm tempted to scream, but that would kill me faster than expected. The oxygen filling my lungs is precious, and I must conserve it.

Vidar writhes in pain and eventually lets go of me, drowned by the large amount of water he's ingested. His face is frozen in an expression of terror and pain, and soon his body is carried away by the current. He becomes nothing more than a shadow fading into the distance before disappearing into the darkness.

My turn is coming.

This distressing thought drives me to claw at the surface above me and strike it. My body hits something hard, and I end up stuck. It's a tree, its branches holding me back. I don't know if they're saving me or, on the contrary, holding me in their claws to deliver the final blow. They tear at my skin as I struggle, but their bites are nothing compared to the cold that has seized my entire body.

A few bubbles of air escape from my mouth; I struggle to keep it closed, but my survival depends on it.

Above me, a shadow looms, then a blurry but familiar face appears as the person rubs the snow on the ice. Niklas. Bathed in moonlight, but also in blue and green hues from the northern lights, he looks angelic. An angel descended from heaven to take me in, to end my suffering.

Am I going to die? If so, leaving this earth while watching the person I love most seems like a beautiful death.

36

Niklas, 25 years old

I've taken control of my life, at least partially. I have my own bar, my finances are in good shape, and I no longer need my father. He knows it, which is why he clings to me and prevents me from leaving. What he doesn't know is that he lost me the day Lovisa came into my life. Whatever happens, no matter how much time passes and my growing hatred toward her, I know we will find each other again, and nothing will separate us. I fucking love her. Yeah, I love her.

***

Lovisa looks like a ghost, frozen under the ice, but Love isn't going to die. I'm going to save her.

I adjust the brass knuckles on my right hand and strike the ice. Again and again. I don't stop, I refuse to, as life slowly leaves her.

"Break! Come on! Break!" I shout as I pound with my other fist.

The ice cracks against my bloodied knuckles. It's so cold, and the rage inside me boils my blood, leaving me no time to worry about the pain radiating through my fingers and up my arm.

She's not moving anymore. I have to get her out of there, quickly!

A large crack forms, and I strike it multiple times, breaking everything around it. My hands touch the icy water. Quickly, I grab Lovisa by the shoulders and pull her out of the lake, grunting. Her body, weighed down by her soaked clothes and cold from the water, falls limply onto me. My heart threatens to stop beating when I realize she's barely breathing.

Not her... I don't want to lose another person I love.

n and then turn her on h   on't
know if I'm doing it right; I'm better at killing than keeping someone alive.

I do this several times without letting up, despite my exhausted body.

"Come on, breathe!"

In the distance, flashlight wave in our direction, several men rush toward us.

"Don't come closer! It's dangerous. Call for help!"

I don't want to take any risks by allowing them to come to us; they wouldn't be of any help to me. I won't let anyone touch her except a paramedic.

Suddenly, Lovisa coughs up water. quickly lift her up to hold her in my arms and let her expel everything from her body. Relief floods over me like a torrent.

I hold her close and lift her face toward mine. Her pale skin and blue lips worry me.

"I had the scare of my life," I admit, my throat tight with emotion.

She smiles faintly, her eyes half-closed, shivering from the cold.

"You saved me," she whispers.

"I wouldn't have allowed you to leave me so easily."

I slide my arm under her knees and lift us up, gritting my teeth. The adrenaline leaves my body, the suppressed pains hit me, threatening to make me buckle. Every step toward solid ground is a trial, and if I hadn't wanted to put Lovisa in safety, I would probably have succumbed to the pain.

"Let me help you," says one of the men hired by Gunkil and Fredrik. "An ambulance is on the way."

He'll have to go through me if he thinks I'm going to let him touch Lovisa.

I shake my head and tighten my grip around her. Her head resting on my shoulder, Love drifts between consciousness and unconsciousness. I'm afraid she'll fall asleep and never wake up. Surrounded by armed men, I walk through the forest, trying not to shiver; I've never been so cold in my life, not even during Hendrik's punishments.

Like a robot, I eventually move forward without really seeing where I'm going. The next events become blurry, my mind jumping from one moment to the next, ignoring what happens in between. I see myself passing the house, thinking of my friend's body lying on the ground. Then I'm in front of an ambulance, and the next moment, I'm lying on a stretcher with Lovisa, refusing to let go of her.

"It's going to be okay," I whisper in her ear, overcome by deep fatigue.

Her face has regained some color, and her lips are a pale pink, but still cold as I steal a kiss from her.

"You should let them examine you."

Her voice is only a distant echo. My vision darkens more and more. Unable to hold on any longer, I let myself go.

***

A freezing tide completely engulfs me. Water seeps through every opening in my body, preventing me from breathing. Pinned to the bottom of the lake, I watch Lovisa drift away from me. Rising higher and higher, her arms outstretched toward me, she screams, "Niklas." I scream after her, cursing the one who tears her away from me. A jolt pulls me out of this nightmare. The blinding daylight forces me to close my eyes. Am I still dreaming? I listen carefully. The beeps of a machine, a cart rolling nearby, and murmurs to my left. I allow myself to open one eye, then the other. Lying in a bed, I recognize the décor of my private room in Dr. Söderholm's clinic. Drawn by the conversation happening nearby, I see Lovisa, also in a bed, in deep conversation with Alfrida. Sensing my gaze, they both turn at the same time and immediately smile.

"You're finally awake," my girlfriend sighs in relief.

Finally? How long have I been unconscious? It's daytime, is it the day after that mess? Or have several days passed?

"When?" I ask in a hoarse voice, that had been quiet for far too long.

My body is sore, hurting everywhere from the mistreatment I endured.

"Three days."

Lovisa and Alfrida come to my bedside, each on one side. I look down at my left arm when I feel it pinned against me again. It's once more strapped up.

I grasp the hand Lovisa offers me and kiss it. Feeling her soft, warm skin is a comfort to my soul. She's safe and sound. Everything looks good, she's not in a hospital gown like me, but dressed in a light pink cashmere sweater and jeans. Her beautiful red hair frames her face, which has regained the colors of a healthy person. The skin of her neck shows some bruises and scratches, and she only has a bruise on the corner of her mouth on the right.

"I'm relieved you woke up, big guy," says Alfrida.

Alfrida runs her hand through my hair to push it back and kisses my forehead. I spent the last few weeks without her by my side, and I must admit, I missed her.

"I'm glad to see nothing happened to you."

She nods, tapping my hand. Her gaze shifts from me to Lovisa.

"Now that you're both awake, I'm going to go, there's much to do at home."

At home. Can I really still call this place my home after everything that happened?

She kisses my forehead again, squeezes Lovisa's hand above me, and leaves us. I look around and purse my lips.

"Where's my phone? I have to call Oscar, I need an update on—"

I abruptly stop.

Oscar is dead.

This memory hits me like a punch to the gut.

Gunkil is dead too.

My brother…

Lovisa brings my hand to her lips and kisses it before placing it on her cheek, she looks at me with sadness, her eyes glistening.

"We lost a lot that night. I'm sorry for Gunkil and Oscar. Their loss is terrible," she murmurs.

I caress her cheek and pull her toward me. She leans against my chest, which wakes a sharp pain. Lifting my blouse, I see a bandage over a cluster of purple bruises.

"You had to be operated again, they put in a new system. Do you want me to call the nurse? I should let her know that you're awake."

She tries to get up, but I stop her.

"Not yet, wait a little."

I don't feel like being prodded and questioned by a stranger, barely awake. Minutes pass and all the events come back to me, but Lovisa also helps by explaining everything she knows. Krigare had fled at the first gunshot and returned when it was all over. The police had stormed Iron House, the massacre was so massive that they couldn't turn a blind eye and an investigation was opened to resolve what had happened. Under different circumstances, this news would have angered me, but I'm far too happy to be alive with Lovisa to care about it right away. As for Alfrida and my men in Greece, it turns out they were not in danger, no threat loomed over them when Rodrigo's guy kidnapped Love.

"Do you know what's been planned for Oscar?" I ask.

Lovisa informs me that Alfrida will take care of it, since he had no one outside of his work. As for Gunkil, his parents will take care of his funeral. They are probably devastated by the death of their son, and I'm the one responsible. I asked for his help knowing he was taking a risk by coming. Guilt gnaws at me, and I'm willing to do anything to ease their grief, but can the loss of a child be erased by any financial means? Finally, I curse myself for not considering Lovisa's situation, which completely slipped my mind.

"The baby," I begin, pushing her back so she can face me. "Is it—"

"No. No… They did a blood test and an ultrasound, but I was so distraught that I interrupted the session. The blood test came back good. I haven't had another examination; I wanted to wait for you."

She bites her lip, looking down at her stomach, her fingers nervously fidgeting with the fabric around that area.

"What are we waiting for? I need to know."

It's important. I need to know if this fateful night took away someone else from us. This being is a part of Lovisa and me, but mostly her, and I know I will love it as much as I love her.

After I signal my awakening, the doctor arrives with a nurse. She is wary of me, and the memory of an aggressive me pushing her away to get dressed and leave comes back to me. I must scare her, which is not surprising. I let her check my vitals.

"Glad to see you're looking better. You're quite a piece of work, Mr. Ekman, has anyone told you that?" says Dr. Söderholm.

"Spare me the lecture, Doc. I know I messed up."

Dr. Söderholm raises an eyebrow and lets out a brief laugh.

"Messing up, you say? You completely destroyed the defibrillator. In twenty-five years of career, I had never seen anything like this."

I pout and say nothing, all I want to know now has nothing to do with my health. I glance sideways at Lovisa, who speaks up.

"I'm ready for the ultrasound. We would like to know if everything is okay."

"About time, young lady," scolds the doctor.

I furrow my brow, about to retort when Lovisa's hand rests on my chest, silently urging me to let it go. Annoyed, I exhale loudly, startling the nurse, who recoils after finishing her examination.

"Everything looks good," the nurse says.

"Good, I'll check with the obstetrician to see if she can see you," says the doctor.

The nurse leaves, followed by the doctor, who reconsiders at the last moment.

"By the way, Mr. Ekman, the next time you assault one of my staff, no matter how much money you invest in my clinic, I'll throw you out and you won't be able to come back. Now, rest well."

I smirk and look at Lovisa, who looks at me questioningly.

"Let's just say I wouldn't let anyone stop me from joining you."

I slide my hand on her cheek and caress the slight swelling on it. She shudders, closing her eyes.

"Did I hurt you?"

"No, it's not that. I was so scared that night, I thought it was the end."

I won't let such a thing happen.

"We've been through a lot. I promised you a trip, remember?" I ask as she nods. "After sorting out all the details here, we'll pack our bags and get out of this miserable place."

The walls of Iron House hold too much pain. It's time for a fresh start. Besides, living in the house where Gunkil and Oscar died would be unbearable for me. Glancing down at my hands, I see Gun's blood on my skin. There's no trace left; yet, the sensation and smell of the warm liquid still envelop me.

"Where would we go?"

I swallow my pain and push away the shadow in my eyes to smile at her.

"Wherever you want. Anything is possible."

The next hour passes in calm. The next hour passes quietly. We discover each other's injuries; Lovisa tells me everything she knows about Iron House, and I tell her about my plan to end it all.

"Absolutely everything?" she asks me, in shock.

"Yes, well, as far as the cartel is concerned. I'll arrange a meeting with my partners to inform them of my decision."

She looks worried.

"Will they let you go that easily?"

"They won't have a choice. Don't worry about that, let me handle it."

Her adorable smile melts my heart and strengthens my love for her.

"We're finally going to be just the two of us then."

"That's what we've always wanted. And if the gynecologist says everything is fine, we could be three, what do you think?"

The thought of losing what could be our child made me realize that I wanted to start a family with her.

"During these past three days, while I was waiting for you to wake up, I've been thinking a lot about our situation. And if, at the beginning, I was really hesitant, now I would like to keep it."

She nervously bites her lip and smiles back at me. We've been through a lot together and now I want to take the step of being a father.

I get up to get dressed, not without groaning in pain. Alfrida brought us clothes for several days. I don't know what will become of her when I get rid of the villa, but she doesn't have to worry about her future, I'll make sure she lacks nothing. Lovisa wants to keep her with us, not as an employee, but as a loyal friend and family member. This option is possible, but the decision is not ours.

A nurse comes to take us to the obstetrician's office. This clinic has almost all the necessary services but is much smaller than a hospital.

The doctor is a woman in her forties. Her brown hair pulled back in a bun gives her a stern look, but when she greets us, a friendly warmth emanates from her, and puts us at ease. I must admit, I'm apprehensive about receiving her verdict.

"Relax," she advises as she sees Lovisa tense up under the probe.

I take Lovisa's hand and turn to the black screen. I squint, trying to understand what I'm supposed to see. Suddenly, she stabilizes the image and remains silent for a few seconds that seem endless to me.

"So?" I ask, unable to wait any longer.

The doctor turns the screen a little more toward us and puts her finger on a gray shape. Her smile immediately relieves me before she even pronounces her verdict.

"Do you see this shape? That's the baby. It's firmly attached. I would like to run a blood test to make sure everything is fine."

"Do you hear that, Love?"

Beside me, Lovisa grabs my fingers and bursts into tears, relieved.

"I'll leave you alone for a few moments."

When the doctor leaves, Lovisa sits up and nestles against me, calming down. I wrap my functional arm around her. I can't help but smile as I look at her.

"The baby is fine. Did you hear that?" I say.

Sitting on the examination chair, with her lower body naked, she might seem vulnerable and defenseless, but she's stronger than ever, her body fought death and kept this child alive, which could have died at multiple times.

"I still can't believe what is happening to us."

"It's only the beginning of good things, Love."

Without her seeing it, I slip the box containing the engagement ring into my pocket. Amidst all this madness, it's still there. That's a sign, right? I take out the black box under the surprised gaze of my pretty redhead.

"When I bought it, I was wondering about the right moment, I couldn't figure out how to propose to you. And I think there won't be a better one than right now."

Lovisa fidgets on the seat, rubbing the paper under her buttocks and blushes.

"Can I at least put my panties back on?"

I chuckle and let her put on that piece of fabric that I'll gladly tear off later, along with her pants. She turns to me, her hands clasped over her mouth to contain her radiant smile.

"Come here," I urge her.

I take the ring out of its box and kneel down, gritting my teeth under the effort. I don't let anything show.

"Oh, Nik…"

"Lovisa, twelve years ago, you managed to enter my heart when, let's face it, I was a real jerk, but you found something to love in me. Since that day, I've loved you too, but my childish feelings are nothing compared to what I feel today."

I take her hand while looking her in the eyes.

"The ordeal of the last few weeks almost led to our downfall. I don't want to spend another moment without you. I love you, Lovisa. Would you do me the honor of becoming my wife?"

Her reaction is what I hoped for. She vigorously nods, her eyes shining with tears.

"Yes! A thousand times yes! I love you so much, Nik."

I slide the ring on her finger and stand up. Lovisa throws herself into my arms. We are caught between laughter and embraces when the doctor joins us and congratulates us on our two good news.

For the first time in a very long time, I finally feel real happiness, and my heart, though medically altered, feels lighter. The weight I've long carried on my shoulders, sometimes crushing, has finally vanished.

Epilogue
Lovisa

Four years later

Music. An ancient art that never dies. I love to hear it in all its forms. Through an instrument, a song, the sound of crickets at night, nature, but most of all, the laughter of a child. And especially one.

"Peter," I call, holding out my arms. "Come see me and stop bothering my students."

A redhead runs in my direction and throws itself at me. His gaze is as lively and mischievous as Niklas's. He's a perfect mix of the two of us. His skin as pale as snow contrasts with his fiery hair.

"I want to go see daddy," Peter says, clinging to me as I stand up.

He wraps his little arms around my neck and watches the students play the violin. He loves music just as much as I do, and when he's not in school, he spends his time flitting between the musicians or strumming a few strings himself. When he's old enough and if he wants, I'll teach him to play seriously.

"We'll go join him, go put on your coat."

After putting him down on the floor, I clap my hands to signal the end of class.

"Don't forget to practice well at home for Friday's show."

My students say goodbye to me and leave, chatting among themselves. I look around the music room, smiling. I've always dreamed of a career in music so, after much thought, teaching seemed like a natural choice. This dream came true a year ago, shortly after Peter's third birthday.

"Let's go, mommy?"

I join him at the entrance and take his little hand, which I love to kiss in the evening during the story I tell him before he goes to bed.

In the car, I buckle him in the back and then start driving through almost a meter of snow. Several years but also several hundred kilometers separate us from Kiruna. Now, we live in a much smaller town, Gällivare.

I drive a few miles before reaching a ski resort owned by Niklas. After we left Iron House, he kept his promise and cut ties with the cartel, and after several hurdles that almost ruined everything, his former associates agreed to his departure. He had to buy his freedom from them, and to do so, he sold everything that belonged to his father. We don't want anything from Hendrik anymore. I thought he would miss that life, but he never mentioned it again, and even if the taste for risk pleased me in some way, I'm happy to be out of it. All he had left was his bar, which he also sold, thus putting an end to his old life, just as I put an end to mine by finally selling my mother's shop. He still owns his vineyard in Italy, and he goes there once a year for business, and we sometimes go there for vacations.

Nik didn't wait to get back in his feet and bought a ski resort, which he improved by offering new services, such as hiking in the nearby forest with new trails or climbing. For a man like him, fond of extreme sensations, this was just what he needed. Fredrik comes to see us from time to time, and they sometimes go into the mountains together for a few days. After Gunkil's death, he quit his bounty hunting profession to pursue a career as a private detective. It involves a lot of research, stakeouts where he observes people, but he's in his element, and he never touched a weapon again.

As for Niklas' heart, since Iron House, no more concerns to report. We have a healthy life with sometimes still some excesses when Niklas fights to save my honor when we go out together. Some things never change, and I must admit that I still like this bad boy side of him just as much. Despite our roles as parents, we remain a married man and woman, for whom the spark and fire still burn. I never tire of him, of his presence, and our long conversations in the evening. He is the one who meant for me; it's written in the stars, as he loves to remind me so much.

His new resolution to become a good man who respects justice and human life began with Jonna and Azerty. If he wanted to kill them at all costs for their sins against us, I managed to convince him that their death would only bring more victims to this terrible war. He still managed to have Azerty expelled to his home country, France. As for Jonna, the restaurant she managed in Kiruna was closed following complaints of unsanitary conditions and food poisoning. To disappear, she immediately left for Australia, where she had always dreamed of going.

"Here we are, buddy."

A spot is reserved for me, right in front of the entrance, it's one of the perks of being the boss's wife.

We enter the sky station. A few customers in ski suits are putting on their skis and heading out. At the reception, several instructors are busy with paperwork or giving explanations to others.

Peter immediately runs behind the counter and comes back with a pouty expression.

"He's not there."

"Hi, Peter! Lovisa," one of the site's employees, greets us. "He shouldn't be long now, he's on his way down."

I take my little fox's hand and carry him to the chairs in front of a bay window overlooking a vast white mountain.

"Look carefully, daddy will be coming from there."

A few minutes pass, then Niklas's towering figure appears in front of a small group of people. His black ski suit contrasts with the snowy decor. He lifts his sunglasses when he sees us at the window. Peter gets up from his chair and starts banging on the glass, calling out happily. Seeing him so enthusiastic at the sight of his father fills my heart with joy. How can such a small being inspire so much love in us? Just like for Niklas, I'm ready to do anything for him.

Nik walks through the door and catches Peter, who jumps into his arms. His cheeks reddened by the cold and his beard wet with snow, my handsome white wolf is still as charming as ever. I kiss him and ruffle the hair of our son.

"He wanted to come see you."

"Daddy! Daddy! You promised we'd use the flying seats!"

We laugh when he refers to the chairlift. Niklas kisses him on the cheek, tickling him with his beard.

"Oh yes, did I promise that?"

"Yes! And you always say that an Ekman keeps his promises."

Niklas continues to smile. His gaze has softened over time; I love seeing this serenity he exudes when he comes down from the mountain. He is finally free.

"And it's important to keep your promises, isn't it, big boy?"

Peter vigorously nods.

"Okay, let's go for that ride and then, let's go home and have a nice hot chocolate. Alfrida whispered to me that she bought marshmallows for you."

Our son's eyes light up with delight. He wriggles in Nik's arms, who struggles to keep him still against him. Before they leave, Niklas kisses me tenderly and whispers in my ear, "There's another promise I made to you, and I intend to honor tonight."

I giggle, stealing one last kiss from him. With a radiant face, I watch them walk away.

Back then, so many bad things were happening to us. We thought that if there was something good coming our way, something was wrong, it was suspicious. But today, every happy day w we spend erases our past, and all the moments of happiness we experience are our reward for the suffering endured. Despite our experiences, I wouldn't change a thing, because it's what brought us to where we are today. You shouldn't regret your past, but accept it to move forward.

Life is a path filled with obstacles that slow us down, make us fall, or even hurt us, but at the end of this road stand beautiful things that are worth fighting for.

Other novels from
WARM PUBLISHING

Scan to easily acess all of Warm Publishing books:

Join also our Facebook Group, Book Warmers, to get the lastedt updates and talk about books and more!

Falling for the Voice
by *Mag Maury*

The sexiest of surprises... and the most unbearable!

My plan was simple: Find a job quickly in order to make rent. And I found one. A waitressing job at the hottest pub in town!

Everything was going smoothly until he arrived: Matt. Sexy. Arrogant. Six feet three of muscles that drive women into a hysterical frenzy at every single one of his concerts.

This guy is really comfortable on stage and oh, so enticing. We girls can try to put him out of our minds but we end up wanting him anyway. And he knows it.

Except me, Charlotte. I say no!

Well... Maybe! After all, I have never really been good at resisting temptation...

My Stepbrother: A Sexual Revelation
by *Sophie S. Pierucci*

Cassie is a highly intelligent young woman... Too much so for her own good!

And she is as daunting as she is intriguing. Carl, the son of his father's second wife, would hardly say otherwise!

Carl is the exact opposite of his steady father. He is a player and a slayer. Afraid of nothing and no one. Except for Cassie when she asks him to introduce her to the pleasures of the flesh.

And when the situation gets out of control, it is too late to turn back, and the two lovers find themselves ensnared in forbidden passion. Forbidden by everyone: society, their parents, their friends.

But how to resist the desire that consumes them?

Roommate with my Boss
by *Erin Graham*

Boss, roommate, fake fiancé... real lover?

Étienne is cold, charismatic, and he never shies away from a challenge.

He masters everything down to the smallest detail... until a little accountant with an unlikely look and flowers in her hair inserts herself into his daily life.

She is whimsical, full of life, laughs at the rules and gets around them, talks all the time except about her past... and she drives him crazy. Yet, it's impossible to fire her.

She needs a job and a roof over her head; he needs a fake fiancée...
Is it a deal?

Kalliopee: A Princess's Sacrifice
by *Koko Nhan*

After years of violent battles, Kalliopee agrees to sacrifice her freedom by marrying the prince of the enemy kingdom in order to bring peace.

In a world where women are treated as slaves rather than wives, she is still delighted to be reunited with her first love, Karel.

However, life is unpredictable, and the horrors of war have transformed Karel into a tough and ruthless heir to the throne, who despises the Viridians more than anything. While he has no qualms about mistreating Kalliopee, his determination wavers when confronted with her striking eyes. In the midst of desire and animosity, schemes and plots, dreams and disillusionment, will the princess's heart endure the price of her liberty?

Touchdown
by *Sonia Birdy*

She's a runner, but the campus star quaterback runs faster than she does!

Rocky has had a chaotic life from which she concluded three fundamental things: life is a succession of problems to be solved, men are assholes to be avoided and promises are only binding on fools who want to believe in them. So, unlike the other girls on campus, boys are not a priority for her. Worse, she sees them as an obstacle to her success!

But during a student party, she meets Jude. Freshly transferred from Harvard to play on Brown's soccer team, Jude is the new star on campus. Handsome and inaccessible, he is the type not to get attached: the perfect candidate for a one-night stand.

But the chemistry is too strong. And though Rocky is determined to run away from him, he is determined to conquer her heart.

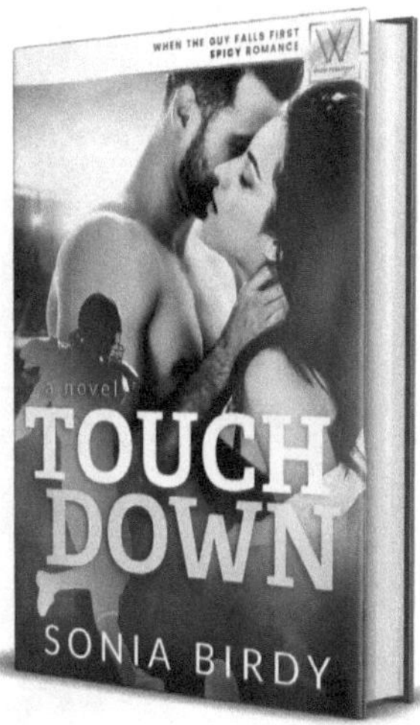

The Courtesan Queen
by *Anna Triss*

After centuries of peace, the four Elemental Clans of Symbiosis are at war with each other. Sylvan, the young King Fuegis, a cruel and ruthless warrior with the ability to control Fire magic, is enslaving the other three kingdoms of Symbiosis, spreading death and terror in his path.

I am Queen Alena of the Glace Clan, which is affiliated with Water magic. I was captured by my worst enemy during the siege of my city. I already know the fate that awaits me tonight. Like the princesses of the other two Elemental Clans that preceded me, I am destined to become the new wife of the tyrant Sylvan.

And tomorrow at dawn... I will be executed.

But queen or slave, I am first and foremost a Glace. I will honor our ancestral philosophy.

"Facing his enemy, a Glace sheds no tears, and never gives up wielding his weapons."

The Private Garden
by *Oly TL*

The most disturbing and transgressive of contracts...

Tiger Sexton seems to have it all. Charisma. Respect. Relentless business acumen. More fortune than he could spend in a life and a sublime wife, Sophia.

When Oceane is invited by Mrs. Sexton for a job interview in one of the restaurants that her husband gave her, the young French tourist knows nothing about this couple. Their name means

nothing to her, people are not her thing. She just wants a job, a place to live and to move on with her life... Sophia's proposal comes at the right time: the Sextons are looking for an *au pair*.

But by opening their doors to her, many other locks are likely to open. Is Oceane ready for this? And what about Sophia, and especially the Tiger lurking in this Secret Garden?

Keep in touch with Missy Heart

Instagram:
https://www.instagram.com/missy_heart_auteur/

TikTok:
https://www.tiktok.com/@missy_heart_auteur

About the Author

Missy Heart was born in Brussels, Belgium, and still lives in the beautiful land of beer and chocolate. At the age of 29, she knew very early on that writing would be part of her life. As a teenager, she wrote extensively on the internet, fueling her imagination through short stories and unfinished stories. But Missy keeps her feet on the ground and has gone to college to become a caregiver and work in a nursing home. She never gave up on her dream of finishing a novel and *after finishing Your Power Over Me will continue on with more novels*. This story was inspired by the beautiful landscapes of Sweden for its snowy scenery, but also for its wild nature.

Her dream is to explore the world and for the moment she is doing it through her novels choosing countries like Morocco, Sweden, Germany, and soon other countries like Scotland, America, Spain…

Mother of two little girls, even for the choice of their first name, she immersed herself in the films and series she loves. The first is called Diana and comes from the heroine Wonder Woman. For the second, it comes from the Teen Wolf series, her name is Lydia.

She shares her life with her partner of 6 years with whom she shares a taste for the imaginary. He pushes her to realize her dream of becoming an author and when their first child is born, she stopped working to be a full-time mother and does everything she could to get published.

When she's not writing, Missy immerses herself in a book, whether on paper or digital, mostly romance, but she also reads fantasy. She also likes to knit, mainly for la Croix Rouge[1], but also for her family.

She has always felt close to nature or the ocean and very much wanted to write by the sea or in a beautiful forest. But with two little girls it's not easy, so she is content with her garden with its palm trees, a little piece of paradise behind her house!

---

[1] Non-profit organisation.

www.ingramcontent.com/pod-product-compliance
Lightning Source LLC
Chambersburg PA
CBHW051428190726
48289CB00001B/92